PRAISE FOR AIMIE K. RUNYAN

Girls on the Line

"*Girls on the Line* brings to vivid life the unknown story of American women who served on the front lines of World War I as telephone operators, working under shellfire and exhaustion to keep frontline officers connected during battle. Philadelphia socialite Ruby battles family disapproval to volunteer at the front, finding camaraderie and sisterhood among her fellow operators, who risk their lives as much as any soldier and fight to be accepted as soldiers in their own right. Runyan illuminates these little-known women of the past in a moving tale of female solidarity and courage."

—Kate Quinn, *New York Times* bestselling author of *The Alice Network*

"An intriguing and original novel inspired by the female telephone operators of WW1, *Girls on the Line* will delight fans of historical fiction. Now is the time for stories about strong, courageous women, and through her heroine, Ruby Wagner, Aimie K. Runyan crafts an absorbing tribute to a group of extraordinary women who played a vital role in the war."

—Hazel Gaynor, *New York Times* bestselling author

"Once again Aimie K. Runyan shines a much-deserved spotlight on unsung female heroes in history. Set during the First World War, *Girls on the Line* follows the arduous journey of an army telephone operator forced to navigate a world of codes and spies and the complexities of love. Brimming with strong women who are easy to root for, this story of loyalty and sacrifice make for an inspiring, heartfelt read."

—Kristina McMorris, *New York Times* bestselling author of *The Edge of Lost*

"Runyan brings America's first women soldiers back to life in a heartfelt tale of love, loss, heroism, and war."

—Elizabeth Cobbs, author of *The Hello Girls*

Daughters of the Night Sky

"Fans of historical fiction or tales of women defying the odds will be immediately drawn in to Runyan's crisp, effortless prose."

—*New York Journal of Books*

"Without a doubt, *Daughters of the Night Sky* is one of the best books I've read this year. Captivating, emotional, insightful, and heart-wrenching, it is a story I will truly never forget. Knowing how accurate the historical details are makes this beautifully written novel even more exceptional. The characters leap off the page and will stay with you long after the final page is read."

—Soraya M. Lane, #1 bestselling author of *Wives of War*

"Fans of *The Nightingale* will be transfixed by this thrillingly original portrait of wartime valor."

—Jennifer Robson, author of *Somewhere in France* and *Goodnight from London*

"*Daughters of the Night Sky* was everything I love about historical fiction. Runyan crafts the perfect balance between plot, characters, and setting, all while educating the reader in an unknown part of women's history. At once compelling, tragic, and uplifting, this is one that I will not soon forget."

—Camille Di Maio, author of *The Memory of Us* and *Before the Rain Falls*

"Aimie K. Runyan breathes life into the gripping tale of the Night Witches—Russian female combat pilots in World War II. A page-turner!"

—James D. Shipman, author of *A Bitter Rain* and *It Is Well*

"Aimie K. Runyan has combined my three favorite literary topics: historical fiction, World War II, and courageous and strong women. She is an incredible historical fiction writer."

—Cathy Lamb, author of *No Place I'd Rather Be*

"A lively and stirring tale of the brave vanguard of female pilots fighting for Russia and, as often, for respect from their male counterparts. As enthralled as I was by this dive into social and military history, it was the humanity of *Daughters of the Night Sky* that won me over: comrades, lovers, and families swept up and torn apart by war. Runyan delivers a well-paced and heartfelt story that fans of World War II novels should not miss."

—Sonja Yoerg, author of *All the Best People*

"*Daughters of the Night Sky* is a compelling World War II story of bravery, determination, and love set within the Forty-Sixth Taman Guards—Russia's all-female pilot regiment. Author Aimie K. Runyan brings four unique women vividly to life: Katya, a superb navigator; Taisiya, her pilot and best friend; Oksana, who risks all for love of her country; and Sofia, the major who leads the women to triumph. Highly recommended."

—M. K. Tod, author of *Time and Regret*

"*Daughters of the Night Sky* is a heart-pounding, epic tale about an incredibly brave squadron of Russian WWII female fighter pilots. Through the eyes of Katya, Aimie K. Runyan takes us through their harrowing adventures and the roller-coaster ride of love and loss in war. Runyan weaves an unputdownable story of bravery, perseverance, and sacrifice. This is a stunner of a novel that I found truly inspiring and well worth the read."

—Kerry Lonsdale, *Wall Street Journal* and Amazon Charts bestselling author of *Everything We Keep*

"A breathtaking novel inspired by a little-known moment in WWII history. Even though I finished *Daughters of the Night Sky* days ago, the scenes are still playing in my head. Katya is an outstanding heroine: a strong woman determined to follow her passion, but also driven by duty and love. And her fellow Night Witches are glorious characters. I miss them and the vivid scenes set within the planes, at the front, and in war-torn Eastern Europe. This is a story I won't soon forget."

—Barbara Claypole White, bestselling author of *The Perfect Son*

GIRLS ON THE LINE

ALSO BY AIMIE K. RUNYAN

Daughters of the Night Sky

Duty to the Crown

Promised to the Crown

GIRLS ON THE LINE

A NOVEL

AIMIE K. RUNYAN

This is a work of fiction. Names, characters, organizations, places, events, and incidents are either products of the author's imagination or are used fictitiously.

Published by Lake Union Publishing, Seattle

www.apub.com

ISBN-13: 9781503904569
ISBN-10: 1503904563

Cover design and photography by Kirk DouPonce, DogEared Design

Printed in the United States of America

Dedicated to the memory of my grandmother,
Helen Louise Petersen, whose inability to lay eggs for the
hungry children of Belgium was the fault of her biology,
not of the generosity of her spirit.

To the wrongs that need resistance, To the right that needs assistance, To the future in the distance, Give yourselves.

—*Carrie Chapman Catt*

Though largely based on numerous journal entries and correspondence from the remarkable women of the US Army Signal Corps, *Girls on the Line* is a work of historical fiction in which I have occasionally taken artistic liberties for the sake of the narrative.

CHAPTER 1

December 6, 1917
Philadelphia, PA

At a party hosted by Mabel Wagner, even one for Red Cross volunteers, it would not do for the table linens to be any less pristine than the bandages we rolled for the boys overseas. There was no detail too small to escape Mother's keen eye, from the shine of the platters on the refreshment table, to the nearly imperceptible flecks of dust on the chandelier. The rugs were brushed and beaten out of doors despite the biting cold and looming snow. The menu was planned weeks in advance and consisted of little Genoa cakes, Linz tarts, oatmeal cookies, and things of that sort that could be made with a modicum of success from corn, barley, or oat flours to spare the wheat flour for the troops. The government urged meatless and wheatless meals at every turn, after all, and there was nothing more fashionable than patriotic sacrifice these days.

Everything was baked to perfection by our hired girl, Evangeline, under Mother's intent supervision and displayed invitingly on the sideboard. During the get-together, Evangeline would be charged with keeping every cup brimming with piping-hot coffee from the service

Mother generally reserved for the holidays. Care was taken to not appear extravagant or wasteful with scarce resources during wartime, but neither would Mother risk having the ladies of the Main Line think that hard times had come anywhere near the Wagner house.

Mother agonized over my clothes, as she had the menu. The maroon satin with ecru lace was too decadent, the gray wool skirt and simple shirtwaist too plain. At length, a simple, brown, velveteen afternoon dress was deemed the appropriate blend of stylish and serviceable for the occasion. We were new to the Main Line, and everything had to be perfect. Money would not buy admittance to society here; only pedigree could do that, and Mother was determined to fashion my older brother Francis's and my way through solid marriages.

Francis and I were barely a year apart in age, and inseparable until the war came. Even when we came of the age and his male pursuits took him out of my sphere for much of the time, we still found ways around Mother's demanding schedules to spend time with each other. There were more than a few lazy Saturday afternoons when we skipped out on social calls to ride bicycles (which Mother forbade me to do) or go canoeing on the Delaware, each of which required trousers. Mother forbade those too, but Francis kept a sturdy pair of knickerbockers and woolen knee socks that he'd outgrown hidden for me in the back of one of his drawers. Keeping them a secret was one of our favorite jokes and sneaking them in with the laundry almost as big an adventure as the out-of-doors exploits that made them necessary. He had hid frogs in my bed, pulled my hair, and teased me relentlessly—and I missed those carefree days terribly. People often wondered at our close friendship, given that we quarreled like cats and dogs as children, but the truth was that we were each other's constant companion and ally. Until, that is, Francis enlisted during the crush to join up in April. Given that his training was in engineering, he was snapped up for the Eleventh Engineer Regiment.

"Tuck up those loose tendrils, Evangeline," Mother ordered as she inspected me. Evangeline hopped to my side with hairpins at the ready and tucked the loose locks up with the rest of my hair. She was a tall, spry girl, with long, nimble fingers perfect for intricate tasks. Evangeline and I had thought the few loose strands softened the look nicely, but Mother preferred things tidy.

"Better. Only a girl with blond curls like yours could make brown look anything other than dowdy," Mother decreed with satisfaction as I twirled for her inspection in the parlor a quarter of an hour before the Red Cross volunteers were meant to arrive. She patted her own mousy-brown locks with a forlorn sigh. My corset pinched at my sides. Since Mother insisted the fireplace in the parlor be kept roaring for the benefit of our guests, the thick fabric of the dress was stifling.

"Very smart looking, Ruby," Father concurred, setting aside the crisp creamy-beige pages of his newspaper. "It's a shame young Nathaniel can't see you looking so lovely while you're hard at work this afternoon. Any of our brave soldiers would be proud to be seen with such a pretty young thing on his arm."

I offered a weak smile at the mention of my fiancé, Nathaniel Morgan. The large ruby ring he'd given me before he enlisted weighed heavy on my hand. He'd thought the choice of stone rather clever. Everyone seemed to think so. He'd been one of the first men of our acquaintance to register in the service when the States entered the war in April, and his patriotic fervor was to his credit. He was a good-looking sort—an aristocratic nose and sage-green eyes that seemed wise beyond his years. He was kind and quick to laugh, and most importantly to Mother, he was from an old and respectable family. If he slid over to the pompous and boring side of things at times, it seemed of little consequence. Marriage, from what a number of my school friends had related to me, was not a thrilling business whomever you married. It seemed just as well to have reasonable expectations.

Father glanced at his pocket watch and stood. He placed his pipe on its tray and smoothed his coat. "I'd best be off before the hens come to brood, eh? I don't think a rooster is particularly welcome once you all get to clucking." He bent down, kissed my cheek, and winked as he tucked the gold disc of his watch back into his pocket.

"I should say not," Mother agreed. "Every time a man ends up at one of these affairs it ruins the entire atmosphere."

"Isn't an extra pair of hands more important than the atmosphere, Mother?" I asked, keeping the cheek from my tone. If she started the gathering out with frayed nerves of my making, she'd never forgive me.

"Don't be difficult, Ruby," Mother said with a dismissive roll of her eyes. "And don't forget Mrs. Lawson is hosting again next Thursday. I expect you with me."

"Mother, I've already begged off two shifts at the Central Office. Any more and Mrs. Trainor may call me on the carpet for missing too much work."

"Watch your slang," Mother said, smoothing out a nonexistent wrinkle on the tablecloth. "We agreed that you may work so long as it doesn't affect your obligations at home. I daresay Nettie Morgan changes the subject whenever your 'job' comes up in conversation."

"Now, now," Father interjected. "There's a war on, and even the great Nettie Morgan needs to realize allowances must be made. She might be Ruby's future mother-in-law, but the work at Pennsylvania Bell is important to the cause. You can't pull her out on a whim to knit socks."

"Knitting socks for our boys on the front, Paul. Don't trivialize what we do." Mother's shoulders straightened, and her features tightened. Father's expression immediately softened.

"Not in a million years, my dear, but take care not to inconvenience the phone company too much. They depend on Ruby too."

"I'll thank you to leave the management of our daughter to me, Paul Wagner." Mother summoned the tone she reserved for ending unpleasant conversations.

"Naturally" was the only acceptable reply Father could give. He shot me a quick, apologetic look. "Enjoy yourselves."

"Ruby knows what we do here is crucial," Mother said by way of farewell, kissing the air near his cheek. In her eyes, it was true. Of course, the Red Cross sent dearly needed supplies to the front, but that was secondary in Mother's eyes. These functions primarily served to allow Mother to garner, for the length of an afternoon, the attention of some of the best society Philadelphia had to offer. My presence was needed to show us as a united front. A doting mother and her devoted daughter. And though Mother would never say it, there was the truth that Nathaniel and I weren't yet married. The war was already a long business, and its outcomes were rarely what we expected. If Nathaniel didn't come home, Mother's search for the perfect match would start afresh. She'd make far more headway with me rolling bandages with prospective mothers-in-law than spending my day pinned to the switchboard.

"They'll be here in just a few minutes, dear. Don't forget to smile. Sit with Nettie Morgan, of course, but don't neglect anyone. Particularly not Mrs. Sinclair or Mrs. Dewhurst." Two of the more influential matrons in the Main Line. One word from either of them would be the making of any woman in Philadelphia, socially speaking. Both had husbands in the Union League, which Father longed to join. Both had eligible sons.

"Yes, Mother," I said, forcing the corners of my lips to turn upward. *A lady is always ready with a smile.* Mother had repeated the words so often they were engraved in my very skull. She studied books on decorum and entertaining the way others studied the Bible.

The get-together was set to begin at two in the afternoon, and by five minutes past, each of the invited guests was seated with her refreshments and rummaging for her knitting needles. Gone were the days of appearing a quarter of an hour late to appear fashionable. What was once common practice was now frivolous. Anything frivolous was now scorned.

"Oh, it is nice to have an afternoon free from the children," Alice Harper, a young matron, confessed as her knitting needles clicked at a rapid pace.

"Are little Robert and James mischief-makers?" Mother asked with an indulgent smile, the sock she was knitting already taking shape. She'd always looked at Francis's antics with amusement. Mine with consternation.

"You'd think it was the boys, but no. My little Louise is the dearest girl to ever draw breath, but even at the age of three, she may be the death of me. I spent an hour hunting for her this morning. I was certain she'd been snatched up from our very doorstep. Can you imagine where I found the little scamp?"

The rest of us shook our heads.

"In Walter's chicken coop of all places," Alice said with martyred grimace. Her husband's wartime experiment in home farming was always a source of annoyance for her. Particularly when the rooster crowed at dawn. "Sound asleep, curled up with one of the hens. And do you know what she said when I asked her why she'd run off? That blessed girl said she was laying eggs for all the starving children in Belgium. She was ashamed she hadn't laid any, so she didn't want to come home until she had a basketful."

"What a sweet girl," I said, careful not to drop a stitch on the khaki scarf that unfurled slowly below my needles. I'd never had much skill with them and envied the other ladies their ability to carry on conversation while producing flawless socks, sweaters, and caps with astonishing speed. "Even she wants to do her part."

"We all must," Mrs. Dewhurst said as her hands manipulated the needles with practiced grace. "Though I'll say it doesn't quite feel like the Christmas season, having all the shopping done so early. I sent packages to Minnie and Robert three weeks ago. By the time the day itself arrives, it will feel like old news."

"The new regulations help save resources for the war," Mrs. Morgan said beside me. "The extra staff in shops, the long hours, and the extra burden on the post are all wonderful for the shopkeepers in peacetime, but a frivolous waste in times like ours."

"Very true, Mrs. Morgan. How are things at the Central Office, Ruby dear?" Alice asked. "It must be terribly exciting."

I sat a little straighter in my chair. "Oh, I'm not sure if 'exciting' is the right term so much as 'interesting.' And busy. I daresay a shift can go by and it seems as though it's been only minutes."

"Well, well," Mother chimed in, not sending me the sharp look I know she longed to. "It is nice for her to have something to do until Nathaniel comes home and she's busy with a family of her own like you, Alice."

"I'm sure you and Nathaniel will have your own brood in no time," Alice said, flashing me a knowing smile. "I think it's marvelous that you've found a way to help the cause for hours a day."

"Hear, hear," Mrs. Dewhurst interjected. "Ruby's work is admirable. I wish more young ladies had such pluck and determination. If more girls were like Ruby, the war would be over by now."

I beamed at the old woman, who smiled at me over her clicking needles.

"The war is going to be over in a trice now that we've sent our boys over," Alice decreed. "My Walter is furious they wouldn't take him, but I've never been gladder of his bad knees in all my life."

Alice never missed an opportunity to mention that her husband had been just as eager to enlist as the other men, and for good reason. Poor Walter had probably considered having the draft board's rejection letter tattooed on his forehead to avoid the accusations of cowardice.

"Have you heard anything from our dear Nathaniel?" Mother asked Nettie Morgan, who was knitting quietly beside me and had made more progress on her fingerless gloves than the rest of us had on our projects.

"Just last week," she replied, offering a guarded smile. I expect she wasn't fond of Mother adopting Nathaniel as "ours" before the wedding. "He's doing as well as can be expected. It doesn't sound like they've seen much action yet. He seems disappointed by that. Anxious to get into the fray as they all are."

"Training takes time," Mrs. Sinclair said. "Let's hope it comes to an end before our boys are put in harm's way."

"Amen," Mrs. Morgan said. "It's a dreadful business, all of it."

"And the work we do here makes it all a little less dreadful for our boys in the trenches," Mrs. Dewhurst said. "Mabel, you've done a fine job today. I don't know that I've seen anyone quite as able to make a gathering both efficient *and* comfortable for old bones like mine. You're to be congratulated."

A polite scattering of applause caused Mother's lips to curl into a smile. As if to punctuate the congratulations, the bell sounded at the door. Evangeline walked calmly but expediently to the door, as Mother had schooled her to do.

I could see Mother counting noses, and I, too, scanned the parlor full of guests to see who might be missing from the party. I couldn't come up with anyone absent other than Hattie Milbanks, who had already sent her regrets, not wanting to spread her cold to the rest of us.

Evangeline reappeared, not accompanied by another volunteer ready to take up her needles for the cause, but alone. A thin scrap of paper shook in her trembling hands as she handed it to Mother.

She was kitty-corner to me, but I recognized the signature yellow of a Western Union telegram envelope. Mother opened it, scanned its contents, and wordlessly handed me the slip of paper before rushing to the telephone we had affixed to the wall in the entryway.

DECEMBER 6, 1917

DEEPLY REGRET TO INFORM YOU THAT LIEUTENANT FRANCIS CHARLES WAGNER, 11TH ENGINEERS, IS OFFICIALLY REPORTED AS KILLED IN ACTION NOVEMBER THIRTIETH.

CHAPTER 2

December 31, 1917

We learned in the next weeks that Francis had been killed in the Battle of Cambrai. His regiment was encamped with the British engineers, and when they were called up, he became one of the first Americans to see action during the war. After months of training behind the front lines, the Americans still waited to join the Brits and the French at the front. In addition to thousands of British soldiers killed, seventy-seven American engineers lost their lives. A small loss for the country, objectively speaking, but the annihilation of an entire universe for my family. My father's pride. My mother's joy. The most aggravating boy in all of Philadelphia, and the dearest one to ever walk its streets. And he was gone.

I'd been given leave from the Central Office until the New Year, and for the first two weeks or so, helping Mother with the memorial service made it bearable. If I ever scoffed at Mother's fussing over social affairs, this was not one of those times. I lost myself in menus and table linens. Anything to avoid confronting the truth. I would never think poorly of an elaborate funeral again in my life. The distraction of deciding between braised chicken and poached salmon made it possible to keep drawing in breath.

But now that we had eulogized Francis, fed our fellow mourners, and sent the multitude of thank-you cards to those who had paid their respects, there was nothing left but to endure the void of his absence, which weighted us all down like leaden shoes. The only acknowledgment of Christmas was the family outing to church. Mother didn't bother to fret over my clothes, though there wasn't much to worry about improving with my black woolen dress. At Mother's insistence, dinner was no grander than any given Tuesday evening. The gifts I had bought for Mother and Father from my wages at the phone company remained unopened in the back corner of my wardrobe.

I was usually one to spring from my bed in the morning, but the listless atmosphere in the house was bleeding me of my vigor. I ambled down the stairs shortly after nine o'clock to find the parlor and dining room as empty as I expected them.

"Have you seen to Mother this morning?" I asked Evangeline, who had busied herself tidying the pantry she already kept pristine.

"Yes, Miss Ruby. She refused her breakfast again. I tried to reason with her, but she wasn't hearing it."

"That's all you can do," I reassured her. "And thank you. I can't imagine we've been the most enjoyable of employers the last few weeks."

"Enough of that. Mr. Francis died in service to his country. If there is a family in all of Pennsylvania entitled to brood, it's this one. Sit and let me fix you breakfast."

"Thank you, Evangeline. And just some coffee, please," I said, patting her elbow. Mother hated it when I acted too familiar with Evangeline. Gossiping with the help about the goings-on in town was not something a refined young woman did, according to Mother. But Evangeline was my age, almost to the very day, and was one of the few girls in my acquaintance who cared for much beyond parties, clothes, and social standing. Better company was hard to find.

"Toast with butter and jam too, or you'll face my wrath," she said with a wink.

"Very well," I said, unable to reply with a jest, as I would have once done.

"It seems a waste," Evangeline said to fill the silence as she placed the coffee in front of me. "All those months training, only to be killed in his first battle."

"Cruel is what it is," I said. "He wanted to fight so badly. They all do."

"He was the best of them," Evangeline whispered. Unspilled tears threatened at her eyes. "I'm so sorry, Ruby. He was *your* brother. I shouldn't carry on like this."

I wiped away tears of my own, for what seemed like the thousandth time in the past few weeks. Giving me a moment to compose myself, she removed the toast from the oven and slathered it with a thick coat of butter and her best strawberry jam and placed it next to my coffee. "But what now?" I asked, looking at the meal that ought to have been appetizing. "Mother refuses help. You have the ship sailing smoothly here. I don't even know where Father has been getting to."

"The office," Evangeline offered. "He's been leaving at the crack of dawn and not coming home until after you've retired for the night. He's burying himself in work."

"That isn't good for him. He needs to rest," I said, indulging Evangeline by eating a corner of one of the slices of toast.

"True enough, but for now it's what's keeping him going. If you want my advice, let him stay at it a bit longer. He'll wear himself out soon enough, take a week's leave to rest, and be much more like his old self afterward."

"So long as he doesn't ruin his health in the process."

"He isn't a frail man, and not all that old. I think it's wise to trust him in this. For now."

"You're probably right," I mused. "But the question is, what do *I* do?"

"I think you should consider taking a page from your father's book. Ring the Central Office, and see if you can't go in for a few hours. I'm sure they'd be glad of the help. Lots of calls coming in for the New Year tomorrow, I'm certain."

"You might be right," I said. "Anything is better than staring at the walls, wondering what I can do to make *any* part of this better."

"Exactly right." Evangeline pulled a brush from her apron pocket and began to style my hair as she always did for the office. A low chignon that wouldn't impede the placement of my headset. Pinned securely enough to stay up for the length of a shift, but not so tight that it would cause my head to ache by the end of it.

"Thank you, Evangeline," I said, patting her hand when she finished.

"Get yourself to the office," she bade. "Do your best to clear your head. It's the best medicine for you."

~

The switchboards at the Pennsylvania Bell Company Central Office spanned the length of the cavernous room. I peeked my head in to see a dozen of my fellow operators sitting on the tall, high-backed metal stools. They answered calls into the Central Office and either dispensed information or connected calls by taking the plug from the incoming exchange and placing it in the corresponding jack of the party they wished to call. The operator rang the third party at ten-second intervals for ninety seconds before asking the original caller to try again at another time. It wasn't particularly straightforward work. Customers had their preferences for how to be rung, and we were expected to honor them. Mrs. Tomlinson had a colicky baby and would rail against us if we rang too long. Mr. Smythe was hard of hearing and expected us to ring for as long as three minutes so he would have time to make it to the telephone. We prided ourselves on knowing this about the people on our exchange, and they loved us for it.

I watched as the operators' hands deftly moved the cables into a humming spiderweb of human communication. As they connected and dropped calls, their efficient movements seemed like something out of a ballet instead of something as prosaic as connecting a call so that a busy housewife could inquire about the cost of three yards of wool serge from the fabric store before making the trip with three children in tow. Their concentration was such that no one saw me at the door, so I padded on down the hallway to the office of our supervisor, Mrs. Trainor.

Her head was buried in a ledger when I knocked softly on the jam of her open door. Her kind, round face lit up when she looked up from her books. "I was surprised at your call, Ruby dear. Have a seat. You have a paycheck coming from earlier in the month, you know. I would have sent it along with a messenger, but I didn't want to intrude during such hard times."

"Oh, well, yes, I suppose. I ought to collect it." In the chaos after Francis's death, I had completely forgotten the two weeks' wages I was owed. I thought of Evangeline, who, even if her own mother died, would not have the luxury of forgetting a single cent she was due. Mrs. Trainor rummaged through the side drawer of her desk until she found the envelope with my name on the front. She passed it to me over her cluttered desk, which she assured us all was perfectly well organized—though only she had the knack for the system of it.

"Thank you, Mrs. Trainor. I hope you had a happy Christmas?" I asked. I smoothed the back of my tweed skirt and sat in the stiff chair opposite her desk.

"Oh, well, it's not quite a proper Christmas without a roast on the table nor enough flour to make plum pudding, but we have to make sacrifices. The fish wasn't bad, but trying to make a fruitcake with half the flour was an unqualified disaster. The children came home for the week, which was lovely. I won't need to ask how yours was, my dear."

"Quiet," I answered. "As you might expect."

"You know you don't need to come back yet if you aren't ready. I haven't got droves of qualified operators of your caliber knocking at my door. Your post is safe for as long as you want me to hold it. I expect your parents prefer keeping you close after—"

"Thank you," I said, cutting her off so she wouldn't have to offer a euphemism. "But really, I find myself at loose ends most of the time. Mother isn't equal to company, and Father spends most of his time at work these days."

"And you thought you'd do the same and keep busy at work?" Mrs. Trainor sat back in her seat and loosely crossed her fingers.

"Something like that."

"I'm glad I was able to find a place for you today. Plenty of the girls will be happy to cut back on their hours to make way for you. New Year's festivities and all."

"I'd be happy to take them. They ought to have the chance to ring in the New Year with their families. I should have come in to spare one of them working on Christmas."

"I'm sure your parents were glad to have you home, even if it wasn't a very gay time, dear. I won't see you damage your health with overwork, though. I can only use you for a half shift today, as this was a last-minute schedule change, and I can't bring you back full-time for another couple of weeks yet, as we'd agreed to. You can leave at lunchtime, have a sandwich with the girls, and, since the weather is tolerable, take a nice, leisurely stroll and do some window-shopping before you go home. It'll do you a world of good."

"That sounds lovely, Mrs. Trainor. Thank you for everything." I smiled, envying her world, where something as small as a sandwich and a peek in the windows at Wanamaker's or Strawbridge's might be enough to make things seem less bleak. I feared we were heading toward a new world, where it would never be that simple for anyone ever again.

For four glorious hours I was too busy to think about the war, Francis, or my heartbroken parents. I connected shopkeepers to their suppliers so they could ask after orders. Wives to their husbands at work, asking them to fetch a quart of milk on the way home. The trickiest was connecting Mrs. Reeve with her daughter in California. Small things, in the scheme of all that was going on, but they meant everything to the people on each end of the line. The dance of connecting plug to jack and back again consumed me, numbed me. I was more grateful than I had words to express. All too soon, Harriet Jenkins tapped my shoulder to let me know lunchtime had come and my shift was over.

The Pennsylvania Bell lunchroom was a windowless, cheerless space where we were usually given a half hour to eat before heading back to our posts. Cramming down a meal in thirty minutes was never agreeable, but at least today I wouldn't need to rush back to my exchange. Without exception, the operators at Pennsylvania Bell were female, and it was rare that a man applied to join our ranks. In many ways, the office had taken on the feel of a college sorority. Three of the girls chattered amiably over their sack lunches. As though the world hadn't been irreparably changed. And for them, it hadn't. They had never even met Francis, and their sadness for his death was no greater than it was for any other fallen countryman. I didn't begrudge their happiness, but it stole the very air from my lungs to see it.

Evangeline, like Mrs. Trainor, had wanted to give me an excuse to stay a little longer, so she had packed me one of her excellent little lunches. I took a place at the table next to Harriet, who had often worked the exchange next to me during the day shifts. Dora and Bessie, fast friends from their first day at the Central Office, were already there poring over the Sunday edition of the *Philadelphia Inquirer* together, hoping for tidbits of news about their boyfriends' regiments in France.

Though I knew they didn't mean to offend, their faces turned ashen as they registered my presence. I was a reminder of the harm they prayed wouldn't befall their loved ones. They were sensible girls, and kind too, but I could see on their faces that there was a small part of them worrying that my family's tragedy might somehow be contagious.

I admitted to myself it wasn't entirely ridiculous. I expected that the mothers in France and England felt like this war was every bit as cruel as the plague that swept over them centuries before. Heartbreak spreading from family to family on the tide of an ill wind.

"Mrs. Trainor was kind enough to find me a half shift," I supplied before they could ask. "I was just looking for an excuse to be out of the house."

"I can imagine so," Harriet said, setting her sandwich aside. "We've all heard the news about Francis, of course. We're so sorry."

"Thank you," I said. "But I've had enough condolences for a bit. I really appreciate the sentiment, though."

"It's good to see you, Rubes," Dora chimed in. "We were worried you might put in your notice, given the circumstances."

"Quite the opposite. I'd work twelve-hour shifts until the end of the war just to feel a part of it if Mrs. Trainor would let me," I said, opening my case and pulling out the lunch Evangeline prepared.

"Wouldn't we all?" Bessie agreed. "Anything to pass the time. It's dull as tombs since the boys left."

"So, what's the news here?" I wanted to turn the subject, though the war was always only a word away from everyone's lips. I'd heard enough of war and longed for meaningless office gossip. Was Gladys, the secretary, still seeing the dashing James from accounting? Had Geraldine, our former colleague, had her baby?

"Three new girls taken on, and I've heard they'll be looking for more in the new year," Harriet said. "We can hardly keep up now, but they're going to have to get more equipment to make use of anyone else. I'm not sure they don't have the cart before the horse." She grabbed a few pages of the paper that Dora had set aside.

"It makes sense to me," I mused. "Equipment can be put in place once they have people trained to use it." I sounded eerily like my father talking shop with his cronies in the radio business. Unlike many men, Father didn't shoo me from the room when he began to discuss business matters. I admired him for it. He even occasionally asked my opinion when something pertinent to my interests came up. It was one of these occasions that led to me being taken on as an operator.

One of his chums who worked in the upper echelon of Ma Bell thought my comments on women in the workplace were well thought out and—more importantly—well enunciated. He suggested to Father that with my genteel speech, coaxed forth from the years of elocution lessons that Mother had insisted upon, I could be of great use to the war effort as an operator. Together Father and I convinced Mother it was the patriotic thing to do, though I think promising her we would set aside the lion's share of my wages for the most elegant wedding trousseau on the Eastern Seaboard was the winning argument.

"Well, there's no mistaking we're in the right business," Bessie said. "Even the War Department seems to think so." She passed one of the middle pages to me and pointed to a tiny square of text on the bottom of the fourth column, straddled between a story about a grain fire in Michigan and an announcement for a charity dance at the local cricket club to benefit French war orphans.

> Women Phone Operators for Army: Washington, Dec. 29. Women telephone operators are being sent abroad for service at the offices of the American forces in France. They have the same privileges and allowances as army nurses. Many army women who have been unable to join their husbands have found a way to do so by qualifying as telephone operators.

"They're not exactly generous with the details, are they?" Harriet observed, having read the little snippet over my shoulder.

"The War Department pays by the letter like the rest of us," Dora quipped, taking a bite of her sandwich. "It might be awfully exciting to go over there."

"And partly daft too," Bessie said. "I can't imagine it's not dangerous work."

"Wars aren't won by men alone," Harriet chided.

"The men need a reason to fight. There's the home front to consider too," Bessie retorted.

I found truth in both arguments but chose not to speak my piece.

"And don't give me the evil eye, Harriet," Bessie continued. "I'd go over in a trice if I spoke a lick of French. I expect that's a requirement."

"I'm surprised they're calling women over," Dora interjected. "I would think with so many men so anxious to go over, they'd train them on the machines."

"How many eager young men have we trained and sacked?" I said. "Most don't last a week. They aren't equal to this work. Men aren't made to focus on a half dozen things at once, as we are. It's how we're able to keep children from jumping out windows, make supper, and iron bedsheets at the same time without running mad."

"True enough," Harriet agreed. "But do you think they'll find enough volunteers to fill the posts? Most older women have children to consider, and the younger ones have families that don't want to send their daughters into harm's way."

"You speak French, right, Ruby?" Dora asked.

"You might say," I replied. It had been my major at Bryn Mawr, though not by choice. Even with Francis as my ally, if there hadn't been a suitable ladies-only institution practically at our front door, I'd never have gotten Mother's blessing to go to university. So, when Mother relented on the condition that French was the only course suitably refined for a young lady, there was no room for me to argue. Prior to college, I'd had ten years of private French lessons with three different mesdemoiselles with varying levels of competence, so I'd been able to advance through my degree quickly, which allowed me to take enough courses in modern history to sit an exam there too. I'd even snuck a few courses in economics and politics in my later terms, when Mother was satisfied with the general bent of my studies.

I toyed with the edge of my napkin, considering Dora's hint.

"Ruby wouldn't put her name in for such a dangerous assignment," Harriet snapped. "Not after what her poor family has been through."

"I think she has a bit more pluck than that," Dora retorted. "Don't you, Ruby?"

"I'm sure there's been some sort of misunderstanding." I gathered up my uneaten lunch and arranged it back in my bag. "I can't imagine they'd send over any woman who isn't in the nursing corps."

"I think you ought to put in for it, Rubes," Bessie said. "Think of all the dashing young men."

"I'm engaged," I reminded her. "They'd be as useful to me as a life preserver in the Gobi Desert."

"There's no harm in window-shopping, even if you have a closetful of dresses," Dora replied, glancing sidelong at me over the rim of her soda bottle. Harriet and Dora threw back their heads in openmouthed laughter. I wasn't able to join in, but it was comforting to see someone else laughing all the same.

I stood and pushed in my chair. "I should be off. See you tomorrow if Mrs. Trainor can find the hours for me."

"We need to head back anyway," Dora said. She removed the page with the army's advertisement before folding the newspaper and returning it to the rack with the others. "Just in case you decide to try for it."

I accepted the paper and folded it small enough to fit into my handbag. I snapped the bag shut as the girls left for the switchboards, then found my way back to the sidewalk outside the imposing edifice. The December wind was cruel, but I couldn't bear returning home to

Mother's moody silence and the void of Father's absence. I took Mrs. Trainor's advice and walked along the streets of downtown. There were grand department stores and smaller boutiques. The Christmas displays, not as gay as in years past, would remain until after the New Year. There were traditional ones with mountains of toys to entice pleading from even the most restrained child; others showed smart new dresses and suits for cunning New Year's Eve parties.

One display showed a trio of mannequin children kneeling eagerly before a pile of magnificently wrapped gifts beneath a resplendent pine tree. Though a thick pane of glass separated me from the tree, I could almost smell the tang of the sap and needles. The trio's mother stood several feet behind them, not absorbed in their merriment, but looking down, unsmiling, at a small picture frame attached to her hand. A short stack of the free YMCA postcards soldiers used to send quick notes home was attached to the other. The father's absence thudded in my ears as loud as the brass band that ushered in the holiday parade each December. Of course the woman in the display was made of wax, not flesh and bone, yet I felt her longing for her deployed husband as keenly as if they were real people.

I placed my hand on the windowpane for a moment and hoped this family would somehow be reunited. The all-too-familiar lump in my throat rose, and I forced myself to move onward before I made a spectacle of myself. I cursed myself for such a reaction to wax figures, but the subtle tribute to the sacrifices of the home front struck a chord in me that the most exuberant patriotic parades had failed to. I imagined what Alice Harper's Christmas might have been like if her Walter had been called up like he'd so desperately wanted. Snuggling those dear babies, bravely making holiday memories despite the ache in her heart. Her family would remain intact, but millions of others had been ripped apart. Some would be reunited, but others, like my own, would never really heal from the loss.

I walked on with no real direction, until the chill forced me to retreat into a café for some hot coffee. A few tables over, two men in uniform, probably days or even hours from shipping out, sat laughing with two lovely young women. The men smiled broadly, proud of their uniforms. So much like Francis. The young ladies smiled too, but it was the sort of smile that didn't reach the eyes. They didn't dare share their fears with their sweethearts, but they knew the dark stretch of lonely nights that loomed before them.

From the depths of my handbag, the single sheet of newsprint sat judging me for my cowardice. I possessed a skill that might help get these young men back safely to their families. I removed the paper from its hiding place, unfolded it, and reread the words a few times as I sipped my coffee. Certainly, they were only preparing a crew of women in case of dire emergency. Certainly, they would find dozens of young women more qualified than I was. Still, there was little harm in sending a letter to learn more.

CHAPTER 3

January 10, 1918

Wasting no time, the telegram from the War Department came on a snowy Thursday some six weeks after we lost Francis. I hadn't truly expected a reply. Commissioning women into the army wasn't how it was done. I was certain that the paper had been fed some misinformation and that if anyone bothered to reply to my inquiry, I would receive a form letter saying there had simply been a clerical error.

I hadn't bothered to tell Mother and Father that I'd written to the army. There was no sense in giving them anything to fret over until there was something to tell them. But as I read and reread the words at the kitchen table after supper while Evangeline waited with martyred patience for me to tell her the news, I knew I had to tell them soon.

"I'm to report next week for testing," I told Evangeline, who exhaled a long breath. She'd been good enough to ferret the letter away for me when the post had come, so I thought it fitting she be the first to hear. "It's right at the Central Office, for the most part, which is nice. If I'm not selected, I won't be out the train fare to Washington or New York."

"Don't talk nonsense. They'll take you, Ruby. They'd be fools not to." She beamed with a mother's pride, and lately she'd been filling that role more often than my own had been able to.

"It's not a done thing yet," I said. "The examinations are apt to be rigorous, and I expect there will be loads of girls clamoring for the posts."

"I'm sure you'll do brilliantly," Evangeline said. "This isn't like you. You're usually so sure of yourself."

"This isn't as simple as doing well or poorly on a test," I said. "If I fail, more competent women will take my place, and that's as it should be. It's whether or not my going is the right thing to do at all."

"You can spend your days here at Pennsylvania Bell or do the work over in France. Do you want to connect housewives to gossip, or the men at the front to the generals?"

"That's rather an unfair question. It's not like all the calls placed here are that trivial, Evangeline. And there's Mother and Father to think about."

"Two more independent, capable people I've yet to meet. And in their hearts, I don't think they'd want to deny you your chance to do your part. But there's only one way to find out." Evangeline's glance drifted up the stairs to my mother's little suite of rooms, which was decorated with lovely rosewood furniture with ivory and pale-pink accents. Soft, feminine, delicate. So very like Mother's view of what a refined lady should be. Evangeline then cast her eyes in the direction of my father's study on the main story. The precise opposite of my mother's private space, it was a masculine haven of dark oak furniture. Draped with deep reds, navy blues, and gold like an English gentlemen's club. Masculine and stoic, but with a sense of quiet grace. I loved the space and, book in hand, availed myself of the plush, navy-blue settee while Father read or went over his ledgers behind his behemoth desk. Father only bid me away when he had one of his headaches, which were thankfully becoming rarer since he'd visited the new optician in town.

"Ask Mother to join us in Father's study," I said, feeling like this would give me something of a strategic advantage. If I barged into Mother's rooms with Father in tow, she'd feel as though her sanctuary had been invaded. She'd be placed on the offensive before I spoke a word.

Evangeline gave a grim nod and padded her way upstairs. I hoped Mother hadn't changed for the evening. If she had exchanged her stiff collars and stays for the comfort of her nightgowns, there would be no prying her downstairs. Like Mrs. Bennet from *Pride and Prejudice*, lamenting over the impropriety of her youngest daughter, Mother preferred to mourn for Francis upstairs and out of the public view. Like Mr. Bennet, I wanted to chortle about the elegance of the custom.

I knocked on the doorjamb to my father's study. He called out his usual "Come in, Ruby girl," though his typical joviality now rested with Francis on the corner of some battlefield in France.

"Come to curl up on your settee, little kitten?" Father asked, looking a tad wistful. "I've missed our quiet evenings. I'm sorry I've spent so much time at the office of late. Dreadfully busy time, you see."

"Of course it has been," I said, offering him a weak smile. And I'm sure it was, but I wouldn't risk injuring his manhood to ask how much of it was added work due to the war efforts, and how much of it had to do with being unable to bear being at home. "Actually, I've asked Mother to join us. I've something rather important to discuss."

"I should hope so," Mother interrupted, taking her place in the large chair next to mine. "What do you mean rousing me from my room at this hour?"

"For heaven's sake, Mabel, it's not even nine thirty." Father's tone leaked equal measures of consternation and exhaustion.

"I've not been well these past few weeks," Mother said with an indignant sniff.

"Neither, I'm sure, has Ruby. And you've been remiss in your duties to her," Father insisted.

"She isn't a child anymore, Paul, and don't you dare accuse me of being a neglectful mother." Her nostrils flared, and I feared that if Father goaded her any further she'd start breathing fire from them.

"Please, both of you. I don't want to quarrel. I wanted to tell you something." I felt my heartbeat hammering in my ears as I formulated the words. "I've written to the War Department. It seems they're looking for operators to serve overseas. I've been selected to report for testing in town to see if I'm qualified for the post."

"That's absurd, Ruby," Mother proclaimed. "Next you'll be telling me the army is conscripting schoolmarms to go teach the displaced children in Belgium."

"Perhaps, Mother. Someone has to do the work that needs to be done. And sadly, there are fewer and fewer men to do it." I laced my fingers tightly, fighting to keep my breath even.

"It took every bit of my patience to allow you to work for the phone company like a common factory girl. I won't hear of you making a spectacle of yourself like this." Mother sniffed in her imperious way. Daring me to challenge her. Each time she did this, I imagined the snort of a bull as he hoofed at the dirt, staring down the unwitting matador and preparing to charge across the arena.

"You forget my mother was a 'common factory girl,' Mabel. I'm proud to see our daughter isn't afraid of hard work, just like her grandmother." Father sat back in his chair, looking in Mother's direction but staring past her at some unknown point on the wall.

"Is that the life you want for our daughter, Paul? Your mother died of consumption, her back stooped, and aged forty years past her time." There was the hint of desperation in Mother's voice. Her beginnings were only slightly more comfortable than Father's. I'd heard only the barest hints about Mother's girlhood, but I'd gathered there had been little time for cheer in her early years, and plenty of nights with an empty stomach, from what I could parse of her scant descriptions.

"Of course not. I don't think working the phone lines in a reasonably comfortable office could compare with twelve hours a day in a dank textile factory." The roll of Father's eyes was almost audible. "I haven't seen too much strain on you these past months, Ruby. Am I wrong?"

I shook my head.

"This isn't the same, Paul. She'd be traveling overseas with goodness knows who and living in goodness knows what sort of conditions and all the while mixing with heaven knows what sort of people. Would you risk our daughter's reputation like that?"

"Mabel, I'm far more concerned that if she goes over there, she'll be risking her *life*. Sort your priorities, woman."

"Don't take that tone with me, Paul. If you don't put an end to this foolish notion, I will."

"Father, I'm a grown woman. I think I can make this decision for myself," I said, finally finding my voice to protest.

"Watch yourself, young lady. You still live under my roof. As it so happens, I'm no more in favor of this scheme than your mother. I think it's rather cheeky that you didn't think to ask before putting your name in at all."

"Given the events of the past few weeks, I didn't think it was worth upsetting you unless I had reason. But they want me to report to the Central Office for testing next week. I almost didn't mention it, since I'd just be going in to work as usual."

"I suppose I can see the logic in *that*," Father said. From the gentle jiggle in his frame, I could tell he was wiggling his foot as he did when he was nervous. "And while I'm not thrilled at the notion, I'll allow you to sit the exam."

"You can't be serious, Paul." Mother's face looked as livid as the time Alice Harper's mother, Tillie, had suggested that Mother's dress was as pretty as the one she'd seen in a New York shopwindow. That Mother's dress actually *was* purchased ready-to-wear, and not tailor-made for her, was completely beside the point. "You'd really give your daughter permission to go overseas, just like that?"

"I said nothing of the sort, Mabel. I'm sure the government is simply reassuring a few progressive-minded eggheads—our president being one of them—that women aren't fit for service. Even if a few exceptional girls, like our Ruby, pass the exams, I'm sure the small number will let Washington know it isn't worth the trouble of sending over a handful of overeager women. Separate billeting alone would be a nightmare."

"What about the nurses?" I said. "They manage to find ways to send over thousands of them."

"And so it has been for over a hundred years. A necessary aid for our boys overseas. It's not the same thing as actually serving."

"As you say, Father," I answered with grim resignation.

"I think you're foolish to allow her to even sit the exams, but my opinion means little, I suppose. Don't come crying to me when the strain of it all sends her into fits."

"It's just a few tests, Mabel. She's sat her share of them before with no trouble. Within the week, the government will see they're better off letting men do the job. This way Ruby can say she tried to do her part and will be happier at home for it."

Mother heaved a great sigh and left the room without comment, presumably to fume in private over my father's recklessness.

"You should have told me sooner, Ruby," he said. "I don't like secrets between you and me. I'd have forbidden you on principle from even sitting the tests, but seeing your mother in high dudgeon did my heart some good. It means she's got something left of her old spirit."

"Your love of antagonizing Mother has saved my skin more times than I care to count," I said with a chuckle.

"Consider it an act of charity to the downtrodden," he said, leaning back in his chair. "She *is* too hard on you. I admit it freely. Or at least when she isn't in earshot."

"And there isn't a secret in this house that Mother can't uncover within seconds, Father. That's why I didn't tell you sooner. Forgive me if I didn't want to endure a lecture before I'd earned one. I hated not telling you, but we've all had enough to deal with."

"I suppose I can't argue with that. For what it's worth, I hope you pass, Ruby. You're a capable young lady, and I know it would make you feel like your months of hard work have been well spent. Just don't be disappointed when it comes to nothing."

"Thank you, Father. I hope I pass them too." For the sake of domestic harmony, I didn't mention that my motives had far less to do with how I felt about myself and far more to do with ending the war.

CHAPTER 4

While the main floor of the Central Office was its usual well-ordered yet cheerful hub of activity, upstairs the tone was one of military solemnity. I'd never had a reason to visit this floor before and knew I hadn't been missing much. The corridors were dimly lit, the doors closed. It was as though the architects had taken pride in creating a space that screamed the word *uninviting* with every eerie flicker of electric light on dismal gray-green tile.

I was one of forty women who waited in hard wooden chairs for instruction. Father would have been floored to see so many women eager to take the exams. And this was just the number the government thought stood a reasonable chance of passing the exam. The number who wrote in was probably much higher. I dressed in a plain suit of gray wool that Mother disliked for being too utilitarian and that I favored for precisely that reason. While some of the other women chatted companionably, I sat poised in my chair, eyes forward, with a small leather notebook and pencil, ready to take down whatever instruction they might give.

At length, a uniformed man who bore an expression of annoyance as comfortably as he would a bespoke suit crossed the room in four long strides and turned on the ball of his foot to face us. He moved with a crispness that could only be contrived from years of army training.

"Ladies, I'm Colonel James Bradford," the gruff man said without preamble. "You're here today because General Pershing is convinced that women alone possess the needed skills to run a proper telephone system, and he is in need of one to win the war. Several thousand women across the country applied to be considered for assignment as operators overseas. You are among the few hundred girls we selected whose applications most closely matched our particular needs. Today and throughout this week, we shall see if your abilities are indeed what you professed them to be in your letters."

Just like Father, he assumed that this was all just an exercise to confirm what he already knew—that women would never prove themselves equal to serving overseas. That we had to embellish our accomplishments to be considered. I felt a pinching in my fingers and loosened the grip on my pencil, lest it snap. I breathed through my indignation at his implication, knowing that if I entered the exams with my nerves already raw, I'd only be proving his assumptions for him. Men could be maddening, and that was true for Father too. One would think that Father would have learned not to underestimate women after being married to a firebrand like Mother, but old habits were hard to kill. He'd always treated me like the exception that proved the rule when it came to feminine competence, and it was by turns flattering and infuriating.

We were summoned one by one from the room by one of Bradford's underlings, whose rank I couldn't determine from the patches on his jacket. Something I would have to learn no doubt, so I made a note in my book to study the military hierarchy after we'd been released for the day. I had expected to be kept busy with endless exams, but there was nothing to do but wait for our names and listen to the ticking of the clock that wore on our patience like waves lapping at a rock: each tick, each wave, eating away until nothing remained but a pile of sand. The waiting was infinitely worse than a stack of exam papers. After about three girls were called, I realized that they were summoning us alphabetically. I groaned inwardly: Wagner would be one of the last names called. If only I'd been born an Abbot or an Adams.

They'll find twenty capable girls before they reach the letter "L," and you'll be sent home. Or worse, they'll test you, just to make you feel important, and then send you a form letter in a week, just as Father predicted.

My toe tapped against the tile floor, and I clamped my hand to my knee to still it. I couldn't indulge these thoughts, or they would prove themselves true—a point Father had made many times: *"The key to success doesn't lie in hard work alone, but more often in believing we are capable."* I took some calming breaths and resolved to stitch the saying on a sampler the next time Mother insisted I busy my hands with a needle and thread.

Some of the girls paced. Others had prepared more intelligently and had brought novels to pass the time. There was a uniformed officer at the back of the room whose only occupation seemed to be to observe us as we waited for our examinations. I wondered if perhaps our conduct in the waiting room might be taken into account in the final selections, so I didn't give in to the desire to wander aimlessly with some of the others. Better to appear that I had control of my qualms, even if stopping the shakes in my hands was a monumental effort. I opened my book and began writing observations about my fellow temporary residents of the waiting room. The tall girl with glossy black hair and a hard expression—she wore fine clothes, but the soles of her shoes were so thin they looked like they'd have holes in them by the time she walked to the examination room. Had she borrowed her dress and coat? Damaged her good shoes in the rain and sent them to the cobbler? I spent the better part of the hour writing nonsense. I hoped at least I gave off the air of looking studious and calm.

"Ruby Wagner," Colonel Bradford's assistant called at last. Only one other, rather forlorn-looking girl remained. Her name was probably Waverly or Wilson, the poor dear. I felt a mild sense of relief knowing at least one other person would have to wait longer than I had. I stood from my chair and smoothed my skirt for long enough to let the blood flow return to my legs before daring to take a step. I didn't think falling on my face before even starting the examination was any sort of auspicious beginning.

I was shown to a small, dimly lit room where instead of an examination booklet or a stern-faced interviewer, I was greeted only by the sight of a candlestick telephone on a spindly table.

"Good luck," the assistant said, closing the door behind him.

The phone rang once, and I tentatively lifted the receiver to my ear and held the mouthpiece close to my lips.

"Hello, this is the adjutant, Ninth Division. Commanding Officer General Smith would like to speak to Colonel DuBois of the Eighteenth Brigade. General Smith does not understand French, and Colonel DuBois does not understand English. You will need to translate General Smith's reply into French and Colonel DuBois's reply into English. Are you ready?"

I steadied myself and willed my "Yes, please proceed" not to sound as though I were trembling.

"This is General Smith speaking." It was the same voice as before. It seemed Colonel Bradford was testing his skills at playacting. "I would like you to tell Colonel DuBois that we are sending four hundred troops to his location on the eighth of April. They will arrive by the twelfth provided their forces can keep the route clear. We are unable to send the medical supplies he requested until the next advancement of troops at the end of the month."

"Very good," I replied. *"Mon Colonel, est-ce que vous me reçevez?"* I asked to confirm that the "French commander" was in fact on the line.

"Oui, mademoiselle. Je vous écoute." The French commander, the self-same Colonel Bradford, responded in admirable French.

I relayed the message carefully, letting every syllable roll off my tongue deliberately, as though I were savoring a morsel of caviar. One muffled word could cost lives at the front. I hadn't had much call to use my French since I graduated from Bryn Mawr, and I noticed an atrophy in my skills I hadn't realized was there. I'd practiced my old dictations and reread my favorite novels to refresh my vocabulary, but there was nothing that could truly replace spontaneous conversation, and there were precious few people in the Main Line who were capable and willing to practice for any length of time.

"Très bien, je vous donne les nouvelles coordonnées. Je tiens à préciser que depuis notre dernier contact nous avons procédé aux changements de rigueur." New coordinates. I snatched my notebook and pencil from my handbag to copy down the long series of numbers. I was just able to open to a blank page before he began rattling off his figures.

"I am giving you new coordinates, as there have been changes since the last message." I translated for "General Smith" before reciting the string of numbers.

"Very good. Pass my thanks along to the colonel."

I exchanged brief pleasantries on behalf of both fictional men and, with a steady hand, replaced the receiver on the hook next to the mouthpiece.

The young officer opened the door behind me, the harsh light of day spilling into the dimmed room. Through my squinted eyes, I could see the hint of a smile at the corner of his lips. "Well done. You've been selected to take the rest of the exams. Only the fifth one today."

There had been at least thirty-five girls called before me. That meant thirty-one of them had been sent home. The other women who had been selected for further testing waited on sofas in a far more comfortable room. They had been offered coffee by Mrs. Trainor herself, and read newspapers in companionable silence.

"I knew I'd see you in here, Ruby dear. Those years studying French couldn't have all been for naught." Mrs. Trainor handed me a cup of strong coffee with a healthy dash of sweet cream. An indulgence in wartime, but one we were apparently entitled to, given the efforts of the day.

"It appears so, Mrs. Trainor. And thank you."

She smiled and retreated to the desk she'd commandeered for the day. Her presence meant that the next exam would likely be a practical one: the switchboards. I was able to sink into my chair and enjoy my coffee knowing that I'd practiced what came next for high hours every workday for the past eighteen months.

I thought of all the kicking and screaming I'd done as a young girl trying to resist the French and elocution lessons Mother had insisted on as soon as Father had become important enough to afford them. My resigned acceptance of them as an adolescent. My teeth-gritting capitulation to Mother's demands for my course of study at university. So concerned with my ability to speak well, she never stopped to consider the importance of me having something to say. Perhaps she thought it was best if I didn't. I couldn't help but wonder how Mother would feel if I told her the curriculum she had designed for me was the most valuable preparation I could have asked for in this endeavor she despised.

For three days, we took written exams, underwent physical examinations that were so thorough I thought I could hear my mother blushing on her settee ten miles away, and were asked an endless series of questions that encompassed everything from French, to technical skills, to our very patriotism. The latter seemed to be of utmost importance. We each had to provide four letters vouching for our love of and loyalty to the country. Mrs. Trainor and several of the other higher-ups at Ma Bell were happy to provide them for me. I took care to stick with my own colleagues and not to ask any of Father's friends for their assistance. While I was sure they knew my motives for joining up were pure, I couldn't know if Father might entice them to say something of my health or demeanor that would make me appear unfit for service.

Beatrice Walker, the poor girl who'd waited the longest, had been the last to make the cut. It seemed fair she'd been accepted, given the hours she was forced to endure in the waiting room. She sat next to me now as we awaited instruction in the disused room on the third floor of the Pennsylvania Bell Central Office. She was the most timid of the group, but not unfriendly. From what I'd gathered, her French was excellent, and from talking to her, I found she was as keen an applicant as the army had ever seen. Two of the other girls were French Canadian. They chatted in French among themselves but were quick to shift to English if they thought we wished to join in conversation. The two others were operators like me, one from Allentown, the other from Princeton, New Jersey. Both had more years than I did at the switchboard and were anxious to join in the fray.

It was hard to know if these women were my competition or my colleagues, but I tried not to fret too much about it. If there were five places and I was the one selected to remain home, then, as I'd told Evangeline, more-capable women would be going in my place. I tried to keep those magnanimous thoughts in my head, but my noble side didn't always prevail. The longer the exams went on, the more I felt my misgivings fade away. I wanted to serve, no matter how dangerous it was. What's more, I knew I was capable.

"Good morning, ladies." Colonel Bradford strolled into the room. He had gained a measure of affability after we had been whittled down to six. It seemed a small number, but perhaps the other training centers in San Francisco and all along the Eastern Seaboard had resulted in enough suitable candidates that he was now convinced that the project had some merit.

"We're going to try your skills on the exchange today. Actual telephone calls, real customers," the colonel explained. "We can't exactly simulate how stressful your work will be on the front, but we want to see how you perform under the stress we're able to muster stateside."

We were escorted down to the main exchange room, a space I knew as well as my mother's own parlor. Harriet was at her usual chair, but Dora and Bessie weren't at their posts. Likely given a day off to make room for us. I hoped they were still being paid, but I had my doubts. Mrs. Trainor gave us some basic instructions and assigned us each exchanges. With a wink, she directed me to my usual place. I appreciated the gesture, but I hoped she didn't feel like I needed the advantage.

"Show us how well you can serve the people of Philadelphia, ladies, and treat every call as though it's as crucial as one on the front lines." The colonel took a place at an empty chair usually reserved for our supervisor.

As she had for almost every shift for eighteen months, Harriet sat on my left. She patted my knee in solidarity, and I flashed her a smile as I placed the familiar headset over my ears. Beatrice was to my right and fumbled with her headset before taking a resolute breath and setting to work.

The first hour was uneventful. Calls from clients to shopkeepers, husbands to wives, and so on. Mrs. Reeve's line lit up, and I felt a tingle.

"Hello, number, please," I said. *Please say California.* Connecting a call to the opposite coast was the biggest challenge I faced at the switchboard and would surely impress the examiners.

"Hello!" Mrs. Reeve yelled into the line. "I'm calling my daughter Ida in San Francisco. Douglas 5734." Despite my gentle indications that she could speak at a normal volume, she was still convinced she needed to belt out her words loud enough to be heard in California without any sort of amplification.

"Very good, Mrs. Reeve. I'll ring you back when I have her." I unplugged her line and rubbed my abused ear for a moment, then began working to connect to the next long-distance exchange. It might take as long as an hour to get Ida on the line, but I hoped that we'd be able to patch the call sooner.

As though the operators from exchange to exchange knew the army was listening on, they patched me through faster than I had ever seen in my months at the switchboard. In a quarter of an hour, I had an astonished Mrs. Reeve speaking with her daughter. Harriet shot me a wink, and I had to fight to keep an impassive professional expression on my face instead of a self-satisfied smirk.

Beatrice wasn't faring as well. She had excelled in the written exams, but I began to wonder if she had ever worked an actual switchboard before. I could see her efforts to calm herself, but her hands shook as she moved to plug each cable into the jack.

"I need to connect a call to a line that's on your exchange," she hissed. "What do I do?"

"Just reach over and plug it in," I whispered.

She leaned over with an unnecessary "Excuse me" and plugged into a jack on the far end of my exchange. In the process of sitting back down, she knocked three calls loose. Luckily for her hide, Mrs. Reeve's call to California wasn't one of them.

"Oh, I'm so sorry!" she exclaimed, too loudly for the office.

"It's all right," I said in hushed tones. "I can reconnect them."

I remembered each of the lines and rang the original callers back to place the calls anew.

"I'm terribly sorry there was a problem with the connection, sir. Please allow me to reconnect your call." Conciliatory, but not overly apologetic. There wasn't a customer on the grid who wasn't used to the occasional broken connection.

The mishap seemed to rattle poor Beatrice even more.

In the course of five minutes, she'd connected three customers to the wrong lines and had at least a half dozen completed calls that hadn't been disconnected.

"That call has been in place for a half hour," I whispered, pointing to a jack in the upper left of her board. "Check back in and disconnect the line if they're finished." I cocked my head and hoped Colonel Bradford wasn't listening on. It wasn't a written examination, but I didn't want to get tossed out for meddling with Beatrice's performance either. "And I'd check in on Mrs. Frederick. She's notorious about not hanging up her line properly. We ask her neighbors to check in on her about it all the time."

The advice seemed to steady Beatrice a bit, and she completed the next two hours without much incident.

Whether she realized she didn't have the skills needed to serve, or whether Colonel Bradford dismissed her, I couldn't be sure, but she did not come back after our eleven-thirty lunch break.

The colonel tapped me on my shoulder an hour before the shift was scheduled to end. Dora waited behind him to take my place, then squeezed my hand covertly before I left and followed the officer to the room on the third floor next to the little training area that he had commandeered as his office while he was in residence.

"Well, Miss Wagner," the colonel said from behind the large, scarred oaken table Mrs. Trainor had procured for him to use as a desk. "You certainly showed your proficiency today." In true military fashion, each pile of papers was rigidly straight—so much so that I envisioned the underling organizing the stacks with a ruler, like Evangeline with her straightedge setting the dinner table with perfect spacing between the dishes and flatware.

"I'm glad you think so, Colonel," I said. "I enjoy my work here at Pennsylvania Bell very much."

"That much is clear," he said. "And you're well liked by both your superiors and peers, which is a credit to you."

Not knowing how to respond to the observation, I nodded.

"I'd like you to answer a final question for me, Miss Wagner," he said, lacing his fingers and leaning forward on the desk. "Why is it you wish to serve?"

"Because, Colonel Bradford, we lost my brother in November, and I know many more families here are going to experience the same before long. And I can't even begin to comprehend the losses for families in Europe. If I can use my skills to help a family to never know that pain, it would be worse than unpatriotic of me not to volunteer. It would be inhuman."

"That is a very good answer, Miss Wagner. It shows that you understand the magnitude of what you will be doing overseas. Your work will mean the difference between life and death. Victory and defeat. I promise you, it won't be pleasant conditions and your safety isn't guaranteed. Far from it. Once you pledge your oath, you'll serve for the duration of the war and as long as your country needs you. Is this still what you want?"

Since I'd learned I'd been accepted for testing, I'd tried to put the thoughts of my own safety aside. I told myself that I could be hit by a bus walking home. That no matter where I served, I'd likely be a good deal safer than the boys in the trenches. The truth was that I wasn't eager to be anywhere near the fighting, but the thought of staying home when I could be useful somehow filled me with more dread than the prospect of German artillery fire. I'd thought there might be a more finite period for my deployment, perhaps a year. But if our boys were sent over with the understanding they would return when the war was won, I supposed it would be no different for us. "Yes, Colonel, it is."

"I'm glad to hear it, Miss Wagner. You'll serve your country well, I'm sure of it." He handed me a dossier from his pile. "Your travel instructions and billeting information, as well as instructions for purchasing your uniform kit and necessary supplies once you reach Manhattan."

I scanned the list of items: uniform coat, skirt, blouses, hat, shoes, boots, gloves, woolen stockings, bloomers, union suits for cold weather, and a whole host of personal items, from iodine to sewing kits.

"The army won't be providing these things?" I asked, mentally calculating the cost of the kit. If it cost a penny under $300, I would have been astonished. I had $35 in my bureau drawer and another $130 in my bank account. I'd have to sort out the other $135 somehow.

"I'm afraid not, Miss Wagner. Like our officers, you'll have to provide your own kit. If you're in need of some financial assistance, American Telephone and Telegraph is in the position to lend it to you." His gaze drifted over my outfit, expensive shoes, and polished leather handbag. I certainly didn't look like the sort who would need a loan, but as was the case with many girls in my position, my money was not my own.

"One last word of advice. Your French, technically speaking, is satisfactory, but you would do well to improve your accent. I'm given to understand that a good number of the other operators going overseas have French backgrounds by way of Canada, their parents' birth, and so on. Listen to them, and try to emulate their style of speech."

"Very good, Colonel," I said, gathering my things. My professors at Bryn Mawr would be disappointed by this, but heaven knew they were fonder of having us work on translations and taking down dictations than working on our conversational skills.

I considered staying in town a bit longer before letting Mother and Father quash my plans for departure, but I opted against it. If I had any chance in winning their approval, I'd do better to break the news to them when I had some measure of control over the timing. I offered up a silent prayer that their morning had been a peaceful one, and then I boarded the next streetcar home.

CHAPTER 5

I'd planned on broaching the subject of my deployment with Mother first. To entrust her with my exam results before speaking with Father would be an unexpected tactic and one that might get her to lower her guard long enough to consider letting me serve. I was home earlier than expected, which would help put Mother in better spirits. She loathed it when I arrived at the dinner table hot, tired, and out of breath because I'd run from the streetcar to make it on time.

I winced as I saw Mrs. Dewhurst seated next to Mother in the parlor, deep in conversation as they sipped tea and nibbled at Evangeline's delicate meringue cookies.

"I hadn't dreamed of seeing you home so early, Ruby dear. What a lovely surprise. Come sit and have tea with us." I swallowed my disappointment at the loss of the opportunity to speak with Mother alone, but charming Mrs. Dewhurst might go a long way in lifting Mother's spirits. I took the free armchair nearest Mrs. Dewhurst and took the tea from Evangeline, who had materialized at my right side like a benevolent genie. I only hoped my shaking hands wouldn't result in a lapful of scalding liquid.

"Of course," I said, plastering on a smile. "Wonderful to see you, Mrs. Dewhurst."

"You're looking well, Ruby," Mrs. Dewhurst said approvingly. "The phone company isn't working you too hard, I take it?"

"Until recently, I've been working a reduced shift," I said. Mother's jawline tensed at the mention of my work, so I hastened to add, "I've rather enjoyed having more time at home to see to things around here. Mother can't do it all herself."

Mother's brow cocked with incredulity, but she offered a satisfied nod. It was at least the right answer, even if it wasn't true.

"I'm surprised to hear it," Mrs. Dewhurst replied. "You always seemed so eager when speaking about your work. I daresay it must be an interesting time for you all at the Central Office with the excitement overseas. I even read they're planning to send over ladies to serve as operators. I don't suppose you've considered throwing in your lot, have you?"

I cast a desperate look at Mother. She'd be mortified if anyone learned I'd sat for the exams, but if I were caught in a lie to Mrs. Dewhurst, it could be disastrous. "Yes, Mrs. Dewhurst. I was actually chosen for further testing."

"I didn't think it was wise at all, but Paul, being the patriot he is, wanted Ruby to have her chance to 'show her mettle,' as he's wont to say. He and I are both convinced that it will all come to nothing, tests or no."

"That's not what my cousin Alberta in Seattle says. According to her, they've sent quite a crew of girls to New York for training. They'll be going overseas in the coming weeks, she's certain of it." Mrs. Dewhurst didn't convey disdain at the notion, which gave me a fluttering feeling in my chest akin to hope. "When do you expect to hear the results of your examination, Ruby dear?"

I cleared my throat and traced with my eyes the intricate patterns on the rug for a moment before meeting Mother's gaze. "I've heard this afternoon. Less than an hour ago, actually." I wanted Mother to know she was the first person I'd intended to share the news with. "I've been selected to go to New York as well. Next week."

"Well done," Mrs. Dewhurst said. "You ought to be very pleased, Mabel. It's a rare thing to see a girl so accomplished in our set. Ruby does us all proud."

For the first time in our acquaintance, I fervently wished to kiss Mrs. Dewhurst's papery cheeks. More important than her praise of me was her use of the pronouns *our* and *us*, which brought my family into Mrs. Dewhurst's inner sanctum.

"I only hope to do my bit," I said earnestly. "Though Mother and Father are—understandably—reluctant to give me their blessing to go. It has been a hard time for all of us, and I couldn't dare defy them."

"Oh, stuff and nonsense," Mrs. Dewhurst said, placing her cup on the side table with a rattle and turning to face Mother. "I expect you're more than proud to see Ruby pick up poor Francis's fallen standard. If I had a daughter, I'd hope she'd have some of Ruby's gumption in her. I can't abide a smart, competent girl wasting herself in the parlor too early in life."

Mother looked at me scathingly, as though I had the temerity to put Mrs. Dewhurst up to defending me. The idea was as appealing as asking Jack the Ripper for directions at midnight while lost in a London back alley.

"Well, it's something to discuss," she said, raising her cup to her lips.

"I shouldn't think there's much to discuss, Mabel, but I won't interfere in your affairs if I'm not wanted. But I can tell you I'd be proud to host a going-away party for her. Send her off with the pomp and circumstance of any of our soldiers."

Mother looked with dread at the bottom of her cup, then placed it back on its saucer on the side table. It was an offer she didn't dare refuse. "If Ruby and her father decide it's the prudent course of action for an engaged young lady to go overseas in such a capacity, I'll not stand in her way."

That night at supper, we'd no sooner sat down to our meal when Mother related the events of the afternoon to Father.

"I don't care if Edna Dewhurst wants to throw Ruby a party for going to the moon. She won't dictate decisions in my own home." Father scowled down at his plate but only picked at the food.

"Paul, be sensible. One word from her could wound your business irreparably. We can't take her feelings lightly, no matter how much I'd like to in this case." The resignation in her voice and the lines of concern on her face made me feel like the most selfish being to ever draw breath. "We wouldn't be in this mess if you'd forbidden the tests in the first place, as I wanted you to."

"I suppose you're pleased with yourself, young lady. Putting us in such a predicament. This is Bryn Mawr and that blasted suffrage rally all over again." Father slammed his fork down on the table loud enough that Evangeline appeared to see if there was a mess that needed to be attended to. Upon seeing Father's purplish complexion and the throbbing vein in his forehead, she disappeared back into the kitchen just as quickly.

I'd never live down my ill-fated attempt to participate in a National American Woman Suffrage Association meeting during my senior year at Bryn Mawr. One of Father's colleagues had seen me and given him a good ribbing for not being able to control the women in his household. I'd never seen Mother and Father angrier in my life and didn't care to repeat the experience. Had it not been for Francis intervening on my behalf, and the fact I only had weeks left before graduation, I have no doubt they'd have pulled me from classes. They never learned that I'd been elected president of the college chapter of the group, and it was just as well. I'd signed up more girls to fight for the cause than any president before me or since. But before Mother and Father could find out, I passed on the baton to the girl I thought best qualified to take my place the following year and disappeared from the movement altogether. Mother and Father held my studies over my head, then my work at Pennsylvania Bell. If my name had been mentioned in the same breath as another suffrage rally, they'd have yanked me back to the parlor, chained to Mother's side until Father delivered me to Nathaniel.

"I'm not happy about it in the least, Father. I'd prefer to make the decision on my own, without Mrs. Dewhurst's endorsement or, forgive me, your blanket opposition to the idea. I'm not a child, and I'm utterly tired of having my life dictated for me." My parents' faces were agape at my pronouncement. I'd tried since those last weeks at Bryn Mawr to keep the peace and had avoided such speeches since then, but there seemed little left to lose.

"Do you think things will be so different when you're married to Nathaniel? Will you go flouting *his* wishes at every turn? That won't make for a very happy marriage, I assure you." Mother's lips pursed, smug, thinking she'd thrown in the trump card.

"No," I spat. "You're passing me from one lord and master to another." Seeing Mother's eyes narrow, I lowered my voice. Father and Nathaniel weren't ogres, and painting them as such wouldn't earn Mother's favor. "I know Nathaniel is what you want for me. He's a good man, and I am lucky to marry into such a family. But I'll spend the next fifty years as Nathaniel's wife. *Fifty years* of duty. All I want is the opportunity to be of service to my country until he comes home. To do something that could make a real difference in defeating the men who killed Francis. It doesn't seem like all that much to ask."

Mother and Father sat silent for a few moments, not making eye contact with me or each other.

"I never once complained about having this engagement arranged for me, as though it was any one of Father's business contracts," I pressed. "I may not be the perfect daughter you wanted, but I *have* tried to obey your wishes."

"This is madness," Mother said, setting her napkin next to her untouched dinner plate and leaving the table without further discussion.

"Very well, Ruby. The decision is yours. And on your own head be it. I just hope that meaning isn't literal in this instance."

I read in my room for an hour or so after Evangeline cleared away the uneaten supper. When I realized I'd reread the same page a dozen times, I gave up on the endeavor, tossed back my covers, and slipped into my dressing gown, not knowing where I might find a retreat from my own thoughts. I considered going downstairs to see if the glow from the fire spilled from the crack beneath Father's study door, but I couldn't bring myself to knock. He'd not be in the mood for conversation. If Mother were still awake, she'd be even less open to discussing the events of the day. That left seeking out Evangeline, who had the door to her room, the smallest bedroom at the end of the hallway, cracked to hear in case she was needed. Her room had been a forbidden sanctuary of my own imposition. She worked so hard with so little respite that coming into her space when she had a few moments' peace felt somehow like crossing an unwritten line of conduct.

"Miss Ruby, come on in," Evangeline said, noticing me before I spoke. She was already in her nightgown, reading letters in bed by the dim light of her lamp. She had a handkerchief in one hand, and freshly shed tears, dried too hastily, streaked her face.

"Have you had some bad news?" I asked, ashamed that I had never thought to ask if she had a brother or some other relative overseas.

"Not as such. Just ignore me." She placed her letters back in the little, intricately painted wooden box where she seemed to keep some of her most valued possessions. Her eyes scanned the room. "I'm afraid I don't have a chair to offer you."

The room was by no means overlarge, but the only contents were a single bed, a tiny bedside table with a lamp that covered most of its surface, and a shabby-looking armoire where Evangeline kept her modest wardrobe. I'd have to ask Father what he could do about finding her a desk for letter writing and a comfortable chair to enhance what little time she had for leisure. If he wouldn't, she could borrow mine when I was gone.

I gestured to the corner at the foot of her bed. "Would you mind?" It was a familiar gesture, but somehow I felt like we were beyond such things.

"Of course not," she replied, sitting up straighter and pulling her covers tight around her chest. "Have you made your decision, then?"

I let out a low laugh. "I suppose you couldn't help but hear."

"No, none of you were speaking in dulcet tones, as it were," she admitted. "I knew the army would pick you. They'd have been daft not to."

"Thank you," I said. "It's nice to have someone under this roof pleased with the news."

"So, do you think you'll go?" she asked again.

"I can't stay home," I said, committing to the decision I hadn't realized I'd made. "I'd never be able to live with myself."

Rather than remind me of the dangers I'd be facing, she peppered me with questions about my training and what testing had been like. When I told her about the kit I was expected to purchase in New York, her eyes went wide.

"Surely your father will give you the money," Evangeline said. "But they wouldn't make it easy for a girl like me to go, would they?"

"I won't ask him," I said. "His consent is all I can bear to ask him for. It's all he has within him to give. Not his blessing. Not his well wishes. Not even his money. I'll accept the loan from AT&T and pay for the uniform out of my wages. I may not be paid a cent for my service, once the loan is accounted for, but it's not as though anyone is depending on my wages."

Having said the words, I was more convinced of the rightness of them. Once I married Nathaniel, he wouldn't give a second thought to whether I'd brought my own pocket money into the marriage. The thought that people lived on less than what he considered to be pocket money was not one I wanted to dwell on just then.

"It doesn't seem right, but I'm sure you know what you're doing." She patted my hand. "I wish I were able to do as much for the war effort as you are."

"You can provide me with an invaluable service, Evangeline. If I'm able to convince them to let me go, look after Mother and Father for me so I don't have to fret over them while I'm overseas."

"That isn't much of a service—they look after themselves well enough. But if it will make you happy, I'll do it."

"You must write to me and tell me how things *really* are. You know I'll never get much in the way of truth out of Mother, and Father's letters will be a rundown of how the business is going. They'll bear more resemblance to a memorandum to the board of directors than a letter to his daughter."

Evangeline laughed, but her eyes looked misty as she cast them back to the wooden box that perched on the bed at her right side.

"I'd be happy to. Did you know your brother, Francis, sent me letters when he was overseas? A dozen in the seven months he was gone."

"No, I didn't," I confessed, taking her hand as she dabbed at a few stray tears that reemerged. "He was the most thoughtful boy."

"I didn't share it before now. I didn't think your mother would approve. There was nothing untoward in them, of course, but you know how she can be." Evangeline glanced in the direction of Mother's room, hesitant, as though Mother would somehow hear the insolence in her tone. "Other boys like him, they look past me. I wasn't invisible to Francis, even though I was the help."

"I can well imagine," I replied drily. I doubted Nathaniel knew half his parents' servants' names. He surely didn't know Evangeline by any other name than "the Wagners' hired girl."

He'd sent her twelve letters since he left. I'd only received two of my own. Mother and Father perhaps four? I looked in her dark-brown eyes, admittedly beautiful. Had Francis formed an attachment to Evangeline under Mother's very nose? She'd be horrified at the idea of her son and heir marrying out of the circle she wanted for us. And now Evangeline's hopes were dashed.

I pulled her close, Mother's edicts about being too familiar with the help be damned. Evangeline returned the embrace, then pulled back and wiped her tears away with the corner of her blanket.

"He was dear to you, Evangeline," I said. "And while Mother is in the confines of her room, I can say I would have loved to have you as a sister-in-law."

Evangeline's chin began to quiver, but she stoically forced it to still. "I'm sure he would have come around to your mother's way of thinking before the deed was done, Ruby. But it was always a delicious fantasy. Married to a good man like Francis and having a life outside of service. A small brood of children to fuss after."

"Did Francis tell you he cared for you?" I asked, taking her hand in mine.

She nodded, swallowing back a fresh wave of tears. "He took me aside right before he left. He asked if I might leave him with a parting kiss to remember in the trenches. H-he said I was the sweetest girl he knew and that he'd hurry home to me."

"Evangeline, if my brother said those things, he would have married you within a month of his return. I promise you that." I spoke earnestly. Some boys were given to false promises and flattery, especially in times like these, when the future seemed so uncertain. Not my Francis. Not *Evangeline's* Francis.

"I would have loved to have you for a sister too." This time it was Evangeline who hugged me. "I wonder if you might do me a favor when you're over there?"

"If I can, of course," I said, sitting back.

She pulled a crisp envelope from the box that was labeled simply *My Francis*, with no address or further information. "I know it's daft, but I wrote him a letter—after. After we had the terrible news. If you could take it to him, wherever he's buried, a little part of my heart would be happier."

I took the letter in my hands and pressed it to my heart. "I'll get it as close to him as I can, Evangeline. I promise you."

Mrs. Dewhurst, true to her word, planned an elegant farewell party with only a few days' notice. Had it been in honor of any other occasion, Mother would have been in awe of her skills as a hostess. The invitation included Evangeline, who wrung her hands as she walked two paces behind Mother. We arrived at their stately home just a few moments past the appointed hour so that my entrance would have the desired impact. I stayed Father's hand on the knocker for just a moment as I steadied my breath, then plastered a smile on my face. A burst of applause sounded as I entered, and I was greeted by not only the faces I expected—the Morgans, the Harpers, and the rest of the Main Line set—but also Mrs. Trainor and most of the girls from Pennsylvania Bell. That Mrs. Dewhurst thought to invite them showed a largeness of spirit I hadn't expected. The girls stood together, chatting among themselves, and my parents and their friends clustered in small groups and occasionally cast a glance over at the girls, who were dressed in plain afternoon dresses suited for a shift at the switchboards. Mother's friends were in smart evening wear, not too formal, but appropriately festive for a party.

Mrs. Trainor, less timid than the girls, came over to our side with a nod to my mother. "We're so proud of you, Ruby," she said. "When Evangeline rang to tell us you were going for certain, I thought I was going to burst my very buttons."

Deep in my marrow I could feel Mother's cringe at Mrs. Trainor's playful use of slang.

"We're all proud of Ruby's sacrifice," Walter Harper said, his arm around Alice's slight frame, towering over her by more than a foot.

"And when is a strapping man like you shipping off?" Dora asked, her head cocked playfully, but arms akimbo. "Or should we pin a white feather to your lapel?"

"Bad knees, I'm afraid," Walter replied, his head ducking by a few degrees. "The medical board won't have me."

"But Walter is doing his part here at home, and admirably too," I said, patting his arm. "His family's factory keeps our men in munitions, and they'd be lost without him to run it."

I shot Dora a warning glare. Jibes tossed at a decent man like Walter would earn her no favors here, especially when there was a barbed hint of accusation behind them.

"Yes, yes," Father interjected. "We have to remember that there is a war movement here at home, and we can't spare every young man from our borders. Some of this white-feather nonsense has gone a bit too far, if you ask me."

"Quite so," Mrs. Trainor agreed. "I find it rather bold for young ladies to criticize young men for not going over, when they don't have to worry about conscription themselves."

Mother pivoted a degree or two toward Mrs. Trainor and offered her an approving nod.

"It makes Ruby's decision to serve all the more admirable in my mind," Mrs. Trainor continued. "And if I might have everyone's attention . . ." She held up her glass, tapping it with her fingernail. The conversation hushed as eyes turned to her. "We've taken up a collection at the phone company in Ruby's honor. We wanted to help cover the expense of her uniform and supplies, to show her that even though we remain behind, we're all with her in spirit." She turned toward me. "It won't be enough to cover the cost of your entire kit, I'm afraid, but it's a small token of our pride for your dedication and service."

She pulled a small envelope from her handbag and handed it over to me. A polite smattering of applause sounded. Everyone raised their glasses and toasted to their contribution.

"Thank you all so very much," I said, the heat pulsing in my cheeks. I hadn't peeked in the envelope, but I could tell it was a considerable amount of money, certainly large enough to be a sacrifice for those who contributed. "I honestly can't accept this. It's far too generous."

Mrs. Trainor put up her hands to block any attempt to return the envelope. "We insist, Ruby dear. I'd go over myself if I weren't twenty years too old for the job. We want you to take a bit of us with you."

"Ruby is quite right," Father chimed in. "It's very generous, to be sure, but we can happily see to her expenses."

"Now, Paul, I think that's rather greedy of you," Walter said, stepping forward and clapping Father companionably on the shoulder. "I believe Mrs. Trainor here is onto something. Helping Ruby with her kit is helping the war effort. You wouldn't deny her friends the chance to send her off properly, now would you?"

"I suppose not, son. I suppose not," Father said.

Walter pulled out his billfold and placed two crisp twenty-dollar bills in my hand. I covered the denomination before the girls from the phone company could see it. Their five-dollar contributions would be felt in their budgets for weeks, while his forty dollars would never be missed.

"Walter—" I began.

"You work hard and finish this war for us, Ruby girl, and it'll be money well spent," he replied. Alice beamed up at him, as proud as if he were donning the khaki himself.

"Hear, hear," Mrs. Dewhurst declared, producing some bills and passing them to Evangeline, who'd come to my side. "It's our duty to see to it this girl is sent off knowing that Philadelphia stands with her." Amid cheers, a dozen or more of the guests reached for their billfolds and handbags to add to the pile of bills that Evangeline now discreetly stashed into my handbag for me.

Mother had turned a rather violent shade of purple but kept a smile plastered to her lips. I was going to hear about this. Father shot me a martyred expression, letting me know my instincts were right and that I wouldn't be alone in my suffering.

Nettie Morgan kept to the fringes of the party, as was her usual custom when she wasn't hosting an event herself. She wasn't shy, so much as keenly aware of the attention she commanded in a room when she mingled more freely. She risked overshadowing the hostess if she played the room, and there were few offenses greater in the Main Line. She had mastered the art of staying to the side of things but keeping her manner inviting so that others felt welcome to seek her out. Once the barrage of contributions had come to its end, she broke from her post in the parlor corner to approach me.

"I have a little something for you, my dear," Mrs. Morgan said, taking my hand. "Not quite as practical as money for your kit, but I daresay Mr. Morgan will be happy to shore up any deficiencies you might have in your funds." I scanned the room to see Nathaniel's father, Albert Morgan, dozing on the sofa, a glass of Mr. Dewhurst's best single-malt scotch in his hand.

"I can't imagine I'll want for a thing, Mrs. Morgan," I said, thinking of the mass of bills Evangeline had stuffed into my handbag. I'd have been shocked if there was a penny less than $500 between the Pennsylvania Bell envelope and the money thrust into my hands tonight. Well more than I'd need for my kit and travel expenses. I'd purchase war bonds with the overage or else donate to the Red Cross.

"It does seem as though you've been well taken care of, my dear. And rightfully so. I can't say I understand the young people these days, but we're happy to support you in this. I wanted to give you a little token of Nathaniel to take with you. A talisman for good luck, so to speak."

She produced a small box from her little beaded clutch and placed it in my hand. I opened it to reveal a silver locket in the shape of a heart, with flowers etched onto it. Inside was a miniature photograph of Nathaniel in his uniform, tall and solemn, though the pride glinting from his eyes softened his expression.

"Such a handsome young man," Mother said, peering over my shoulder to see what Mrs. Morgan had given me. "I'm sure Ruby will treasure it."

"Of course," I agreed. Mother removed the necklace from the box in my hands, and fastened it around my throat. Mother and Mrs. Morgan didn't need to know it would have to stay stowed in my case when I was in uniform.

"You must promise me one thing, my dear," Mrs. Morgan said, taking my hands once more. "News from the front has been so scarce. I know Nathaniel must be horribly busy with training, but it's hard for Mr. Morgan and me to be in the dark. You'll be in the middle of everything, information-wise. If you hear anything about Nathaniel, you'll be sure to let us know."

"Of course, she'll be happy to," Mother supplied on my behalf. "I expect she'll be just as glad to hear the news herself."

"If I'm able," I said. "Secrecy is paramount to winning the war, if all the posters are to be believed. I don't want to make promises I can't keep."

"Very sensible, my dear," Mrs. Morgan said, patting my arm.

"I can assure you that if I see him, I'll remind him that regular letters home wouldn't come amiss."

"Good girl," Mrs. Morgan said with a polite titter. "Though I'm sure few of the boys can be bothered with such things. I'd always wished we'd had a daughter as well as our Nathaniel. You know the old saying 'My son is my son 'til he takes a wife, but my daughter's my daughter for the rest of her life.'"

"Well, you needn't worry on that score, my dear Nettie," Mother said. "I know our Ruby isn't the sort of girl to slight her family-in-law, no matter how devoted she is to us."

In my mind loomed a vision of thirty years of Christmases, Thanksgivings, and Easters where each set of parents cajoled their only child to attend the festivities with them. Each and every family event stood to be a battle. Mother would be understanding at first but would grow resentful. I expected Nathaniel's mother would be much the same.

I was then pulled away by Harriet and the rest of the Bell girls, who wanted to give me a parting hug before finding the streetcar home. They had work in the early hours and hadn't the luxury of lingering.

"Make sure you give the best-looking doughboys our names, will you?" Dora said with a kiss on my cheek. "Nothing quite as dashing as a man in uniform, is there?"

"I think we'll all be a bit busy for that sort of thing," I quipped, with a playful cuff to her arm.

"Never too busy for love," Harriet supplied. "And just because you're spoken for doesn't mean you can't do some good publicity for your pals back home. Just remember, I like the tall, dark, and handsome ones. Save the baby-faced ones for Bessie."

Bessie stuck out her tongue. At nineteen, she was one of the youngest employees in the building. A fact Harriet rarely let her forget.

"Jot down your orders, and I'll see what I can send back for you," I said with a laugh. "I'll miss you all so very much."

"The war will be over in a few weeks, and you'll be back in the seat next to mine in time for spring," Harriet predicted. "Just you wait and see."

"Your lips to God's ears, my girl," I said, though my smile didn't go very deep. The odds were that I'd worked my last day at the phone company. Once the war was over and Nathaniel came home, I'd be preparing for the wedding in earnest. My arguments for holding a job would become fewer and fewer.

Mrs. Trainor joined the girls and towed Evangeline along with her. "You have your Evangeline here to thank for our collection," she said as she kissed my cheeks. "She was the one who mentioned that the army was requiring you all to pay for your kits. She hated the thought of you depleting your nest egg before your wedding, and we all agreed."

"Evangeline is a wonder," I said. "Especially when it comes to sticking her nose in my affairs." I winked in her direction.

"I'm not even a little sorry, Miss Ruby," Evangeline said, adopting the "Miss" Mother insisted on when company was present. "I couldn't bear the thought of you leaving without a proper send-off."

"Too right," Mrs. Trainor said. "Though I ought to be furious with you, leaving me shorthanded like this. Replacing you won't be an easy task."

"You know, Mrs. Trainor, the perfect solution might be closer than you think," I said, surprised this was the first time I'd considered the idea. "Evangeline is as smart as they come and has a lovely speaking voice. I don't think you could do better."

"Please don't go giving people ideas. I'm sure I'd never be able to figure it all out." The shade of vermilion in Evangeline's cheeks matched her fiery hair.

"I'll be the judge of that, young lady," Mrs. Trainor said. "I want to see you in my office on Monday morning."

"But what about your parents?" Evangeline said. "Surely you don't want to leave them in the lurch?"

"They won't be throwing many parties over the next few months, and I daresay keeping house for them alone won't take all your day. You could work half shifts and have plenty of time to look in on Mother and Father. And gain some work experience outside of service too."

"It's all settled," Mrs. Trainor said. "I won't take no for an answer."

"Very well," Evangeline said. Though her tone was resigned, I saw a glimmer of excitement in her eyes I'd not seen before.

CHAPTER 6

"No packing light, that's for certain," Evangeline said, looking at the pile from the pharmacy that I had heaped on my bed. A mending kit, several toothbrushes and a liberal amount of brushing powder, a hot-water bottle—things the army thought necessary for our deployment. Evangeline had spent the day with me at Wanamaker's department store and the pharmacy amassing the items for my kit. Only my uniform, hats, insignia, and shoes remained to be purchased from the military tailor in New York. "What do you think the baking powder is for? Do they expect you to poison the Germans with cakes?"

"Knowing my skill in the kitchen, one of my cakes would do the trick," I said as I unwrapped my new nightgowns. "It's probably in case of an upset stomach or the like. Again, necessary if I end up cooking."

"Hush now, you've made progress in the kitchen," Evangeline scolded as she sorted. "You just need more practice."

"Speaking of practice, are you excited for your chat with Mrs. Trainor on Monday? I can go over some of the basics with you before then."

"Don't you think I'm daft to try?" Evangeline asked, not looking up as she folded my new nightgowns. "I can't imagine they'd have any use for me. And I'll have to wear my Sunday dress every day of the week until I have wages enough for a new one. Everyone will laugh at me."

"Enough of this dull stuff," I said. "Let's go through my things for you. I've got a closetful of clothes that will go untouched until I get back, and they'll get you through until you can get things you like. You're taller than I am, but the hemlines are going up, so that won't matter too awfully much."

I reserved three of the most practical suits of clothes to take along with me but let Evangeline pick and choose from the rest. Chances were, styles would have changed so much by the time I returned home that I'd not miss anything she wanted to keep. Not to mention Mother would insist that I have new things suitable for a young matron once I was married.

"I fear I'm interrupting quite the gabfest," Father said with a knock at the open door.

"Home already, Father? Evangeline and I are just going through some things."

"You've got quite the collection to take with you, my dear," Father said, eyeing the parcels that still littered the bed.

"Indeed, I do," I said.

"Then my contribution to the war effort will come in useful." Father motioned into the hallway, and a young man carrying a large leather steamer trunk entered the room.

"Just place it at the foot of the bed," I ordered.

"Thank you, Dennis," Father said, slipping a bill into the delivery boy's hand. "Evangeline, I do believe Mrs. Wagner could do with a cup of tea. If not, you ought to take ten minutes to yourself and enjoy one." Evangeline excused herself with a quick curtsey and a small smile at Father's manner of dismissal.

"Thank you, Father. I'd been meaning to ask to borrow Mother's, but I hadn't worked up the courage."

"I don't blame you," Father said with a wink. "We ought to send *her* overseas. She'd have the war over in a snap, wouldn't she? She simply wouldn't stand for the nonsense to continue on any longer."

"She's our secret weapon," I agreed. "I'll make sure General Pershing smuggles her over at the first opportunity."

"Good girl," he said. "I hope you like the trunk. I thought at first it might be a bit too elegant for your purposes, but the war won't last forever. You'll need a nice trunk when Nathaniel takes you gallivanting."

"I wonder if he'll want to," I said. "He may have had enough gallivanting for one lifetime."

"You could be right, my dear. Though I expect the lure of Europe in peacetime will call him back soon enough. There's hardly a year gone by when Nettie Morgan hasn't spent at least a few weeks in London or Paris."

"You know, if you intended this for an early wedding gift, you ought to have used my married name on the nameplate. You've had them engrave REW, not REM."

"Well, my dear, in at least this small way, you'll still be a Wagner. Until you're in need of new luggage, at any rate."

"Always," I agreed.

Father bridged the gap between us and scooped me up in a hug, as he used to do when I was small.

"This whole venture of yours is harebrained and foolish, you know," he said, kissing the top of my head. "And I couldn't be prouder. Just promise me you'll do nothing to put yourself in danger. We've had quite enough heartbreak in this house."

I nodded, willing the tears not to spill over onto my cheeks. "Of course, Papa."

Mother, apparently having turned down Evangeline's offer for tea, entered my room, her arms laden with clothes. I released Father and braced myself as she bustled about the room like a cyclone.

"I thought the trunk would never get here," she said, setting the pile on my writing desk. "Why you didn't go with Strawbridge's, Paul, I'll never know."

"I'll leave you ladies to it," Father said, shaking his head. Mother said nothing but opened the lid of the trunk.

"I hope you have space enough. I can't imagine what the army is thinking, expecting you to take half a pharmacy with you."

"I expect because we can't count on the French pharmacies still being open in the advanced areas." *Or still standing.*

"Well, it's no wonder Evangeline thought you'd need to pass the hat to pay for all this. I ought to send her packing for it, though. It was mortifying."

"She's been good to us for the past two years, Mother. I'll be furious if you do anything of the sort." I folded my arms over my chest as Mother began undoing all of Evangeline's work and sorting things to her own liking.

"Well, heaven forbid my feelings are taken into account. That would never do." She examined the interior of the trunk and made no disparaging comment. At least one thing met with her approval. Her gaze shifted to the two short piles of clothing I'd set aside to pack.

"Lord, I knew I couldn't trust you to do this yourself. Are you going to wear the same clothes until they're threadbare like a pauper's?" Mother shook her head. The only clothing I'd laid out were the nightgowns and undergarments the army included on the list, along with two plain suits in brown and gray wool I'd reserved from my own wardrobe. A third suit in a finer maroon tweed I'd wear on the train and save for any nicer occasions that might come up. It seemed enough to get me through until my uniform could be tailored in New York. A few novels and a family photo were the only luxuries I brought with me. Anything more seemed like an unnecessary burden.

"Look what I have for you." She held up a lovely afternoon dress of dainty lavender satin with ecru lace. There was a small bunch of silk flowers attached to the sash at the waist. Just the thing for a smart tea with Main Line society in spring.

"It's beautiful, Mother." I didn't meet her eyes and looked instead at the pile of clothes she planned to add to the—rather restricted—confines of my new trunk.

"You don't like it," she assessed. "Whatever is the matter with it?"

"Not a thing. Truly. It's a gorgeous dress, but I'll be in uniform."

"You can't mean to tell me you won't have any time to socialize in Paris. You'll have need of a few smart things."

"I don't know if I'll be stationed in Paris," I said, trying to veil my exasperation. She never fully grasped that France and Paris were not the same thing. "And no, I don't expect to be out of uniform at all while I'm overseas." I'd not been given much instruction on that score, but I knew the officers and enlisted men brought no civilian clothes and only a very few personal effects. I had no reason to believe we would be treated any differently.

Mother sat down her pile of velveteen and satin to look over the folded garments on the bed. "You haven't even set out proper underthings. Where is your corset?"

"I'm not taking one, Mother. You've heard the decree from the War Industries Board. I took all of mine to have the metal repurposed for the war. You ought to do the same."

"I most certainly will not. What is the point of the war if we all slide into barbarism? What are you planning to wear, for heaven's sake? Or were you planning to run free like a wildebeest?"

"A brassiere and army-issue bloomers, Mother," I said, trying to put things back in order as she rummaged through them.

"And they expect you to go without a corset? A girdle?"

"Yes, Mother. I expect they need us agile enough to move quickly. They won't have much patience for the impediment of a corset on an operator any more than they would an infantryman. And I'll have you know there wasn't a single corset to be seen at Wanamaker's this morning. I don't expect they'll come back into fashion once women get a taste of freedom."

"I don't know what you've gotten yourself mixed up in, Ruby, but get it out of your system while you're over there. The Morgans won't stand for it. I'd forbid it in the first place, but your father overruled me."

I thought of Nettie Morgan finding the temerity to address my undergarments and had to stifle a laugh. I could almost feel the heat from her imaginary blush, daring to even approach such an indelicate topic.

"Mother, I'm not going over for the express purpose of embarrassing you or the family. I just want to do my part."

"You can do your part here. The Red Cross—"

"I know what you're going to say, and I'm sorry I can't always do what makes you happy. I have tried. I hope you know that. All the same, this is where I'm needed." I stood aside as she, unhearing, continued to rifle through the piles of goods, reorganizing as she saw fit, removing a few required items, and adding the impractical garments with abandon. "Mother, I appreciate you going to the trouble of getting me new things, but I don't think it's wise to take them."

"You've always been stubborn, and your father encouraged it. You get it from him, you know."

Father, being one of the most tractable men I'd ever known, was hardly the source of my stubbornness, but I held my tongue. I suspect that in his youth, Father had been a lump of clay; he made something of himself only because he had Mother prodding him into the figure of the man he became. She ought to be proud of her role in his success, but she would never claim it. She preferred to stuff me in a corset and pinched ballroom slippers to follow in her footsteps.

Mother filled my trunk with the delicate dresses and frilly underthings that I would be forced to lug through Europe. In the end, it was a lighter burden to bear than her unmet expectations. I'd need four porters just to carry the thing down a gangplank. Shaking my head, I removed my ruby engagement ring and the silver locket from Nettie Morgan and placed them in the jewel box on my dresser. There they would remain until I returned. It was just a little less weight to bear on my shoulders.

CHAPTER 7

January 14, 1918
New York City

I'd visited Manhattan a few times over the course of my youth, and it had impressed me each time. The vivacity of the people and the energy of the city were qualities we couldn't fully emulate in Philadelphia. Though I wasn't a backwater bumpkin, I could not help but feel daunted by the city that could swallow a person whole without ever taking notice.

I reported to the gleaming new AT&T headquarters on Broadway. The stone pillars seemed rooted deep within the earth itself and stretched up to the heavens. The lobby gleamed with polished marble that reflected my figure almost as clearly as a mirror. The click-clack of my low-heeled boots would have been deafening, but it was covered by the sounds of dozens of other people's hurried footsteps and the intense buzz of what sounded like very urgent conversations. Then again, everything in Manhattan always seemed to be of critical importance, whether it was or not.

I found the room designated for our orientation on the tenth floor of the massive edifice. I'd arrived a few minutes before our briefings were set to begin and peered out the window. There was no hope of seeing much in the distance, the view being obscured by other behemoths of concrete and steel, but watching the people below scurrying about in the light flurry of snow was fascinating. The carriages whose numbers were decreasing. The motorcars and trucks that were becoming more numerous. Bicycles darted between them, more daring than I thought they ought to be. It was dirtier, grittier, and less friendly than Philadelphia, but infinitely more interesting. There were thirty or so women gathered in the room before we were called to take our places.

A tall, uniformed gentleman—it seemed as though the sight of a man in civilian clothes was becoming a bit of a novelty—addressed the room, which was now buzzing with the excited chatter of the women who would be crossing over with me.

"Ladies, I'm Captain Ernest Wessen. Welcome to your training. We have a tight schedule for you, but I'm afraid compared to what you'll be up against overseas, this will be a breezy summer holiday, despite what the weather might have to say on the matter." A number of us chuckled at the attempt at humor. "Today you'll be given orders as to where you'll be staying in the city, get fitted for your uniforms, and so on. Once all those administrative matters are seen to, you'll spend the next few weeks learning the military hierarchy and getting briefings on topics of importance related to your time overseas. Your government thanks you for your service. We received thousands of letters from interested young women, and you were among the elite chosen for service. You should be immensely proud to be sitting in this room today."

I felt the tingling of gooseflesh at the captain's words. The reality that I would be going overseas was sinking in, but I didn't feel the nag of fear lapping at my toes like cold ocean waves.

"I need to see Miss Fairbanks, Miss Wagner, and Miss Henderson in my office. The rest of you will kindly head out the door to the left to have your photographs taken for your passports." The captain gestured to an open door, which led to a vast corridor. The girls filed out, but a tall young woman with mousy-brown hair crossed the room to Captain Wessen, as did a shorter woman with a crop of black curls.

"Millicent Fairbanks," the tall woman said, extending her hand to the captain and then to me. "Pleased to meet you." Miss Gloria Henderson and I followed suit.

The captain led us to his office. It was a small, windowless room that was clearly designed for storage. Yet another broom closet enjoying the glory of a wartime promotion. The three of us barely had room to take our places in the folding chairs without giving the other a concussion.

"The reason I've called you here is to inform you that Miss Fairbanks has been selected to serve as chief operator for your group, and Misses Wagner and Henderson as supervising operators. The three of you have shown not only exemplary skill at the switchboards, but also a knack for training and leadership that makes you ideal for the post."

Millicent turned white as the plaster on the walls, and I was certain I wasn't any rosier. I'd worried that helping Beatrice at the switchboards during the exams would get me in trouble, but perhaps they'd seen it as an aptitude for teaching. I couldn't imagine that their learning about my involvement with the suffragists' chapter at Bryn Mawr would have worked in my favor, but logic wasn't something to seek out in the upper hierarchy of the US Army.

"You will each have roughly twelve women under your command. Two of those will serve as your assistants. You will direct the training of the women under your command and be responsible for their conduct. They will salute you as they would their superior officer. We urge you to remember that while you may become very close to the women in your squadrons, it's best to keep distance between yourselves and your subordinates. It will help everyone adhere to the chain of command."

"I've never commanded anyone before," Millicent said, her hands clasped in her lap.

"You will find that we're all called upon in wartime to do things we've never done before. More often than not, things we didn't think we were capable of. You'll find yourself equal to the task, Miss Fairbanks. I'm certain of it."

"I hope you're right," she said.

"I have no choice but to be correct about all of you, Miss Fairbanks. If this mission of ours is a failure, it could cost us the war. If you've been led to believe otherwise, we've expressed ourselves badly."

Millicent, Gloria, and I left with a salute. An awkward one, owing to our desire not to jab anyone in the ribs.

"That was terrifying," Gloria finally managed to breathe as we searched for the corridor where the others waited for their photographs.

"It was meant to be, I'm sure," I said. "The captain wants us scared so we take this thing seriously."

"Well, it worked," Millicent said. "I don't know the first thing about saluting or marching or any of this army stuff. I had no idea they'd go and make me chief operator, of all things."

"None of us do," I reminded her. "Not one of us has a bit of military experience. Neither did most of the boys at the front. You're no worse off than any of us."

Millicent's expression brightened a bit. "I suppose that does help," she said. "I wish I had your confidence, though."

"If there's one thing I learned from my father and all his business dealings, it's that success is usually pretending you're capable of doing something until you are."

A soft knock followed by the rattling of keys sounded at the hotel-room door.

"You are decent, yes?" someone with a heavily accented, lilting voice called before opening the door completely.

"Yes, yes," I replied. "Come in."

The young woman was perhaps twenty-two years of age, with dark golden-brown hair pulled into a loose knot at the nape of her neck. Her dainty black hat, adorned with a single white silk rose, was placed at a saucy tilt. She had startlingly green eyes, the sort that missed nothing. Her nose was slim and graceful, her lips full. Her blue suit of clothes was plain, but she wore it well. The picture of a Gibson girl in all her radiant health and beauty. I felt the prick of jealousy in my throat but swallowed it back. Soon enough we'd be in uniform and it would be our skills, rather than our looks, that mattered. Wouldn't that be a refreshing change?

"You are Ruby Wagner, yes? I have been told to room with you," she said, fluttering as she set down her case.

"Yes, though you have me at a disadvantage, Miss—?"

"Oh, *pardon*. I am Margot St. Denis. Pleased to meet you." She placed her suitcase on the floor and extended a hand. "I'll be under your command as your *assistante*, Miss Wagner. I am sorry to have missed today's training. My train was very late coming in from Portland. But with a war on, this sort of thing is to be expected, I suppose."

"Ah, you're from Maine. I've heard it's beautiful there. I've never had the chance to visit."

"It is," she confirmed, placing her case on the bed nearest the wall. She turned her head to take in her surroundings. "As many lakes, forests, mountains as a person could want. This is a lovely room, isn't it?"

"Very," I agreed. For all Mother's fretting that I'd be living in flea-infested taverns, she couldn't have found fault with the Prince George Hotel. The air was laced with the scent of orange oil and freshly laundered sheets. The tall, dark walnut headboards on the beds gleamed from regular polishing. The crisp linens sparkled as white as those in the most pristine hospital but were softened by cheerful floral wallpaper and quaint, if bland, paintings of idyllic countrysides that likely existed nowhere outside of the artist's imagination.

"Did you grow up in Maine, then?" I asked as Margot set to unpacking her two suits of clothes and few personal effects.

"Trois-Rivières in Quebec. Papa moved us to Maine when I was twelve." She snapped her case shut and closed the closet doors.

"That explains your lovely accent," I said.

"Ah yes, my accent." She narrowed her eyes. "Because of it, the phone company would not hire me for the switchboards, though I placed highest on their operator exams. They stick me in an office typing all day instead. You Americans loathe nothing so much as a foreign accent."

I thought of Father's annoyance when he had to do business with foreign brokers. His difficulties parsing their words made him feel stupid, which was one thing he could never abide. The issue would only be compounded over the telephone. "That's a shame," I said. "But now you can put all your knowledge to work for a higher cause."

"This is true," she said, placing her case in the far corner next to mine. "And when we get back home, perhaps my service to the country will make my accent seem less important to Ma Bell, no?"

"I should think so," I affirmed, choking back my doubts. *"People recognize their peers by their manner of speaking,"* Mother had insisted daily when I would complain about the tedium of the speaking exercises. The world was changing, to be sure, but I wasn't certain a big company like Bell could change to keep pace with it. "I'm happy to help you with it if you want. My French accent isn't what it could be either. An exchange of talents, so to speak?"

"You have a deal." Margot stuck out her hand to shake on it.

"Brilliant. We'll trade afternoons. You can be student first since it was my idea."

"*Fantastique*—fantastic," she corrected herself. "But not today, if you don't mind."

"Of course, it must have been a long trek."

"It is long in normal times. Add the confusion of a war and it is simply dreadful."

"In that case, let's go find some supper. I'm not sure they had anything planned for this evening. Between you and me, I think they are improvising more than they'd have us know."

Color drained from Margot's face. "Perhaps we can find a little grocery? Or just a little sandwich?"

She was likely famished after her trip but had been expecting the army to provide for her. Based on the decadent lobby and our posh furnishings, I figured the hotel restaurant had to cost the earth. "There's a little diner a block south of here. My treat."

"That is gracious of you," she said, reclaiming a small handbag from her belongings and assessing her reflection in the full-length mirror that dominated one corner of the room. She adjusted her hat and jacket, then smoothed her skirt. She had circles under her eyes from travel, but only food and sleep would cure those.

We walked companionably down the streets of New York, chatting about the wonders of the city and our lives back home. Her brother, Antoine, was in the service too. He'd joined up with a Canadian regiment soon after the war started and was notoriously poor about writing home. Margot's father, Jacques, had brought them to Maine ten years before because work had been scarce closer to home. Though he learned that the streets south of the Longfellow Mountains were no more paved in gold than the ones to the north, he'd made a decent living working for paper mills after earning the respect of his supervisors and working his way up the ladder until he passed two years before. She spoke of her father with affection, and while my own father had an easier time making his way in the world, I could see a similarity in their characters. I could only imagine the pain she'd felt in losing him. If anything were to happen to Father, I'd be left without an ally against Mother and her insisting ways.

I pushed the painful thought away and told her a bit about my own parents, glossing over Father's successes a bit and trying to paint Mother fairly. I told her about Francis. I spoke of Evangeline like a sister and of the happy times working for Bell. Margot had anecdotes about her colleagues in the Portland branch and made no attempt to hide her envy of the operators who, it seemed, lorded over the secretaries and other staff. I was grateful we didn't have the same atmosphere in Philadelphia.

"And I was the only one from my branch to be selected this time," Margot said with a satisfied smile. "There were others who did well, so I expect they will be called soon, but I was first."

I smiled at her as the waiter placed menus in front of us. "What can I get you ladies to drink?" the waiter asked as we opened our menus. The custom in casual restaurants annoyed me. My choice of beverage might depend on what I wanted for my meal, which I could not have begun to choose, but shooing a waiter away long enough to make the decision was almost always met with visible disdain. Based on stories Harriet's brother, who worked in a bistro not far from our office in Philadelphia, had told her about what waiters and chefs did to the food of problem customers, I had no desire to annoy anyone.

"An iced tea, please," I said, thinking it would pair well enough with any of the entrees I glanced over on the menu.

"The same for me, please," Margot added with a smile.

Rather than be charmed by her sweet demeanor, the waiter rolled his eyes. "I can hardly understand you with that accent."

"I-I apologize," Margot stammered. "I will have the same as my friend."

The waiter let out an exaggerated sigh and muttered something about "foreigners" under his breath.

"Excuse me," I intervened. "There was nothing hard to understand about her order. Or are you hard of hearing?"

The waiter's grip on his notepad grew viselike at the inference. "I can hear perfectly fine, miss. It's she who can't talk right."

"I promise you, young man, there is nothing wrong with her manner of speaking. I suggest you remember this if you want our business." I was now sitting ramrod straight and could feel my mother's coldest glare on my face. For once I was glad for the loan of it.

"It makes no difference to me, lady. Why should I serve some Frenchie? They can't even fight their own wars."

Margot averted her eyes and looked down. I could see the trembling in her hands only because I was looking for it.

"This young lady is a Canadian-born American. Furthermore, she is in service to this country and will be going overseas to do her part. Don't you dare presume to speak down to her."

"I don't see a uniform," he spat. "You're lying."

Margot found some of her gall and hurled it at him. "We'll be in them soon enough. Where's yours?"

"I haven't been called up yet, not that it's any of your business."

"The lady you just insulted didn't have to be called up," I retorted. "She volunteered. As did I. Do you still think you ought to be running your mouth, young man? What would your employer say?"

The pimple-faced boy stammered what sounded like an apology, but I'd had my fill of his gall. I stood from my seat and said loud enough for the entire diner to hear, "I don't think I care to spend my money in a restaurant run by cowards who insult servicewomen. Let's find someplace else, Margot."

A number of people applauded as we exited the restaurant, and a couple of tables even cleared out, leaving uneaten food behind. The diner owner tried to race after us, calling apologies, but I took Margot's arm in mine, and we didn't give him the satisfaction of looking backward.

We walked for more than a half hour in silence. I could feel that Margot's shaking had stopped, but I still waited for her to break the silence when she was ready.

"Does this place look nice to you?" she asked. A rumble from her stomach punctuated her words. It was an Italian restaurant—they all were in this neighborhood, apparently. I'd not had much Italian food, even in Philadelphia, where there was plenty of it to be found, but I had enjoyed what little I'd sampled.

"It looks lovely," I said, glancing in at the inviting room, which was warmed by candle glow and red-checkered gingham tablecloths. We stepped inside and were immediately whisked to a quiet table in the corner by a waiter whose accent was so thick, there would be no chance of him paying any mind to hers. Her shoulders lowered by inches as she pored over the menu.

"I think the time for iced tea has passed, don't you?" I asked Margot, preempting the waiter's question. "How about some chianti?"

"Oh yes," she said. "That is the finest idea I've heard all day. I am glad they made you supervisor." The waiter scurried off with a smile in search of a bottle.

"My willingness to calm nerves with cheap wine *was* one of the determining factors," I said deadpan. She laughed for the first time since we met, loud enough to receive arched eyebrows from the nearby table.

"*Mon dieu, ce goujat.* I should not have let him bother me," she said.

"Anyone would be upset by such a thing," I said, patting her hand. "But do your best to shake it off. We can't let little vermin like him rattle us. We have bigger things to be getting on with."

"This is very true. Though I try not to think of the—bigness—of it?" she said. "Only what I must do each day. One day, I can handle. A whole war? Only armies can do such things."

"You're a wise woman, Margot. And I'm glad to have you with me. I'll be grateful for every level head under my command. Though I confess: commanding was never what I thought I'd be doing."

"From what I have seen, you're very good at it," Margot said, and thanked the waiter as he placed a glass before her and filled it with the velvety-red liquid.

"I hope you're right," I said.

"I have never had this 'pizza' before, have you?"

"No," I confessed. "Though it seems we're meant to share it. Which one shall we order?"

"I am not too brave this evening. The *Margherita* seems simple enough?" she asked.

It wasn't long before the waiter came back with an enormous flat circle of bread that could have easily fed a family of four. The zing of the tomato sauce added life to the stolid flavor of the cheese. The chopped leaves of basil married the two together.

"This is *magnifique*, really," Margot said between bites. "I am glad I haven't been measured for my uniform yet."

I laughed, knowing what Mother would say if she saw me eating my fill of anything. But she was not there, nor was her disapproving *tsk* as we finished the entire pizza.

I considered suggesting a streetcar but was glad for the walk back to the hotel, despite the dark and the chill of night. Perhaps we should have been more worried, but with all the trouble overseas, it seemed everyone was too preoccupied to cause much trouble at home.

Back in our room, we changed into our nightgowns, the wine still causing us to giggle more than we might otherwise. "Thank you for standing up for me today, by the way," Margot said as she arranged herself in bed. "I ought to be used to it by now. We are picked on in Portland too. They think we are stupid and *paresseux*—lazy—no matter how much we show them otherwise. But it is rare that anyone stands up for us like you did."

"Please don't mention it," I said. "He deserved an earful."

"It was fun to see," Margot admitted with a giggle. "You will have the Germans back in Berlin single-handedly if you use that tone with them."

"Then I'll be sure to do so at the first opportunity," I said, wishing it were true.

~

The comfort of our lodgings at the Prince George was a temporary luxury. By the end of our first week, we were sleeping on cots in a New Jersey tavern, which was much closer to the flea-infested hovels Mother had warned would be my reality for the duration of the war. There were forty women in our group, each of whom was to salute Millicent. Then Gloria and I as supervisors were next in command, then the assistant supervisors like Margot, then the rest of the operators. That part of the military hierarchy we had down easily enough. The rest I had to pretend I knew and help the others muddle through. My girls were coming along passably well in marching—though I'd not want them to stand inspection yet. We spent hours on the roof of the AT&T building doing calisthenics, marching, and drilling. I would have preferred to have more hours getting some of them up to speed on the switchboards, but I had no power to set the schedule.

"Keep up the pace, Miss Porter," I called when Sadie, a statuesque woman from Maryland, lagged two paces too far behind the woman in front of her. Her eyes lanced daggers at me, but she quickened her step. She didn't like me, but it wasn't in her nature to be defiant toward someone in authority. She was likely five years older than I, and I suspected she resented that I'd been made supervisor and she hadn't even been given a place as an assistant.

"This is getting tedious," called Luce, the French-born San Franciscan, in her lilting accent. "How much longer must we march on this silly rooftop?"

I wanted to agree with her. The stylish boots—the most serviceable I owned—had created at least a half dozen blisters on my toes and heels in the two weeks we'd been training. But I couldn't give in to my discomfort any more than I could indulge Luce in her boredom. "Until you all learn to do it right," I said. "We're soldiers now. Our boys overseas have been training far longer than we have, and we must be able to keep up with them, mustn't we?"

"That's right," Margot agreed, though I knew she was no more fond of the marching in the biting February wind than anyone else.

The women from the East Coast were, as a rule, compliant. Bless them for it. The three westerners in the group—Luce and Addie from San Francisco and Vera from Seattle—were less apt to accept regulations without a barrage of questions. Ruth from Denver was fiercely independent, and I don't think she cared for the orders and rules any more than the rest of the westerners, but she was a serious and steadfast girl and gave me no headaches. We continued our drills for another hour before we were relieved to go downstairs for lunch in the cafeteria and an afternoon on the switchboards.

"It's too bad they can't hire a proper cook." Hazel, a diminutive girl from Boston, sighed, looking down at the forlorn sandwich and rather anemic pasta salad on her tray as she took a place next to me. The cafeteria cooks were scrambling to keep up with the needs of the influx of operators training for duty overseas, and the challenge was compounded by shortages of wheat, sugar, and almost everything else.

"Think of what our men are eating at the front," I said. "I'm sure many would be grateful to be eating so well."

Hazel ate in silence, perhaps annoyed at my remonstrance, but it had to be done. If we vented every complaint or let ourselves wallow in homesickness, we'd all be miserable. Worse, we'd be ineffective. Margot and I separated at mealtimes to change the course of conversation when it took a negative turn. I hated censuring them. Nothing they complained about was really out of order, but if they couldn't handle the challenges of training, then service overseas would be unthinkable.

Every one of us had an extra bounce in our step as we walked down the corridor to the switchboards. The experienced operators were thrilled to work the busiest exchange in the country, while the others were anxious to get more practice. I smiled at their enthusiasm, wishing

I could have my turn at the boards as well, but that was the sacrifice I was called on to make. Ruth, Hazel, and Sadie were the best on the boards by a wide margin, and so I entrusted much of their training to Margot. She also looked over Eleanor—a Canadian-born girl living in Michigan who was a newer operator but learning well enough. Ruth was so skilled as an operator, she was one of the rare few who didn't speak much French who was called on to serve. Luce and Margot, our native speakers, took turns tutoring her in the evenings and at odd moments. She was an eager pupil and quickly gaining in proficiency. Vera, Luce, and Mary were new to the switchboards, having been chosen for their French skills and not their knowledge of the phone system, so I looked over them myself along with our youngest operator, Julia, who was exceedingly capable but unsure of herself.

Margot's half of the switchboard was running as smoothly as a ship in good wind. The experienced operators were learning the quirks of their neighbors, and though we'd only been working together for a couple of weeks, they could predict each other's movements and connect calls on an adjacent exchange without distracting their neighbors as they worked. My girls were coming along, but I could still notice a pause when Julia was speaking to a customer and Vera had to reach over to plug in a jack on her exchange. Mary took a little longer than some of the others to locate the right lines off of her exchange as well, but she was remarkably capable at placing long-distance calls. Perhaps her years teaching French at a Washington, DC, prep school had given her voice the tone of authority that made operators in other cities eager to connect her calls quickly. An enviable skill.

After we had put in three hours in training at the switchboards, Captain Wessen summoned us to one of the rooms commandeered for training purposes.

"Please wait in the line that corresponds with the first letter of your last name," he commanded. "Your uniforms have arrived. You will be expected to wear them at all times starting tomorrow morning."

Uniformed personnel stood behind four tables where large bundles waited for us. We were all anxious to look like servicewomen. One step closer to France. To Francis. To the war.

The buzzing in the room wasn't the usual nervous drone, but a genuine excitement to be properly outfitted. When I received my bundle, I felt a thrill at the sight of the navy-blue wool Norfolk jacket and matching skirt. There were a cap, blouses, and a number of other items tucked into the heavy parcel, and I could well understand why I'd had to part with such a princely sum for the ensemble. I longed to tear into it like an eager child at Christmas but didn't want to struggle to keep it all together on the train back to New Jersey.

The following morning, I exchanged my nightgown for the sleek-looking navy-blue uniform. The skirt was short enough that it brushed the bottom of my calves. Unused to such a short garment, I would have to fight the urge to tug it lower.

"These bloomers are the most ridiculous thing I've ever seen," muttered Margot when none of our operators were in earshot. "My grandmother wouldn't be caught dead in something so . . . dowdy."

"I doubt she ever wore such short skirts," I said, tightening the jacket's belt around my waist. I was still unused to seeing my silhouette without a corset and hoped I didn't look as boxy as I felt. The freedom of movement was glorious, though, and would be indispensable overseas. I smoothed the starched white collar at my neck and straightened my armband, complete with supervisor's laurel framing the transmitter insignia that indicated our belonging to the US Army Signal Corps.

"What do you think?" I asked Margot, wishing we still had the luxury of the full-length mirror in our shared room at the Prince George.

"You look like a woman in charge," Margot replied with satisfaction. "Properly in the army."

Just before breakfast time, a courier came around with a large number of parcel boxes from the AT&T headquarters.

"To ship our civilian clothes home," Margot explained as she read the note. "We're not to take any with us."

I looked at the straining trunk that was near bursting with skirts, frilled lace blouses, and corsets. "I'll need two, I'm afraid."

I packed each of them to the brim, tied them off with twine, and scrawled my parents' address on the top. It was a mark of great maturity that I didn't add "I told you so" below it. I'd follow it that night with a postcard explaining the return of the clothes, once the temptation to gloat subsided. The poor courier collected them all, and I felt worlds lighter as I saw him hobbling off under the weight of all the parcels. For the duration of the war I wouldn't have to agonize over what I wore for every occasion or fret over which handbag went best with my shoes. I was both excited and scared that for once in my life people would have to look beyond my clothes.

On the train ride into Manhattan, I noticed a shift. People got up from their seats and offered them to us. Perfect strangers waved to us.

"You go there and do us all proud," one older man said before exiting the train. "Do it for those of us who can't go over." We gave our solemn promise, and he descended from the train with a smile.

We'd been scattered about the city and nearby in New Jersey in various makeshift residences provided by the YWCA, so I got to see the entirety of my squad uniformed for the first time. Today there was no complaining about marching. Each girl had the glint of purpose in her eye with each salute and about-face.

When we were given the signal to break for luncheon, I nodded at their crisp salute.

"Well done, ladies. You look like soldiers today, and you marched like them too. Keep it up, and we'll be marching back home in no time."

CHAPTER 8

March 2, 1918

We stood on the dock in New York Harbor, the cold winds of early spring swirling about us like frozen vines of sprawling kudzu. We waited for permission to board our vessel, a proud old ship called the *Celtic*. It was one of four White Star Line ships—including the *Baltic*, the *Cedric*, and the *Adriatic*—that bore the moniker "Big Four" at the turn of the century. The largest and most luxurious on the seas when they were new. From the stony looks on my operators' faces, it was clear they remembered all too well the newspaper articles, the icy photos, and the horrific tales of the survivors from another White Star Line ship that boasted the same "most luxurious" designation more recently. Our enemy was far more sinister than an iceberg and a distracted crewman, however. We couldn't fault nature for sinking a ship, but we owed the Germans no such kindness. They'd proven themselves more than adept with their submarines, and we undertook the crossing knowing it might be the most dangerous part of our service.

We milled about the docks for most of the morning, never straying far, and never for more than half an hour. I'd never made the crossing before, and it never occurred to me the monumental task it was to get a passenger load of nearly three thousand people safely boarded.

Margot's face drained of color when we saw three pair of men carrying stretchers—their contents protected from prying eyes by the cover of white sheets.

"A German spy," Millicent supplied, walking up behind us and answering the unasked question. "I heard the rumor earlier this morning. I'd hoped it was an exaggeration, but it seems to be true. Thankfully we managed to take him down before he got any more of our men. But there's no chance he was working alone. They're like cockroaches. You can kill one, but there are hundreds more you can't see scurrying about in the dark."

Mary shivered next to me, though I couldn't tell if her revulsion was in response to the fallen spy or the cockroach analogy. Given our weeks in the tavern in Hoboken, we were well versed on the latter. "Good God. Here in New York."

"It's the price we pay for entering into the fray," Sadie offered.

"I don't think we were safe even before then," I mused. "We're too big for the luxury of neutrality."

"Well said, Ruby," Millicent said. "Why don't you all go find some coffee? I think there's a shop just a block inland. It'll do you good to stretch your legs on firm ground while you have the chance."

I nodded my approval at the suggestion, knowing good coffee would probably be scarce on board, and I didn't dare guess what might await us in France. Only Margot, Luce, and Hazel decided to leave the dock with me, however, the others preferring to stay with Millicent in sight of the ship.

The shop was what one would expect near the docks. Small, busy, and utilitarian. It was run by an Italian family, and they kept the menu simple: strong coffee and Italian pastries. There were no frills like those at the dainty tea shops and cafés Mother favored in Philadelphia. A small table opened up, and we scooted together to make room. Our coffee cups covered every inch of the tiny table, so we kept our gloves and handbags on our laps.

March's chill hadn't given way to the feeble warmth of spring just yet, so the hot coffee was as restorative as a crackling fire after a trek through the snow. I added a little cream to my own, Luce and Margot took theirs black, and Hazel seemed to prefer her cream and sugar with the barest hint of coffee flavor.

Luce shook her head. "You should just have ordered a glass of warm milk if that's what you wanted."

"Oh, mind your business," Hazel said, sticking out her tongue as she might do to an impudent older brother, causing a round of titters from the table.

"You're in good spirits for your crossing," a uniformed man seated next to us observed. "What time are you shipping out?"

"They haven't—" Luce began.

"I don't believe that's your concern," I interjected, remembering the German spy.

"It's all right," he pressed. "I'm one of you." He gestured to his uniform, which looked the part. He angled himself in his chair so his sergeant's stripes were prominently displayed to the room. He was determined everyone would see he wasn't enlisting as a simple private. But as authentic as the uniform appeared, it could have been acquired by fair means or foul.

"If you were meant to know, they would have told you," I said with a glare. I caught Margot, Hazel, and Luce's eyes and silently warned them not to offer any more information. We hadn't even been told if we were sailing to England or France, and it was just as well. The less information we had, the less likely that information could fall into enemy hands. The sergeant, if that's what he truly was, went back to his own coffee with a smirk. Chances are I was being overly cautious, but I wasn't going to risk anyone's safety on the guise of being polite.

My coffee lost its appeal, but I waited for the others to finish theirs before we found our way back to the docks just within the half-hour limit. Millicent was beginning to scan the crowd for our whereabouts. I wished there had been a way to bring her back a cup, but transporting coffee in a flimsy paper cup wasn't a practical option. I mentioned the uniformed man to her, and she said my response was absolutely right. She promised she would mention it to her higher-ups, but there wasn't too much that could be done. Asking questions wasn't an offense until something was done with the answers.

After an hour more milling about the docks, we were allowed to board at last, and all eleven of the women in my squad stood together on the deck of the ship as endless lines of doughboys boarded after us.

"Handsome devils, the lot of them," Addie commented in a whisper.

"It's the uniform," Luce observed. "It can make the plainest boy look like a man."

I nodded, remembering how grown up Francis had looked the day he shipped out. How natural Nathaniel seemed to look in his officer's uniform. It suited his swagger.

I heard a sniffle next to me and saw that Hazel was dabbing at her eyes with a dainty handkerchief.

"It's quite something, isn't it?" I said, giving her a quick hug.

"So many of them won't be coming back home," she whispered. "They've just said goodbye to their mothers and sweethearts for the last time. It's awful."

"They're doing their duty," Sadie scolded. "Just like we are."

"We won't be carrying bayonets," Hazel commented. "We won't be in the trenches."

"They're brave men," I said in a tone softer than Sadie's. "And we owe them very much, but look at their faces, Hazel. They're proud to serve. Just as I know you are."

"Hear, hear," Margot chimed in. "Don't bury them all yet. Americans have fight in them. The Germans won't roll over us—just you watch."

We were eventually shown to our bunks—second-class accommodations that had been rearranged to fit twice the number of passengers as in the days when it escorted the wealthiest people across the ocean in splendor. We were cramped, but nothing like the troops, who had been sent to spend the next two weeks in steerage accommodations. The ship was capable of making the trip in ten days. A week if the winds favored her. But we'd been told that it would take us closer to two weeks because we would be joining a crew of escort ships that would protect us and help us avoid detection by the German U-boats.

Though Vera and Luce seemed stoic enough about our departure, some of the others seemed to leave their usual exuberant smiles back on the docks, Hazel in particular.

"Hurry up, ladies, and claim your bunks. I want us to stay together as a squad," I called. I saw Millicent nod her approval out of the corner of my eye. The comportment of the girls was on her head, but if the supervisors maintained authority and insisted that the girls continue to toe the mark on the crossing, the load on Millicent would lighten. Not to mention it would make regaining full authority that much easier once we reached our bases. No one grumbled, but they tossed their cases in the nearest five sets of bunks and began to settle in as best they could.

For the next hour, Luce and Margot drilled us on French, at my request. It was harder to worry about the first lurching of the ship out of the harbor and into the open ocean when we were focused on the proper conjugation of the verb "*vouloir*" in the past conditional. By evening, the girls had gotten over the worst of their jitters and were in better spirits when we joined the rest of the passengers for dinner.

"Oh Lord, I didn't think what almost two weeks on a ship with an English cook would mean," Margot whispered to me, not wanting to appear a hypocrite for her grousing. The dinner consisted of a dry-looking chunk of meat, which may have once been beef, paired with an unappetizing gray sauce. I would not be able to rebuke anyone for their complaints, but I stifled my own. Not looking at the contents of the tray and eating quickly were the two easiest ways to make it through the meal.

A familiar face rounded the corner into the dining hall: the sergeant from the coffee shop. He spotted our table and approached with a glint in his eye.

"I told you I was one of you," he chided. "It was a test. I wanted to see how good you girls are at keeping your tongues from wagging. You did well."

I widened my eyes at his impertinence. "I'm glad to know I made muster with you, Sergeant." My tone dripped with acid. "I hope I manage to do the same with officers who matter."

He stood, blinking at my rebuke before finding his place at a table at the other end of the room.

"That was amazing, Ruby, but aren't you afraid he's going to tell the higher-ups about what you said?" Hazel asked, a tremor in her voice.

"He's a sergeant. From what I can tell, each and every one of us outranks him. He had no right to 'test us' at all. I've half a mind to tell the higher-ups what *he* did. It would probably earn him more than a tongue-lashing."

I had endured all of the meal I could and took my mess kit to the filthy cleaning stations where we were all expected to clean our own dishes in the same putrid water. Then I retired to my bunk, followed soon by Margot.

"Don't let that idiot bother you," she said by way of greeting.

"He doesn't," I said. "His arrogance does. He has no right to act like he's our superior."

"No, but we must get used to it," Margot reasoned. "They will assume we don't know what we're doing until we show them otherwise. It might not be just, but there is no sense in fretting about the way things are. We will change it when we are able."

~

A few days into the voyage and half the girls were down with seasickness. That night, the sea was as rough as one might possibly endure. Even the mighty *Celtic* swayed in the waves. I was one of the few spared, which was surprising given my inexperience with sea travel. I supposed one was born with a solid stomach or one wasn't, and experience wouldn't help much either way.

I checked in on Mary, who'd been sickest of the lot.

"Sleeping peacefully now that the contents of her stomach are thoroughly disposed of," Sadie reported at the door, looking a little martyred. "But her color looks much better."

"Good," I said. "Offer her tepid water and bread if she wakes. And try to get rest yourself."

"I've got things under control," she snapped.

"I can see you do," I replied, ignoring her tone. "Good work."

I tucked into my own bunk room, where Margot still looked miserable. She stifled her moans of discomfort but hadn't summoned the strength to leave her bed.

"I ought to help you look in on the others," she said, taking shallow breaths between words.

"Just close your eyes and ignore the world for a bit," I encouraged. "You'll be of more use to me if you're well rested tomorrow."

She grunted an affirmative, and I left her to continue my rounds.

"Chief Operator Fairbanks is unwell," Gloria announced, poking her head out from the bunk room they shared. "She looks positively emerald green."

"Poor dear," I said, and looked in. True to Gloria's description, Millicent was greener than an Irish meadow, and her brow was glowing with beads of sweat.

"Has she been ill yet?" I asked.

"No," Gloria replied. "She hadn't complained of anything until about twenty minutes ago. She said she had a headache and needed a lie down."

Millicent pulled the blanket up to her chin and mumbled something I wasn't able to parse. When she shivered, despite the reasonably comfortable temperatures in the bunk rooms, I stepped over to her bedside.

"This isn't seasickness," I said. "She has a fever. Damn and blast. This is the last thing we need on board a ship. Go fetch the ship's doctor."

Gloria bounded out the door with an alacrity I'd never seen in her before. I sat on the edge of the bunk and held Millicent's hand, hoping it was just a brief, passing illness, the kind that set in fast and burned out quickly. The spring brought with it a nasty bout of flu, and if she wasn't quarantined, we'd end up with a shipload of sick soldiers.

Millicent's symptoms were dire enough to garner the ship's doctor's quick attention. He arrived in the bunk room, half a pace behind Gloria, within a quarter of an hour.

"Fever," I said. "No vomiting. I can't get her to tell me what else might be wrong."

The grim-faced man, well into his forties or fifties, and probably considered too old for frontline medic work, looked her over. He listened to her breathing with his stethoscope, and I could see the furrow in his brow decrease by a fraction.

"Her lungs are clear, thank God," he announced. "Not the flu that's been making the papers."

I wrapped my arms around myself. "Do you have any idea what it is, then?"

"Any number of things. The best I can do is leave you a few aspirin to keep her fever down, but she's not going to be fit for service, potentially for weeks."

I exchanged glances with Gloria. The doctor looked into Millicent's throat and then pulled back her blanket to examine her limbs. Her arms were a mass of angry red welts.

"An allergic reaction," he pronounced. "A severe one. If I were a betting man, I'd lay odds it was the smallpox vaccine you all had before you left. This is rare, but I've seen it once or twice before. When did you get your shots?"

"Three weeks ago," Gloria answered. "Though I think Millicent went later because she had to speak with Captain Wessen. Maybe two weeks ago?"

"That's the right time frame," the doctor mused. "The good news is that she won't infect anyone."

"What can be done, Doctor?" I asked as Gloria clutched my hand.

"Not much on board this damned ship," he muttered. "We'll have to get her to a hospital as soon as we touch dry land. And hope and pray it doesn't cause swelling of the brain. Try to keep her cool and comfortable. I'd see about transferring her to the infirmary, but she's probably more comfortable here. Can you spare someone to keep an eye on her?"

"Yes, Doctor," I said without hesitation. Taking care of Millicent seemed far more important than drilling and marching, no matter what the army might say about it. We could take shifts to make sure she wasn't alone.

"Dear God," Gloria muttered as the doctor left. "What do we do?"

"We carry on," I said. "You keep an eye on her for now, and I'll look after the others."

"Very well," Gloria said. "I'll keep vigil here as long as she needs me."

"Rest if she's resting," I said. "We don't need you run down too."

The news of Millicent's illness was going to spread like its own virus among the operators. A half dozen heads poked out of bunk rooms when they heard me emerge into the corridor. I decided it was best not to pretend it was anything less than serious.

"The doctor is doing his best, but she's very ill, I'm afraid. She's resting comfortably enough now," I said. "I trust everyone else is feeling reasonably well?"

"Nothing we can't handle, Ruby," Eleanor said. "Mary and Addie have seen better days, but I don't think anyone's seriously ill."

"Good," I said. "Do we need anything other than some more bread and water to settle stomachs? I'm going to let the higher-ups know about Millicent. The doctor seems to think she'll be out of commission for quite some time."

"The world's largest vat of coffee come morning," Luce said as Vera made retching sounds from inside the bunk room. "Best to give them notice now, no?"

"This is an English ship. I expect they're tea people."

Luce muttered something in French that I certainly had never learned from a professor. I didn't need a dictionary to parse its meaning.

"I don't think that's the sort of expression you'll need at the switchboard, Operator Roussel, but I commend your efforts in keeping your vocabulary on point. I'll ask about coffee."

The ship was a floating city, and finding my way to the radio room took time. The lieutenant who was at the controls was absorbed in his work, but when I mentioned the content of the message that needed to be sent, he was quick to agree. I estimated it was only four in the afternoon on the East Coast, though it was closing in on seven in the evening in the middle of the ocean. I hoped the message would be intercepted by the day staff, which might have the ability to react.

The reply came within a quarter of an hour:

FAIRBANKS PLACED ON MEDICAL LEAVE INDEFINITELY PENDING TREATMENT IN UK. WAGNER TO REPLACE AS CHIEF OPERATOR.

I held the transcribed message in my hand, which shook. Millicent was days from reliable medical care, and I was now charged with leading the entire First Telephone Group into service. Turning back to New York would have cost time we didn't have, but I'd held the foolish hope in the back of my mind that the army might have considered the option. I wanted to wire them back and insist that Gloria be given the chief-operator job, but I knew either I'd be met with a reprimand for shirking my duty, or worse, they might relieve me of duty altogether and send me back as soon as I reached dry land.

I went up to the deck of the ship, though the waves were still relentless. I didn't dare step too close to the railing, but I leaned against the damp exterior wall of the dining room, watching the churning black waters. The salty spray perfumed the air, cleansing my nose of the odor of illness and close quarters.

I'd have to take the advice I'd given Millicent and go down to the girls as though I had a plan in place. As though this promotion was utterly routine. As though I had no doubts as to my ability to lead these women into war.

The night air on the English Channel stung our faces like a torrent of angry hornets. We were blanketed in fog, forced to anchor a few miles off the coast of France until the mire lifted and the crew of our ferry across the channel could see well enough to navigate the murky waters. We stayed on deck, wearing all the clothes we had in our possession as well as bulky life vests. The threat of German attack was so certain, we didn't dare lower our guard long enough to go belowdecks to sleep. If they bombed us, our survival would depend on a quick evacuation. I confess, not all my shivers were on account of the swath of fog that kept us trapped at sea. And this was our second night encamped on the ferry, unable to move through the beclouded sea.

It seemed cruel that after nearly two weeks of interminable rocking, appalling food, and relentless nausea, we ended back aboard another vessel, but so it was. The *Celtic* was needed to fetch more troops from the port in New Jersey, so they lost no time by extending our sea voyage long enough to take us all the way to France. The Allies depended on the troops—this we understood. But while no one spoke the thought aloud, we all wondered if we had been delivered into the hands of the enemy to be obliterated before we had the chance to be of service.

I took Margot's hand in mine, and despite the barrier of two gloves between our hands, I could tell hers was as icy as my own. She gave me a stoic smile and returned her gaze to the fog-veiled sea. Like the rest of us, she scanned the open waters for any sign of attack from the Germans. With their submarines, we would be too late to act by the time they made themselves obvious. We all knew this, but we searched the waters—what little we could see of them—nonetheless. It felt better than doing nothing if we could not sleep.

Our brief hours in England had gone by in a whirr of activity as we were ushered off the ship and onto the ferry with hardly a moment to adjust to the sensation of dry land. The first thing we noticed as we descended from the ship was the lack of men. We had expected the usual array of male porters and crew members carrying equipment and loading cargo, but women labored in their places. Every man fit to fight needed to be sent to the front, which left only the very old, the very young, and those who had been lamed to the point they could no longer serve. They were replacing the men already fallen as best they could, but it was clear that England, if not defeated, would bear the scars of this war for generations.

Our major task during our brief stay in England was entrusting Millicent to the care of the nearest army hospital. She was out of the worst of the danger, but it might take weeks or months to recover her full health. The doctor told us they would likely treat her until they were certain she could handle the return journey, then send her back home for discharge. She was such a capable operator, the loss of her service was going to be a blow to our unit. But just as soon as we saw her settled, we were whisked onto the ferry to continue on to France.

I could hear a gentle weeping next to me and looked over to see Hazel bent over, quietly sobbing into her knees. I went to her side and wrapped my arm around her.

"I can think of a dozen reasons for tears right now. Which one is it?" I asked, keeping my tone as light as I could. "But whatever you do, please *try* to stem the tears. We don't need to flood the boat."

Hazel let out a girlish giggle and dried her face with the back of her woolen sleeve. "Take your pick. Hungry. Tired. Cold."

"Fair enough," I said. "I can't do much about the cold and tired, but I can ease the hunger a bit." I rifled through my little rucksack and fished out an apple I'd bought from the ship's canteen our last day aboard. I hadn't gotten around to eating it, owing to some last-minute drilling we'd been called to on the decks. Drilling and calisthenics aboard the ship were quite the spectacle to behold. Even our most graceful operators couldn't compensate for the ebb and flow of the gargantuan ship.

Hazel accepted the apple gratefully, and her cheeks regained a bit of color from the nourishment. A few of the others gazed with poorly concealed longing at the small morsel of fruit that was now nearly gone. I'd have given Father's fortune to give them all a hot steak dinner. Woolen blankets. Anything to ease their discomfort.

I took to pacing the decks to warm myself. Time had a way of playing tricks on us after so long at sea, and I couldn't tell how many hours were left before the sun would rise again, hopefully to burn off the fog and see us off to the coast of France. But even that thought could give me no comfort. If the sun rose and shone bright enough to clear the path for us, our cover, too, would be lost.

Fatigue weighed heavy on us, but tempers remained cool. I was proud of my girls, who huddled together against the bitter night. I racked my brain for something to help, but I drew a blank. I'd spent so long with Mother contradicting every decision I'd made, I'd grown accustomed to her supplying the "correct" course of action before taking a step.

"What should I do?" I whispered to Margot. "They're miserable."

"Lead them," she whispered back, her eyes piercing. "Get their minds off it."

I shook my head at my own indecision.

"Let's walk," I suggested to my squad. "It'll stave off the cold better than any blanket."

Each woman rose at my suggestion and followed my lead, walking briskly around the deck of the ferry, and the other two squads soon followed suit.

"Well done," Margot whispered. The creases of worry on the brows had lessened noticeably.

"It was always my father's response to anything," I said. "'*Whatever the problem is, take a constitutional. It may not solve the problem, but at least you got some fresh air to clear out the worry.*' He was right about that more often than not."

"He sounds like an astute man," she said. "He must be proud."

"He seemed to be," I said. I didn't avow to her that his pride was tempered with fear in almost equal measure.

The rays of sun breached the horizon shortly after that, and there were a few gasps and muted shrieks when the ferry made a terrible screeching sound. Had the Germans spotted us once the cloak of night lifted? The screeching gave way to the rumbling whirr of the engines, and at last the metal tub began to creep toward the French coast.

I was able to breathe deeper as soon as I felt the firm ground beneath me, though I knew I'd just set foot on the most dangerous place in the world.

"Are you afraid?" Margot asked, reading my expression as we walked off the pier and toward the train station.

I was, but somehow stilled the shaking of my hands and the quaver in my voice. "Incredibly. But I'm pretty sure that before long we're all going to be busy enough not to notice."

CHAPTER 9

March 26, 1918
Chaumont, Haute-Marne, France

The town of Chaumont, under normal circumstances, would have been charming. The old part of town was a tight coil of stolid stone buildings with graceful red-tile roofs that dated back centuries further than anything in Philadelphia. It was just 150 miles to the southeast of Paris and had been chosen by General Pershing to be the seat of the American Expeditionary Forces, or AEF, headquarters. The HQ building, a mile to the north of the town center, was nearly bursting with staff who never seemed to sleep. Though the fighting was nearly 250 miles to the north, one would think it was next door.

We'd been forced to leave most of our group behind in Paris, with tears and embraces as though we'd all been friends for years. Indeed, it felt as though we had. It seemed strange to think we'd likely never see many of the women we trained with ever again, but we always knew we'd be scattered to the offices where we were needed most. Only seven of us were sent to headquarters, as the higher-ups wanted to keep the signal-corps group in the advance area small until the systems were all well in hand. Poor Gloria was left to console her own squad, which was bound for Tours. Another small band would stay in Paris. Even the most stalwart of the girls was afraid to some degree, but now that we'd all crossed the Rubicon, none of us wanted to be left behind to be "featherbed soldiers hundreds of miles from the front." Margot was promoted to supervisor and would serve in my command. Mary, Hazel, Luce, and Vera were under my charge, and I could not have chosen a better squad in terms of their range of skills. Unfortunately, Sadie Porter was also assigned to Chaumont, which didn't sit well with either Sadie or me.

We were housed in comfortable lodgings organized by the YWCA across town, which meant we would have a good six miles of walking over the course of a day. Upon our arrival, we met the head of our house, a Mrs. Stella Grant, who had the unenviable task of finding lodgings for all the signal-corps girls coming into the region, organizing social events for us, and, along with myself, acting as chaperone.

Mrs. Grant was the sort of woman who looked cheerful no matter the circumstance. She was forty years old and had signed on with the YWCA once her husband, Jim, had been called up. "Better to come over and help the cause than to sit at home and stew," she said. As she expertly knit away at some socks while we were becoming acquainted, I sensed that she was of the ilk that couldn't bear to sit idle. Despite all the energy that seemed to leach out from every pore of her being, she was a soothing presence. After only a few hours in her company, I was convinced she was the perfect woman for such a big job.

I was to report with two of the girls to get a tour of the facilities and to begin transitioning our group in to relieve the men for other duties. Margot, as supervisor, was entitled to one of the spots with me, and I awarded the other to Mary, who was looking a bit cagey. I could tell that Sadie felt as though she should have had the spot, being the oldest, but also that she was mollified I'd chosen her friend and not one of the others. Mary and Sadie were older than the rest of us, and they had formed a sort of bond. But while Sadie was resentful of being led by younger women, Mary had a far kinder disposition. I expected it was born of her years as a high school French teacher, a profession that would have taught her, if nothing else, patience.

Major Weaver, who it seemed was my direct supervisor, sent a driver to spare us the walk on our first day, which was an unexpected kindness. Though subdued by the proximity of war, the town was still charming. The red-tiled roofs and the smooth cobbles of the streets were as inviting and vibrant as those of any of the villages we'd passed on the way from Le Havre. Despite everything, I felt incredibly lucky to call such a place home, even for a short while.

The young sergeant who drove us in gestured with pride to the headquarters as we approached. The stone building was indeed impressive, but less so than the hive of activity it contained. Every man who walked the corridors moved briskly and with the unmistakable mask of purpose. I felt the sweat pool in my palms. Would we ever find our place as a cog in this massive machine? The sergeant deposited us with Major Weaver, a short, wiry man who looked as though he'd had one more cup of coffee than was good for him.

"Lavatory," he barked, pointing with his right hand as we jogged to keep up with him. "Clerical offices." Finally, when we reached the end of one impossibly long, dim hallway, he barked, "Telephone services." And left with the briefest of introductions to the officers on duty. Lieutenants Drake and Bradley, assigned to desk work after injuries sustained at the front, looked as harried as someone juggling hot embers.

"I've never been happier to see a woman in my whole life, and that's saying something," Lieutenant Bradley said with a wide smile. The right side of his face was scarred badly, but one could tell he had once been incredibly handsome. Lieutenant Drake was missing his right leg, but he was in otherwise remarkable health and spirits.

"We're glad to be here," I said earnestly. "It doesn't seem Major Weaver is all that happy to be here, though. I don't think he said three words together on our tour."

"Never mind him," Lieutenant Drake said. "He's been growling for a week about being sent a pack of girls to run the office. We've tried to tell him that you'll do a better job of running the phones than we can, but he's set on sulking."

"Well," I said, unable to find a suitable comment about Major Weaver's reluctance. "It looks like you've got a good setup so far."

"We've done what we can," Lieutenant Bradley said, sitting up a bit straighter in response to the compliment. "But we're not real operators like you. We both look forward to learning your tricks of the trade. We'll continue on with the night shifts once you ladies are all settled in. It's quiet enough we can manage without making ourselves look like fools."

"I doubt you look like fools," Mary said affectionately. "But it'll be good to get to work."

"Then let's," I said, taking my place next to Lieutenant Bradley and looking over the board. It was a simple one, outdated by perhaps ten years, but we'd heard it was better than what the French had been using. I took out my leather notebook and began making notes about possible strategies for organization. There were five switchboards, each with a tall metal chair that resembled a high-backed barstool. It was evident that those at headquarters were working to add in even more stations to make use of all of us.

As though our arrival had been announced, the boards started lighting up, and I took up the first line. "Number, please?" I said, summoning my cheeriest tone from my days at Pennsylvania Bell.

I heard some faint breathing and muffled background noise, but no voice responded.

"Hello? Number, please?" I repeated.

"My God, a real American girl?"

"Yes, and I'd be happy to connect you."

"I've never heard a sweeter sound in all my days."

The sun was feeble on Easter morning as it rose over the little house. We'd arrived in Chaumont less than a week before. We breakfasted well that morning, Mrs. Grant having procured some real butter and bacon for the holiday meal, though we couldn't linger overlong. Margot led the Catholic girls to Mass at the little church nearby, and Mrs. Grant and I collected the Protestants for a little service at the YMCA. The chapel was makeshift to say the least, with rickety chairs for pews and an altar fashioned from a board resting on some precarious-looking sawhorses. The only indication of the importance of the celebration was a sparkling white altar cloth with some simple embroidery and low candles. Someone had thought to bring in some spring flowers too. Their vibrant colors seemed out of place in the somber room, but they were a welcome breath of life all the same. It wasn't like the lavish displays at the Episcopal churches back home, and I was glad for the simplicity.

I tried to follow the good bishop's homily, but I found myself distracted by the sight of the soldiers, some of them badly wounded, who were praying with heads bowed, utterly indifferent to the drafty, bare floor on which they knelt. Back home, I'd always had a bad habit of looking about during church instead of listening to the priest or reading along in my prayer books. In my study, I noticed that apart from the children, the young men always struggled the most to keep themselves still and focused. Their desire to be outside with their chums, driving with their sweethearts, or tucked in at the supper table was written as plainly on their faces as the hymns in the songbooks that lined each pew. Today these men's attentions did not waver. Their prayer was sincere, and it was the same for all of them. Let the war end. Let me be spared. Let the world go back to some version of the normal it had once been. I wondered if that last prayer could be answered, but I had to hold out hope. If not for my own sake, for theirs.

As we left the YMCA, the faces of my girls seemed a bit more relaxed since when we embarked the ship weeks before. I had no way of knowing which of them were particularly devout, but I think their serenity had a great deal more to do with an hour spent in the company of countrymen, hearing a service as familiar as a nursery rhyme, than it did with anything the bishop had to say. Mrs. Grant left us at the fork in the road to return home to her duties, and the rest of us continued on the extra mile and a half to headquarters.

Margot's girls came in about fifteen minutes after us, though only half our number was needed for the quiet telephone traffic we had on Sunday shifts. I hadn't expected the weekends to be much of a reprieve, but it seemed that even battles slowed on the day of rest, though it was certain not to last. As thankful as I was for the calm, however, I much preferred to sit at the boards myself than watch others as they performed their duties. Time inched on when work was sparse, but it positively dragged when I had to leave it to the others.

Little Hazel looked wan as she connected a call, and I saw her hands shake as she plugged the jack into the line. Her skin had the unhealthy pallor I'd seen on Francis when at university he'd spent too many days indoors with his nose in books and his rear on a laboratory stool. The clock was at a quarter to one, and we'd be dismissed for our half day soon, when the less efficient male operators would take our places.

"I think we need a picnic luncheon today, ladies," I announced as the men entered and waited expectantly for their spots at the boards. "If you care to join me, we'll go for a little amble by the canal. It'll do us all good, eh? Anyone who stays indoors by choice on a day like this deserves a court-martial, in my mind."

"I'm for it," Margot asserted immediately. "I've seen nothing other than the streets between the house and here. I'm going to grow moss if I don't have a change of scenery."

Luce begged off, wanting to write letters and catch up on her washing. Hazel looked noncommittal, as though she wasn't quite sure the invitation included her.

"Come on, Hazel, it won't be a party without you," I insisted.

She looked at me sideways.

"*Oui*, you must come with us, *cocotte*," Margot urged. "It would be a shame for you to stay indoors with the old women, no?"

She made no reply but followed us to the mess hall, where we beseeched the chef to fit us up with some odds and ends we could take with us in our satchels. The sprawling hills were still wet with spring dew, but we forged on, forgetting the damp grass that clung to our ankles. We happened along some obliging logs and settled in to eat our haul from the mess, such as it was, and admired the expansive green countryside that seemed bristling with energy at the prospect of the lush summer ahead. The rolling hills were indifferent to the cacophony of shelling, sirens, and the rattle of the machine guns far off to the north. Only the chirping of birds and the rustle of the wind through the tender new branches of the beech trees seemed to matter here.

"You wouldn't think there's a war on," Hazel mused, eating a morsel of her cheese. "It seems so peaceful."

"It is," I agreed.

"I wish Mother could see this place. And my sister. They'd go mad for a nice vista like this. But at the same time, I don't want them anywhere near this place."

"C'est logique," Margot reasoned. "I've always wanted to bring my *maman* to France. To see the land of her ancestors, to be in a place where her accent would be thought quaint. But if you gave me a million dollars right in this moment, I would keep her safe at home."

Hazel stood, and we joined as she continued to stroll. Her eyes shone bright as she gazed out over the hills that went on for miles with nothing but vineyards and trees, dotted sparsely with little red-roofed farmhouses. Only the train tracks scarred the earth, and even then, it didn't detract from the view. "I've made such a stupid mistake. I wanted more than anything to come, and now that I'm here, I know someone else would have done so much better than I. I'd ask you to send me back, but I don't deserve a place on the boat."

"Nonsense," I said. "You're one of the best on the boards, when you're not brooding, and your French is better than mine. We need you."

"You're kind," she said, pausing atop a small hill that looked down onto the tracks.

"No, I speak the truth. I've no reason to flatter you. If I thought I could replace you with someone more able, I would. What we're doing is too important for me to do otherwise."

Just then, one of the long trains with freight cars labeled *40 hommes 8 chevaux* came through, loaded with well more than the forty men the cars were meant to hold. They were Frenchmen on their way to the front. They had the haunted look of starved dogs who had spent far too long on the streets scrapping over a measly pile of bones. We waved to them all, and they rewarded us with brilliant, if weary, smiles. They used what energy they had to call out to us and wave like we were crowned princesses instead of simple telephone girls.

"You keep the men in contact with their generals, Hazel," Margot reminded her. "That is no simple task."

"No, it isn't," Hazel agreed, but said no more. I hoped that the majority of her moodiness stemmed from homesickness and the usual bad humor that came with the deprivation of creature comforts in wartime. I'd have to contrive a way to keep her distracted until she settled in, and decided I'd consult Margot on the matter when we had a second alone.

The rest of Easter was a cheerful time, as much as could be managed. Mrs. Grant had found a way to procure a real chicken dinner as a celebration, and all the girls were alight with joy to have such a decadent reminder of home. No fancy French sauces or heavy wines to detract from the delightfully simple roasted chicken, potatoes, carrots, and green beans. I tried not to think of the trainload of young soldiers heading eastward on the drafty, rattling cars toward the gates of hell instead of having a nice Easter dinner in a warm house. I tried not to think of the mothers and sweethearts who already pined for them. I tried not to think of how Francis would never join us for a holiday meal again. Though I tried to concentrate on the lively conversation around me, I couldn't eat my portion of the lovely dinner without continuously reminding myself that another such treat might be a long time coming.

But each bite, each laugh, each funny story and fond remembrance was a reminder of the sweet-faced French boys on the train who might never be coming home.

CHAPTER 10

April 2, 1918

"I can't believe you scheduled Vera today again," Sadie complained loudly as she took her spot at the board next to Mary. "She's had three full shifts three days in a row. You ought to be bawled out for favoritism."

The girls had been anxious to get to their posts, which made me proud, though I could do without the jealousy. During a battle, we were the only immediate line of communication between the men at the front and the generals behind the lines coordinating the attacks. Betweentimes, we expedited communication between our own camps and those run by the British and the French. We'd arrived in France almost a year after the men, but it was just in time for us to see the men into their first battle after the disaster at Cambrai that cost us Francis. It was only the second battle we'd fought as an independent army.

"Scheduling is my prerogative, Miss Porter, and I am under no obligation to explain my decision-making to you." My voice was louder than I intended and garnered a questioning look from a pair of officers passing in the corridor.

"I just don't think it's right," Sadie continued in lower tones more appropriate for the telephone office. "If you can't accept feedback without biting our heads off, you should be relieved of command altogether."

"Your opinion is taken under consideration, Miss Porter. And if you want to avoid a reprimand for being late, I suggest you get to your seat. You're three minutes late for your shift."

I kept the fury from my face, but I wanted more than anything to punch a hole in the wall. Given the sturdy look of the walls at general headquarters—or GHQ—it was just as well I was able to channel my anger. I didn't need a half dozen broken bones in my hand in addition to my freshly soured mood.

Margot met my eye as she whispered some advice to Hazel about the infernal codes we were forced to remember for every location in creation. It was made clear that we'd be forced to learn a whole new set just as soon as we'd learned the ones we'd just been given, and the cycle would repeat for the duration of our time here.

"Ah, you asked me to relieve you for a drink of water and a trip to the lavatory," Margot said to me. "How careless of me." She spoke loud enough so that she was sure Sadie could hear. She took my position peering over the shoulders of the girls as they worked.

"Very kind," I said crisply, and turned out of the room. Once outside, I leaned my forehead against the cool plaster on the corridor wall. I took deep breaths until I felt the rushing blood drain a bit from my face. Perhaps Sadie was right. I didn't have the temperament to lead. But I was stubborn enough not to allow the infuriating girl to be the reason I was demoted.

"Miss Wagner, just who I was looking for." Major Weaver approached from behind me. "I'd like a word in my office, please."

I followed him to the spartan room that served as his office and sat opposite his desk. I wondered if he didn't have a full-time sergeant whose sole responsibility was keeping his desk in pristine condition.

Moving a stack of papers or borrowing a pen from its ordered surface would have been like desecrating the *Mona Lisa* by scrawling my name on it with red lipstick.

"I'm very sorry that the scheduling isn't to everyone's liking just yet," I began without preamble. "Miss Porter is just overeager to do her bit. We all are."

"What? Oh, well, those sorts of things are to be expected." The furrow on his brow betrayed that he really didn't have the foggiest idea what I was referring to. A golden band on his wedding finger had the settled-in look that made it seem as if his finger and the ring had been fused together for centuries. I suspected he had more than a little experience feigning understanding in the name of expediency. "I've actually asked you in here to discuss another matter altogether."

"I hope you're pleased with our work so far?" I gripped one of the arms of the chair, hopefully in a manner he couldn't see.

"Indeed, yes. You've been here a week and you've managed to increase our call rates fivefold. Nothing to complain about at all." He looked sheepish at the admission, given his curt welcome. At least he seemed the reasonable sort of man who wouldn't ignore results in order to preserve his pride.

"I'm glad to hear that."

"Yes, well, we do have one concern. About your Miss Brooks."

"Hazel?" I asked. "She's only had three shifts since we got here. Surely we can give her some time to adjust?"

"It isn't her performance, Miss Wagner. Nothing seems amiss on that front. We have reason to believe she's in contact with the other side. We need you and Miss St. Denis to keep an eye on her. You need to report to me if you see anything at all that doesn't seem right. I'd like you to swing by every day about this time and brief me on what you observe. I'll be asking the same of Miss St. Denis a little later. Don't warn her about this conversation, however."

"Understood, Major," I said, having loosened my death grip on the chair's arm. "Whatever you need. But if you think she's a spy, why not send her home before she can leak any information to the Germans?"

"Because that would plug only one little leak. If we keep her on, and she is involved, we just might be able to stem the flow of the entire blasted river, so to speak."

"That seems dangerous," I cautioned, despite the implications that I was questioning his order. "What if she's able to pass on vital information?"

"That's why you're here," he replied. "You and your supervisor are never to leave her alone, and you won't entrust her with the most sensitive information. There is no way to keep it all from her without getting her suspicions up, of course, but we'll guide you through what to do."

"Very well," I said, as though I might have anything to say on the matter. "It's a shame. She seems so lovely."

"Spies usually are," he said. "It makes them good at their jobs."

"Likely so," I agreed.

"Dismissed, Miss Wagner. Carry on with the good work."

"Thank you, Major."

I walked the fifty paces back to the telephone office, and they seemed to go on for a country mile. That sweet Hazel Brooks could be a spy seemed about as likely as Mother joining the suffragettes.

The room was abuzz as the girls placed calls every few seconds. I watched as Hazel's lithe fingers pulled two plugs from jacks and connected a line to an adjacent board in a single beat. She was a neat little thing, always well groomed and impeccably mannered. She seemed on the brink of tears half the time when she was alone with the other operators and me, and I'd ascribed it to simple homesickness and a gentle spirit. I'd been impressed that when we were at the office, she'd been able to gather her professionalism. She was always ready with a smile, even for the surliest general. Now I realized that sweet smile might be covering up more than a longing for her mother and her own bed. It might be covering up a deceit that could cost people their lives.

~

"Do you really think sensitive little Hazel Brooks is capable of such a thing?" Margot asked me that night as we settled into our beds. Despite Mrs. Grant's good cooking and a pleasant evening, I felt the knots in my neck clenching tight and growing tighter the more I thought about having to spy on one of my own girls.

"It's hard to imagine," I said. "But if I were a German seeking to extract information from us, I wouldn't exactly pick some weaselly-looking man with shifty eyes and a thick German accent, would I?"

"I imagine not," she said with a low laugh. "It's too terrible to think of."

"It is," I said. "We can't let her out of this house without one of us with her. We'll have to think up excuses that won't make her suspicious. I know we're going to bungle this whole mess. I'm not trained for counterspying."

"We can only do our best," Margot replied, rolling onto her back. "And hope that she has done nothing wrong."

"I hope that's enough," I said. "I just wish they'd found whatever evidence they have on her before we'd come over."

"That is always the way," Margot says. "When life has a chance to make itself easy, it usually finds a way to be difficult."

"Amen to that," I said. "To think, even six months ago the biggest worry I had was what dress to wear to the next Red Cross function. And how to keep Mother from contriving a reason to force me to quit Bell."

"The day I was hired at Bell was one of the proudest of my *maman*'s life," Margot mused. "Even if I was only a secretary. How different your family is from mine. Not working was never a choice. I was lucky to find something more interesting than work as a maid or a nanny."

"Mother was worried Nathaniel and his family would find me too 'common' for holding a job," I said. "I doubt a Morgan woman has worked outside of the home since before they came over on the *Mayflower*."

"You would think he would be pleased to have a clever and capable wife," Margot said.

"Clever and capable aren't the hallmarks of a good society wife," I said. "At least not on the surface. The men prefer wives to be pretty, sweet tempered, and good with dinner parties. They have no idea how shrewd their wives really are. Most of the men owe their success to their wives, but they're so discreet in their scheming and politicking, the men never find out."

"And it would make you happy to be this sort of woman?" Margot asked. "To boost your husband's ambitions and have none of your own?"

"Nathaniel is a good man," I said. "Grasping for more seems greedy, I suppose."

"I just cannot imagine a woman who is bold enough to serve her country in wartime being happy in that sort of life," she said. "That's not the Ruby I know."

"You only know this Ruby," I said. "The one back home is much more biddable."

"She doesn't sound like much fun."

"Perhaps she isn't," I admitted, pulling my blanket up to my chin. "But she has a better chance of living in peace with my mother than this Ruby does."

"Ah, mothers can be a trial," Margot agreed. "My *maman* always preferred my older brother, Antoine. He returned to Quebec a few years before Papa died. He signed up early on. There wasn't much sympathy up there for eligible men who didn't volunteer."

"It was the same back at home," I said, thinking of sweet Walter Harper. "But it has to be even worse in Canada."

"We—they have been in the fray longer," she said. "War shortens tempers, and people have a tendency to act in ugly ways because of it."

"Does your brother know you're here?" I asked.

"I sent him a letter from New York," Margot said. "I haven't got a reply yet, but that doesn't mean much. He may have written to Maman, and there hasn't been time to get a letter from her yet."

"I'm sure he's well," I said, hoping I wouldn't be raising her spirits only to have them dashed.

"I have no reason to believe he isn't," she said. "And I will cling to that until I hear otherwise."

"You're a smart girl," I said.

"Yes, you are lucky to have me for your assistant," she proclaimed.

"And so remarkably humble," I chided.

"What use is there in that?" she said. "There is much to be said for bravado. Remember this when you go home to your Nathaniel."

"For someone who gives romantic advice so freely, you've never mentioned a boyfriend," I teased. "Or do you prefer to leave behind a string of broken hearts?"

"Precisely right," she said. "I collect them like some men collect coins and stamps."

"Very funny," I said. "I should hire you out to entertain the troops. I'm sure they have need of a good comedian."

"There was a nice young boy back in Maine. David Lewis. We used to ride in his car sometimes and go for picnics. But his mother didn't approve of him going out with a 'French girl.' He stopped talking to me on her orders. Then he signed up for the war. And so it is."

Evangeline's face popped into my head. Mother would have directed the entirety of her wrath at her head if Francis's attachment to her had ever become known. "I'm sorry his mother was so shortsighted. Any woman ought to be delighted to have you as a daughter-in-law."

"I am *charmante*," Margot conceded. I didn't need the light of the kerosene lamp to see her wink. "But alas, charm with empty pockets does not feed a family. He could not face life without his parents' money, and they would have probably disowned him for marrying me. But then again, if he loved me so very much, he would have married me and made his own way in the world. No girl is good enough for a mother's baby boy. A man knows this and follows his own mind."

"Do you think you'll look for David after the war?" I asked. "It may have toughened him up a bit."

"Bah. I'm not sure he deserves a second chance," she said. "But he might get lucky and the war may make me a more compassionate soul. *On verra.*"

"We'll see, my foot. I'd be surprised if you aren't married within a month of the war's end. Two if you make him work for it."

"Better make it three," she said. "I can hold a grudge just as well as my French foremothers."

CHAPTER 11

April 12, 1918

The spring was timid in its arrival to Chaumont, but once it arrived, it was nothing short of breathtaking. The wildflowers that blanketed the hills outside of town were a glorious riot of color that made me lament my lack of artistic skill. The color couldn't be captured by the subtle shades of gray in photographs, and my clumsy sketches would be a mockery of the countryside, so in my memory alone they would live. I thought about Mother's flower beds, which would soon be awakening for spring, and felt a pang of loss at not being able to see their magnificent display that year.

Things were well enough in hand that I was able to leave Margot in charge at the switchboards for half a day at times, and I was desperate to find a laundry that Friday in order to freshen a few of my blouses. I cast an eye over at Hazel, who had just come on duty, and then looked to Margot. She replied with a wink that I understood to mean *I'm watching her, don't you worry.*

Luce and Vera had the afternoon off as well, so we began the trek back to our house so I could fetch my laundry. They'd decided to accompany me and do a bit of shopping, which was a welcome addition, but before we'd turned onto the main road, a medic in a truck pulled over by our side.

"Good afternoon, ladies, and welcome to Chaumont. There isn't a soldier in France whose spirits weren't lifted by your arrival," he said, removing his cap. "I'm Lieutenant Andrew Carrigan."

"What a lovely thing to say, Lieutenant," Luce replied. "We're proud to be here to do our duty."

"Well then, I wonder if you wouldn't mind adding one more to your considerable workload. I have a hospital full of wounded soldiers who are in desperate need of some good cheer."

"We'd be delighted," I said. Laundry and shopping could keep for another day, and I had been curious to see what the conditions were like in the army hospitals. I didn't know if Francis had died instantly or if he'd lingered in a hospital, but I had wondered what sort of attentions he was given if the latter were true.

The lieutenant, a young man whom I guessed to be just a little older than myself—perhaps late twenties—drove us to the hospital in the army truck that rattled ominously as it lurched forward.

"The hospital is pretty well equipped, given the circumstances," Lieutenant Carrigan explained. "But of course we're constantly low on supplies. Nothing as bad as the field hospitals at the front, though."

"I can only imagine," I said, thinking of the countless bandages I'd rolled back at home. I'd have to write to tell Mother how truly appreciated those efforts were.

"Have you been to the front, Lieutenant?" Vera asked, wedged between Luce and the truck door. "I expect it's terribly exciting."

"Yes, miss, I have," Lieutenant Carrigan replied. "A couple of drives with the English. And 'exciting' isn't the word I'd use. It's a lot of waiting around in ankle-deep mud and hoping you're spared when the 'excitement' happens. The new recruits come in fresh-faced and ready to take on the Hun single-handed. That enthusiasm gives way to dread pretty quickly."

"How long have you been overseas, then?" I asked.

"Since January of '17. I volunteered with the English, who were more than happy for another medic, let me tell you. I only just got transferred back to the AEF. I was on light duty after a nasty bout of the Spanish flu last month, and then they let me come serve with my countrymen."

He looked hearty enough, but I could see his color hadn't fully recovered. He looked to be the sort that would bronze under the sun within minutes, but clearly he had spent all of the winter and spring indoors.

"You volunteered so early," I mused. "That was months before we entered the war."

"I knew we'd have to enter before too long. My father thought I was a fool, and I broke my mother's heart, but I figured the more men I patched up before the States joined in the fray, the better off we'd be when we did."

"Very forward thinking, Lieutenant," Luce observed.

"I couldn't imagine we'd avoid taking sides for much longer," he said. "And it was a good way to get some more experience before medical school. A family friend helped arrange it all."

I'd given Francis and Nathaniel credit for their bravery when they enlisted before the draft, but to enlist with England was something altogether different. The way his dark eyes shone when he spoke of medical school betrayed that serving on the battlefield was a small price to pay for reaching that goal. I wondered if there was anything Nathaniel cared about that passionately.

"So, you won't be leaving medicine behind after the war?" I asked, wishing I could have thought of something more interesting to say.

"Not if I have a breath left in my body," he said, his grip on the steering wheel tightening in determination. "I've wanted to be a doctor since I was seven years old."

"How wonderful," I said. I tried to swallow back the envy that rose from my core. The prospect of a profession beyond the domestic sphere was a fantasy I rarely indulged for fear it would consume me. I'd yet to find anything, however, that stirred such excitement in me as medicine so clearly did in the young lieutenant.

"Here we are," he said, pulling the truck in front of a large building that had not been designed to serve as a hospital but that, like so many things—and so many people—had been repurposed. My eyes met his when he offered me his hand as I stepped down from the truck. I felt a tingle of heat rise to my cheeks, and I scoffed inwardly at my foolishness.

Lieutenant Carrigan escorted us in, and we were greeted by rows upon rows of hospital cots with men suffering from various degrees of illness and injury. Bandages were soaked crimson with blood, and men moaned in their beds, begging for relief.

There was a group of three nurses near the entryway, likely the only other American women in town. I had opened my mouth to greet them, but they shot the three of us a poisonous stare and scattered to tend to patients.

"Friendly," Luce said. "I know I washed today, and I don't think either of you two smell. I wonder what's got them in a dither."

"I grew up with sisters," said Lieutenant Carrigan, "so my best guess is that they're not happy to have other women in town to steal the soldiers' attention away from them."

"Nonsense," I said loyally. "There are more than enough young men around if that's what they're after. I suppose they think we've overstepped the mark and are making their work look less valuable. Something of that sort."

"You might be right," Lieutenant Carrigan said, eyeing the women, who still took furtive glances back at us. "But don't pay them any mind. Just go chat with the injured men like you would any chum. Anyone who looks up to speaking. Whatever you do, just try not to stare. It's the one thing they can't bear."

"Of course," Luce said, flashing him a bright smile. "We'll have all these men on their feet and dancing before we leave."

"Be careful with that lot, then," Lieutenant Carrigan said, winking as he gestured to a row of beds. "Those are the men recovering from surgery. My commander will have my hide if any of them drop stitches."

"Understood," Luce said. "No fox-trot for them. Perhaps a gentle waltz."

"A few might be up for a tango, if you take it slow," he said with a laugh.

We dispersed throughout the hospital, stopping at each bed where the soldier looked as though he had the strength to carry on a conversation. I visited with a sergeant from Maryland who'd been shot in the shoulder a few days before. Luckily the injury missed anything vital, but he'd be without the use of his right arm for quite some time. There was a private from Boston who was keen to talk about home, and another from Michigan who missed his mother's cooking so much he could have written a dissertation about the exact flavor and consistency of her pot roast.

"Where are you from?" a raspy voice called from a cot as I finished chatting with the young Michigander. I walked over to him and pulled up a doctor's stool that had been left in the walkway.

"Philadelphia," I said as I sat down. "Born and raised. You?"

"The very same," he said. "You're from the Main Line. I can hear it in your voice." He made a weak attempt at a smile. His color was positively ashen, and his forehead was damp with sweat. I took a spare cloth from the little table by his bed and mopped his brow. I looked up to see if I could attract the attention of a doctor or a medic, but none were in my field of view.

Mother would have been happy to know the Main Line had seeped its way into my voice. "Right on the first try. You have a good ear, Sergeant."

"Willie Macomb," he supplied. "Pleased to meet you."

"Ruby Wagner," I said. "What part of town are you from?"

"If you breathe a word of it to anyone, I'll denounce you as a dirty liar, but I'm from Germantown," he chuckled, which caused him to break into a fit of wheezing coughs.

"No jokes for you, then," I said once the coughing had calmed down. "I'll do my best to be dull."

"I don't think that's possible for a pretty girl like you, if it's not too bold to say."

"Handsome young sergeants like you can call me pretty all they like," I said, patting his hand.

"This uniform does more for a fellow's reputation with the ladies than any single thing I've ever seen," he declared. "It's a shame I won't be able to make use of it."

"Don't say such things," I chided, now taking his hand in mine. It was ice cold, and his skin was clammy from fevers that surely had crested and waned for hours. "These doctors seem to know what they're doing."

"That they do," Willie admitted. "But they're just doctors. They aren't magicians, and I'm afraid that's the only thing that could save me now."

I wanted to contradict the young man, but I could hear his breathing growing shallower. I scanned the room once more, hoping Lieutenant Carrigan or one of the other staff members would pop into view. "Let me go find one of the doctors, Willie. They'll be able to help."

"You can help more than any of them," he said, barely above a whisper.

"What do you need?" I said, brushing a tendril of drenched hair from his forehead.

"Sing for me?" he asked. "Any old thing."

I blinked for a moment, then thought of the old lullaby my mother crooned by my bedside when I was grievously sick with measles as a little girl. I had only the dimmest memories of the illness, my fever had been so high. I remember Mother crying when the doctor examined me. I remember Father's face looking grimmer than I had ever seen. Above all, I remembered Mother singing the sweet words about starlight and dewdrops.

Beautiful dreamer,
wake unto me.
Starlight and dewdrops
are awaiting thee.

Sounds of the rude world
heard in the day
led by the moonlight
have all passed away . . .

Mother hadn't sung it much since that time, but as I sung the lyrics now, I realized that she wasn't singing me back to sleep; she was coaxing me back to life. I held Willie's hand and hoped my song would be the same balm for him as it had been for me, until Lieutenant Carrigan placed his hand on my shoulder. He took Willie's hand from mine and checked for a pulse.

"He's gone," he said quietly.

I was grateful I was still seated. "My God, I'm sorry. I should have come to get you, Lieutenant. I didn't realize—"

"No, no. There was nothing we could do for him. He lasted longer than we thought he would. We managed to clean out the shrapnel, but he was already infected. He's been lingering for a week."

"The poor boy," I said. "I can't even bring myself to say 'man' in his case."

"Nineteen years old," he said. "It's a damn waste. But you sang him over to the other side. I'm sure he died happy, listening to that lovely voice of yours."

"How do you do this all day long?" I asked. "Look at the faces of men you know are going to die? Can a person get used to such a thing?"

"The day I'm used to it is the day this war has killed me too," he said. "But we carry on because we have to."

"Well said, Lieutenant."

"Andrew, please," he said. "May I call you Ruby?"

"Of course." It was a bit forward, but these were strange times, after all.

He moved to pull the sheet over Willie's head, but I stopped his hand. I ducked over to kiss Willie's forehead before he was taken away with the other casualties.

"I just thought his mother might rest a little easier knowing he'd had a last kiss. Not that the telegram will mention such things," I explained lamely. I shuddered remembering our own sheet of waxy yellow paper. How I'd longed for just a few more sentences explaining what had happened to Francis. If he'd suffered. If he was alone. "Do you think I could write to her?"

"Yes, or I can do it for you," Andrew offered. "I'd been planning on sending word as soon as . . . the worst happened. I'm hoping my letter can beat the official telegram, but it's not likely. I could send a note from you along with mine if you can hurry."

"I will," I promised. "I'll do it now and come back around this evening if that suits you."

"That would be grand," he said. "And Ruby, you did a great thing today."

I shook his hand and left Luce and Vera with their patients, who were all brightened by the presence of lively American girls. I walked back out into the fading light of late afternoon. The walk back home now seemed twice its usual length. With every step, my heart ached for the mother, who didn't yet know that the boy she'd rocked to sleep as a baby, whom she nursed through all the trials of childhood, was gone before he'd truly had the chance to live.

⸻

If I'd had an unending supply of paper, I would have littered the little secretary desk in the corner of the parlor with a mountain of failed drafts of the condolence letter to Willie's mother. But as my supply was limited, and wasting any resource seemed downright unpatriotic, I stared at a blank sheet for over half an hour wondering what in the world I could say that might bring the poor woman some solace. In the end, I opted to write simply, removing my own emotion from the equation so that she would have room for her own. I let her know he didn't seem to be in much pain, and that he was not alone when he passed. That the doctors had cared for him and done their utmost to make him comfortable. I knew in the end, it would be of little real comfort to her, but they were the things I would want to know in her place. The things I know Mother wished she knew about Francis. I folded up the words in an envelope and pressed it to my heart, which broke for the woman who had lost her precious boy.

Luce and Vera made it in from the hospital, along with several of the girls coming off shifts at GHQ, just before six o'clock, when the smells of Mrs. Grant's good cooking began to waft from the kitchen. She'd tracked down some decent beef, and I could feel the rumble in my stomach despite the activities of the afternoon.

"I hope you have a bit to spare," Luce announced to Mrs. Grant, who had emerged to greet the girls. "We brought home a guest. Andrew—that is, Lieutenant Carrigan—is parking the truck."

"He came home with you?" I asked, incredulous.

"He said you had a letter for him, so we invited him to dinner to save you the trouble of walking into town," Vera explained, giving Luce a sidelong glance.

"Kind of you," I said. "Though I'm not sure we should have taken Lieutenant Carrigan from his duties."

"I had the evening off," he supplied, entering through the door Mrs. Grant opened for him. "And I wasn't about to pass up the opportunity for a meal in such pleasant company."

"You're very welcome here," Mrs. Grant said. I offered introductions, and she ushered us all to the dinner table, where we had an unusually good dinner of steak, steamed carrots, and creamed potatoes. Not the best steak I'd had in my life, but one of the best meals I'd had in weeks.

"What important work you do, Lieutenant," Mrs. Grant said, always eager for lively conversation when officers came calling.

"Thank you, though no more important than what these ladies are doing keeping headquarters connected to the front. Or compared to what you're doing to keep them safe."

"You're too kind. They're such good girls, it isn't much work at all. Ruby has the hard task, really. Chief operator is a big job."

Andrew's eyes widened in surprise. "I had no idea. You're young for such a position." Sadie stifled a derisive snort, which I rewarded with a glare. I'd not have the lieutenant spreading tales that the signal-corps girls were anything less than impeccably behaved.

I pointed to the patch on my shoulder that included the signal-corps transmitter, which designated that I was an operator. The laurel below the transmitter designated the rank of supervisor, the lightning bolt that of chief operator. "We're all young—they hadn't much choice but to choose a young woman to lead."

"They chose well," he said. "I've heard nothing but praise for your group since you arrived."

"Thank you," I said. "It's nice to hear our work is appreciated."

"So much so, I know some of the officers have put on a hunt to find a piano for your parlor so they can woo you all with their musical abilities when they come calling. And you them. I know I'd love to hear Miss Wagner's lovely voice again."

"That is a rare occurrence, Lieutenant. If they want to hear my voice, they'd do better to place a call."

Andrew chortled. "It's a shame, though. You have talent."

"Do you really think they might be able to get us a piano?" Hazel asked, her face brighter than I'd seen it since I met her. "I'd love nothing more."

"When I tell them that, I'm sure they'll search to the ends of the earth to get one for you."

Hazel beamed and began to chatter about her piano lessons. None of us suspected she had such a musical bent.

The meal slowed to its end, and one by one the girls excused themselves to set about their evening activities. It was always a pleasant time of day, when we retreated to our quiet pursuits like letter writing and mending.

"I ought to be heading back, I suppose," Andrew announced as the clock loomed to quarter of eight. He'd be expected back at base by eight and would only have moments to spare.

"I'll see you out," I said, as Mrs. Grant had already started in on the dishes.

I walked him to the edge of the porch, and I saw him eye the hulking green truck with regret. "It was the nicest evening I've had in ages, Ruby. Thank you."

"We love having callers," I said truthfully. "It makes the evenings seem like a party."

"I hope you don't mind if I call often, then," Andrew said. "I'd like to get to know you better."

"I'm sure the girls would enjoy that very much," I said. It was true. Not only was he more than pleasant to look at, but he brought a much-needed levity to the house too. We were so intent on excelling at our work that I worried our seriousness would lead to exhaustion in the coming months. His wit, his charm, was a respite from the war, a respite that we'd need more and more.

"I hope that includes you, Ruby."

"Of course," I said. I shook my head, patted my pockets, and produced the letter for Willie's mother. "The letter! I nearly forgot. And it's why you came, after all."

"Oh yes," Andrew said, accepting the note. "I'll get it in the post with mine at first light. Sleep well, Ruby. I hope you and the others will come to the hospital regularly. It does us all good."

"Whenever we can be spared," I promised, though the thought of repeating the day's heartbreak made my stomach drop.

I retreated inside as his truck rattled down the street. Luce and Vera giggled like schoolgirls on the sofa.

"What is wrong with you?" I asked, arching a weary eyebrow.

"You are completely oblivious, aren't you?" Luce said, exasperated. "He didn't come for the letter any more than we came to France to see the Eiffel Tower. He likes you."

"I'm sure you're making things up in your head for your own amusement," I said, rolling my eyes. "You'd do better to read a good book and let the poor lieutenant alone."

"Say what you will, Chief Operator Wagner, but he hung on every word you spoke at dinner and barely looked at the rest of us," Luce insisted.

"It's true," Vera added. "My brother looked at Ida Plummer that way once, and now they have three children and another on the way."

"Ah, the future foretold," Luce said, rubbing her hands with glee. "I predict a wedding and a baby for you within a year of the war's end."

"Very likely," I snapped. "I have a fiancé somewhere here in France, and I'm sure the lieutenant will be as eager as the rest of us to go back to life as it should be."

I huffed back up the stairs to my room, glad to have the space to myself since Margot was working a later shift that night. I wrote to Nathaniel, mostly to spite Luce and Vera, and I hoped the army could direct it to him. It was full of pat well-wishes and hopes that army life was at least bearable. I'd not written him since I sent a telegram from New York informing him that I was being deployed, and another letter was rather overdue.

> *Things are quite comfortable here. The girls are as cunning as they are sweet, and I am sure we'll be of use to the war efforts. I've promised your mother faithfully to report on your well-being, so I hope you'll find the time to send word as often as you can. I'm sure it will save her sleepless nights . . .*

I shook my head when I realized I ought to have said "us both" instead of "her" with regard to the sleepless nights but signed off the letter as it was rather than use up more paper for another draft. I offered little information about what we were doing in Chaumont, partly for safety reasons, partly because I knew he had no interest in this part of my life. Unable to contain my thoughts well enough for sleep, I pulled out another sheet and wrote to Mother. Truth be told, I missed her. Her mood was always brightest with the spring blooms, and we'd always found common ground in the garden.

For some reason, I was compelled to tell her all about Willie and how I watched him slip from this world to the next. I didn't burden her with my sorrow, because I didn't want her next letter to be filled with pleas for my return. But I did want her to consider that it was possible—however remotely—that Francis had not been alone as he died.

CHAPTER 12

June 12, 1918

Andrew became a regular guest at the house, and while he was pleasant enough company, his frequent visits led to teasing from Margot and the others that I could have done without. He'd become such a fixture in the house that he could hardly have been excluded when Mrs. Grant organized a celebration for Hazel, Vera, and me, who all had June birthdays. His birthday was midmonth as well, so I couldn't contrive a reason to exclude him from the dinner that wouldn't have hurt his feelings.

Mrs. Grant spent the better part of the day preparing the feast. We all stared at the spread, indulging with our eyes before we gave our stomachs that pleasure. Though we never wanted for food, it was usually plain and a bit stodgy. No one complained, but the occasional slice of cherry pie or peanut biscuits would have gone a long way to break the monotony of stews, soups, and dried meats with stale bread.

"This is an absolute miracle," I breathed. "Is that honest-to-goodness apple pie? It looks better than any birthday cake I could have dreamed up."

"Tarte tatin," Mrs. Grant said with a nod. "Thinner than our apple pies at home, but the glaze and crisp crust are an improvement, in my mind. And we've managed to whip up a real *brochet à la champenoise* for you all. And just a tipple of champagne to go with it for good measure."

She gestured to a platter with fresh lake pike stuffed with mushrooms, onion, and carrots, all swimming in a butter-and-champagne sauce. There was the barest hint of the local delicacy—gray truffle—shaved on top. We all ate with only the sparsest conversation for at least a half an hour as we reveled in the exquisitely prepared dishes, unwilling to let our palates be distracted by anything so mundane as conversation. The fish flaked with the merest touch of the fork tines, and the taste of the pike managed to carry through the strong flavors of the vegetables and the decadent sauce.

"Mrs. Grant, this was the best thing I've had since my mother's own cioppino. Bless you for this." The look on Andrew's face was rapturous as he savored each bite. *Cioppino.* His mother must be of Italian descent, which explained his easily bronzed skin.

"My pleasure, my dear. No matter how dire things are, there's no excuse to miss an occasion for celebration. Perhaps especially then."

"Hear, hear," I said. "This was truly a vacation from everything, Mrs. Grant."

"Then I've been successful beyond my wildest expectation. My treat to myself will be tucking in early tonight, since I have all my chicks under one roof. I'll trust you to behave yourselves," she said with a wink.

"Goodness, that fish was good," Hazel said with a contented sigh.

"I'll have to find a recipe for Evangeline," I said, leaning heavily back in my chair.

"You call your mother by her first name?" Andrew asked, refilling my glass of champagne before seeing to his own.

"No, she's our hired girl. She's my age or a year or two older. She's quite a good cook, but not all that inventive. She's young, though, and I'm sure her repertoire will grow with time."

"You should serve this at your wedding," Vera said, gathering plates for the wash. "I'd think a French dish would be fashionable enough for a society wedding on the Main Line, and a reminder of the time you and Nathaniel spent here."

"A lovely idea," I said without much conviction. There was little chance I'd be consulted on the menu.

Andrew's face blanched. "Ah. A rich fiancé *and* a maid? I see you're set up quite nicely."

"My father and I work," I explained. "Keeping house is a big job. Mother needs someone since I'm not always there. And I promise you, that gets cast in my face regularly. Mother would much rather it was me."

"And I suppose the poor girl has a room in the attics and one afternoon off a month?" Andrew stared at the bubbles in his glass rather than at my face.

"As a matter of fact, her room is just down the hall from mine. And she can take off the time she needs. Mother has never once refused her." I pushed the slice of tart away, having lost my appetite in the face of Andrew's accusations.

"Not that she'd dare ask and risk her job." He placed his champagne glass down on the wooden table with an audible clink.

"Now why are you acting like this all of a sudden? Evangeline is our employee, yes. But she's also my friend." I wanted to tell him all about the letter to Francis that sat in my trunk, waiting for me to lay it at his grave, but I would keep their secret. It wasn't mine to share, especially not for the sake of winning an argument.

"Really? You take her shopping with all your other posh friends from the Main Line? To hold your pocketbook, maybe?"

"*Vraiment*, Andrew, I don't think this is necessary," Margot interjected.

"Isn't it? Aren't you tired of seeing your sisters working for her kind? You're lucky you got clear of service, and you know it."

"I know I am. But I don't think Ruby and her family are like you say. And it isn't fair for you to judge them before you know them."

"Just like everyone is so kind to you? They hear your accent, and doors slam in your face. People just like her."

"Ruby isn't doing the slamming, Andrew. And I'm willing to find these things out for myself. Don't be a *goujat*."

Another time, I might have smiled, remembering her description of the impertinent waiter in New York, but remained impassive. "Thank you, Margot, but save your breath. I'm going up."

"A fine way to treat a servicewoman," Margot said, ignoring my injunction. "On her birthday celebration, no less. When has she ever been unkind to you?"

Andrew smoothed his hair with both hands. "Margot is right. Please don't leave. Damn it, I'm sorry, Ruby."

I turned to face him fully while gripping the arms of my chair to keep them from a less dignified office, like throttling his neck. "Are you determined to think the worst of me, Andrew? If that's true, I don't see any reason for us to bother with any sort of friendship, as you claim to want. I assure you I have no need of friends of that sort. I'm not that desperate for company."

"Maybe," Andrew said, "it's that I don't know what to make of a girl who has every creature comfort within her grasp but worked the switchboards anyway. Or one who came over here when no one expected her to."

"Maybe you should think about the fact that I'm here, Andrew. Maybe that will tell you everything you need to know."

"It depends on why you're here. Plenty of people are here for the glory and fame, and I can't say I hold that in such high regard."

"Not that I owe you an explanation, but my brother was killed in action in Cambrai. He believed in this cause, and I suppose I couldn't bear to think of his work left undone."

Andrew paled at my confession. "I'm sorry, I had no idea."

"Of course you didn't know. You were too busy formulating your half-cocked opinions of me to find out for certain."

"I deserve that. And worse."

"Will wonders never cease? We're finally in agreement on something."

"Listen, Ruby, I'm sorry I acted like an idiot. I hope you'll forgive me."

"To what end, Andrew? We're here together to win a war. We don't need to be chums for that to happen."

"I know that. But I can't stand to think that you hate me."

"I don't hate you, Andrew. I think you've got an idea in your head about what I am and where I come from that is about a hundred and eighty degrees off-kilter, but I haven't given you more thought than that. You haven't given me any indication that you're worth the trouble."

"I can't argue with that, Ruby. I truly can't. I'll leave now." He downed the last inch of his champagne with a swift motion of his wrist. "And for what it's worth, I really am sorry."

The party broke up with Andrew's departure, and I wasn't disappointed by it. Margot and I settled in, and as I replaced my uniform with my nightgown, I was suddenly oppressed under the weight of my own fatigue.

"I'm sorry Andrew behaved like a . . . *jackass*," Margot said as she pulled back her covers. "Did I get it right?"

"Impeccably," I said. "But it isn't your fault. You needn't apologize for him. You didn't act like Robespierre, ready to drag me to the guillotine."

"Yes, he was ridiculous. Especially since you didn't suggest that anyone eat cake," she said with a snort.

"Very funny," I said, wishing I had a spare pillow to toss at her. "I don't think Marie Antoinette ever actually said that, by the way. We're both maligned."

"Innocents, the both of you. But if you forgive me, Madame Antoinette, I don't think it was the maid that upset him."

"What do you mean?" I asked, sitting up a bit straighter.

"Vera mentioned that you were engaged. Did he know this?"

"I suppose not," I said. "I don't think I've had reason to mention Nathaniel to him. I'm not sure what difference it makes."

"Perhaps it matters to him more than you know," she said. "I do hope that you'll forgive him, in time."

"I'm not sure the occasion will arise. I expect he'll stay clear of us. It's a shame for the girls, but I'm sure other officers will be eager to come calling."

"You may be right," she said, though her tone implied otherwise. "But if he apologizes a second time, you should consider listening."

"I promise nothing," I said, turning on my side. "But since you seem to like him so well, I'll do my best to be civil."

Week's end came and went with the typical flurry of activity. Then, with Monday's shift behind me, I walked into the house just before six in the evening to find the off-duty girls and Mrs. Grant running about in a panic.

"What on earth is the matter?" I asked, observing the frenzy. "Are you expecting the Germans to invade? What do you know that GHQ doesn't?"

"General Pershing," Hazel said, trying to control her panting breath. She'd been out in the garden beating the dust off the sofa cushions, her cheeks reddened from rushing about. "He's coming to do an inspection. A full inspection."

"Good Lord, when?" I asked, taking one of the cushions from her hands and placing it back where it belonged on the sofa. Mrs. Grant kept an impeccable house, but I instantly morphed into my mother, seeing dust and chaos everywhere.

"Within the hour," she said, her voice shaking. "He's going to think we're a bunch of slobs."

"Not if we get to work," I said. "Everyone, make sure your beds are made and all of your personal effects are orderly. Preferably stored in your trunks if they can be." The girls were working piecemeal on a half dozen jobs at a time, accomplishing none. Even Sadie complied without any derisive remarks and tucked in the corners of her bedcovers with crisp efficiency.

We spent the next half hour scrubbing and dusting. Mrs. Grant had all but locked herself in the kitchen and would allow none to help her efforts to make it sparkle. I called for everyone to cease when the general was a quarter of an hour away so they had time to ensure their uniforms were pristine. Hazel changed into a fresh blouse, having sweat through the one she'd been working in, and Mary attended to the hem of her skirt, which had become a bit frayed. Like a mother, I looked them over, searching for unsightly smudges on their cheeks or flyaway hairs.

"You'll do," I pronounced as the women filed into line to greet the general. I hadn't seen them look quite so crisp since the day our uniforms arrived in New York. "Just stand tall and answer any questions like you know what you're talking about."

General Pershing arrived five minutes before the allotted time, which surprised none of us. One could hardly be effective at leading an army if one didn't have a profound respect for punctuality. He cut an impressive figure: tall and lean with white hair and a trim mustache. He walked with efficiency and spoke with economy, but there was a twinkle of keen intelligence and an inescapable humor in his dark eyes if a person took the time to look. I imagined he couldn't have kept his wits about him without that spark of mirth. As Father said back at home, many men feel as though they have the weight of the world on their shoulders, but General Pershing actually does.

"You're running a solid operation here, Miss Wagner," he said in response to my salute. He offered me his hand. "Your country is grateful for your service."

"And I am grateful for the chance to give it, sir," I replied, shaking his hand firmly. "I think I can safely say we all are."

"Very good," he said. "And you and your operators are comfortable?"

"Mrs. Grant has been exemplary," I said. "We couldn't ask for a more attentive caretaker. She is my right hand here at home, just as Miss St. Denis is my right hand at the office."

He shook both of their hands with a "Thank you for your devoted service," which caused Mrs. Grant to flush scarlet.

Once he'd shaken hands with all the girls, he took a quick tour of the home. Guided by Mrs. Grant and me, he and several of his underlings looked at every bedroom and even our lavatory.

"There's nothing left but the kitchen, sir," I said as we returned to the front parlor.

"Oh, I always like to look at the kitchens," he said. "You can tell more about how something is run by how the kitchen is maintained than by asking a hundred questions."

I led the way, Mrs. Grant trailing the general, quietly wringing her hands. He made a thorough inspection, even peering into the bread box, and gave the captain who followed him a nod.

"Exemplary," he said. "Carry on, ladies. We need your hard work now more than ever."

He left with another flurry of handshakes. We all waited a full minute after the door closed behind him before erupting in applause and laughter.

"I swear on my mother's grave I thought I was going to suffer a coronary on my own kitchen floor," Mrs. Grant said, sitting dramatically in her favorite chair near the fireplace.

"It's a good thing you keep it so clean," Margot replied. "Just think, the general himself took the time to come see us."

"And why shouldn't he?" I said loyally. "We're doing as much for the war effort as the men at the front. The general has the good sense to see how necessary we are."

It was true: none of us would have been here if he hadn't insisted that women were needed to fill these posts. A more traditional man would have plodded along with male operators because bringing women into service was "not the way things were done." I could almost hear those lines in my mother's practiced alto tones.

Hazel looked out the window, though General Pershing and his entourage had long gone. Her expression was downcast, and she padded back to her room without a word to anyone.

"We have to find out what she's up to," I whispered to Margot when the others had gone about their evening pursuits after dinnertime. "We can't risk having her in the office if she's sending secrets to the other side."

"I'm afraid you're right," Margot said. "Though I hate to think her capable of treason."

I scanned the room to ensure none of the others had curious ears, but all seemed invested enough in their conversation. "I hate to think it of any of my girls, but if I were looking for sensitive information, ours would be one of the first offices where I'd install a spy."

CHAPTER 13

June 16, 1918

"I'm very sorry about your headache," Margot said a little too loudly at the bedroom door for all the house to hear. "I'll take your shift this morning, and if you're feeling able, you can relieve me this afternoon."

"Nice and subtle," I said in a whisper, shaking my head.

"Bonne chance," she whispered back, straightening her cap in the hall mirror and closing the door behind her.

Hazel's comings and goings had never given cause for suspicion. She was a model operator, always early to her shifts, tidy, and efficient. But the visit from Pershing the previous day was a reminder of the sensitive information the army entrusted us with each day. We couldn't risk it falling into enemy hands. With each report to Major Weaver, I hoped he'd relieve me of this duty, but he insisted on continued surveillance. Rather than wait for the evidence to appear, I'd decided to look through her personal effects that morning to see if she was concealing anything that might suggest she'd been in contact with anyone on the wrong side of the war. Or, if the heavens smiled on me, some proof that she'd definitively cut off all ties months and months ago. In either case, it felt better to do something other than trail her around.

I waited a full quarter of an hour after the girls had gone to their shifts and Mrs. Grant had gone to do the marketing. I couldn't risk Hazel's return, or Weaver would never learn the truth. Nor would I have the others witness what was now the most loathsome duty I'd had to perform so far.

I entered the room Hazel shared with Mary and Sadie, every inch of it still as pristine as it had been for Pershing's visit. I looked through the contents of her trunk and found nothing but her clothes and a few novels. Nothing seditious, nothing that might even be considered unseemly for a young woman in service. I likely couldn't say the same for the novels in Luce's trunk, but thankfully I hadn't been called upon to root through her things. I looked in pockets and leafed through books to see if there were any letters or any hints that she'd intercepted any of the codes that were meant to be kept secret.

I was about to give up the search as a bad job and to tell Major Weaver that if Hazel was up to anything improper, she was good enough at her job to hide it from anyone with my amateur sleuthing abilities. If he wanted to catch her, he could bring in an expert who could do it properly. Then I felt a twinge in my gut, remembering the days of my girlhood when I would hide penny candies and funny papers under my mattress to keep them from Mother's prying eyes and Francis's covetous grasp. I lifted the corner of her mattress and found a small stack of envelopes, all addressed to her. The return address appeared to be for a military base in Germany, and all the letters were dated from the months prior to our departure.

I hesitated at the invasion of privacy, but I sat on the edge of Hazel's bed and opened the most recent of the letters.

Meine liebe, Hazel,

It is hard to think it has been two years since last I held you in my arms. Hard to think it is now more than a year since I was conscripted into the army. If only my father had listened to yours and we had stayed with you in Boston. No matter how unwelcome we were, it would have been better than this. I will not bore you with the details of the trench, mein Liebling, for I know you have imagination enough to know what things are like for us. It warms my heart to know that you will be closer to me, though I wish you were safe at home with your parents. I trust you will use that good head of yours to stay safe while you live among the French. They may be allies to the Americans, but my heart cannot ever fully trust them. You are a young woman of honor and duty, but remember that chief among them is to stay safe and well for—

Dein Heinrich

I read a few more. The content seemed innocent, apart from the fact that it confirmed Major Weaver's suspicions that Hazel had been in contact with enemy nationals. These were simple love letters to a young girl from her beau, but I was not to be the judge of whether her actions made her unfit for service. I set the letters in my lap, buried my face in my hands, and rubbed my eyes and temples. She was one of the best operators I had, and we'd be crippled without her, but I had no choice but to take the letters to the major immediately. Whether their contents were innocent or not, he had to know.

I was convinced it wouldn't be enough to send her home. There was no way they could bar her for having contacted a family friend before her service. She must have kept her old love letters for her own sentimental reasons, and there was no proof she'd sent him anything since she began training in New York. Perhaps this would be proof enough she *hadn't* done anything nefarious enough to merit discharge, and we could leave the whole investigation behind. I felt the knots unravel in my core and stood, ready to exonerate her. Certainly there was no crime in her having been in contact with this Heinrich before joining the army. If it made her unfit for service, that would be unfortunate, but there was nothing in them, from what I could tell, that would toss a court-martial in her lap. At least I could bid a not-so-fond farewell to my days in counterspying.

Not wanting to delay the unpleasant business, I made the trek into GHQ in forty-five minutes instead of the usual hour. I took the corridor to the major's office that did not wind past the phone offices, and had the good fortune not to run into any of the girls who might have gone to the mess hall or the lavatory. The major was poring over his reports when I knocked at the door.

"General Pershing came as close to raving about you ladies as I've ever seen him do," Major Weaver said as he motioned for me to sit. "You should be very proud."

"I am, sir," I replied. "Though the general's visit isn't the reason I've come to see you. I'm afraid you were right about Miss Brooks."

"I see we have more reason to be proud of you," he said, straightening his tie. "What have you found out?"

I produced the letters from my bag. "They all seem to be from a beau of hers in Germany. Heinrich. All are from long before her service."

"Heinrich Steiner. Serving in Germany, but of Austrian birth. His father, Jakob, runs a very successful jewelry business. He met the Brooks family in Boston just before the war broke out."

"If you knew all this, why did you need my help?" I asked.

"We didn't have proof that they were still in contact. We intercepted a few letters between their fathers some time back, one of which implied their children still had a fondness for each other. Miss Brooks was on the ship over when the connection was discovered, so we allowed her to keep her post. Some of the higher-ups thought there was a slight chance she might lead us to some useful information, but I don't think that's likely. Just a pair of star-crossed lovebirds, unfortunately."

"The letters seem pretty innocent," I said. "And nothing since before she left Boston for training. Does this mean we can finally go back to normal?"

"No, we can't risk it," Weaver said. "Even if the letters are as they seem on the surface, we can't be sure she wouldn't try to continue her correspondence. She could leak sensitive information without even realizing what she's done. We need you to put the letters back as you found them and keep your eye on her. We know the task is an onerous one, but there's really no one else in the position to do it."

To Hazel, I was her supervisor, her den mother, and her chaperone all in one. The major was right: only Margot and I would have the cover of authority we needed to control and monitor her whereabouts.

"Understood, Major," I said. "We'll continue on as we have been."

"Very good, Miss Wagner," he said. "See that you get those letters back before she notices they're missing. We don't want to put her on her guard."

I hurried back to the YWCA house and stashed the stack of letters under her mattress, hoping she'd not notice anything amiss. If she were a spy, she wasn't a particularly clever one, hiding something so potentially damning under her mattress. Surely someone involved in true espionage for the Germans would have an elaborate hidden compartment in her trunk or some such. By the time I descended downstairs to implore Mrs. Grant for a cup of tea, there was no need for me to feign the headache that had kept me from duty that day. There was some solace in having one less falsehood to bear.

CHAPTER 14

I heard the *slip-slap, slip-slap* of Major Weaver's polished oxfords on the tile floor that led to the telephone offices. Hazel looked up at me, and Mary discreetly rolled her eyes as she jotted down key points of the conversation she was translating. It was rare the sound was followed by news of any pleasant sort—especially when it came toward the end of my shift—but I made a point of perfecting a professional expression for just such occasions.

I turned to greet the major when he appeared at the doorway, and was surprised to find he was accompanied by a tall, slender man who looked to be in his early forties. He had military protocol seeping from every pore, and apparently greater skill at walking down a corridor undetected.

"Miss Wagner, we have a visitor from Tours. Captain Fielding requested special permission to see how you're running things here. Perhaps so he can take a few pointers back for the ladies in Tours, I suppose?"

"Miss Henderson is more than capable of running the Tours office," the captain replied.

"That she is," I said loyally. "We trained together in Manhattan. She's as fine an operator as we have in the signal corps."

"Quite right," Fielding chimed in. "We thought the reverse, actually. That we might be of some use to you."

"Has your service from us been anything less than satisfactory?" Major Weaver asked, clasping his hands behind his back. "I've not had any complaints come across my desk on that score."

"Satisfactory isn't exemplary," Fielding replied, straightening his tie.

"I'm not sure what you mean to imply by that, Captain, but I'll leave you to it. Miss Wagner will take any of your suggestions under advisement, I'm sure." He left, casting me a parting, apologetic glance.

"I know you're reaching the end of your shift, Miss Wagner. I was wondering if we might share a meal in the mess hall before you return to your billet?"

There was no means of politely refusing a superior officer, and I cursed my position in the army hierarchy that made me his target. "Of course," I said, mustering a weak smile. Half the girls cast a glance sideways at me as they filed out and made way for the evening crew that had come to take their posts. Even Sadie had the good grace to shoot me an apologetic look.

Captain Fielding and I took seats in the mess hall, the metal tray of food looking just as unappetizing as it had at lunchtime. Sickly-gray chicken and mashed potatoes that looked like they were mixed with liberal amounts of plaster of Paris were a far cry from Mrs. Grant's good cooking.

"How many operators are under your charge, Miss Wagner?" Fielding asked between hurried bites, not looking up from his tray.

"I started with six, but these days we have ten on a regular basis, Captain. We get flurries of ladies who come for a bit of field training before heading off to other offices here in the east and along the front." I took a bite of the potatoes and endeavored not to gag at the cold, mealy mess.

"Do you feel like you're able to give the trainees sufficient time at the boards before sending them on?" he continued. I bit the tip of my tongue for a moment to stop my reply. We had two months of training in New York, and often several weeks of closely supervised practical experience before being sent on to key locations. With few exceptions, we were experienced operators before they took us on. Our boys rarely had the benefit of such extensive training when being sent to a new post. He had to assume that we, being ladies, somehow needed more coddling.

"It's never ideal, but we manage," I explained after a calming breath. "In most cases, my own operators work fewer hours."

"And do you feel like this puts your regular operators at a disadvantage when they return to their posts?" the captain asked, finally looking up from his meal. He looked like a house cat who had stumbled upon a grounded bird and was all too anxious to pounce upon any weakness.

"Not in the least, Captain. They aren't novices on the switchboard and won't lose their skills with a few extra half days to themselves. Most use their downtime to study the codes, to see to their personal chores, and to get the exercise their bodies are denied while sitting at the boards for such long stretches. Just like our men at the front, my operators perform all the better for having some rest."

The captain's lips pursed, and he returned to his chicken. Had I offended him by comparing my ladies to soldiers? He oughtn't be. We'd taken the same oath they had—from the privates in the trenches to General Pershing himself—and were every bit as dedicated to winning the war.

"Do you believe the office would be run more efficiently with fewer permanent operators?" he continued. "So as to make room for the trainees as they come through?"

"No, sir," I said firmly, placing my fork down with a metallic clank against my tray. "We don't have trainees coming with any sort of predictable frequency, and it would be impossible to run the office with fewer women when we don't have surplus staff."

"I see," he said. "Perhaps if we were more creative with transferring your inactive operators to other posts in the area while you have trainees in residence?"

"Let me make sure I'm rightly understanding you. You propose ferrying my operators around from post to post at a moment's notice—making them learn new office procedures, and exhausting them in the process—all to prevent a few half shifts? That seems like a recipe for the sort of mistakes that cost soldiers their lives." I pushed the tray away and crossed my arms over my chest, unable to share a meal with this man any longer. The cook would grouse at me for wasting food, but I'd find an obliging bin if I had to.

"I'm simply trying to explore every avenue for increasing efficiency within the signal corps, Miss Wagner. The operations at GHQ are vital, and we can't afford for them to be anything less than flawless."

"Can you say that your operations in Tours are flawless?" I asked. "Can you really sit across from me and say that your office has reached such peak efficiency that you have the time to come here and criticize what we do?"

"I am simply—" he repeated.

"I respect your concerns, *Captain*"—I pronounced the title slowly, disdainfully, as though it were the basest of curses I was being forced to repeat—"but headquarters cannot risk being understaffed. I assure you, we are not lazing idle here." I could have lectured him about the benefit of our hospital visits. The boost to morale when we hosted suppers. The joy Hazel brought when she played the piano for guests. I saved it, though. He was not my commander and was due no such explanation.

"I'm so sorry to interrupt your conversation, Chief Operator Wagner, but I've been asked to tell you that there's a matter at the YWCA house that needs your attention sooner rather than later."

The captain and I turned our heads to see Andrew standing at attention at the head of the long cafeteria table. The captain looked at him with consternation, I with relief.

"Thank you, Lieutenant," I said. "I'll go back immediately. You'll forgive me, Captain, but I cannot neglect my duties any longer."

I left the tray of uneaten food where it was and marched out of the mess at a brisk clip, Andrew following a pace behind and to the left as though I were a superior officer.

"At ease, Lieutenant," I said wryly, stopping in the corridor. "You have no idea what you just saved me from. What's going on at the Y? Has Margot finally killed Sadie?" Worse, had she encountered some evidence of Hazel's wrongdoing? That, Andrew couldn't possibly know.

"Not a thing, that I'm aware of," he said. "But I know exactly what I'm saving you from. A court-martial for slugging that pompous nincompoop right in the nose like he deserves. I couldn't stand to think of you spending the night in a holding cell, no matter how satisfying it might have been to let him have it."

I wanted to argue that I had better mastery of my temper than to make such a public display but thought the better of adding to my list of wrongdoings by telling a bald-faced lie. "Thank you," I said.

"Let's keep walking before he gets wise, shall we?" he said. "Neither of us wants to find out how vindictive the captain might be if he discovers my little sham."

"Good idea," I replied, turning to continue to the building's exit. "You're intent on saving my bacon this evening."

"It's the least I can do. If you want to repay me, let me take you on an outing tomorrow as a peace offering. I hear you have a half day, and I can usually get one of the doctors to lend me a truck."

"Let me guess who informed you about that," I said, silently cursing Margot. Part of me wanted to be stubborn and find an excuse to say no, but I couldn't justify spending the energy on holding a grudge. "But you're right: our friend Fielding thinks that we've got too much leisure time as it is. Just as well he doesn't see me out for a stroll."

"Thank you for accepting," he said. "If you'd refused, I'd have deserved that and worse for the way I acted."

"It must be nice to be a man," I mused.

"How do you mean?"

"You think you hurt my feelings. One might put it another way: you insulted an officer—or at least the equivalent of one—in front of her subordinates. If I were Major Weaver, would you be able to buy forgiveness with a drive out into the country? Would you have the gall to ask?"

"No," he said, tucking his hands in his pockets.

"No, you'd be scrubbing a floor or peeling potatoes until your hands were bloody—if he was feeling generous." I turned and continued down the path that led back to the house, though the gravel crunching beneath Andrew's boots still sounded behind me. "Why are you following me?"

"Because I'm trying to think of a single thing I could do to make this right," he said. "And I'd like you in earshot when I come up with it."

"You could begin by making a proper apology," I said. "It's always a good place to start."

"I *am* sorry, Ruby. I was thoughtless, rude, and needlessly cruel. I am sorry I said it, and sorry I embarrassed you in front of the others. I hope you can find it within yourself to forgive me."

I looked into the depths of Andrew's dark eyes and saw nothing but truth reflected back.

"Better," I said. "And you won't pull such a thing again?"

"On my honor," he said, holding up his right hand. "I'll be on my best behavior in your presence from now on."

"That sounds as dull as a lecture on wallpaper glue. How about you just try not to lay into me for no reason?"

He extended his hand. "Fair deal," he said.

"I'm still angry at you," I said, accepting the handshake. "But at least you're man enough to admit your mistakes. That counts for something in my book."

"That's something to build on. May I pick you up at seven tomorrow morning, then?" His head cocked to one side as he waited for my answer.

"That sounds fine," I said. "Am I allowed to know where you're taking me?"

"Someplace that suits a woman of your character—that's all I'll say for now," he said with a wink.

We continued on, chatting about mundane details of our lives back at home. The time passed so quickly in his company, I was surprised when we found ourselves at the gate out front of the house. I ascended the steps and stifled a chuckle as I noticed the rustle of the curtains in the front window as prying eyes retreated to more innocent activities before I opened the door.

He arrived as promised in the morning, a large metal thermos full of coffee and a few pastries from a local shop taking up the space between us on the bench seat.

"I thought a light breakfast would be in order," he said. "We've got an hour's ride ahead of us. And no, I'm not telling you where we're going. Just enjoy your pastry. That old baker glowed like a tot on Christmas morning. He'd managed to procure a good-sized bag of flour for the first time in weeks. He seemed happy to be back at his trade."

"He found the right trade," I said, taking a bite of the flaky *pain au chocolat* once we'd made our way onto the main road. I thought about pressing him about the destination, but I decided to let him keep his secret awhile longer. "It astounds me that the French aren't all the size of houses. They know their way around the kitchen."

"Italians too," Andrew added loyally. "French pastries are good, but there's nothing in this world that compares to my mama's cannoli."

"You seem very fond of your mother."

"Isn't everyone fond of their mothers?"

"You know what I mean," I said. "Everyone *loves* their mothers. They just don't always *like* them all that well."

"I suppose I understand that," he said, turning the hulking green truck onto the highway heading north. "But you're right. My mama is a remarkable woman, and I think the world of her."

"That's refreshing to hear from a young man," I said, looking out as the red-tiled roofs of Chaumont gave way to rolling green hills. I'd never once heard Nathaniel speak of his mother with anything other than a vaguely tender indifference. "Most prattle on about their fathers. Or themselves."

"I expect that's a fair accusation of my sex," he said. "I suppose when a boy is raised by a man who looks at his wife like she was an angel from heaven, Mary Pickford's better-looking younger sister, and the cure for polio all rolled into one, he can't help but admire her."

"It's wonderful when children are raised in a home where parents love each other so deeply. It sets a healthy example." Despite Mother's stiff demeanor and Father's bristling, there was always a tenderness between them that no amount of refinement could scrub away.

"It does," he said. "I hardly ever went out with girls back at home. If I couldn't see them the way Dad sees Mama, I didn't see much of a point. They met on the crossing to America from the old country. He was from Ireland; she was from Italy. They could scarce hold a conversation, but the moment he set eyes on her, he promised to make himself worthy of her. He worked his fingers to the bone, but they were married six months after they arrived in the States."

His eyes were fixed on the road ahead, but his gaze looked remote. Perhaps thinking of a girl who'd fallen short of the mark? "Hardly ever" wasn't "never." I felt the subtle prick of jealousy climb up my spine but ignored it. His romantic interests had as much to do with my life as the political goings-on in some remote village in Guatemala.

"What a lovely story," I said. "And what is it your father does?"

"He's an auto mechanic. And a darned fine one. He repaired carriages and helped run a stable when he first arrived in the States, but he saw the promise of the automobile and got trained up. It was a side business at first, but it's growing into a roaring trade."

"I imagine so," I said, remembering the automobiles rushing along the streets of New York like blood coursing through arteries. We'd only seen a handful of vehicles since leaving Chaumont that morning, and it was lovely to see the countryside without the other cars spoiling the view. "He sounds like a forward-thinking man. My father saw the same promise in the radio, and he's done well with it. Though I expected your father's work might have something to do with medicine, given your enthusiasm for it."

"No, our family physician, Dr. Keeley, is responsible for that. He's a second father to me, and I don't think my own dad would object to my saying so."

"Did he save your life when you were a tot?" I asked. "Get you over a nasty bout of scarlet fever or some such thing?"

"Nothing so dramatic as that," he said. "He treated me for a stutter when I was a boy. Mama dragged me from specialist to specialist whenever we had enough money to go. Speech exercises in front of a mirror. Silence for days. Marbles in my mouth until hell wouldn't have it. None of it made a lick of difference. Then one day when I was seven, my baby sister, Colleen, came down with a bad cold and Mama took her to see the new doctor in the neighborhood. Since Dad was working, I had to tag along. He asked me a question and noticed the stutter. Told Mama to save the money she'd been spending on all the quacks and get me singing lessons instead. Opera, preferably."

"And it worked?" I asked, astonished at the notion. My own elocution teachers were fond of marbles themselves, and I'd been one of the lucky few who hadn't experienced swallowing one.

"Like magic. It wasn't overnight, but it strengthened my diaphragm. Changed my breathing patterns. After a few months, I'd improved so much Mama sent me every week with fresh *crostata*, *panna cotta*, and *zuccotto* to thank him. He gained twenty pounds."

I couldn't restrain an unladylike laugh. "And you were so impressed with him you decided to follow in his footsteps."

"More or less. On one of my first deliveries—with Mama's famous amaretti cookies, if memory serves—I asked why voice lessons had worked. He explained basic anatomy to me like I was a grown man instead of a bratty kid. It was hard for me not to look up to him."

"Did you keep up with your singing lessons?"

"Until I finished high school," he said. "I loved them and wasn't half-bad, if I say so myself. But in the end, I knew it wasn't the life for me. Too many nights growing up with sparse suppers to deny an opportunity for a regular paycheck. And I could hardly keep up with it when I started taking university classes. Working for my dad and taking courses was all I could handle."

"That must have taken a lot of dedication, managing both at once," I said. More than once Francis had complained about the intensity of his course load, and he didn't even have Mother's social demands to contend with, let alone a job.

"I had more than a few nights without sleep," Andrew said. "But it was the only path to medical school, so I stuck with it."

"I admire your determination," I said, glancing through the side window. We'd entered a tiny but well-ordered village. An elderly woman, clad from head to toe in black with a starched white apron, swept her walkway. She looked up at us with world-weary eyes and went back to her chore. A young matron hung her laundry on a line as her children played with a brown leather soccer ball in the garden. "So, you don't sing anymore?"

"Only for my family if they get it in their heads to ask. With three sisters and a brother, it's enough of a crowd for me."

After another half hour or so, he pulled the truck to a stop. "And here we are, my dear Miss Wagner. Our destination."

He parked in front of an unremarkable stone house in a quiet neighborhood tucked in the center of a sleepy little village. He stepped down out of the truck and came over to my side to offer me a hand. "Welcome to Domrémy," he said. He gestured to the small house with a funny, slanted roof. "Joan of Arc was born here. The house has been rebuilt enough times you can hardly consider it the same building, but plenty of her family called this place home. I thought you two had enough in common that a pilgrimage here was in order."

"I don't believe in false modesty, but I think you hold far too high an opinion of me," I said, approaching the building. I felt my knees tremble just a bit as I walked. "Hasn't she been made a saint?"

"She's been beatified, not canonized," he said, pulling from his Catholic upbringing. "Though I'm sure that's coming in a few years. Saint or no, I like to think she'd be proud to have a sister-soldier pay her home a visit. We ought to bring all the girls here if we can manage a holiday."

"I'm sure they'd love it," I said, lowering my voice to a whisper as we entered the house. It seemed somehow more sacred than any church I'd ever visited.

A few other American soldiers, silently paying respects, left shortly after we entered. The house was about the size of our drawing room back at home and was almost completely bare, save for a few relics. The beige stone walls revealed none of the tale of the legendary woman who had begun her life in their confines. I wondered what this place might have been like with a fire crackling merrily in the large stone fireplace. Her mother would have tended the soup in a cast-iron cauldron that hung over the fire while Joan played on the floor. When she was older, perhaps she played in her father's fields with the other children who lived nearby.

But there was no trace of life. No heavy, scarred table where her mother might have chopped vegetables or careworn mattresses where they might have slept. Instead, one simple statue and the plaque attributed to the noblewoman who had commissioned it were all that remained as tribute to her extraordinary life. Unlike grander statues, this one depicted her with an appropriately childlike face, cast downward. She wore not only the armor and boots she was typically depicted in, but also a calf-length skirt which betrayed her sex. She clutched her sword to her bosom; her expression was solemn, almost fearful. My breath lodged in my chest, knowing something of the dread she felt.

"Penny for your thoughts," Andrew whispered, standing beside me.

"I'm not sure they're worth that much," I said. "It's just that she knows what's coming. It's not like the paintings that show her like a warrior queen charging against the enemy. She's just a girl. And she knows that this divine mission of hers is probably going to kill her."

Andrew looked as though he were going to take a step closer to me but then thought better of it. "I knew you'd understand each other. Would you care to take a stroll around the village before we go back? Or do you want to stay awhile longer?"

Another uniformed soldier entered, and it seemed just as well to let him enjoy the place in solitude, as I'd been able to do. "We should go," I said, but paused briefly to sign the registry at the door. Not that anyone would ever care that I'd been here, but somehow it felt right to leave a tiny piece of myself behind.

The sunlight assaulted our eyes as we left the dark little house behind. American soldiers wandered the streets, smoking cigarettes and laughing at private jokes.

"There seem to be more Americans here than French," I said.

"The training camp at Neufchâteau isn't ten miles from here," Andrew said. "It's become a favorite place for them to visit on their half days. Joan makes for a good draw."

"It's incredible," I said. A breeze kicked up and caused the tall grasses in the open field outside the village to ripple in the wind like the muscles of a lithe dancer bounding across the stage. "No wonder she had visions. I would think anyone who grew up in such a beautiful place like this couldn't help but have them. Thank you for bringing me here, Andrew."

Not taking my eyes from the windswept fields, I took his hand for a moment, squeezing it in mine, before letting go. I felt a quickening in my chest that was followed almost immediately with the pang of disloyalty. Nathaniel deserved better than me taking my half days in the countryside alone with other men, no matter how splendid the outing, nor how charming the company.

"I hope this means you forgive me," Andrew said. "I'd like to be friends."

Friends. Nathaniel couldn't object to that. Though aside from Francis, I'd never considered any young man to be a friend. At home, the young men kept to their circle and the young ladies to another. There were no casual outings as friends. There was courtship.

"Friends," I said, extending my hand for him to shake. I doubted we'd see each other after the war, and there was enough animosity in the world to make prolonging my quarrel with Andrew seem foolish.

We stopped inside the ancient church, just a few paces from her birthplace, that Joan and her family attended, and walked the steps where the village lore claimed she'd seen her visions. Once we felt we'd done our duty by Joan, we wandered the little hamlet until the time required us to return to headquarters.

"I'd love to know what set you off at the birthday party," I blurted out once we left Domrémy behind us. I studied his profile as he pondered his response.

Andrew propped his elbow on the window ledge and rested his head against his fingers. "Mama worked as a maid my entire childhood while Dad scraped by with his repair jobs. I saw a half dozen families take advantage of her kindness. I'm not keen on the whole concept of maids and the like." The muscles in his jaw were clenched. I supposed some particularly foul memory must have been pulling at him.

"I promise we aren't like that," I said. "Though I'm sure no one thinks they are."

"Thank you for saying that," he said. "I'm sure each and every one of Mama's employers thought they were being magnanimous when they paid her an extra twenty-five cents for working three hours late."

"I wouldn't say Mother is easy to work for, but she's always been considerate of Evangeline. She's the first help we ever had, aside from a nanny who helped a bit in the kitchen when I was small. We weren't always well off. Father made his fortune in the last fifteen years or so. We all remember what a 'normal' life is like. Watered-down porridge, patchwork on elbows and knees. All of it."

"I guess I gathered you'd always been well-to-do. You certainly carry yourself that way."

"Thanks to Mother. Comportment lessons. Elocution. French. From the moment she saw Father's potential to launch us into Philadelphia society, she invested every spare penny to make sure we'd be ready to take our place in it."

"She sounds . . . rather conniving? Is that the right way to put it?"

"'Conniving' isn't wrong, though I'd say 'shrewd' is more accurate. She's a more astute scholar of people's character than I've ever met. And she knows that mistreating a servant is base behavior of the worst kind. She'd never stoop to it."

"You do mean it, don't you?" Andrew asked.

"I do. And I truly consider Evangeline a friend. She's a smart girl, and kind too." I'd have been proud to call her my sister, but the knowledge that she'd no longer have that chance stung too much to speak aloud. "All this talk is making me homesick."

"Same here, but it is nice to talk about home sometimes," he said.

"It's a reminder of why we're doing this. What we're protecting, and what we have to lose."

Too soon we pulled into headquarters. I exited the truck as quickly as I could before the sight of Andrew dropping me off could cause chatter. Margot beamed as I entered the room to relieve her for her afternoon off.

"You left early this morning," Margot said. "I thought you'd have yourself a little *sieste* on your half day."

"Lieutenant Carrigan took me for a drive." I tried to impart the news as though it were as uninteresting as reheated oatmeal.

Margot raised her eyebrows. "I didn't think you were on such friendly terms."

"He rescued me from that awful Captain Fielding," I said, lowering my voice. "I felt refusing him would have been rather petty."

"Definitely. But an unchaperoned drive with a young man?" She placed a hand on her hip. "My, my, Mademoiselle Wagner, *bon travail*."

"Keep it up, Mademoiselle St. Denis, and you'll not see another half day off for the duration of the war."

"Ah, but for the joy of taunting you, *ma chère*, it would be a worthy price."

CHAPTER 15

June 21, 1918

The German troops had been relatively quiet for a couple of weeks, and we all got the feeling that our side was scurrying to regroup for a counterattack. The Germans had thrown all their might into their attack in early June, but we'd managed to hold them back from the road to Paris. The stories that came out of the attack at Belleau Wood were horrifying. Entire battalions of troops marooned in the woods, pinned between barbed wire and German machine guns. The marines finally secured our position in the area, but they paid for it in flesh.

That afternoon, Sadie and Hazel, along with a half dozen trainees bound for Neufchâteau, worked the lines. The traffic was light, but it gave the new girls a chance to ask questions without slowing anyone down. Some might have thought the calm was reassuring, but in truth we just dreaded the surge of activity that would invariably accompany the next drive on either side.

"You have a visitor, Chief Operator Wagner," Major Weaver announced at the door in the loud whisper we'd asked him to use.

I turned back to see a familiar face next to the major's in the doorway. The even features of Nathaniel's patrician face, his perfectly groomed, copper-brown hair and matching mustache, and his impeccable uniform made him look like something from a recruitment poster. I gave my head a little shake as though to wake myself from a stupor.

"My dear girl, but it's good to see you," he said, coming over to my side without regard for the quiet we needed to run the office. I wasn't filled with the urge to take him up in my arms, and the display would only have served to embarrass him anyway, so I placed a decorous kiss on the air above his cheek. "I ought to strangle you for coming anywhere near this godforsaken place," he said, "but I can't bring myself to be anything but glad to see you."

"I—it's good to see you too, Nathaniel," I said, conjuring up a smile.

Sadie shot me a poisonous look, covered her mouthpiece with her hand, and hissed, "*Some* of us are working."

I restrained a scoff. "Take my place for an hour once you finish your call. You've wanted a chance to supervise."

Sadie's eyes widened, but she nodded in agreement. I wondered if I wasn't playing the part of the wary mother giving in to a petulant child and if I'd pay the price for those few moments of peace.

"Take the rest of the day," Major Weaver said. "I can assist Operator Porter." He gave me a significant glance. He knew next to nothing about running a switchboard, but Sadie wasn't privy to the importance of keeping Hazel under constant supervision.

I led Nathaniel out of the office and onto the grounds, where we could speak without being overheard.

"How on earth did you manage to come here?" I stammered once we were out under the unremitting June sun.

"My commanding officer had business in Neufchâteau. I managed to persuade him to let me do the errand for him so I could pay you a visit."

"How long are you here?"

"Only a few hours, I'm afraid. I'm to report back to Neufchâteau by eight tonight and will be on the morning train back north." I had been able to parse from his letters that he'd been stationed somewhere near Belgium, but the censors always managed to block out precise locations. Finding me at GHQ would have been a much simpler task. "I hope the surprise is a welcome one?"

"Of course it is," I said, once again drawing my lips into a smile. "Shall we find you something to eat? The mess will be closed for lunch, and it's a bit early for supper, but I'm sure we can find an obliging restaurant."

"I was able to find something for lunch before I drove here," he said, offering me his arm. "But I wouldn't mind a stroll on such a nice day after being cooped up on trains and in meetings for the last week."

"That would be lovely," I said, pointing him on the prettiest route that would lead us out into the countryside.

"You're looking well, my dear," Nathaniel pronounced, looking me up and down. "Your mother wrote to me, you know. She was terribly worried about you signing on. I wish you'd consulted me. I'd never have condoned it."

I closed my eyes and swallowed a retort. *He's going to be your husband. You'll have to get used to asking his opinion about things.* "Father understood that I couldn't bear to stay home and do nothing."

"I wouldn't dismiss the work the women are doing at home as 'nothing,' Ruby. Don't be unkind."

"That isn't what I meant to imply, but you can't deny that you need orders from your general more urgently than you need fresh socks and wool caps."

"Let's not argue," Nathaniel said. "I'm here for only a few hours. We ought to make the most of it."

"You're right. I'm just glad Major Weaver was willing to relieve me for the afternoon."

"Chief operator," he said. "I can't say I haven't boasted to the other officers about you. It's rather impressive. Where does that rank fit in the scheme of things? Something like a lieutenant? Captain, even?"

"It's hard to say," I admitted. "We're certainly treated with more deference than the enlisted men but are expected to salute the officers. Somewhere in between the two, I suppose. No one quite knows what to do with us."

"Well, it's something wholly new. I've heard they've allowed women to serve in the navy and the marines as well. I expect they have them doing clerical tasks and the like to free up the men for combat."

"How marvelous," I said. "It's wonderful they have the chance to do their part."

"You don't think it would be better for the men to know their wives and daughters are safe? There is the home front to think of."

"Of course there is, but if bringing over a few thousand women out of millions will end the war faster and save lives, I'm not one to disagree."

"I suppose that's hard to argue against. But with all the changes in the world, it's tempting to cling to tradition, don't you think?"

"Not especially. It seems the surest road to disappointment. Change is the only constant, as the philosophers say."

"I'm afraid you're all too right about that, my dear," he said.

"How bad is it at the front?" I asked as we turned onto a lane shaded with thick trees. "Really and truly."

"We trained on French soil for almost a full year," he said, his color growing chalky. I gripped his arm in support. "And no bit of it could prepare us for the trenches. There isn't a memoir, moving picture, poem, or song that can do the horror of it justice." He was quiet a moment, then said, "I never got to tell you how sorry I am about Francis. I was gutted to hear about him. He was always the best of us."

I patted his hand in silent thanks. I remembered more than a few occasions when Francis had been left out of social gatherings where a word from Nathaniel would have meant seamless inclusion. But his words were sincere, and Francis wouldn't have wanted me to hold a grudge. I held Nathaniel's arm a bit tighter.

"No one should have to see the things you've seen, Nathaniel," I said. "For that, I'm truly sorry."

"I'm not," he replied, looking off into the distance. "If this really is the war to end all wars, if it means our sons will be spared from the trenches, I'm happy to serve."

Our sons. He spoke with the confidence of a man who would survive the war, and I was glad of it. He clung to hope, or at least would have me think he did.

"Do you want a large family?" I asked. We'd never had the time alone to discuss such private matters, and this might be my last chance to ask before we were married.

"I haven't given it too much thought," he said, glancing down at the dirt road beneath his boots. "Now that you ask the question, I feel I've been remiss about it."

"The war has been a bit of a distraction," I said drily.

"More than once I've kept myself awake with the knowledge that we might already be married with a child by now had it not been for the war. I suppose I've always imagined a larger family than my own. Being an only child was rather lonely, as you might expect, and being the only heir, the usual maternal fussing was amplified tenfold. But I find overly large families to be wearisome. Vulgar, even, when taken to extremes. Three children? Perhaps four if we take a liking to it?"

"That seems reasonable," I said.

"Strange having this conversation here," Nathaniel said, gesturing to the path before us. "It seems better suited to a private discussion in our sitting room after dinner, out of earshot of the maids, rather than a dusty road in the middle of a war zone."

"Am I making you uncomfortable?"

"Not at all. You're probably right. It's best to have an understanding before it's too late."

"Too late?" I asked. "What do you mean?"

"It's just that marriage . . . complicates things. Once a couple is married, these big decisions can become treacherous. The party who has to compromise ends up resenting the party who held their ground. Or if both must compromise, they resent each other. If there is an understanding beforehand, it breeds less animosity."

"Spoken like a man who has read his share of legal jargon," I said.

"More than my share. I have to say, it's nice to talk about the future with you. To think about the way things will be . . . after. It's reassuring to believe that the world may somehow resemble its old self once the war is over."

"Will it really, Nathaniel?"

"At least in one respect it will," he said, stopping on the side of the road, raising my fingers to his lips. "No matter what happens, we'll build a future together. We'll secure our families' futures and be a force for good back at home."

We wandered back into town, discussing the latest news we'd had from the Main Line, and all the minutiae of army life, until the sun was lowering in the sky and he had to make his way back to the encampment at Neufchâteau.

"I wish I could stay longer," Nathaniel said. "Please keep yourself safe, my dear." He brushed a curl off my face.

"And no heroics for you either," I said. I reached up with my free hand and traced the side of his cheek with my finger. Our eyes met, and he leaned in. I angled my face so he could lower his lips to mine, but instead he placed a chaste kiss on my forehead.

An ice-cold frisson slithered up my spine at the realization that this was how my future would be. I would have the good fortune to marry a kind man who cared for me—who respected me, even. But I would never be able to stir real passion in him, no matter how warm and affectionate I was toward him. I imagined growing colder and more aloof as the years went on, each little rejection driving another sliver of ice through my heart.

But I'd made my promises to my family, and I would keep them.

CHAPTER 16

June 24, 1918

As we filed into the telephone offices that morning, we were greeted by the sight of a small booklet in front of each station.

"Ladies, we have a gift for you," Major Weaver said as the girls took their places. "A book of codes we are to use in order to keep any telephone communications the Germans may be able to intercept as vague as possible. We call it the Potomac, after the river back home. The book contains three-letter codes for common words used in communication. We expect you to familiarize yourselves with the codes, use them in accordance with the directions listed, and above all else, protect their secrecy with your very lives."

I flipped through the booklet, about fifty pages in length, four columns wide. In the first twenty-five pages, the first and third columns contained words or short phrases, the second and fourth had sets of three random letters that we were to use as code. *Assist* became "BLU," *behind the lines* became "MXY," and so on. There were multiple codes for each letter. "C" might be "LFP," "EZR," or "DFP." If a word needed to be spelled out, we needed to vary which one we used, to make decrypting the code as hard as possible. Instructions said to avoid double letters by using different codes for each "O" in *boot*, for example. There were codes for frequently used affixes to speed things along, as well as numbers. The second half of the book reversed the process so the codes could be translated back into comprehensible words.

"This is going to make things more complicated," Sadie said, rubbing her temples as she leafed through the book. "This will take weeks to learn."

"Let's hope the code is in play that long, Miss Porter," the major said. "The moment we have reason to believe the code has been compromised, all extant copies will be burned and another will be issued. The fewer times we have to do this, the better for all of us. On that note, the first group you must memorize is 'DAM.' It means 'code lost.' If this code is transmitted, you are to advise Miss Wagner or Miss St. Denis at once, and she will inform me so that the book-destruction protocol can be set into effect. Use of the code begins today."

When Major Weaver exited the room, our heads were all still buried in the laundry list. No one groused, but the enormity of the task before us hung heavy. We'd have to memorize the codes in order to transcribe them with any reasonable speed. Phrases like *casualties heavy* ("LAS") and *we are losing heavily* ("WBS") delivered a blow to the gut as I read them.

"We can do this, ladies," I said, snapping the book shut. "We've all studied foreign languages before. What's a thousand or so codes?"

As might be expected, the abrupt introduction of the codes slowed down our rate of communication that day, but after several hours the girls were becoming more adept. Vera and Mary were particularly quick at deciphering them, and I noticed them being able to translate back into English with fewer and fewer glances into the primer. Sadie and Hazel struggled more, but there was still improvement by the end of the shift.

By the time we were to head back to the YWCA house, the girls looked as though they'd worked a triple shift, and I couldn't blame them for it.

Major Weaver returned as the clock clicked over to five in the evening, when the night shift was to relieve us. Presumably he was there to brief them on the codes, as he had done for us.

"Go on ahead, ladies," I said. "I'll catch up with you." Given the new protocol of the day, Major Weaver would want a briefing on how things had gone, and that would likely take the better part of a half hour.

"Be sure to verify the number of codebooks at the beginning and end of each shift," the major said to Lieutenant Drake, who now led the night crew, and me. "That number should be twelve. If at any time you see a discrepancy, alert me immediately."

I gathered the primers. Eleven. I recounted twice more to the same result.

"One of the girls must have scooped one up with her things," I said, wincing.

"Chase them down, Miss Wagner. And let them know in the future they're not to leave this room."

I bolted from the office, hoping the girls were taking the usual path back to the YWCA house. It was ten minutes before I caught sight of them.

"Stop!" I screeched, attracting the attention of every shopkeeper on the street. "Margot, Hazel, all of you!"

The girls turned, brows arched. "What on earth is the matter with you?" Sadie said, the roll of her eyes as dramatic as any stage actress's.

"Which one of you took a primer?" I asked. "One is missing."

Sadie reached into her satchel and produced the book.

"I was going to take it home to study," she explained. "Is it a capital offense to try to excel at one's post?"

"Major Weaver says I'm to inventory them at the beginning and end of the day. If you want to study, you have to do so in the telephone offices."

"Nice and quiet place to read," Sadie scoffed. "A wonderful environment for memorizing."

"Anything else will put our troops at risk," I said with a bark. "It's not about us. Now I'm going to return this to Major Weaver before they have to burn a six-hour-old code. Explain to Mrs. Grant why I'll be late for supper."

I felt the cold trickle of sweat down my back by the time I returned to the telephone office. I placed the code in Major Weaver's waiting hands.

"Who took it from the room, Miss Wagner?" the major asked without preamble.

"Sadie Porter," I said. "She was hoping to study it. It's a lot to remember."

"I was hoping it was our Miss Brooks," he said. "It would be nice to put an end to this whole investigation. Speaking of whom, I'll ask that you remain vigilant in your surveillance of Miss Brooks. Now that the code is in play, we can't risk any part of it being compromised."

Mrs. Grant greeted me with supper, not too badly lessened for having been reheated, though my appetite wasn't equal to it. I ate in the kitchen and enjoyed the silence of the house, as the girls were scattered upstairs in quiet pursuits.

"You would prefer to be alone, no?" Margot asked. I jerked around to see her at the door. "I am sorry to frighten you, but I entered two full minutes ago. I've rarely seen anyone so intimate with their thoughts."

"What a lovely way of saying 'brooding.' You needn't leave. I'm happy for some company."

"Did the major call you out for the primer?" she asked, taking a seat opposite mine at the small kitchen table. "It wasn't your fault he waited five minutes too long to pass on his instructions."

"No." I poked at the florets of broccoli with disinterest. "But he mentioned Hazel again. He seemed disappointed it wasn't she who took the book, so we could be done with the investigation. It seems awful that he wants her gone."

"He wants one less headache. One can hardly blame him." She rose to pour herself a glass of milk, then resumed her place and lowered her voice. "Listen, there is no need to fret. We keep an eye on her, and it is the best thing for everyone. If she's innocent, us keeping an eye on her will confirm it. If she isn't—well, it's unfortunate, but we'll be protecting everyone."

"I know you're right," I said, forcing down a bite of chicken.

"I think most of us are surprised by the duties falling into our laps," Margot said. "You know, my brother, Antoine, has been promoted to sergeant. I'm sure much is the same for him."

"Congratulations to your brother. I'm glad you've had word."

"Yes, it is good to be able to pass on news to Maman for him. With me, he knows he doesn't need to compose a great ballad. He can simply tell me he is well and complain about the food. I can elaborate on the details for her. He was never much for writing."

I smiled, thinking of Francis. He had a fair hand with words, but the only one who'd received regular letters was Evangeline. The thought of Evangeline's letter to Francis in my trunk upstairs weighed heavy. What if it had been Hazel who managed to leak information that got Francis killed in Cambrai? It couldn't have been Hazel herself, but there might be another seemingly innocent girl just like her who gave the enemy the information they needed to mow down his regiment.

Knowing how many of us had loved ones at the front, Hazel might be deliberately putting them in harm's way.

"Where is Hazel now?" I asked.

"In her room with Mary and Sadie. Reading a novel."

"Did you happen to see what it was?" I asked, pushing the plate away.

"*Little Women*," she said. "Nothing scandalous."

"No," I said. "Wholesome and American as apple pie."

An unholy wail of the air-raid siren sounded overhead like the cry of a brokenhearted banshee. We'd had our share of *alertes* before, but always in the dead of night, not in the hours before bed.

I bounded to the kitchen door, Margot a pace behind me. "To the cellar!" I bellowed to the girls upstairs. I already heard the thundering of feet down the stairs as the girls ran from their bedrooms. Most were in nightgowns, but all had thought to grab shoes or boots before descending, as I'd ordered them during past drills. Fleeing in a nightgown would be cold, inconvenient, and embarrassing. Fleeing barefoot would be impossible.

I stood at the top of the stairs that wended down to the dank cellar where Mrs. Grant stored potatoes, onions, and carrots. I'd also had it stocked with water, emergency rations, candles, and medical supplies in the event of a true attack. In one corner loomed a massive metal tub where we were to wash our clothes, but it was so large, not even the tallest of us could reach in to give anything a proper scrubbing. We were left to wash our necessities in the bath and sinks upstairs and take the rest to the indelicate care of the laundresses in town.

"We ought to hide in the tub," Margot joked. "There isn't a German bomb that could even dent it."

"We'd be playing right into their trap," Vera retorted with a wry laugh. "We'd be trapped in there for weeks until someone thought to come look for us, and we'd have died of starvation by then."

The others were not in such high spirits. Hazel was as gray as concrete, and even the usually buoyant Luce was gaunt. Mary started whispering the "Our Father" to herself and was joined by Mrs. Grant and Sadie. Some of the Catholic girls chimed in with the "Pater Noster."

I remained silent, listening for the drone of the German zeppelin followed by the crash of bombs. The screech of twisting metal and the roar of collapsing stone. The only sounds were the miserable howl of the sirens underscored by the softly muttered, melodic prayers of the women in my charge.

"Do you think they're coming this time?" Margot asked in a whisper.

"An attack so early in the evening seems strange," I said close to her ear. "Which is all the more worrying." There was no sense in dipping my fears in powdered sugar for her.

She returned a grim expression but did not join in the prayers. We heard what sounded like the rumble of trucks on the road above, and though no one spoke the words aloud, the question on every face was *Are they ours or theirs?*

Our previous *alertes* lasted a quarter of an hour. A half hour at the most. We had been below ground for over an hour, and the sirens still blared.

"Try to sleep," I commanded when the prayers had come to their end. "This won't give us a reprieve from our morning duties, and I won't have you making mistakes."

Wordlessly, the women lounged out and tried to make themselves as comfortable as they could, despite the cold stone floors. Some shut their eyes and tried to ignore the muted noise of the world above, but most were unable to even give the pretense that they could rest while we had no idea what might be unfolding over our heads.

CHAPTER 17

The sirens didn't go silent for two hours, at which point we ambled, our aching muscles protesting, up the stairs. The street in front of the house seemed as calm as ever, though a few army trucks rumbled past as we surveyed the scene. Sleep was hard coming, even in the comfort of our beds, and the morning approached with a relentless speed. Again, at four thirty, the alarm sounded, and we were called from our sleep to the dank cellar. No one bothered trying to rest after that. The sun was rising in the east when the alarms died, and we emerged to the surface again.

We all reported early for duty, bleary-eyed and rumpled. Not a member of staff looked better rested than we, and the smell of coffee wafted through the corridors like fine perfume in a Parisian boudoir. I rotated girls in at shorter intervals, hoping to keep their attention as sharp as possible. Despite their fatigue, I didn't see a single dropped call, bungled code, or botched translation.

Andrew was waiting at the door to the telephone office when we finished our shift and made way for the evening crew.

"How did you ladies fare last night?" he asked. "You look as bright as roses despite the late hours."

"You're a skilled liar," I said, glaring through narrowed eyes. "Probably just as well you don't speak the truth today. Any idea what the *alertes* were about?"

"The medical staff usually isn't privy to that sort of thing, but I can say the beds in the hospital aren't much fuller than yesterday."

"Thank heaven for that," I said.

"You've got that right. The rumor I heard was something to do with the chemical weapons the Germans are messing with. There must have been some sort of scare. The engineering units are doubling up their efforts to come up with a defense. They're doing some practice attacks tonight on the experimental gas field. A pal of mine invited me to come watch and said I could bring you ladies along. I can take you in the ambulance if you want."

The thought of an evening out caused the fatigue to weigh on my shoulders like a leaden jacket, but the expressions on the girls' faces were so hopeful, I couldn't deny them, nor could I let them go unescorted. I gave my consent and had an obliging sergeant send word to Mrs. Grant that she could forgo dinner. We piled into the ambulance, which was really a glorified farm truck with a covered bed that had been haphazardly painted in army green. The road to the gas field was pitted, and we jostled about like dried beans in a can.

"Bless you, Carrigan, you brought real live women." A man greeted Andrew with a clap on the back. He wore the insignia of a lieutenant and spoke with a Brooklyn accent that wasn't as polished as Andrew's.

"They wouldn't want to miss this," he said. "They're an adventuresome lot, our operators."

"The best kind of lady, if you ask me," the lieutenant said. "Introduce us, man."

"Miss Ruby Wagner, this is Gus Hendricks, a pal of mine from back home, and the backbone of the Thirtieth Engineers. Gus, this is Miss Wagner, chief operator of the First Telephone Group, and her merry band of miscreants."

My "merry band" erupted in girlish giggles at Andrew's pronouncement, and I could scarce keep my eyes from rolling back into my head. He made individual introductions, and we were escorted to the mess hall, which had once been a farmer's cottage.

"You won't be dipping too far into your own rations?" I asked as Gus showed us to our table. "Six extra mouths to feed isn't a small matter."

"You wouldn't deny us the chance of entertaining you properly," Gus said, holding a chair out for me. "We don't have much occasion for hosting young ladies out here, but when we do, we take pride in doing it right."

"Of course," I said, patting his hand. They treated us to some of the best steak we'd had since the States, and real honest-to-goodness cake. They draped rags over their arms, pretending to be elegant French waiters as they presented the meal.

"We should fire the cooks at GHQ and bring these men in," Sadie declared as she pushed away her clean plate. "We'd all gain fifteen pounds but have a fine time doing it."

"I'm for it," I said, raising my glass of water. "If you're as good with weapons as you are in the kitchen, the war should have been over months ago."

"Ah, Miss Wagner, we've just begun to fight," Gus said, batting a roguish wink in my direction. "If you ladies are finished, come on outside and inspect our work."

Gus and his men took us on a tour of the "dummy" trenches they'd dug to simulate the effect of their weaponry on the men in the actual trenches off to the northeast.

"Imagine those poor boys living in the muck, day after day," Hazel said. She sighed and looked down into the muddy bog. The engineers scurried about in them, preparing for their tests, but they'd have the luxury of leaving them tonight for proper barracks. Hazel looked intently at the hum of activity. Had allowing her to come been a mistake? What information could she be gathering to send over to the enemy? She was in full view of some of our newest weapons and would see them deployed. Would she know enough to send anything of use to the other side?

But denying her the chance to come while allowing the others would have just raised suspicion. She was one of us and had to feel as such until Major Weaver had reason to remove her from service.

It was full dark when we assembled out on the western corner of the field, a safe distance from the terrifying machines of war that loomed on the opposite edge. With a signal, the night sky morphed from inky blue to fiery, brilliant orange as the liquid fire—thermite, they called it—rolled over the field like angry molten tidal waves. The deafening boom of the shells as they flew overhead in the direction of the forest caused some of us to cower. I could see Andrew's brow covered in a sheen, though he didn't flinch at each crash. He'd seen this before, and not in any sort of "practice attack." He'd lost his fellow men in battle, seen firsthand the devastation of these weapons.

I wanted to hold his hand. To let the part of him that longed to run for cover know that, even though I hadn't shared his experience, I could empathize with it. Instead, I tucked my hands in my pockets and kept my eyes on the tapestry of fire and destruction the engineers wove for us.

The dummy trench they'd designated as the "German Front" was completely engulfed in flames. Had real men occupied the trenches, those who survived could not have been considered the lucky ones. In that moment, I realized that hell was in no sense theoretical.

CHAPTER 18

June 29, 1918

"You managed to clean your suit," Margot said approvingly as I reported for my half day on Saturday. She'd shown me how to spot-clean the wool with gasoline. I never thought I'd miss Chapman's Dry Cleaners, but I'd have traded in a month's pay for the convenience of it now.

"I smell like a broken kerosene lamp," I said. "But I didn't burn down the YWCA house, so I'll call it a victory. My blouses didn't fare as well at the laundress's, though. They're dirtier than when I sent them in."

"These Frenchwomen are not keen on pleasing their clients," Margot agreed. "It must be nice to have so much business they cannot be bothered with such things."

"More evenings perched over the bathtub," I said. "I'll have to ask Evangeline to send more cleaning powder. I've yet to see any worth having here. How was the shift?"

"It went well." She snapped the fixture on her handbag. "Quiet, but not completely dead."

"Very good," I said. I peeked into the office, where all the women were either busy connecting calls or reading over the codebooks. "Where is Hazel?"

"She's been here all morning," Margot said, just noticing the vacant station at the boards. "She must have gone out the other door with Vera just now. They both have a half day coming."

"Damn," I cursed in a whisper. "We've got to find her. Did they mention any plans?"

"Vera spoke of walking into town to see if any shops were open. She's in need of some new stockings."

"Good," I said. "That narrows things down, so long as they stayed together. I'll run after them. I can tell Hazel I need her this afternoon."

"Better coming from you," Margot agreed. "I'll stay on here. You go."

I wanted to burst off running but knew that if Hazel saw me sweating and out of breath, she'd know I had come tearing after her. I immediately recognized Vera's tall frame as she waited for the clerk at the shop nearest GHQ where stockings had at least a fair chance of being found. Hazel wasn't with her.

"Where is Hazel?" I asked. "I need her back at GHQ."

"She's gone down the road to check on Delphine. Apparently her mother has been unwell, and Hazel thought she might be able to lend a hand." Delphine was the local girl that Mrs. Grant engaged to help with the deep cleaning. She was a pleasant young thing and had become a favorite with the girls.

"Kind of her," I said. "I'll go catch up with her. I'll see you this evening."

"If you wait for me, I'll join you," Vera said, her eyes shooting daggers at the clerk. "I can hope the girl here will come help me before I'm too old and decrepit to put the stockings on by myself."

"Don't be silly," I said. "Enjoy your shopping, and get some fresh air."

"You don't need to tell me twice. See you back at the house."

My pace quickened as I scanned the street numbers on the rue Chartier, where Delphine lived with her family. I was glad I'd happened to overhear her mention it to Mrs. Grant once and that I'd somehow committed it to memory.

Within ten minutes, I came upon the house, or rather Hazel standing at the door, speaking with Delphine, who looked tired and harried. A far different creature from the well-groomed maid who tended our house three days a week. Hazel offered her a crisp bill from her handbag—I couldn't tell for sure, but it looked like twenty francs, which was no small sum. Delphine handed Hazel an envelope that was tucked into her blouse and never took her eyes off the blue-and-white banknote in her hand. Hazel looked equally captivated by the missive in her hands. If it wasn't from Heinrich, I'd polish Mother's silver for a month.

Hazel turned to walk down the steps without a parting word to Delphine. She flipped over the envelope, sliding her index finger under the flap to open it as she walked.

"Hazel!" I called, loud enough for some of the neighbors to turn their heads.

She looked up at the sound of my voice. Her large, greenish-brown eyes widened further, resembling those of a doe contemplating whether she ought to run to the safety of the thicket or remain still, hoping the hunter would miss his mark. In most cases, either choice ended badly for the deer, but running would make things infinitely worse for Hazel. She would have Major Weaver and every resource at his disposal to track her down.

"Hazel, I need you to come with me," I said, making my voice softer. "I promise they will treat you fairly." There was no sense pretending I didn't know whom the letter was from.

"They'll court-martial me," she said, looking behind her. There were enough people milling about and sweeping sidewalks to slow her escape.

"Not necessarily," I said, hoping it was true. "But they absolutely will if you run. You know they'll find you, Hazel. Probably within hours. Be smart, tell the truth, and you might get discharged home with your freedom intact."

Tears welled up in her eyes and spilled over onto her high cheekbones as she walked to my side and handed me the letter before I had to demand it from her. "I had to know if he was still alive," she whispered as I tucked the letter away. "I didn't think a letter would get through to him, so I wrote a letter to his parents in Vienna. I simply asked if they knew he was well and had them send their letter to Delphine. She needed money for medicine for her mother, so she was willing to post the letter for me and receive the reply at her home. It cost me forty francs, but I had to know."

"An expensive letter," I said, taking her gently by the arm and leading her back toward GHQ. Forty francs was worth almost eight American dollars. Enough to buy a week's groceries for a family. More than enough to cover the medicine that Delphine's mother would need.

"It was worth every *centime*," she said. "You're engaged. Imagine not knowing if he's dead or alive for the better part of three years."

"I wouldn't go to the risk of sending him a letter if it could jeopardize our men. Heinrich's parents now know where you are. What if they deduce that you're with the signal-corps girls? What could be done with that information?"

"I didn't think of that," she said. "They wouldn't tell a soul. They're good, honest people. They've known Daddy for years."

"They might be, but what if the Germans find out they've been in contact with you? You know they're going through the mail. How long would they last under interrogation before they gave up your location? Fifteen minutes? Half an hour? God only knows what methods they use to get information."

She blanched. "What have I done?"

"You made a rather large mistake. I just hope it hasn't cost you more than your post. You know I have no choice but to take you to Major Weaver."

She nodded. "I hope you know I meant no harm," she said as we turned onto the street where GHQ loomed like a fortress. "I just wanted to know if he's—if he's still alive."

"I know, Hazel," I said. "I know you care for Heinrich, and I'm sure he's every bit as nice as our own boys at the front. For your sake, I hope he's well."

"Major Weaver is going to take the letter, isn't he?"

"I can't imagine otherwise. I'm sure they'll have every cryptographer in the building studying it for hidden code within the hour."

"Can I please read it? If I'm going to be sent home in disgrace, can I at least have the consolation of knowing?"

"Fine," I said, my hands shaking as I pulled the letter from my jacket pocket. "I'll see what I can parse."

"It'll be in English," she said. "They loved practicing the language when they came to Boston."

I thought of the previous letters Heinrich had sent. It *was* too bad they'd gone back to Vienna. Instead of facing Major Weaver's wrath, she might be at home with two green-eyed babies with their mother's chestnut hair and some trace of their father. A roguish dimple? Perhaps a strong aquiline nose? Heinrich might be in service to the US, translating or some such. It was such an easy decision in retrospect, but they almost always are.

I looked at the letter. I could paraphrase its contents so she wouldn't be able to decipher any code. I knew this might land me in a court-martial of my own, but the extent of my military discipline didn't extend this far. It contained only one line:

> *Feldwebelleutnant Heinrich Steiner laid to rest*
> *August 2, 1917.*

"I'm so sorry, Hazel. He's gone. He died last year." I wrapped my arm around her.

Her face crumpled, and she placed her head in her hands to gather her composure. "I think I knew it all along. When I thought of him, the warmth in my heart was replaced by a stone in my gut. But it's better to know."

"I hope it was worth the price," I said, resuming our walk toward headquarters. "And if Weaver asks, you were able to glance at the note before I could stop you."

She nodded. "I'll never forget this kindness, Ruby."

"I'm glad you think of it that way," I said. "Because it certainly doesn't feel like it."

I escorted her into Major Weaver's office. When his sergeant saw that I had Hazel in a grip by the arm, he pulled the major from a briefing to meet us in his office.

"Miss Brooks sent a letter to Vienna, and it seems today she got a reply." I handed the letter over to him. That the contents were in English didn't seem to surprise him.

"I know it was wrong, Major. I hadn't been able to get a letter over the Austrian border from home in over a year. All I wanted was to know if he was well. I meant no harm."

"Who sent the letter for you?" he asked. "One of the signal-corps girls? A besotted young sergeant?"

"No, sir. Just one of the people here in town in need of money. I needed a civilian address to get the reply." Her hands were clasped in knots on her lap. She was so focused she hardly blinked.

"It seems you thought of everything, didn't you?" he asked.

"I didn't want to cause any trouble."

"Well, you failed in that, Miss Brooks. You've caused a great deal. And I take it the reply isn't what you hoped for."

"No, it isn't, Major," she said. "Heinrich was a good man who happened to live in the wrong country."

"An unfortunate fate to befall many over the course of history," Major Weaver mused. He stood, and we scrambled to our feet, as military custom dictated. He offered me his hand. "Thank you for your diligence, Miss Wagner. I'll continue this questioning in private. I'll trust you to be discreet."

"Of course." I shook his hand, then turned to leave. I paused briefly, then placed my hand on Hazel's shoulder. I couldn't fathom that her actions were anything other than those of a lovesick girl who missed her beau, but that was for Major Weaver to discern and not me. Thank heavens.

I went to the telephone offices to relieve Margot. She came to the hall, her eyes asking the question she dared not voice.

"It's all over," I said. "Go take what's left of your afternoon. I'll find you a few more free hours later this week."

"I'm happy to stay," Margot said, rubbing my bicep. "You look like you could use a rest. I'll take my half day another time."

"I need to stay," I insisted. "Switchboards and headsets are far more useful to me than a sofa and a novel right now, I assure you."

~

A sergeant with a harried expression was sent for Hazel's effects the very night she was removed from the house, and we didn't have so much as a parting goodbye. Margot looked somber as we gathered around the dinner table, and I ate the dry meat and stewed carrots Mrs. Grant placed before me, only out of politeness and an awareness of the suffering of others who would have been grateful for the meal.

"Where has Hazel gone?" Sadie asked between bites of the tough beef. "We have a right to know." Mary cleared her throat, a signal meant to urge Sadie to soften her tone. It was rarely effective.

"I can't tell you what I don't know," I answered truthfully. She might be on her way to a ship that would take her home or locked up in an army guardhouse somewhere awaiting more interrogation. Major Weaver would likely never disclose all the facts to me, as Hazel was no longer under my charge. "I do know that her beau was killed in action, so I suspect she's asked for discharge."

"Hazel never mentioned a beau," Sadie pressed, cocking her head to the side. "And if he were killed in action, she'd want to stay on to do her part. I don't buy this for a second."

"Sadie, calm down. I'm sure they have their reasons." Mary's eyes were pleading as she addressed her friend. Her years as a teacher had made her a peacemaker. I was glad she'd taken a liking to Sadie, who had few gentling influences.

"I don't like it one bit," Sadie said, stabbing her filet with her fork and sawing with her knife as if to punctuate her words. "Something seems shifty. I think our Miss Wagner here isn't giving us the whole truth."

"No, perhaps I'm not," I conceded, placing my napkin by my plate. "Because people entrusted with more authority than me have ordered me not to and I have the good sense to obey them. A trait you'd do well to acquire, Miss Porter."

"Did you have Hazel sent away?" Sadie said, setting her fork down with a thunk. "I bet you were jealous of her. She was the best on the switchboards, and it made you look bad for the brass."

"Oh, there you are," I said, raising my arms in exasperation. "I'm going to send away one of our very best operators and leave us shorthanded—potentially handicapping our office for weeks or more—because I'm insecure in my own abilities. That will do wonders for my reputation with the major, now won't it?"

"Who is replacing her?" Mary asked, shooting Sadie a pointed look.

"That's just it. I have no idea when, or indeed *if*, they'll send a replacement. We'll have to make do for a while."

"Well, isn't that just a fine kettle of fish. Extra shifts for all of us," Sadie said, heaving a sigh.

"Yes," I replied, pushing back from the table. "And since you've claimed to be so eager for the work, you'll take hers for the next week."

"You can't—" Sadie began.

"Yes, I can," I interrupted, standing. "And if you don't like it, take it up with Major Weaver. I trust you know where to find his office. Good night, ladies."

I went up the stairs two at a time, barely resisting the urge to slam the door so hard the window would rattle. I wouldn't give Sadie Porter the satisfaction of knowing she'd gotten to me. I flopped on the bed to wallow with a sinking feeling in my gut.

Margot followed a quarter of an hour later and began to change out of her uniform.

"For what it's worth, you did the right thing," she said after a few minutes.

"What are you referring to? Hazel or Sadie?"

"Both," she said. "Sadie needs to be put in her place. And if Hazel really is innocent of wrongdoing, she's better off at home to mourn her sweetheart. If she'd stayed and anything went wrong, eyes would have fallen to her. Deserved or not. She stands a much better chance of avoiding trouble if she's home. You may have saved her from months in a jail cell."

"If this is the right thing to do, then why do I feel so terrible?" I said, sitting up in my bed. "When I was a girl, my father always told me that if I listened to my gut, I'd make good decisions in life. Keeping Hazel's secret? I felt sick. Turning her in? I felt sick."

"Your father has been blessed with a simple life, where right and wrong were perhaps a bit more obvious," Margot said, sliding into bed. "He never fought in a war. And this war? It's as much like the one his father fought as a canary is like an eagle. No rows of soldiers shooting in open fields with people looking on from their picnics. Your father gives sound advice, but much like the horse and carriage, I fear it's becoming a bit outmoded."

When I was a girl, my father had spoken so often of my grandfather, Sterling Wagner, hero of the Union and pride of his family, that

I could practically see the Battle of Gettysburg unfold before my eyes. Father had made war seem courtly, like a gentlemen's blood sport. There were no trophies and foxtails in the trenches, though, nor victory luncheons with flowing champagne.

"You're probably right," I said. "I just hope I'm not becoming outmoded along with them."

Margot laughed from her bunk. "You're working with telephones, some of the most sophisticated equipment at the army's disposal. I think you'll manage to keep up with the times for a while yet."

CHAPTER 19

July 11, 1918

"Going to a dance in uniform seems about as festive as going to a wedding in black," Vera complained, looking at her reflection in the mirror. "What I wouldn't give for some silk and satin for one evening."

"You look more fetching in a uniform than in the fanciest silk gown in a Paris shopwindow," Luce said, stepping next to Vera and giving herself a once-over in the mirror, then smoothing the front of her jacket.

"You're more practical than I am," Mary said. "That's why I'm working so hard. The sooner this war is over, the sooner I can go back to lavender, periwinkle, and Kelly green. Muslin, satin, poplin. If I never wear navy blue again, I'll live a happy life. Though I won't forgo wool for winter."

"San Francisco would be miserable without wool," Luce agreed. "Less rain than Seattle, but you have to wade through pea-soup fog for six months of the year."

"The truck is here," Margot called from downstairs. "And Lieutenant Carrigan has threatened to leave without us."

"He wouldn't dare," Mary said as we descended. "He wouldn't risk making Ruby angry a second time by having her arrive late and out of breath to the dance."

"I wouldn't suggest it," I agreed. "It will cost him more than an outing to the countryside to make it right this time."

We piled into the covered bed of an army truck and crossed town to the large hall the army had rented for a bit of a late Fourth of July celebration. The room was cavernous and plain, but the red, white, and blue bunting cheered it up considerably. Anyone who could be spared from duties was allowed to attend, and even the highest-ranking officers were pleased at the prospect of an evening where we might forget, if only for a few hours, the atrocities happening to the northeast.

"I feel like a kid with a nickel in a candy shop," Luce said, looking at the assortment of servicemen eager to dance with the few women in attendance. "How can a girl choose just one?"

There was a proper American band playing bright, lively music. Though men outnumbered women handily, it didn't dissuade anyone from taking to the floor. Andrew took my hand and pulled me to the dance floor in a mad one-step just as soon as we entered.

"I hadn't really planned on dancing," I said, trying to keep pace. My schooling in dancing had been limited to the classic ballroom variety. Mother wasn't keen on ragtime, so there weren't many chances to learn the crazy new dances like the turkey trot or the bunny hug.

"How on earth could you come to a dance with lonely soldiers and sit on the sidelines?" he asked. "Why, that's worse than selfish. It's cruel. Downright unpatriotic."

"I doubt Nathaniel would approve."

"You think this Nathaniel character of yours would reject a dance with a pretty girl if he had the chance?" Andrew asked with a sidelong glance. "More importantly, would you expect him to?"

"No, I suppose not," I said.

"I didn't think so," he said. "You wouldn't begrudge him some fun after all he's been through these past months. Now do him the courtesy of thinking he'd be just as considerate of you."

"I suppose you're right. It's for the good the soldiers' morale, after all."

"Like I was saying. Patriotic duty."

Once the dance was up, a sergeant cut in for a fox-trot, then a captain for the Castle walk, then on and on until I was certain my feet would be a solid blister in the morning. Not one of the signal-corps girls sat out for a single dance. Even pragmatic Mary was smiling as a stout young lieutenant from the radio office led her about the floor. I found myself glancing across the room to Andrew. One of the nurses had coaxed him out for another one-step, even faster than the last.

The tempo of the music slowed, finally, and the couples paired off for a lilting waltz.

Andrew cut across the room, pulling me close. "Patriotic duty," he reminded me.

"Patriotic duty, my foot. But finally, a dance that's my speed."

"You've managed to keep up tonight." I could feel his fingers splay on the small of my back, and he urged me another inch closer. I felt an unfamiliar twinge within me at the intimacy of his touch. The desire to pull away to maintain my composure warred with the instinct to inch closer still. "Admit it, you've enjoyed yourself."

"This *is* nice," I agreed, accepting his nudge. "Nathaniel isn't much for dancing."

Andrew didn't meet my gaze and appeared to swallow his first reply. "I'm sure he's got other qualities. Like letting you dance with me, since he doesn't care for it. He's not the jealous type, is he? I wouldn't want to stir up trouble."

"Women tend to be more forgiving of these things," I said. "Though in truth I couldn't tell you if he's the jealous kind. I've never given him any reason to show that side of himself."

"Then do yourself a favor before you walk down the aisle and find out. Write to him about the dance tonight. Tell him you enjoyed it. Better to know what you're getting into beforehand."

I thought about the advice from the girls back at home. *"Marriage is never exciting business. At least if you need to get to know each other, you've got something to talk about for a while."* I thought about the unguarded conversation that Nathaniel and I had during our brief hours together while he was on leave. I couldn't imagine he'd be equal to another such discussion until we were married.

"For a man who professes to have little liking for courting," I said, "you seem wise beyond your experience."

"A wise man observes the world in which he lives," Andrew said with mock solemnity.

"You're a regular fount of knowledge this evening."

"Most evenings." He winked. "You'd know this by now if we spent more time together."

The tingling spread, filling me with a warmth. I wanted to close the gap between us, but I didn't dare indulge myself. It's not that I didn't trust the others not to spread tales. I didn't trust myself. The song wasn't over, but I took my hand from his shoulder. "I'm sorry, Andrew. I think I need to sit for a little while."

"Of course," he said, ushering me to the folding chairs to the side of the room. "Can I get you some punch?"

"Don't worry about me," I said. The nurse he'd danced with looked over at us keenly, obviously hoping for another round on the dance floor. "Your friend would like a dance. Don't neglect her on my account."

Andrew opened his mouth to respond, but he closed it just as quickly. He looked over at the nurse, a pretty, petite brunette with large eyes and a kind smile. The sort of girl perfect for caring for the sick. The kind that would make a doting mother. "If you're sure."

The waltz ended, followed by a fox-trot that was nearly as slow. The sweet strains of the violin bounced against the wood-paneled walls.

Andrew crossed to the sweet-looking nurse and took her in his arms. Did he hold her as close? I convinced myself he kept a few more inches between them. I tried, with less success, to convince myself it didn't matter if he did.

~

"I have a bone to pick with you, Lieutenant Andrew Carrigan," Luce crowed, her French accent thicker for her fatigue. Andrew offered her his hand as she hopped down from the bed of the rattling green army truck.

"I've never been more terrified in my life, Mademoiselle Roussel. Tell me my offense so I can strive to make amends," Andrew said with a flourishing bow, then stood again to offer Margot assistance.

"I'm afraid it won't be that easy," Luce said. "You're simply going to have to stand court-martial and answer for your crimes. To the parlor with you."

Andrew was all but dragged by the girls into the house and forced to sit in Mrs. Grant's favorite chair. He swore an oath on the *Oxford English Dictionary* to tell the complete and unvarnished truth.

"Lieutenant Carrigan, you are hereby charged with the following acts: overt fraternization with the American Red Cross nursing staff—"

"I'm a medic, I can hardly avoid—"

"And, more egregiously," Luce interjected, "neglecting the women of the US Army Signal Corps at a social function. How do you plead?"

"I can only hope to throw myself on the mercy of this—very fair and impartial—tribunal. I am only one man, and I have yet to figure out a way to dance with more than one lady at a time. In my defense, I did dance with your chief operator. Twice. And if memory serves, there wasn't a single dance where any of you went in need of a partner."

"Do you offer any defense against the first charge?" Luce pressed. "You were seen dancing in the arms of the same—rather homely—nurse twice in the course of the same evening."

"Come now, don't be mean," Andrew said. "Nurse Caldwell isn't homely." Noticing the mock horror in Luce's face, he hastened to add, "Of course, she can't compare to any of you. It was an act of charity, really. How could she hope to compete with you all for the attention of the men in the room? I was simply performing an act of kindness for a colleague."

"Likely story," Vera said. "I believe he's become fond of the enemy. Tell us, Lieutenant. Are you sweet on this Nurse Caldwell?"

Andrew looked at me, pleading for mercy. I offered him none.

"No," he said. "She's a nice girl, but she's not my type."

"What is your type, then?" Mary chimed in, getting in on the fun. "The tribunal would very much like this information for the official record."

Andrew looked down at his hands for a moment, then met Mary's gaze. "Usually the sort I can't have."

Only Margot dared cast a glance in my direction.

"We've heard his testimony," I said, stepping forward. "And while Lieutenant Carrigan's comportment this evening wasn't blameless, as head of this tribunal, I can't see that he's committed any punishable crime. We'll release him on his own recognizance, on the condition that he is mindful of his social allegiance at future events to the ladies of the signal corps. Do we make ourselves clear, Lieutenant?"

"Yes indeed, ma'am," Andrew said, standing from his place and offering a smart salute. "I won't fail this house again."

"Very well, Lieutenant. Dismissed."

Andrew made his farewell and dashed to his truck before the ladies of the tribunal could appeal my decision. He clearly had been raised with sisters and knew escape was the wisest course of action.

"The lieutenant does seem keen on you," Mary commented from her place on the sofa, removing her cap and tucking her hairpins into the side. "He seems like a nice young man."

"I suppose he is," I said. Desperate to change the subject, I turned it back on her. "Have you heard from your sweetheart lately? Any idea how he's faring?"

Mary seldom mentioned her beau, I sensed because she thought it unprofessional. The excitement of the evening seemed to lower her inhibitions, though, and a smile tugged at her lips as she spoke. "Just yesterday. Jim's stationed somewhere near Belgium, from what I can decipher. Miserable, as you can imagine, but whole and healthy. Every letter and postcard is pure relief in paper and ink."

"You hear from him often, then?" I asked.

"Every week since I got over here," she said. "You don't hear from your Nathaniel so often?"

"Nathaniel's mother has been wonderful about keeping me up to date," I said. "I'm grateful for it."

"I'm sure," Mary said. "It's nice you'll get along so well with your mother-in-law. It's murder when you don't."

"Amen to that," Sadie interjected. "My older sister could hardly stand to be in the same room as hers. Such a spiteful old creature. Like she wanted to keep her boy to herself for the rest of his life. It's absurd."

"Mrs. Morgan is lovely," I said. "She's always been gracious to me."

"Gracious?" Vera asked. "That seems rather . . . formal?"

"Welcome to Philadelphia society, my dears," I said with a chortle, leaning back in my chair. "Boston and New York have nothing on us."

"I heard a quote once," Mary said. "In Boston, they ask what a man knows. In New York, they ask what he's worth. In Philadelphia, they ask who his parents are."

"Mark Twain," I supplied. "And he got the bead on it for sure."

"So, if your mother-in-law is 'gracious,' how do you describe your Nathaniel?" Margot asked. While some of the girls got a glance of him during his brief visit, he was still much of a mystery to them. I didn't speak of him often.

"Kind," I said. "Loyal to his country. Serious."

"An ideal soldier," Mary said approvingly.

"He is," I agreed. "He was so eager to join up once we entered the war. The proudest day of his life was the day he put on his uniform."

"Sounds like a good man," Mary said.

I nodded. The day he had enlisted was the only time I could think of when our parents had allowed us the opportunity to spend a few hours together unchaperoned. He wanted me to go with him to the army recruiting station. *"For luck,"* he'd said. His mother couldn't bear to go, which I was better able to understand after we lost Francis and my own mother had been pulled into a Red Cross meeting. He signed his papers with a raucous round of applause from the other young men waiting their turn. They seemed pleased to see a "swell" like Nathaniel joining their ranks. After we left the recruiter, he took me to the restaurant in the Bellevue-Stratford Hotel. It was a gorgeous, imposing building, popular with our fathers and their associates, and gaining in favor with Nathaniel too. He'd enjoyed a flame-kissed tenderloin, still red in the middle with a perfectly seasoned crust. I'd had filet mignon that was as decadent as chocolate cake. We chatted companionably throughout the meal. He was giddy to do his part, and I was proud he was so willing. I'd heard some of the stories of the young men wanting to "make a memory" with their sweethearts before going "over there." I knew Nathaniel had been raised to be a proper gentleman, but I expected that underneath all that grooming, there was a red-blooded man with the same needs as all the others.

I'd prepared myself for the possibility of an invitation upstairs after dinner. I knew Mother would be horrified at the idea. She'd be certain he'd leave me alone and ruined. But if the stories were to be believed, our men would need the comfort of these memories to keep them going. I was waiting for him to make a gentle suggestion that perhaps

I might be interested in seeing some of the artwork in the upstairs hallways. I wondered if he'd discreetly procured a room key. I placed my hand on his knee to give him some reassurance that his advances wouldn't be rebuffed. He merely patted my hand and shifted his weight. I pulled back and knotted my fingers in my lap. The meal ended, and no invitation was made. He drove me home in his Monroe roadster, the top open to the fledgling sun of April. There was a polite kiss on my cheek before he pulled away to share the news of his enlistment with his parents. I watched as the car grew small and I was left only to wonder if the feeling that enveloped me was laced with more disappointment or relief.

CHAPTER 20

August 25, 1918

Headquarters, while never still, seemed positively humming when we reported for work. Faces that had seemed lined with purpose now looked furrowed with deepest determination.

"What do you think is going on?" Sadie asked me just above a whisper as we turned down the hallway toward the telephone office.

"I'd wager anything we're going to make a push into the German lines," I said, my voice flat. We wouldn't have unlimited chances to make a success of the campaign if this one failed. We didn't have the troops to sacrifice, nor the supplies for an endless siege. The British and French were long since at the last of theirs too. We had to do this right the first time.

"It's just as well," she replied. "We need to get on with things and end it once and for all."

"I think you're right," I said. She offered me a rare smile as she took her place at the board. The longer things lingered, the worse it was for the men at the front. I had to think a decisive strike was the best course for the army, but of course it wasn't for me to speculate on strategy.

I heard the telltale swish-click of Major Weaver's oxfords on the tile floors in the hallway. The creases of worry in his brow were plain to see as he appeared at the doorway. "Miss Wagner," he said, just loud enough to be heard, motioning for me to join him in the corridor.

He handed me a telegram, and from the look on his face, I could see he knew its contents.

PREPARE TO LEAVE IMMEDIATELY.

"Were you briefed about a new assignment?" Major Weaver asked.

"No, Major. I have no idea what this could be about."

"Very well, go home and pack whatever you need. I'd be ready for less-than-ideal conditions if I were you."

"Yes, sir." I saluted, then scurried back into the office and gave command to Sadie. She looked bewildered but didn't ask questions.

"You can handle this," I said. "You know how to lead these girls."

"Are you coming back?"

"I have no idea. You're in charge until you hear otherwise."

She perked up at the notion of her newfound authority. I hoped I hadn't created a monster or that, if I had, she'd be someone else's problem for a good long while.

By the time I reached home, I felt the sweat plastering my curls to my forehead and my lungs burning from exhaustion. I'd run nearly the whole way in my woolen suit under the August sun. There was no choice. If I didn't rush home to pack, I'd risk being sent off with nothing more than the sweaty clothes on my back. I'd not expected the house to be in uproar when I returned, but Margot and Vera were flying about like the place was on fire. They'd had the morning off and had the advantage of an extra hour to pack.

"Mrs. Grant was sent off this morning to find us lodgings," Margot said. "I don't know where they took her. I'm not sure she even knew herself. They haven't told us anything other than we're going with you."

"Thank God for that," I said, flinging open the lid of my trunk, which I'd hoisted onto the bed. "I'd hate to head off to parts unknown all by myself." I began tossing in the sparse contents of my wardrobe and personal belongings without care for how haphazard I'd look for days after arriving at our destination—wherever that was to be. I thought of the horrified expression Mother would wear once she saw the rumpled condition of my blouses.

"Something funny?" Margot asked without looking up from her considerably neater trunk.

"Just thinking of home," I said, removing a blouse to fold it more neatly. Though I hadn't thought I'd acquired much, I struggled to fit all my belongings in my trunk and suitcase. I'd need to stow some unmentionables in my laundry bag in order to bring it all with me. Who knew if I'd have the chance to return this way, and I didn't want to burden the girls with the task of forwarding things to me.

"Glad it's a happy thought," Margot said. "Where do you think we're going?"

"Closer to the front is my only guess," I said. "I can't imagine it being anything else."

"I hope you're right," Vera chimed in from the doorway. "How exciting would that be? I'd hate to get sent all the way back to Tours or something, so far from the action."

"I wouldn't rule it out, but I don't see them sending any personnel west," I said. "We've got to be preparing for a push. And a big one at that."

"It's about time," Margot said. "If we don't act, the Germans will win out of sheer stamina."

Less than thirty minutes later, a car pulled up to the residence. Andrew, stony faced, knocked on the door. "I'm to take you to Colonel Lucas at Neufchâteau," he said by way of greeting. "As soon as we can get there."

"And they sent you?" I asked. "Can the hospital spare you?"

"I'm taking some supplies to Neufchâteau and collecting a couple of injured men. I volunteered to save someone else the trip since the ambulance can haul all your gear."

Andrew looked as cheerful as a pallbearer as he helped load our trunks in the bed of the Model T ambulance. Margot and Vera claimed what was left of the space beneath the canvas canopy for themselves before I could object, so I clambered up front next to Andrew. Margot opened the screen between the ambulance bed and the cab so she and Vera could try to maintain a conversation, though it was a challenge between the partition that separated us and the rumble of the engine.

"Do you know where we're going after Neufchâteau?" I asked, hoping he might have been briefed better than we had.

"No," he replied. "They told me only where to drop you off."

"You're not telling us something," I said, studying the grim line of his mouth and the subtle twitch in his jaw. "I can see it in your face. Out with it."

"They're deploying troops from Neufchâteau. To go to the front."

Vera let out an excited whoop from the back. "You were right. I'd hoped you were."

"It was the only thing that made sense," I said.

"I'd guess you'll be there by suppertime," Andrew said. "Though I wish I were wrong."

"You don't want us to go do our part?" I asked.

"Within a hairsbreadth of German artillery fire? God no. I wouldn't want any of you girls near it."

Margot cleared her voice in a way that I knew meant *See, I told you he's crazy for you, you* idiote. I silenced her with a stare that could have turned her to stone, but she still smiled innocently and crossed her arms over her chest.

"Your heart's in the right place," I admitted. "But the war will be over sooner if we're there to connect the men to the generals farther back. You know it."

"I do, but I sure don't like it."

I felt an urge to censure him for being overly protective when it wasn't his place to fret over us but said nothing. It would serve no purpose to bait him when he was motivated only by concern for his friends.

We pulled into Neufchâteau in the early afternoon, where Eleanor Campbell and Addie McMillan, who had trained in New York and made the crossing with us, were waiting for us with gigantic smiles. I hugged them both like sisters.

"It's been such a grand time here! Tell us everything about headquarters!" Addie demanded before we'd even pulled apart.

"We'll have time enough on the way to Ligny-en-Barrois," Eleanor supplied. "It's quite the haul from here, I understand."

"Is that where we're going?" I asked. "We haven't heard a thing."

"That's correct, Miss Wagner," Colonel Lucas supplied as he approached us. "We're glad to have you coming with us."

"Happy to be here, Colonel," I said, saluting the man I presumed would be my new commander.

"I'm afraid you've missed lunch, and we have to be on our way. We hope to make it before dark, but that's a bit optimistic at this point."

"Very good, Colonel."

Addie and Eleanor showed Vera and Margot off to the car that would take us on to the front, but Andrew held me back gently by the crook of my arm.

"Please promise me you'll be careful," Andrew said, his voice so low I strained to hear him. "Pay attention, and listen to your gut. I'm begging you."

"I promise," I said, offering him a gentle squeeze to his upper arm. "I won't try to be a hero."

"Good," he replied. He stooped and kissed my cheek. "You can forgive me for that indiscretion later."

It was an act of sheer providence that we arrived at Ligny-en-Barrois in time to eat at the mess hall with the others. The plain stew and hard bread was probably less than stellar, but we sure couldn't tell, hungry as we were. The troops actually cheered as we entered the mess, and I have to say it felt nice to be so welcomed. We shook hands with the men around us, and we ate until we felt warm and sleepy. As night descended on the camp, an eerie hush enveloped us. Everyone knew how close the enemy loomed and how lethal an attack could be under the cloak of darkness.

A spry young captain gave us a quick tour of our offices. Three switchboards with three chairs in a tiny room. There was a packing box fit to be used for a desk, and not a single other piece of furniture. Oilcloth covered all the windows, so no light could peek through after dark, and someone had placed piles of sandbags below them. "This office looks like my *grand-père*'s *cabane à sucre* in the woods outside Trois Rivières," Margot said. "I hope we don't have a strong wind. They'll find pieces scattered in Italy if we do."

"It's perfect." I ran the tip of my finger along the switchboard closest to me. "This is what a battlefield office should look like. Simple, efficient. It's the finest in the whole AEF, if you ask me."

"I'm glad you think so," Colonel Lucas said, entering behind us. "Your equipment isn't as sophisticated as what you had in Chaumont—there's no mistaking that. The hours will be long, and you'll be handling the G3 boards—lines reserved for the areas actively engaged in combat. I can't stress enough how vital your work will be here, but you wouldn't have been called up unless your superiors thought you were the best they had."

"We're equal to the task, Colonel," I said. "I have confidence in my operators and their abilities. You'll be glad to have us on board, sir."

"I already am, Miss Wagner," he said. "Be sure to bring your helmets with you when you come on duty, and Captain Brown here will get you each a gas mask to have with you at all times. Carry on, ladies."

Eleanor looked wide eyed as the colonel closed the door behind him. "Nice, light task we've been charged with, eh?"

"It's what we all wanted," I said.

"That it is," Addie agreed. "I didn't come over expecting champagne and roses."

I patted her on her arm. She was the blond-haired, blue-eyed sort that seemed almost breakable in her porcelain beauty, but in training she'd always surprised me with her resolve. I was glad to have her with us.

Captain Brown seemed proud to show us to the lodgings that Mrs. Grant had been able to procure for us. It was a proper French house, not far off the main square. Though old fashioned, the quaint little place was just as lovely as the plush rooms we'd enjoyed at the Prince George Hotel back in New York. There was a pleasant courtyard that would be a riot of colorful flowers in spring, though I hoped we'd all be safely home before it had the chance to bloom again.

"Not half-bad," Vera said, inspecting the parlor. "Though we'll miss having electricity. We were spoiled in Chaumont."

"That we were," Margot agreed. She pulled back a drape to reveal oilcloth covering the windows, just as we had at our office. "Though I don't think we'd get much good from the electric light. We won't be allowed to use it after dark."

I nodded. "And let's face the truth, ladies. I don't think we'll be here all that often in daylight hours. I don't know Colonel Lucas well, but I'm sure he wasn't joking about the long hours. I'm making it policy from now on that if you are not working or eating, you should be sleeping or resting."

The girls mumbled their agreement, and we divided up between the two rooms: Vera, Eleanor, and Addie taking the larger room, Margot and me taking the smaller.

Our room had real canopied beds and candy-pink wallpaper. It was the sort of room I would have reveled in as a girl, though such extravagances were beyond us back then. I wondered who the home had belonged to. Perhaps a wealthy family who had retreated to the relative safety of the west but who wished to be of service by donating the use of their home to the YMCA, who in turn gave Mrs. Grant permission to have us housed there. I would have made a point to ask some of the neighbors who hadn't retreated west themselves, but I doubted we'd have the time for social calls like we did in Chaumont.

"Well, if we don't have much time to sleep, at least we will be comfortable when we do," Margot said.

"It will help," I agreed. "And no three-mile hike into the office every day."

"Thank heaven for that," Margot said. "I'll let my brother, Antoine, drive me everywhere when I get home. I don't care how dusty and grimy his truck is."

It was late, and we were due at the office in the early hours, but I was too jittery from travel to consider sleep. Margot and I unpacked our uniforms into the armoire and arranged the rest of our belongings as best we could in dim light. The last thing I did was hang my helmet and the gas mask on a hook next to the bed, ready at a moment's notice. I removed the gas mask from its pouch and held it by the mouthpiece. I stared into its vacant eyes. I imagined the thousands of young men in the trenches, wearing the same masks for hours on end. Rich, poor, well connected, friendless—everyone was the same in these masks.

Did these masks make it easier for the Germans? Did it take away our humanity? Did the sameness allow them to see our troops not as brothers, fathers, and husbands, but instead as soulless, warmongering automatons? Then again, they hadn't hesitated to use the gas projectors even when they could see our faces. I remembered the fields of fire near Chaumont and knew we were just as willing to unleash terror. The artillery fire started up shortly after I climbed into bed. This close to the front, I would have to learn to live with the lullaby of mortar fire.

CHAPTER 21

September 5, 1918

"How nice it is to be able to change with some light," Margot said by candlelight as she pulled on her nightgown. "I'll never get used to fumbling in the dark."

We'd been dismissed an hour earlier than usual and, for the first time since our arrival, got home before twilight gave way to full dark, so we had the luxury of a few minutes' use of candles before I had to enforce the nighttime ban. "Enjoy your sleep," I said. "They wouldn't have let us go early if we weren't going to need it."

A few moments later, I made the call for lights out to Eleanor, Vera, and Addie down the hall and extinguished my own. It wasn't a quarter of an hour later when Addie let out a horrific banshee's wail. It was promptly followed by a series of loud thuds against the wall their room shared with ours, interspersed with mad giggling. Margot and I flung back our covers and dashed to the adjacent room. We were greeted by the sight of the girls, each with a lit candle in her left hand and one of her army-issued boots in the right.

"Dear God in heaven, is the mattress on fire?" I asked. "Because that's the only reason I can think of that would warrant such a commotion. Blow out those candles before you burn down the house or the brass sees us. Or worse, the Hun."

"It is, in a manner of speaking," Addie said, directing our attention with her candle. "Cooties. Bedbugs. They're everywhere."

"Oh Lord," I said, now seeing the hundreds of little insects pouring out from the ancient wallpaper. "We're infested."

"You can say that again," Vera said, slapping at herself. "I can't sleep in this house. I'll dream they're crawling all over me, even if we squash every last one."

"Well, we can't have the girls in Chaumont thinking we're living like queens, can we?" Margot asked. "Sadie would never let us live it down. She'd have you believe they're all living in a mud hovel by the side of the road and we are all ungrateful shrews. We should send her a letter tomorrow and tell her."

"Send her a few of the bedbugs with it," Vera said, folding her arms over her chest. "We have plenty to spare."

"Bah, where is your sense of adventure?" Margot asked. "This is a story to tell your grandchildren. Better, it's one to woo men with. They'll never refuse a woman who can face the Germans and the cooties without blinking an eye."

"Absolutely," I said, patting Vera on the back. She'd gone from alabaster to "Dingy New York City Concrete" in color, and I was worried she might go screaming all the way back to Seattle if she didn't have some encouragement. "It's a golden opportunity for impressing even the most stalwart soldier."

"If you say so," she replied noncommittally, blowing out her candle. "But I appreciate your well-intentioned lies all the same."

"I'll see about getting a fumigator in the morning," I said. "Let's try to get some rest in the meantime. We can't afford to be sloppy in our work."

"If we are, it's because we're being chewed alive in our sleep," Eleanor groused.

"It doesn't matter to the boys in the trenches why we make mistakes. They pay for them regardless," I snapped. "Now get some rest. That's an order."

We'd just settled back in when a thunderous knocking came at the front door.

"*Mon dieu*, who is it?" Margot asked, sitting up and rubbing her eyes. "It must be two in the morning."

"Shhh," I warned. "I'll go find out. If there's trouble, you all climb out the bedroom window."

I wrapped my robe tight around me and went to the door, my knees wobbling as though my bones had been boiled into gelatin.

I tried to peek out the window, but the oilcloth coverings revealed only a silhouette in uniform. I couldn't tell whose, though I doubted the Germans bothered knocking.

"Who is it?" I called, grabbing a heavy book from a nearby table.

"Lieutenant Carrigan," Andrew's voice, unusually gruff, barked from the other side of the door.

I exhaled with relief and opened the door to find him looking as sleep deprived and careworn as I felt.

"What are you doing here, Lieutenant?" I asked, the evening air cool enough to make me pull my robe tighter around me.

"I've been sent to find out what on earth is going on here," he said in a voice that closely resembled a grizzly's growl. "We could see lights flickering from your north window from a half mile away."

"The girls were trying to rid us of some bedbugs," I said. "I told them off for lighting the candles, and I'll see what can be done about the pest problem in the morning."

"The Germans could have mistaken your flashing lights for signals." His stance was still rigid, his arms crossed over his chest. "If you think there's a sweeter target for them, I assure you there isn't. Double up on your oilcloth and confiscate their candles if you have to. Damn it, Ruby, you promised me you'd stay safe."

"I'll remind the girls how serious it is," I said, fighting the urge to pat his arm. "But what are you doing all the way in Ligny?"

"I requested a transfer. I've spent my share of time 'taking it easy' behind the lines. I got here twenty minutes ago, and my first order of duty was to bawl you out for the window before the Germans could do the deed for me."

I nodded, swallowing hard at the bile that rose in my throat. I clutched the book tight to my chest.

"What were you planning to do with that book?" Andrew asked.

"If you were with a pack of Germans that overran the camp while we were sleeping, I was going to do my best to bash your head in with it and run like mad."

Andrew turned a sickly shade of gray. "I don't think the *Petit Larousse* dictionary is all that effective against a German Luger."

"It's what I had," I replied simply. "It might have been enough to give the girls time to escape into the woods. I'll see if I can convince them to publish a bigger dictionary. Would that be better?"

"Christ," Andrew said, shaking his head at my joke. "You're going to get yourself killed."

"Not when we have the entire First Army looking out for us," I said earnestly. "You all would never stand for it."

"If wishing could make a thing true . . . ," he muttered. "Listen, I have something for you, and I want you to promise to keep it with you at all times." He pulled a small pistol, barely larger than a pack of playing cards, from his back pocket, and a tiny tin of ammunition from another.

"I don't think it's really all that necessary," I said, looking down at the impossibly small firearm. I couldn't imagine something so small being able to take a life, but I was sure that, if shot properly, it was equal to the task. And given that Mrs. Grant had returned to Chaumont, the duty to protect the house and the girls was mine alone.

"Listen, if the Germans come knocking, that pistol will be as useful as a concrete life vest. They swarm like bees. But . . . if the worst should happen, it just might give you a few seconds to get away. You might take one of them down with you. It's a little better than nothing, and I'll sleep better knowing you have it."

"Fine," I agreed, accepting the pistol gingerly in the palm of my hand, eyeing it with distrust.

"Thank you," he said, his voice strained. "I'll teach you how to use it properly when we both have the time, but it's not complicated."

"Shouldn't I be the one thanking you?"

"You took the gift, and I'm grateful. All I ask is that you be careful out here and don't be afraid to use that pistol if it comes down to it."

"I promise," I said, wishing I felt as resolute as I sounded.

He left the barracks without another word, and I retreated to the bedroom, where all four girls waited.

"Who was that?" Margot asked.

Vera pointed to the gun in my hand. "A better question, *what* is that?"

"Lieutenant Carrigan," I said. "He's transferred along with us, and just dressed me down for the lights. He gave us this in case of the worst." I opened the lid to my trunk and stashed the revolver in one of my ruined blouses I kept on hand for cleaning.

"Heaven forbid," Addie said with a shudder.

"To bed," I ordered. "And I won't hesitate to follow the lieutenant's directives and take your candles if anyone tries such a thing again."

Addie and Vera nodded and left for their room. I flung myself back into bed, then stood again and took the helmet and gas mask off their hooks and placed them on the floor beneath my bed before retreating under the covers. Though it was only fifty miles from headquarters, the front line seemed a world away from the relative calm of Chaumont.

"I hate it when you're right," Vera muttered less than a week later as she checked the time. It was quarter to eleven at night. She and I had been on duty since midmorning, and there were still calls being placed. It was the busiest day we'd had since we'd come to Ligny, but not by a wide margin. "I don't think I've had more than four hours' sleep together since I got here."

"Sometimes I hate it when I'm right too," I agreed. "You and Eleanor go home. I'll make sure the men get off to a decent start." I'd sent Margot and Addie home four hours earlier to sleep. The cannons hadn't ceased since then, so I hoped the opportunity hadn't been wasted. One of the advantages to life in Ligny was that I wasn't relegated to peering over the other operators' shoulders as they worked or chaperoning their excursions. I got time on the boards, and I'd found I'd missed it.

Only a few calls came in during the half hour I waited for the relief staff to show up, though the fatigue caused my hands to shake as I disconnected a call that had ended. The two young signal-corps men, Lieutenants Oakley and Shreve, both looking a little more refreshed than I was, took over the boards. They must have learned to sleep in daylight amid the constant rattling and rumbling of the war machines. I envied them.

"What's the code for Saint-Mihiel again?" one whispered, covering his mouthpiece.

"Podunk," I said. Code within codes. Spelling out false place-names, where each letter couple was represented by one of three possible three-letter combinations. It was too easy to crack them otherwise. Double letters, common prefixes and suffixes, and unique letter combinations gave it all away if we didn't mix things up. Place-names were protected with special care, even more than in weeks past. Even if the Germans intercepted the word *Podunk*, they'd still be clueless. Though the girls and I tried not to speculate too much among ourselves, we knew that a big drive had to be coming. If the Germans caught wind of the location of an attack, all could be lost. We had to remember new code names almost daily, and our efforts weren't aided by the lack of sleep. That these men only covered the quietest hours of the night didn't help them retain the information either.

Colonel Lucas arrived just a few minutes later looking as haggard as I felt. "I'm afraid I'll need you back at three."

I bit back the *Are you serious?* that was on the tip of my tongue and replied with a crisp "Yes, sir."

Captain Brown, dear that he was, saw me home in the pouring rain. I had the advantage of a good rubber coat and boots, while his gear was far thinner. I made no attempt to dissuade him from coming along, though. We always told the men we were happy to make the short walk on our own, but they insisted on escorting us when duties kept us this late. Our safety was a point of pride with these men, and I wouldn't begrudge them the satisfaction of protecting us, no matter how unnecessarily. The orange glow to the east lit our way, and I still jumped a little with each boom of the cannon. By now it came as natural as a sneeze.

Margot didn't register my arrival, and I tried not to mutter a curse as I set my alarm for two fifteen just as my clock struck midnight.

It seemed as though mere minutes had passed when Captain Brown returned to collect me, Margot, and Addie to report for duty.

"Let us go with you," Vera protested. "We're no worse off than you. We don't want to miss the end of the war."

"Don't count your chickens. Margot and Addie got several hours more sleep than you did, and I'll need you two alert enough to handle things this afternoon when the rest of us are spent. Report at eight, and not a moment sooner unless I send word."

The girls grumbled their way back to their beds, but I understood their enthusiasm.

The colonel watched with widened eyes as we took our places at the boards ten minutes before we were scheduled.

"The first wave will go over the hill in one hour, ladies," he said. "You'll be connecting vital orders to the front all day. Whatever you need to keep going, you let us know."

Lieutenants Shreve and Oakley were relieved of duty but were commanded to stay on site during the push. Both took the opportunity to fall asleep on the narrow benches someone had thought to bring in. Their gentle snores came wafting almost instantly but thankfully didn't distract from our work.

"Show-offs," Addie muttered.

I connected calls at a speed I hadn't seen since our biggest crushes in Philadelphia. I had every right to feel exhaustion course through my veins, but I felt nothing but the drive to keep working.

"Operator Eighteen, how may I connect you?" Though we were all anxious with the drive, I didn't let the nerves into my voice. If the men on the line sensed we were calm and unfazed, it could only help them to remain so.

"Tell Lieutenant Oakley there's trouble down the line and we need him on it ASAP," an unidentified voice barked, and immediately hung up. I turned and saw his sleeping form hadn't budged.

"Lieutenant Oakley," I called. "You're needed on the line."

He didn't stir.

"Lieutenant!" I snapped. I had no idea if our connections were in danger of being severed, but that seemed the likeliest scenario. "Get up!"

"You won't be able to wake him with a sound," Margot said. "They've all trained themselves to sleep through hell itself. You'll have to shake him."

I removed my headset and jostled him. Gently at first, then violently, until he and Shreve both fell to the floor.

"You're needed on the line, Oakley," I said, exasperated. He shook his head for a couple of seconds, then rushed for the door. Shreve had reclaimed his place and was back to snoring within seconds.

Colonel Lucas reported at six that the push was going well, but the lines were so busy we hadn't time to do more than acknowledge the news with a brief smile.

Eleanor and Vera came on at eight, relieving Margot and Addie to grab a quick breakfast at the mess. When they returned, I let Margot take my post for a fifteen-minute break to grab some food of my own, and allowed her to stay on to relieve the others as needed, provided she rested while she could. Addie went home to get some proper sleep and was to report back in late afternoon.

The rush lasted all day, though by suppertime it calmed enough I was able to relieve everyone but Addie, whom I kept on for another two hours. I was almost surprised when Oakley and Shreve returned for their night duties—the time had seemed to pass so quickly.

"You must be dead on your feet," Oakley said. "We've got things here. Go get some sleep. Colonel Lucas can't know you're still on duty or he'd have sent you home hours ago."

"I'm perfectly fine," I said. "I'll just go wash up a bit and help you keep up for another couple of hours."

The men shook their heads but, to their credit, didn't argue.

I found a basin of cold water near the infirmary and splashed the revivifying liquid against my face.

"How long have you been on duty?" a voice asked from behind me. Andrew placed a hand on my back. I felt the world spin, but I steadied myself with his other hand. "How long have you been on duty?" he repeated. "I heard that you'd come on at three this morning."

"That's right," I said. "The lines have been mad all day."

"Where are the other operators?" he asked, turning me around. "Has the night crew come on?"

"I sent the girls home to sleep a while ago. I was just going to make sure the men have it all under control. I'll be fine for another couple of hours." I knew the words weren't true as soon as I spoke them, but I wouldn't give him the satisfaction of hearing me admit defeat. The world had begun to spin, and Andrew's arms were the only thing keeping me from sinking to the ground.

"Nothing doing," he said. "You're going home and getting some sleep. Doctor's orders. And I'll tell Colonel Lucas to send you back home if anyone sees you here before six tomorrow morning."

"You're not a doctor yet," I said, still gripping his hand.

"Good enough for Uncle Sam," he replied. "I'm taking you home myself. If you give me any trouble, I'll carry you up to your room and tuck you into bed myself."

"I think you'd like that a little too well, Lieutenant," I whispered. "I think you have ulterior motives."

"You need sleep. My only motive, Miss Wagner, is keeping you from falling ill on the job. It's more work for me, and I've plenty to be going on with." He guided me on the makeshift trail toward the main road that led into town.

"So, you're being selfish, is that it?" I asked, leaning my head against his shoulder.

"Precisely." He tightened his grip around my waist. "Selfish."

"Can you tell me something? Why did you request a transfer? You could have stayed safe behind the lines."

"The men who need patching up are here, not in Chaumont. The end of this war is coming, Ruby. For better and for worse, and I'll have more of a chance to make a difference at the front. Just like you, though you'll do no one any good if you fall asleep at your switchboard tomorrow."

"Is that the only reason, Lieutenant?"

"The only one that matters, Miss Wagner," he said, walking me up the front steps and knocking on the door. Margot's footsteps quickly sounded in the entryway. She answered blearily, long since changed into her nightclothes and tucked into bed.

"I thought she must have found a cot in the camp somewhere," Margot said. "I didn't imagine she was still working."

"See that she makes it up the stairs without breaking her neck, please," Andrew said, passing me off to her. "And she could do with a lecture on not trying to single-handedly win the war."

"We'd all still be there if she hadn't ordered us home. If you think any of us would listen to that lecture, *mon ami*, you haven't been paying much attention."

CHAPTER 22

September 20, 1918
Souilly, France

We got word late in the afternoon that we, along with a good portion of the men stationed in Ligny, would be moving closer to the front in just a matter of hours. Souilly was so close to the fighting that the sound of artillery fire hung in the air like cheap perfume. Inescapable and grating. Our little office, housed in the makeshift wooden barracks, was as spartan as our space in Ligny. We were housed in the barracks next door, where we slept on cots with bedrolls, just like the soldiers. It was a far cry from our billet in Ligny, but mercifully we'd yet to see any bedbugs.

The last drive against the Germans had gone well, but it wasn't the definitive strike we'd hoped for. The battle still waged on, and the phones were as busy as ever. We continued putting in long hours, but I kept to the day shift, when the traffic was at its worst. I rotated two girls per night for the night shift to help the men with the call load, and we still had to put in twelve to fourteen hours a day to keep up with the demand. My girls had grown pale and thin, but none wavered in her pace. Margot came in at noon to work the transition shift and to relieve me for a quick lunch and breath of fresh air. I was ready to hop from my post to the mess when I saw her face. Her cheeks looked flushed, beyond what the caress of crisp September air and our harried departure from Ligny might have caused.

"Are you feeling all right?" I asked.

"Not wonderful," she said. "I'm sure it's just a cold, though. It will pass."

"I want you home," I said. "I'll take your shift. Unless you have a fever, in which case I want you in the hospital. Let me feel your forehead."

She obliged, leaning her head forward a bit.

"You have a fever. A good one at that," I assessed. "Eleanor, take my exchange until further notice. I'll see if I can dig up some of the signal-corps men to cover me once I see Margot settled."

She gave me the "OK" sign and answered a call on my board just seconds later.

I put my arm around Margot and guided her toward the massive series of tents that served as our field hospital.

Andrew saw us as we approached and dashed over. "What's the matter?" he asked, supporting her from the other side.

"Margot has a fever," I said. "I'd like to make sure it's nothing before I send her home to bed."

Andrew ushered us inside and had Margot sit in a spindly wooden chair. He kneeled before her and felt her forehead as I had, then checked her swollen glands and the whites of her eyes.

"Sore throat?" he asked.

She nodded in reply.

"Headache?"

"Everything aches," she replied, her voice raspy.

"Shit, shit, shit," Andrew muttered under his breath as he stood. He turned to me, his expression somber. "Spanish flu."

I felt my knees weaken, but I steeled my composure. "What can we do for her?"

"She hasn't taken any time away from the switchboards, has she?"

"Colonel Lucas needed her at Bar-le-Duc a few days ago, before we came to Souilly," I said. "Aside from that, no."

"We'll have to let them know. Though with soldiers coming in from every camp in creation, it could have come from anywhere. Damn it all."

"Operator down?" the head doctor, a Major McMurray, asked when he saw Andrew checking her breathing.

"Stay back, Spanish flu," Andrew barked.

"For God's sake, get her out of here. She'll kill them all off in forty-eight hours with one sneeze." Dr. McMurray made a sweeping gesture to the injured men, all more susceptible to illness than healthy people would be.

"I know that as well as you do, Doctor. But where I can take her?" Andrew pressed. "She needs treatment."

The doctor looked thoughtful, then motioned to a vacant tent a few feet from the hospital. "It's not much, but you'll be close by if you need counsel. I don't want anyone coming in or out of that tent without a full scrubbing, do you hear?"

"Yes, sir," Andrew replied.

How we'd manage such a thing without running water, I had no idea. "What about the barracks? She'd be more comfortable there."

"Not unless you want every operator down with it," Dr. McMurray said. "You'd better hope she hasn't already infected the lot of you. Wait here. Carrigan, get her settled, and I'll pass off the supplies we can spare to Miss Wagner."

Andrew disappeared into the darkness of the tent, the good doctor back into his hospital. I paced in the mud between the two as I waited for the doctor to amass his supplies. He emerged ten minutes later with a box with some clean rags, a few vials of russet-brown powder, and some gauze masks, and thrust it in my hands.

"Won't you come look over her?" I asked. "I'm sure Lieutenant Carrigan would be grateful for the assistance."

"I'm sorry, miss, but I can't risk another member of the medical crew getting sick—myself included. I need every man I have for patching up the men we have coming through here by the boxcar load. Wear one of those masks, and if he needs anything, knock at the door."

He returned to the infirmary, and I stood at the closed doorway, blinking in disbelief.

I followed his orders and placed the mask over my nose and mouth, and I turned to the tent. Already Andrew was at work, making Margot comfortable with the spare bedding.

"This is what he gave me," I said, passing him the box. "Tell me what I can do."

He sat on a folding chair, rifled through the contents of the box, and rubbed his temples, exhaling. He put on his own mask and began organizing the haphazard box.

Just then, Vera and Addie appeared at the door to the tent. "We saw you come in here," Vera said. "Why isn't she in the field hospital?"

"Stop there!" Andrew roared. "Do not come one step closer."

"Spanish flu," I explained. "We're quarantined."

They both took a step backward, holding one flap open so they could speak to us. "Can we help?" Vera asked.

"I need milk and clean water from the mess," Andrew replied as he placed a mask over Margot's face. "And some cups and spoons. Leave it right where you stand, and yell that you've left it. Don't even lift the flap of the tent. If you see anyone so much as sneeze, you tell Dr. McMurray. Do you understand?"

The skittering of boots on gravel was their response, and the milk and water were delivered within ten minutes.

"What can I do?" I repeated. "Anything."

"Fill one of the cups half full with milk," he said. He handed me one of the glass vials containing the russet-brown powder. "Mix this with it, and help her drink it."

I followed his command, my hands shaking as I poured the milk into the tin cup and opened the glass vial. "Cinnamon?" I asked as I recognized the scent.

"It's said to help lower the fever," he said. "Though I'm not sure how much stock I put in it. I'm sure he doesn't have aspirin to spare, so it's the best we can do."

I lowered Margot's mask and held the liquid to her lips. "Please drink," I urged her. I could tell as I held the back of her neck that her fever had risen dangerously high. The glassiness in her eyes had replaced her usually keen expression, and I felt it hard to keep my breath even.

Andrew dipped one of the clean rags into the cold water and placed the compress on her forehead. It made her wince, but it was the best we could do to lower her temperature.

For two hours, Andrew and I took turns dosing her with the concoction of cinnamon and milk and applying the compress to her burning forehead. She grew incoherent, then listless and pale.

"Christ," Andrew muttered. "I'll take the Germans over this damn plague. I can patch bullet holes. I'm useless against this." He threw the rag into the water pail and buried his head in his hands.

I walked over to him and wrapped my arms around him. "You're doing all you can with what you have. Don't give up on her yet. She's strong."

Andrew pulled me into his lap and held me to his chest for a few moments. I thought he started to speak a few times, but no words came.

"You're not useless, nor am I," I repeated. "Tell me what can be done. If I have to drive into the heart of Germany myself to get medicine, I will."

Andrew pulled me tight and released me. "Go ask the doctor for a transfusion kit."

I opened my mouth to question his reasoning but thought better of it and ran to the field hospital to do as he asked. Dr. McMurray raised a brow when I made my request, but he ducked back into the infirmary and returned wearing a gauze mask of his own. He held a large wooden kit like an apothecary's box. I followed him to the tent, and he passed the kit off to me before he stopped at the entrance.

"What are you up to in there, Carrigan?"

"Some of the doctors in Chaumont were talking about how they'd had some success in treating the flu with blood transfusions from patients who survived. I had it last March when I was with the Tommies."

"Are you sure you know what you're doing, lad?" he asked. "It seems risky to me."

"No risk at all, sir," he said. "If this goes poorly, she dies in an hour. If I do nothing, she dies in an hour. If it works, she just might live."

"You don't have time to blood-type her," he pressed.

"I'm O-negative," Andrew replied, rolling up his sleeve. "Universal donor. If you haven't noticed, a good amount of the blood you have on hand is mine."

"On your head be it," the doctor said. "I wish you luck."

"You can have the mess send me a meal," Andrew said by way of thanks. "I'll need it after this."

"Sounds like you've been entitled to double rations as it is," the doctor said, retreating.

"I'll need your help," Andrew said, turning to me. "I can set up the kit, but you'll have to insert the needle into my arm to extract the blood. You aren't faint at the sight of it, are you?"

"No," I said, hoping that was true. I'd not had enough experience with it to know one way or the other.

Once he hooked up the rubber hoses to the beaker, Andrew guided me through how to insert the needle into the vein in the crook of his elbow.

"Well done, first try," he said. "I've seen proper doctors who need a half dozen tries to get it right."

"Beginner's luck," I said.

"Massage my arm to help the blood flow," he ordered. "It's awkward to do myself."

I obliged, running my thumbs along his vein as he showed me, and it wasn't long before the beaker was filled with the thick red liquid. I bandaged the puncture site and watched as he reversed the process for Margot, holding the beaker of life-saving fluid above her arm to encourage the flow into her own veins. When he was finished, he bandaged her and set about cleaning the kit so it could be used for other patients.

"What's left to do?" I asked. I looked down at Margot's face, which looked perhaps a bit rosier after the transfusion, though I wasn't sure it wasn't my own wishful thinking.

"Hope and pray," Andrew replied, latching the kit shut. "Aside from some aspirin, there's not anything more the best New York surgeons could do at this point. And let's throw in a good word that this doesn't spread to the whole camp."

I held Margot's clammy hand in mine and watched the gentle rise and fall of her chest. Her breathing didn't seem strained, and she appeared to be sleeping peacefully now, which I took to be a positive sign.

"Thank you," I said. "Whatever happens, you've taken better care of her than anyone else here would. You'll make an excellent doctor one day."

"I hope you're right, Ruby," he said, kneeling by my side and resting his head on my shoulder. "I know how much she means to you."

Despite myself, I pulled down my mask and kissed a bare stretch of cheek that wasn't covered by his mask. I longed for nothing more than to curl up in the safety of his arms and find the comfort of sleep, but we continued our vigil by Margot's side until dawn crested over the ruined lands in the east.

Though we tried to keep the disease contained, we had fifty cases of the flu before the next nightfall. By lunchtime, the first men began to show symptoms, and Addie too. By dinnertime, Andrew and I could no longer house the patients in the tent where Dr. McMurray had quarantined us, and we'd spilled over into another. By eight, we'd lost two men and seemed in danger of losing more. Some of the privates were given masks and had been ordered to bury the bodies a good distance from the camp. I didn't need to see their faces to know this was the worst task they'd been charged with yet. The only silver lining was that while Margot was still incredibly weak, the disease showed no signs of progressing further. Her heartbeat was stronger, and I thought her color was improving slightly, though that might have been too optimistic of me.

I'm sure I felt the rumblings of my stomach and the siren call of sleep after thirty-six hours awake, but as wave after wave of infected men were sent to our care, I could no sooner indulge them than go and fight for the enemy, though I worried for Andrew. He'd given transfusions to the first two who fell after Margot, and all three were showing marked signs of improvement, but he couldn't weaken himself by donating more.

"You look like you need sleep," I said, knowing he'd be no more likely to sleep than I, but the dark circles under his eyes and the gray cast to his skin were worrying. "Can't Dr. McMurray spare another medic or two?"

"Not likely, unless he's ordered to," he answered. I must have looked as though I were going to berate the doctor for his callous decision, as Andrew cut me off. "He's not wrong. We're about to launch the biggest push yet. If we lose too many medics, we lose the war. But I'm going to treat these last four with the cinnamon and milk. See if anyone else needs anything."

It was a request we had little ability to satisfy. We'd come to the end of the meager supplies Dr. McMurray ceded to us, and it was doubtful we'd have access to more before the Red Cross intervened with fresh supplies and medics. I aided Andrew as he ministered to the last of the men and checked in on Margot. She was alert, but very weak. I checked her breathing, which now sounded strong and regular, thanks to Andrew's early attentions. The disease hadn't the chance to attack her bronchial tubes, so she'd avoided the most dangerous of the symptoms. Addie's skin was wan, her breathing raspy, but she spoke clearly enough I felt she'd be able to pull through. The ones we'd lost had failed within hours, developed brown spots on their cheeks, and had horrific nosebleeds toward the end. If they managed to last more than three or four hours from the onset of the fever, there seemed to be at least a reasonable chance of pulling through. I wet a few rags with cool water to help lower fevers, but there was little else I could do for them.

"We're getting some sleep," Andrew ordered at last.

"Yes, sir," I said without irony. It was a miracle neither of us had slumped over onto one of the patients and begun snoring. "But we're out of cots."

"Welcome to the US Army, darling. There have been men sleeping on the ground since this godforsaken war began."

"Fair point," I conceded.

He took two blankets and laid them side by side as close to the kerosene heater as he dared and tossed a third blanket in my direction. "Since you've not had the misfortune to spend a night in the trenches, I'll save you from the worst of it and give you the space next to the heater."

"A true gentleman," I said.

"My mother would be proud," Andrew said with a full-throated laugh as he settled in next to me.

"I'm sure she would be. Even setting aside your chivalrous behavior. You did good work today."

"I tried."

I could hear the strain in his voice. One of the boys who had died was barely eighteen years old. There was no way to justify the loss.

"Do you think we'll get more supplies soon?" I asked. He scooched closer to me and the source of the heat, and I tried not to think of his arm brushing against mine. "I know Dr. McMurray has to conserve what he's got . . ."

"It all depends on the Red Cross. I'm sure they'll divert supplies if they can, but if I learned anything in the spring, it's that if one camp has an outbreak, more will follow. They can't deplete their stock for us and leave every other unit to fend for themselves."

"Try to get some sleep," I said. "And let's hope we have some reinforcements in the morning."

Andrew made a muffled noise that sounded like an affirmative as he burrowed under his thin blanket. "Thank you for helping me," he whispered as he drifted out of consciousness. "I couldn't have done this alone."

"I wasn't about to leave you and Margot to your own devices," I said, though in my gut I worried for how things were progressing in the office. Eleanor was leading things, but I'd heard no updates beyond that. She was a capable operator. More than capable. But she'd not had the chance to lead as supervisor in the long term before, especially not when the phone traffic was at its peak before a major offensive.

Instead of offering a reply, Andrew pulled me against his chest so that my back contoured against it. His hands didn't wander, nor did he whisper anything suggestive in my ear. Nevertheless, I should have asked him to roll back to his own space. I should have nestled under my blanket and done my best to ward off the chill, but the warmth of his arms was too inviting. Soon his even breathing gave way to soft snores. It wasn't right to sleep ensconced in his strong arms, but it would have taken a woman stronger than I to resist him. I let myself melt into the embrace and slept soundly, feeling safer there than I had in months.

I thought I felt the brush of his lips against my forehead as he rose the next morning, but it was so fleeting it might have been the work of my imagination as I drifted back into wakefulness.

"The Red Cross is here," Andrew said, handing me a cup of hot coffee as I stood and stretched my aching muscles. He gestured to the pair of rickety chairs and took his place next to mine with his own steaming cup. "They haven't brought much, but there are three trained medics to take over for us. Some tents for an emergency hospital when others fall ill. A bit of aspirin. It's better than nothing. You can go back to the switchboards after breakfast. Since you haven't shown any signs of the illness, McMurray won't keep you quarantined."

"That's wonderful," I said, feeling my spirits sink, despite myself. I should have been glad to return to the comfort of my barracks and the duties I was trained for.

"I'll miss working with you too," Andrew said in a low voice. "You'd have made an incomparable nurse."

"I don't think I'm cut out for that work, but thank you for the compliment all the same."

He tucked a tendril of hair behind my ear absentmindedly, as if it were his own. I only too clearly remembered the warmth of his body next to mine as we tried to sleep on the frozen ground, and I took a step back from him. I turned, wordlessly, and emerged blinking into the fledgling morning sun to face the ordered chaos of the camp.

CHAPTER 23

October 3, 1918

"Go get some lunch," Vera bade me as I disconnected a call. I'd been rubbing my temples after deciphering a half dozen encoded calls. We'd been through several "river" codes and were just getting used to the Colorado code, which we'd received a week before. "FGC VNY": *Ammunition exhausted, awaiting instructions.* "QOJ YOX": *Intense machine gun fire.* "LUB": *Men missing.* The messages came out awkwardly at times, but their meaning was generally clear. And they might be meaningless the next day if we were forced to revamp the codes.

"I suppose I should while there's food to be had," I said, passing her the headset.

I stepped out into the autumn sun, which was bold and beautiful for the first time in days, though not enough to dry out the rivers of mud that coursed through the camps. I felt the pop-pop-popping of the ligaments in my back as I stretched to my full height, and felt the grumbling of my neglected muscles as I crossed to the mess. I'd spend my next free day walking, I vowed. I'd atone for all the hours I kept my muscles idle before a switchboard.

The men lucky enough to have time to eat sat in rows in subdued silence, with only the discordant symphony of bombs and artillery fire to accompany their meal. Each ping of a bullet was reflected in their haunted eyes. There was little conversation. I took the tray of food, whose warmth was the only thing to recommend it, and sat alongside the men and ate without tasting.

The walk back to the office took me past the field hospital. Having passed the care of the flu victims on to the Red Cross nurses, Andrew had finally resumed treating the wounded brought back from the front. I had no idea how many men we'd lost to the illness, though it seemed we were lucky. From what I could discern at the switchboards, other camps had lost hundreds of men over the course of a few weeks. Addie and Margot were spared, though it sapped their strength for days. Once Major McMurray cleared them for work, there was no keeping them from the office, though I made sure they got day shifts and plenty of sleep. Vera, Eleanor, and I took up the slack, and I could see the long hours wearing on them. I watched closely to make sure signs of illness didn't start to manifest themselves on top of the dark circles under their eyes and their pallid skin. I'd have given a year's wages to have another two operators with us, but there was no pulling them from their stations at present. There wasn't a telephone office in France that didn't feel the same crunch that we did.

As I passed the field hospital, I noticed Andrew leaning against the pole of the tent that housed our makeshift evacuation hospital. His white hospital garb was smeared with a streak of crimson that appeared to sever him in two. His arms were clutched around his chest as he drew a cigarette to his mouth with a shaking hand.

"I didn't think you smoked," I commented.

He started at the sound of my voice. I'd heard him say more than once it was a frivolous habit. He wanted medical school too badly to waste the money on such an indulgence.

"I d-don't," he said, looking down, almost with astonishment, at the thin white cylinder that quivered between his index and middle fingers. "N-not really. McMurray handed me one of his and ordered me to take a break."

His childhood stutter had returned, and his hands shook.

"Far be it from me to argue with doctor's orders," I said. "You look tired."

"It's b-beyond that, Ruby. I—" He stopped himself short, frustrated by his fragmented speech. He didn't have to say it. Day after day, they patched men up, nursed them back to health, then sent them back to the front, only to see them brought back under a sheet two days later. And sometimes those were the lucky ones.

I closed the gap between us and caressed his biceps. It was bold, but the impropriety of it scarcely registered with me. "You're one of the most valuable men here, Andrew."

He looked down at my hand, dropped his cigarette, and extinguished it with the toe of his boot, then took one of my hands with his free one and pressed it to his lips.

"W-what's going to be left, Ruby?" he asked, not looking for an answer. "Are w-we going to look back in two years and wonder what the hell the point of this damn mess was?"

"Probably," I said without flinching. "But how would things have gone if we'd done nothing? If we'd let the kaiser do as he pleased while his generals stockpiled enough weapons to destroy us all?"

He wrapped an arm around me and tucked me in to his chest for a moment, letting go with reluctance. "Y-you're stronger than I am. I sh-should be ashamed, b-but I'm just proud of you."

"I can't afford for the girls or anyone else to see me act weak. I have to have my little crises in private. Don't think I haven't cried myself to sleep more than a few times since I got here. And not just because I was overtired. I couldn't do what you do, Andrew. I knew that from the first day I visited your hospital in Chaumont."

"Y-you held Willie's hand. You sang to him as he died." He looked off into the distance, perhaps trying to recall the exact contours of the boy's face.

"You remember," I said, blinking. There had been thousands of men under Andrew's care since then.

"I w-wish I could remember them all. They deserve it. But I could never forget young Willie. I-it was the day I met you."

"Stay strong," I told him, ignoring the sentimental comment. "Bulgaria has sued for peace. The colonel thinks Austria won't be far behind. This could all be over within weeks."

"From your lips . . ." He trailed off. "I'm a d-damn mess."

"Sing," I ordered. "You'll feel better."

"Y-you're crazy. In the middle of an army camp. I-it hardly seems the time."

"The US government disagrees with you. They've spent a pretty penny to send every sort of performer over here to entertain the troops. Try it."

He shook his head. "It's a n-nice idea, Ruby, but I can't. I'll get through this somehow."

I squeezed his hand. "I know you can, Andrew."

Dr. McMurray emerged from the flap in the tent. "I'm going to need your help with an amputation in ten minutes, Carrigan. Sergeant Whittaker's leg needs to go."

"G-goddamn it all," Andrew said under his breath.

"I know, son. You did all you could to save it, but once the gangrene takes hold, there's nothing to be done. I'm sorry. Take another minute of fresh air, and come on in."

Andrew raked his fingers through his hair, expelling a great breath. He grabbed my hand and pulled me into the tent.

He stood to the side of the doorway and filled the air with his rich tenor voice.

A te, o cara, amor talora
Mi guidò furtivo e in pianto;
Or mi guida a te d'accanto
Tra la gioia e l'esultar . . .

The doctors and nurses stopped in their duties, and the men who were equal to conversation stopped in their chatter. I would have traded the world to understand the Italian, but I found the meaning didn't really matter. For the three minutes the aria lasted, Andrew was the picture of bliss. Every muscle in his face that wasn't used for the creation of sound looked more relaxed than I had ever seen them. The eyes of the men, for a few shining moments, looked assuaged of their pain.

When he finished, the soldiers, nurses, and doctors applauded, then scattered to their duties. It was as though the moment never happened, but the air under the tent somehow didn't seem as heavy.

"Thank you," Andrew said, brushing a faint kiss on my cheek before running toward the curtained partition of the operating ward.

CHAPTER 24

October 30, 1918

By late afternoon, I could feel the fatigue pulsing up my calves, like being tickled by cold, bony fingers. I'd grown used to the uncomfortable tingle of muscles that demanded rest. There was going to be a push tomorrow, and we were needed every moment. Austria's forces had all but collapsed two days before, and everyone thought they had to be on the point of signing an armistice. We couldn't afford to slow down our siege and lose our advantage if we wanted Germany to follow suit. I'd been on duty for eleven hours, and I could feel the welcome embrace of my bedcovers waiting for me in the barracks. The sun was still high in the sky, but we could now sleep in plain daylight with no difficulty. There was something wholesome about the hunger and exhaustion born of hard work. At odd times I wondered if I'd ever be able to adjust back to the type of sleep one gave into out of custom and boredom.

Margot came in with Vera to relieve us, and I absentmindedly offered her thanks as I passed her my headset. Eleanor, Addie, and I stumbled out, blinking against the too-bright sun. We had turned on the path to the barracks when Addie grabbed my elbow.

"Where is all that smoke coming from?" she asked, pointing to a billowing gray column that engulfed the southern half of our camp.

"It's the barracks," Colonel Lucas called, emerging from the rickety building that served as his office, his face tight with concentration as he rushed to summon more help. "Save what you can."

The five of us removed the switchboards and all the equipment we could lift until the men could assist us. We managed to get all the necessary equipment safe from the dangers of the fire and the buckets of water the men were using to quench it. The smoke had grown thick, and Eleanor's body was racked with a nasty cough. I wrapped my arm around her and hoped she hadn't inhaled too much smoke.

"Just take slow, even breaths," I advised. There was so much commotion, I couldn't begin to go about finding medical staff to see to her. For all I knew, the hospital was being cleared out and the staff wouldn't be able to see to her anyway. "You're going to be fine. Just try to calm yourself the best you can."

After a few minutes, her hacking seemed less intense and she was able to take a proper breath. I didn't care for her sickly pallor, but I was convinced that she wasn't in any immediate danger, though I'd have given anything for an oxygen tank to return her to a healthy shade of pink.

We'd been so concerned with the office, we'd hardly taken notice that our own barracks were among those going up in flames. I had a brief moment of panic, wondering how we'd manage with no spare uniforms or personal effects, before I noticed the flames that threatened the pylon that loomed over the camp. If the flames reached it, the exchange would be down for days. If the exchange were down during the drive, hundreds—more likely thousands—of lives would be at even greater peril. I gnashed my teeth at the idea that something as stupid as a stray cigarette had caused such devastation, and shivered at the idea that it was something more sinister.

I held Eleanor's hand—she'd gone white watching the flames that fed ravenously on the wooden structures. I heard Margot murmuring the Ave Maria in Latin, and I recited a few prayers of my own. I'd never included a pylon in my prayers before, but if there had ever been a time when ordinary objects were more deserving, I had yet to hear of it.

Finally the bucket brigade, aided by calm winds and good luck, managed to quench the blaze. The afternoon was spent sorting out the remainder of our effects. The soldiers had performed a minor miracle by saving a healthy share of our possessions before the fire had really taken hold. Some letters from home and one of my best blouses were gone, but my loss didn't sting as badly as Eleanor's. She'd lost her beloved late grandmother's prayer book, which had been entrusted to her as a talisman against bad luck.

Having given the book up as lost, she brushed away a few tears as she climbed out of the ruined building,

"I'm so sorry," I said to her, giving her a quick hug when she returned to us. "It's a terrible loss."

"It does rather seem like a bad omen, doesn't it?" she said, wiping away the last of her tears.

"Or it could have done exactly what it was meant to do," Addie supplied. "You weren't lost in the fire, thank heaven, and that's what matters."

"Too true," I said. "Everything else can be replaced, even if it isn't exactly the same." Though I said this, I was almost limp with gratitude when I discovered Evangeline's letter to Francis was unscathed, tucked inside one of my novels for safekeeping.

"Allez, les filles," Margot prodded. "Let's go find out where we are needed."

They sent us to some unfinished, windowless barracks with cracks in the floor so large that grass and weeds could grow up through them.

"Our very own garden," I said with a snicker. "How cheery." The sun hadn't even fully set, and the cold already seeped in through the floor like frigid water coming in through a sinking ship.

We relocated our things and set about reestablishing our housekeeping, which wasn't a long business given that we hadn't brought much with us and now had even less to sort out.

"I don't think Eleanor is quite well," Margot whispered to me. "Should I see if the hospital can see to her?"

"I'll do it," I said. "Making her walk in clean air may be the best thing for her. What's left of the smoke is at least blowing in the opposite direction now."

Eleanor followed me, with only minimal protests that she wasn't ill enough to bother the doctors with her troubles—not a good sign, as she was always the first to avoid the doctor's tent. Mercifully the field hospital had been spared and was operating as usual by the time we arrived. One of the doctors took a look at her and strapped an oxygen mask to her face. Within a few minutes, her color had improved and she looked more like her old self. I was dismissed to make room for others, and left her, visibly more cheerful, in the care of the good doctors.

I returned to the path that led to our new makeshift barracks, pulling my cloak tight against the chill of the evening.

"Ruby!" a voice called from behind me. I turned to see Andrew racing toward me. "I-I mean Miss Wagner. Thank God you're all right."

"I'm perfectly fine," I said. "Miss Campbell breathed in some smoke, and that's the worst of it."

"Thank God. Major McMurray took me to one of the field hospitals up the line to help with some evacuations. All I heard when I got back fifteen minutes ago was that we'd lost several barracks, and yours was among them. Someone said he'd seen you at the hospital and I—" He took a breath. "Well, does anyone know how it started?"

"Not as far as I've heard," I said. "It's been so dry, it could have been anything. A spark from a generator. A stray ember from a cigarette. I'm just happy the exchange was spared."

"So long as you aren't hurt . . . ," Andrew said, his face pale.

"Thank you so much for your concern, Lieutenant," I said. Despite myself I clasped his hand for a moment. "But we're all going to be just fine."

Andrew took a step closer and lowered his lips to mine. I was too astounded to react, but simply let myself feel the warmth of him against me. I knew I should have pulled away, but I melted into his embrace. He smelled of liniment oil and hard work, but it could have been the finest Castile soap, as intoxicating as it was. When he pulled away, I could do nothing but blink in surprise.

"God, I shouldn't have done that," he breathed, running a finger down my cheek. "I'm so sorry, Ruby."

"I-I," I stammered, waiting for the air to refill my lungs. "It's all right, Andrew." *I liked it. It was wonderful.* Those words were on my tongue but all I could utter was *"It's all right."*

"I'm sure you have a lot to do," he said, looking at the ground. "Again, I'm so sorry."

I watched as he walked back up toward the hospital, and I could still feel my heart thudding against my chest.

"You look pale," Margot said as I entered the temporary barracks. "Is Eleanor going to be all right?"

"She'll be fine," I said. "She just needs some oxygen and rest. I'll go back to collect her in a couple of hours."

"Then why do you look like you just watched a hanging?"

"It's really nothing. I just spoke with Lieutenant Carrigan is all."

"Have there been some developments with the drive tomorrow?" she asked, looking up from the rumpled pile of signal-corps uniforms the men had rescued from the burning barracks.

"Not that I know of, and I'm not sure he would know at any rate." I took a blouse from the pile and started folding it.

"What aren't you telling me, Mademoiselle Wagner?" Margot asked, now standing with her arms akimbo. "I know you well enough to see when you're keeping something back."

I wanted to tell her that about the kiss. I knew she'd be understanding. She wouldn't berate me for kissing a man when I was engaged to another, especially when there was a war on. I simply couldn't bear to speak the words aloud. Not because I'd not stopped Andrew from kissing me, but because in those brief seconds, Andrew made me feel more alive than I had in all the hours I'd spent in Nathaniel's company. That betrayal was far worse than any physical misstep.

"It's nothing of importance, Margot. Perhaps another time? We ought to get some sleep."

She eyed me suspiciously but crawled into her bunk, just as I did the same in mine. The smell of smoke still clung to the linens, but I paid it no mind as Andrew's kiss lingered on my lips. The cold air blew in from the cracks in the floor, and I shivered despite the layers I'd pulled atop me. None of it compared to the chill that I felt in the depths of my heart.

CHAPTER 25

October 31, 1918

Hell is always depicted as a pit of fire. I think Lucifer got it all wrong. If he really wanted to keep souls in everlasting torment, he'd bog them all down in the mud of eastern France. Sometime in the night, the skies opened up and showed no signs of relenting. While we were glad we'd be spared more fires in the barracks, slop-filled boots and continuously chilled feet were the steep price we paid for the reprieve. We arrived at the office just after dawn to reestablish the lines in sturdier barracks away from the fire damage. With the excitement of the fire and the ceaseless barrage of German and American guns, I doubt any of us managed to scrape together more than a couple of hours of sleep. We sat, clinging to the warmth of our coffee mugs every second our hands could be spared, as the boards lit up like a Christmas display at Wanamaker's, with people behind the lines desperate to reach the front. Lord only knew what they feared had happened to us.

"What in creation took so long to get a connection?" a voice roared over the line from GHQ in Chaumont. Sadie Porter. She was now running the office, and it seemed her temper hadn't mellowed. "We've been trying to connect to you for hours. What are you doing over there?"

"My apologies. We've had a bit of an emergency here." I'd been instructed not to speak about the fire to anyone. If the Germans intercepted the message, they might be able to deduce that the First Army headquarters was at Souilly.

"What sort of emergency is important enough to keep you from answering the phones all night long? The evening shift couldn't get through either."

"I can't discuss this any further," I said, tapping the tip of my pencil against the scarred wooden table. "May I connect you with someone?"

"Honestly, this is a disgrace," Sadie continued. "Major Weaver has been waiting to speak with Colonel Lucas since last night."

"It was unavoidable," I said, placing the pencil down before I snapped it in two. "I'll be happy to connect you now."

I patched through the call, then removed my headset and rubbed my temples against the looming headache.

Margot looked over, her eyes voicing her question for her.

"Sadie Porter is her usual charming self," I said. I regretted ever mentioning her as a suitable replacement. The title of supervising operator was more than her ego could possibly manage to keep in check.

"Ah, I cannot say I'm surprised," Margot clucked. "She is a sour woman."

"Bitter," I corrected.

"Bah, I think both words work for her."

I couldn't disagree.

Margot continued, "Making her the senior-most operator at GHQ was one of the army's biggest mistakes during the course of this war."

"A bit of an exaggeration, but it's on the list," I said.

The barrage of gunfire punctuated every sentence. We spoke louder into our headsets, struggling to hear and be heard over the artillery fire audible on both sides of the line.

The switchboards didn't slow down until it was well past ten at night. By the time Margot and I had passed over the lines to the night operators and begun stumbling toward the barracks, I wasn't quite sure how my feet managed to wade through the muddy paths and keep me reasonably upright. As I neared the door, I considered the wisdom of falling into bed fully clothed. I'd look rumpled in the morning, but I wouldn't have to go to the trouble of dressing.

I heard a piercing shriek from the other side of the door and felt my fatigue slip away like a satin dressing gown. I flung open the door, wishing I had Andrew's pistol tucked in my boot. Vera was perched on the side of Eleanor's bunk, holding her hand. Addie was upright in her own, her eyes fixed on Eleanor, who was shaking with sobs.

"What's the matter?" I asked, crossing over to them, Margot a pace behind. Eleanor looked pale but thankfully didn't show any sign of illness. The camp could ill afford another bout of flu.

"It's the guns," Vera said, concern lining her face. "The constant barrage is getting to her."

I sank next to Vera and patted Eleanor's knee. The sound of a mortar shell's wail caused her to coil up in a ball. When the resultant crash dissipated from the air, she uncurled, breathing heavy.

"Just ten minutes," she said, nearly incoherent. "Couldn't they stop for just ten minutes?"

"I know, sweetheart," I said, my voice sounding much like my father's when I'd come to him with a scraped knee as a girl. "Hopefully this means it will all be over soon. Neither side can keep up like this forever."

"God, it feels like forever," Eleanor said, sitting up and wiping her cheeks. "I don't think I'll ever get a proper night's sleep again."

"You will," I promised her. "And hopefully soon. I need you at your best tomorrow."

The reminder of her duty sobered her, and her breathing took on a more regular cadence. We ended up fashioning earmuffs for her with a scarf and a pair of clean socks—one for each ear. It wouldn't block the noise entirely but would at least muffle it, so she might be able to convince herself that danger was farther away than it really was.

"Thank you," Vera whispered once Eleanor was finally resting quietly. "She started screaming, and I felt useless."

"I've felt useless more times than I care to count since we got here," I admitted. "I hope she sleeps. If she can't, we'll have to send her back from the front. Back to GHQ, or even farther west. Or home."

"Home," Vera said. "That word sounds almost foreign nowadays, doesn't it?"

"C'est du chinois," Margot agreed. "And it seems as far away as China too."

"Let's buck up, girls," I said. "We'll be back there soon enough. And we can hold our heads high, knowing we did our part when we go marching home."

Margot was right, though. Mother's parlor, Red Cross knitting parties, and all the comings and goings of the Main Line were worlds away. I wondered how many weeks it would take for me to get used to regular sleep and decent meals again. It would happen all too soon, I expected. Too soon before dutiful, quiet Ruby reemerged and took my place.

I ended up exchanging my uniform for my nightgown, feeling far more awake as I climbed under the covers than I had when I left the office. The gunfire and the crash of artillery still sounded to the east, and the unsubstantial walls of the barracks were barely able to dampen the hellish din. The sounds of Eleanor's faint snoring reassured me she'd likely be able to take her shift in the morning. The night before, I'd heard the muffled sound of Addie's crying into her pillow. The week before, I'd had to keep Vera from breaking a cheeky sergeant in half with her bare hands. Margot was more stoic than the rest, but there was an unmistakable look in her eyes that told me she was near the limits of her endurance.

The men on the front—on both sides—had to be in the same spirits. It seemed the outcome of the war wouldn't be decided by might alone but by who was able to keep from snapping first.

CHAPTER 26

November 11, 1918

"It's over!" Colonel Lucas flew from his office just before eleven in the morning with the energy of a much younger man. "The damned Germans finally signed."

The sound of gunfire was still in the distance, and the crashing of bombs still echoed. We had all been waiting for the news since the day before. We'd heard bits and pieces from radio communication that the Germans were on the verge of armistice, and from the influx of German prisoners into the camp, we believed it had to be true. With every flash of light at the boards, we hoped for the news that we'd all been delivered to the other side of the war and that we could begin rebuilding what was lost.

"Thank God," I said, fighting the urge to collapse with relief. "But why are we still fighting?" I asked, gesturing toward the gunfire to the east.

"The cease-fire is at 1100 hours. The eleventh hour of the eleventh day of the eleventh month. I'm guessing the politicians think they're being poetic or some such. We've got to get through to the front lines."

"What's the status of the telegraph lines?" I asked.

"Bad shape. More lines down than up it seems."

"We'll get through," I said. I connected the colonel to the nearest command post and passed him my headset.

"The Germans signed the armistice," he bellowed into the line. "Cease-fire at 1100 hours! Repeat, cease your fire at 1100 hours!"

I could hear an emphatic "Yes, sir!" from my headset.

Addie stayed at the boards, but the rest of us spilled out of the office into the reluctant November sun. The clock struck eleven. The popping of the guns slowed. None to the south. None to the north. Then a hush to the east.

Margot took my hand, and I felt the air in my lungs clamoring for release.

From some far-flung corner of the camp, someone let out a cry that seeped into my very marrow. It was joy and agony all in one. The fighting was finally over, but so much had been lost in the endless fields of mud. The landscape of the world and of every man, woman, and child in the path of the machine of war had been irrevocably changed.

I felt myself sink to the ground, mud and all, and let the tears flow down my cheeks unfettered. Margot sank beside me, and I wrapped my arms around her and planted a kiss on the top of her golden-brown head. For a few minutes, we just sat, watching the men shout and jump. Embracing each other like brothers. Crying openly, unashamedly. In this moment, there was no pride. No conceit or vanity. Just brotherhood.

"*Mon dieu*, we have been praying for this day for months. Years, really . . . but it doesn't seem like such a thing is possible. What do we do now?" Margot wiped her cheeks with her sleeve and smiled at the sight of a nearby group of soldiers who had begun singing a rowdy song fit for a seedy tavern.

"I know," I said, hugging her close. "Tomorrow we're going to get up and follow orders. There is plenty of work to be done for months to come. But today we celebrate."

"I've never heard better words come from your lips," Vera said from behind us. She and Eleanor, having heard the news, had come over from the barracks. We stood up, perfectly indifferent to the thick layer of mud that had to be decorating our rear ends. Eleanor handed each of us our tin cups, which she must have rooted out from our supplies. Vera pulled a bottle of champagne from the bag that had, up until today, carried her gas mask.

"We've been on our best behavior since January, ladies," Vera said. "I think it's time to let down our hair a little." She opened the bottle with a practiced hand and poured the first of the foamy liquid into my cup, careful not to spill the least drop. Ours wasn't the only bottle to appear from the depths of barracks and tents, though the men sprayed more on each other and up into the air than they drank.

"Such a waste," Vera muttered, clucking her tongue and shaking her head, completely insincere in her admonishment.

"Come now, there *isn't* a war on," Addie said, joining us and accepting her cup. "Let them have their fun, mother hen."

"I think they would have more fun with the champagne in their bellies rather than in the mud, but I won't criticize anyone today," Margot proclaimed. She raised her cup, and we all followed suit. "To the end of this damned war, and a bright new future."

"To the US Army Signal Corps," Eleanor added.

"And to the finest operators in the whole US Army," I said. "I've never been prouder in my whole life."

Not worrying about shifts or duties for the first time in months, all five of us retreated into the office, taking turns attending to the inevitable dribble of calls that came through as the details of peace began to take shape. Margot and I scraped the mud from our backsides with the dull knives from our mess kits, trying to keep our fits of giggles from being heard over the lines.

Along with the champagne, Vera had provided us with a veritable feast of jams, crackers, cookies, and all sorts of treats from our modest stores. We'd eaten these luxuries so sparingly, it seemed more than decadent to eat our fill.

The bubbles of the champagne still tart on my tongue, I felt the muscles across my shoulders uncoil.

Andrew joined in the celebrating after a few hours, when McMurray released him for his dinner break. He gratefully partook in our little feast and even enjoyed a half glass of champagne, which was all he would permit himself while he was on shift.

Judging by the bags under his eyes, I figured he hadn't slept in over twenty-four hours and still had several more before he'd be able to crawl into his own bed. He sat down and placed an arm around me, and I hadn't the heart to insist he remove it. It was just a few moments before I felt his head rest against mine and heard his breathing grow even with slumber.

"Shall we wake him?" Eleanor whispered.

"Let him sleep awhile longer," I whispered back. "He has a little time left on his break."

His weight against me was solid and reassuring, and it wasn't just for his sake that I wouldn't have him disturbed.

As Andrew slept at my side, Eleanor connected a major from GHQ with one of our captains just behind the front, who was likely still holed up in a trench with a bulky, unreliable field telephone. Did he have a bottle of champagne? How long before he'd get a soft bed and a hot meal? It wouldn't be long in coming for him and the rest of the men who had survived the war. I turned my head and nuzzled Andrew's neck, my lips brushing featherlight against his soft skin so as not to wake him. That he and the rest of the men were finally safe was the best comfort I'd had in months.

CHAPTER 27

December 14, 1918
Paris

I stepped outside the YWCA-run hotel and paused on the stoop to survey the street below. The insincere midmorning sun engulfed the street in a weak halo, but the icy breeze gave no false promises of a mild winter—it carried daggers. I found myself glad for the sturdy tan gloves Evangeline had gifted me. There was a hesitance in people as they emerged from their houses and into the light of the postwar world. The street where we stayed had largely been spared from the bombs dropped by the German Gotha bombers, but the next street over had a massive crater the size of four automobiles. One building had been obliterated, and close to one hundred people had been killed. Entire families gone. Almost every neighborhood had a similar story, and it was infinitely worse in the east.

But they emerged from their homes just the same and set to the daunting task of rebuilding their city. The able-bodied surviving soldiers worked alongside the men who had been too old to serve, the women, and even the children. They cleared debris, replaced windows, and rebuilt crumbled facades as best they could with scant supplies. They swept the rubble of the war from their streets and began the trickier business of learning how to move on in a family where beloved husbands, brothers, and sons would never return home. I had only the barest taste of what some of these families had endured. I'd yet to hear from Nathaniel, but there were so many regiments trying to get word home to their families, the mail was worse than congested. He'd been stationed near Belgium, and I expected he was busy rebuilding with the rest of us.

"You look like you stayed up too late listening to good jazz and drinking bad gin," a familiar tenor cooed from the bottom of the steps.

"Nothing quite so scandalous, nor so fun," I admitted. "Sixteen solid hours on the switchboards, and despite a decent night's sleep, I'm still sluggish. President Wilson arrived yesterday, and they managed to prolong the armistice in the nick of time. Here's hoping they get a proper peace treaty signed soon."

"Hear, hear," Andrew said. "I'd heard they'd put you all through the wringer these past few days, which is why I'm here. Nothing for it but some French coffee. Best in the world, though if you breathe a word of that to my Italian mama, I'll deny it to my dying breath. Which would happen just as soon as she heard of me saying such a thing."

I chuckled at the image of the feisty Italian mother's wrath but felt a tingle at the idea I might ever have the opportunity to meet her. I didn't know this woman, but I sensed she would be able to read my feelings for her Andrew as plainly as pages in a book.

"I can't say no to that," I said.

"Good. There are a few cafés still up and running in the quartier. One or two of them are even decent, though it'll be a year before anything is back up to snuff."

He offered his arm, and I took it, trying not to think of how I enjoyed the feeling of my hand as it rested in the crook of his arm. He took me to a quaint little café that might have been suitable for a postcard had it not had boards still on the windows. The waiters, perhaps still buoyant from the armistice festivities, provided us with cheerful service that would have rivaled the homiest family restaurant in the Midwest.

He ordered for us, knowing both what would be best from the French menu and what the restaurateur would be likely to have available. He avoided anything with flour, which was still scarce since the Germans laid waste to the fields to the east.

In the end, I was presented with coffee as dark and rich as I'd ever tasted, a mixed fruit juice, and a minuscule hunk of baguette served with jam. Nothing like the mountains of bacon and eggs from home, but at least it was flavorful and fresh, if not plentiful. My uniform already hung considerably looser than it had upon my departure, and I was sure my ribs would be visible under it all if I were brave enough to look.

"It'll be years before the crops are what they were," Andrew said as he looked down at his emaciated pastry.

"It's going to be a hard winter," I agreed. Neither of us spoke the painful truth that the war wasn't finished claiming lives.

"Enough of this. You have the day off, yes? Spend it in Paris with me. Let's see what we worked so hard to save."

The prospect of a day alone in Andrew's company was as enticing as it was out of bounds. The memory of the kiss we shared in the woods outside Souilly still haunted my mind like an unsettled specter.

"Come on now. A couple of friends can spend a day together, can't they?" he prodded, reading the nature of my thoughts. "Let me show you the city before they send us home and we have to go back to whatever 'real life' is going to look like."

I had a vision of myself trapped in an endless series of parlors, paying calls to people as interesting as faded wallpaper. Would this be my last chance to see Paris? I might be sent home the day they finalized the peace treaty. I might be kept on for several more months. I had no way of knowing if today would be my last chance to see Andrew before one of us was sent home. I tried to ignore the ice that crept into my veins at the thought, but the shiver I emitted wasn't due to the December air.

"All right, but back before curfew. I'm not going to end my service with any disciplinary action on my record."

"Sensible," he said. "Especially considering we don't know how long our service will last."

"True," I replied. "I'd imagined that once the war ended, we'd be sent home in a matter of days. Maybe weeks. It hadn't occurred to me how much work there would be left."

"We were all focused on winning the war. Thinking about the aftermath was a bit presumptuous."

"Amen to that."

"I know just how to celebrate today," Andrew declared. "We're going to see something I've been longing to see my whole life."

"The Eiffel Tower."

"Nothing so touristy as that. You and me, we're people of culture and refinement, aren't we? Never mind that I'll never get the smell of iodine off my hands. I hope your boots are comfortable, because we have a walk ahead of us."

It took some time to traverse the city, but Andrew led us at last to a lavish garden in the middle of a posh neighborhood just south of the city center.

"Welcome to the jardin du Luxembourg," Andrew said as we passed through the gates. "Once a backyard fit for royalty, though it seems shabby in comparison to present company."

I swatted his arm in mock annoyance. "It *is* gorgeous," I said. "Though it's not exactly the season for sauntering in the garden."

"True enough, but we're not here to see the plants. We're going to the museum at the Palace."

"That seems like a very 'dignified' way to spend the afternoon," I chided.

"Isn't that what you wanted? I was thinking we could have high tea later. Perhaps listen to a public discourse on temperance?"

I poked him playfully in the ribs. "No need to tease, you brute."

There wasn't a crowd milling about, given the falling temperatures, but a few people braved the chill to breathe in the late-autumn air. Their clothes were a little shabbier than they might have been, their faces more drawn and gray, but they walked with the nonchalance mastered only by the Parisians. There were no sirens, no drone of planes overhead, no telltale char marks where bombs had landed.

"You could almost pretend things are normal," I mused aloud.

"It gives a person hope, doesn't it? That the world might actually heal from all of this."

"Oh, I have no doubt the world will be just fine. It managed perfectly well before mankind came to be, and I wonder if it won't be better off without us once we're gone. I just wonder how the rest of us will carry on. Humans are frail creatures, and I wonder if we haven't broken an entire generation of men."

To this, Andrew said nothing.

He didn't offer his arm as we mounted the steps to the museum, but instead took my hand in his and laced his gloved fingers through mine. When we checked our coats and gloves at the desk, he claimed my hand once more, this time his bare skin against mine. I should have protested the familiar gesture, but it wasn't in me to refuse the warmth of his palm clasped against my own.

"It's a remarkable collection," I said, admiring the delightfully vibrant palette of a portrait of two girls playing the piano. I'd not frequented many art museums in my time, feeling that one stodgy portrait in hues of black, gray, brown, and cream looked much like another. This painting was full of life and light.

"It is," Andrew agreed. "And all the more remarkable because the artists are all still alive. Or rather recently deceased. Mama told me that once the artist dies, they either send the artwork to the Louvre if it's good enough or sell it off to private collectors and such."

"I wish I knew more about art," I mused, stepping closer to look at the brushstrokes of a slight woman dancing at a barre in her white tights and flowing tulle skirt that highlighted her trim figure and athletic lines.

"I'm no expert myself, though I always enjoyed flipping through Mama's books. This Renoir fellow isn't half-bad, is he?"

"No, he's brilliant. I've heard of him but never thought I'd have the chance to see his work for myself. He knew the world didn't need another portrait of an aristocrat. These are real people."

"Exactly," Andrew said. "This one looks a bit like you. *La Liseuse*."

He pointed to a portrait, fairly traditional by Renoir's standards, of a woman engrossed in a book. She had blond hair curled up atop her head like a massive red-gold crown. Her eyes were completely absorbed in her tome, a gentle smile tugging at the edge of her full ruby lips.

"People have said worse about me," I commented. "She does seem lovely. I wonder what she's reading."

"Perhaps a novel. I'd wager it's something scandalous from her canny smile."

"Probably not a book of sermons," I agreed. "Not if she kept company with Renoir, anyway. Look at the way he plays with light. It looks as though it's bouncing right off her skin."

"You have the eye of an artist." He stroked the back of my hand with his thumb, and I pretended not to notice.

"Nothing of the sort. I just know what I like."

"How lucky for the painting," Andrew mused, his eyes diverting from my face to another tableau.

"What do you mean?"

"You're going home to marry the boy your parents hand-selected for you," Andrew said, struggling to keep his tone nonchalant. "How can I hope to compare with someone who comes from the right part of town, from the right family?"

"I've never asked you to compete, Andrew. I'm engaged. I know we've become friends, and I won't pretend . . ." I lowered my voice. "I won't pretend the kiss we shared wasn't wonderful. But strange things happen in war. I truly didn't mean to lead you on. I hope you don't blame me for it."

"You honestly think this is all about the kiss?" Andrew asked, his voice just above a whisper, his lips nearly touching my ear. "I fell for you long before that kiss. From the first day I saw you walking on the road toward GHQ. I finally knew what my father felt when he first laid eyes on my mother."

I swallowed hard. "I'm sorry, Andrew. I'm just not sure what to say. I shouldn't even be here with you."

"Listen, Ruby. I know that I shouldn't impose my company on you. Your Nathaniel will be able to provide you with the silks and diamonds a girl like you deserves. I'd be a selfish ass to try and come between you and him. I just wanted one day in your company. One day without duty, gunfire, and mayhem. A souvenir to take home from the war, if you will."

I closed my eyes and, despite my better judgment, leaned my forehead against his solid chest. He wrapped his arms around me and ignored the people milling about, who were likely giving us curious expressions. I could feel him lower his head and inhale deeply.

"My God," he breathed into my ear, "you smell like lilies and jasmine. In a war zone. This is killing me. If I thought you loved him, I could endure it for you. But to imagine you a slave of duty and convention for the next fifty years guts me like a goddamned bayonet."

I took in his own musky scent, always tinged with the scent of iodine and disinfectant, and could not remember ever being close enough to Nathaniel to really get a sense of how he smelled. The two or three times he'd kissed me had been chaste. But now, locked in a simple hug, I worried passersby would be able to hear the beat of my heart as it bounced off the marble floor. For all his goodness, Nathaniel's affections had only roused a vaguely pleasant warmth in my core.

"I'll take you back to the Y," Andrew said, pulling away. "But I have a gift for you. You can toss it into a drawer when you get home and never look at it again, but it will make me happy to know you have it all the same." He took a small parcel from his pocket and placed it in my hands. The packaging was one of his embroidered handkerchiefs, tied with a crimson ribbon. I loosened the bow to find a cuff bracelet skillfully carved with various little flowers. He slipped it onto my right wrist and kissed the soft skin above my pulse, a liberty he'd taken so quickly I might have imagined it but for his guilt-tinged expression.

"I-it's gorgeous," I stuttered, my composure eluding me.

"I carved it from a shell casing," he admitted. "It gave me something to do to keep from running mad when I knew they were firing behind the front lines. I spent my days imagining this moment, when I could give it to you, knowing you were safe."

"It means more to me than all the diamonds and silks in the world," I whispered. More than the ruby ring that sat safe at home, nestled in a box on my dressing table. But that I could not voice.

"I'm going to keep my promise and take you back," Andrew said, reaching up to stroke the side of my face but dropping his hand as he thought better of it.

"No," I said, louder than I intended. I took his hand back in mine. "You wanted a day. That doesn't seem too much to ask."

Wrapped in the late-autumn frost and oblivious to the cold, we strolled along the Seine. We spoke of everything and nothing for the better part of the afternoon. At some point Andrew released my hand and placed his arm around my waist. I fell silent often, drinking in the sensation of his nearness. Memorizing it like a beloved sonnet.

"Dinner and back home?" Andrew asked as the sun began to hang low in the sky. "I know you don't want a dressing-down for missing the eight o'clock curfew."

"That sounds lovely," I said as he ushered us to a likely-looking street that seemed to be gearing up for an evening of food, wine, and song.

"The Parisians are ready for a party," I observed. "They deserve one."

"They do indeed," Andrew agreed. "And Paris is usually more than ready to throw a grand one. Like my neighbors in Brooklyn who could fill a table with food and strike up a band at a moment's notice for the flimsiest of reasons."

I thought of the weeks of planning Mother could put into a simple tea. A real party could take a month or more to orchestrate, and she wasn't the exception on the Main Line. "I don't have any neighbors like that. But they sound awfully fun."

"Brooklyn may be rough around the edges, but that has its advantages, I suppose."

"I've always thought the anonymity of living in a place like New York would be exhilarating. Even if you—I don't know—fall on your face in public or get spattered with street muck, no one would know you. Philadelphia might be a large city, but if I were to accept a ride in a carriage or a car from someone my mother didn't approve of, she'd know about it before I came in the door."

"It can be exhilarating. It's also lonely. If people are calling your mother to let her know you've taken a ride with an unsavory character, it means they care about you."

"I suppose that's true."

"But for the time being, I'll be glad for the fact that you're here and unchaperoned." Andrew leaned in and brushed his lips against the top of my cheekbone. "So long as you permit me to take a few innocent liberties."

"Be careful, I might take a few myself." I winked, despite myself.

"It's not taking liberties if they're given freely, my darling girl." He held the door open to a little restaurant on the corner and placed his hand on the small of my back as I crossed the threshold. There were no white tablecloths and flickering candles for us. A corner booth in a noisy brasserie with scarred wooden tables and dim lights suited us better. They served us sole meunière in a butter sauce so decadent, it was all I could do to keep from licking the back of my fork.

"God, but the French know their way around a fish." Andrew rested his hand on my knee. The gesture was familiar enough I ought to have stopped him, but I hadn't the determination to rebuke him. His touch felt as comfortable as a thin silk shift on a warm summer night.

"That they do," I agreed. I refrained from mentioning that Evangeline might be glad to have the recipe. I wouldn't darken the evening with the specter of our disagreement.

"Do you have to be so . . ." Andrew withdrew his hand. "I have to stop torturing myself. Let me take you home. It'll be close enough to curfew after we cut through the city anyway."

"Actually, my pass is for midnight," I confessed. "It's been so long since I used one, the brass has all but told me I can have an all-night pass whenever I want one."

"Why are you coming clean now?" Andrew asked. "You don't want to put your good name at risk by staying out that late with me."

"I promised I would spend a day with you, and the day doesn't end at eight o'clock. I won't skip out on my promises."

"Well, I'll never say I don't believe in miracles after today," he said in a low voice. "Dancing?"

I nodded, and we shivered our way a few blocks over to a dance hall, where a band was playing with more enthusiasm than skill. Andrew wrapped his arms around me, and we swayed in time to the tinny music. I felt his warmth through all the layers of his woolen uniform and drank in the scent of him.

"I wish tonight could last forever," I whispered into his chest.

"The memory will, my love," he murmured. I wondered if he was even aware of the endearment he'd just offered, or if he was speaking in his dreamy haze. "That can be enough."

After a few dances, he pulled me over to the bar, where he ordered two cocktails. His was a simple whiskey and soda, while mine was a vibrant purple concoction.

"What have you ordered me?" I asked. "I'm not sure if it's charming or terrifying."

"Both," he answered. "I've heard them called amethyst martinis. They're made with parfait amour. A bit old fashioned, but it used to be a popular liqueur with the smart set over here—with the ladies, anyway. Try it."

"Perfect love?" I translated. "Are you slipping me a love potion, Lieutenant?"

"If only such a thing existed. But no, I'd rather have you of your own free will."

I placed the glass to my lips and let the chilled liquid rest on my tongue before letting it roll back into my throat. Notes of rose, citrus, vanilla, and the barest hint of anise played on my palate.

"It's incredible," I said, taking another taste. "Like it doesn't belong to this world."

"I've often thought the same about you. Too beautiful, too sweet to be real. I thought you two might enjoy each other."

I leaned in and kissed him, not caring who looked on. "You're ridiculous, you know."

"Just one martini for you, then, darling. I don't want to go from ridiculous to foolish."

He pulled me back to the dance floor. Three dances melted into a half dozen, and although there were more than a few soldiers looking for a partner, no one dared to intrude to ask my favor.

"If all we have to take back home with us are memories, I want to make another," I said, leaning in closer and pressing my lips to the bare skin of his neck.

He stood back a mere half pace to look at me, his brow arched, questioning.

"Surely we can find somewhere to be alone?"

"Ruby—" Still clutching me to him, he looked off into the distance over the dance floor.

"What is it?"

"Nothing, my darling." He gave up any pretense at restraint and kissed me deeply right on the dance floor, ignoring the shrill whistles and jeers from a few onlookers. "I survived a war—a broken heart can mend."

Andrew found us a room in a hotel in the Sixth Arrondissement. One of the quiet neighborhoods where Parisians really lived and tourists rarely found their way.

"Are you sure?" he asked, the room key raised in his hand, but stopping short of the doorknob and the point of no return that certainly lay on the opposite side of the threshold.

"I am." I allowed no equivocation in my voice. If I hesitated, if I faltered in the least, I knew he'd have me back in my room with the signal-corps girls within the hour. If I was to spend the rest of my days in the Main Line, leading the life I was expected to, I needed this night. I needed to know what real passion felt like. I knew this could be a fatal mistake. I might do better to go on as before, not knowing what I was missing, but in that moment all that mattered was him. I couldn't break the promise I'd made to my parents, to Nathaniel, but I could take this night for myself.

The door creaked loudly as he opened it, as though announcing to all of Paris what I was about to do. It was a plain room with a double bed and ratty little chair. Despite being shabby, it was as clean as any posh hotel in New York and tended with pride.

"You and this Nathaniel haven't . . ."

"Heavens, no. Mother would never allow us that kind of privacy." I refrained from mentioning the afternoon at the Bellevue when I wondered if Nathaniel might take advantage of the lapse in supervision. If he had, would I be here now? Perhaps I'd be anticipating my marriage to him more if I knew what was in store. I pushed the thought from my head and pulled Andrew into my arms.

"There is a chance he might notice." Andrew practically turned a violent shade of vermilion at the thought. He pulled away and down on the edge of the bed.

"That isn't a worry for tonight," I said, unbuttoning my uniform jacket and placing it onto the chair. I wasn't sure how to proceed, so I crossed the room, sat on his lap, and tentatively kissed the soft skin at the nape of his neck.

"This is going to kill me," he murmured, his eyes closed as I began to unbutton his uniform jacket.

"Should I stop?" I asked, my hands hesitating. I prayed he wouldn't pull away.

"No, God no."

I divested him of his jacket and shirt and admired the muscles of his chest, made hard from endless hours of hard labor under the hood of a car in his father's shop. I traced the chiseled lines of his torso with the tips of my fingers before he let out a low growl and pulled me to him, lowering his mouth on mine. His kiss began assertively, his tongue exploring eagerly, but escalated into desperation. A low moan escaped from his mouth into mine, and I responded by gripping him closer.

"Show me what to do," I whispered into his ear. I had a vague idea of how the business was done, but it was something Mother had told me my husband would teach me when the time came. All questions I had ever dared ask on the subject were met with stony silence.

"I'm no expert," he whispered, now cradling me against him, his lips brushing against mine as he tempered his need. "But I think we can manage. If you're really sure."

"I really am, Andrew. I need this more than you know. But there can't be a baby."

"I've got us covered," he whispered. "The Brits have been passing condoms out like candy since the war started. A more prudent line than our own government's, if you ask me. I found an obliging shopkeeper who still had some in stock."

"So, the thought crossed your mind, then?" I said, finding the courage to slide my hands below his belt to cup his buttocks.

"More times than I should admit," he said. "But I had no expectations for tonight, my darling girl. Just a vague hope."

"Let's not waste scarce resources, then. That would be unpatriotic, after all."

"We can't have that," he agreed. His fingers found the buttons of my blouse, and I found myself clinging to him, breathless.

"My God, you're an angel," he crooned in my ear as he lowered me to the bed.

My only response was a muffled whimper as his hands continued to explore. "Please" was the only coherent word I could find.

"My love," he whispered as he obliged me. "My love."

"Yours," I breathed. And let myself surrender, unashamed.

CHAPTER 28

Andrew returned me to the YWCA with seconds to spare before my curfew. He'd be a few minutes late for his own pass, but he wasn't horribly worried for the consequences as he left me with a parting kiss. Mrs. Grant, who had come to Paris with us, was waiting for me in the hotel's front parlor. The deep crease of worry in her brow had lessened since the armistice but had not dissipated completely. When one of us missed curfew, she now had the usual concerns of a mother figure. A broken-down car, a sprained ankle—everyday misfortunes. She didn't have to worry we'd been taken by a stray bomb blast or a gas attack.

"Nice evening, Ruby?" she asked as she sipped at a cup of tea. She motioned for me to take the armchair next to hers.

"Very," I said, hoping the truth of how I'd spent the evening wasn't etched on my face. "Paris is a lovely city. I'm grateful I've had the chance to see it coming back to life."

"It does seem to be," she said. Her duties kept her occupied much of the time, and she rarely had the chance to spend much time away from AEF headquarters or the YWCA hotel.

"You've had a telegram," she said, handing me the thin envelope. "I hope it's nothing urgent, but I wasn't sure where to send a courier to look for you."

I tried to avoid blushing at the thought of an army courier finding me in Andrew's arms. "No, I wouldn't have expected you to," I said with a dismissive wave. I felt flutters in my stomach as my hands fumbled with the envelope. Mother hadn't had anything urgent enough to say that couldn't be included in a letter, and Father hadn't done more than sign a little note on Mother's messages since I'd left.

It was from Nettie Morgan, Nathaniel's mother:

> NATHANIEL INJURED, WE FEAR SERIOUSLY. HOSPITALIZED IN BOULOGNE-SUR-MER. VISIT HIM AND APPRISE US OF HIS CONDITION, IF POSSIBLE. GRATEFULLY, NETTIE MORGAN.

I passed the telegram over to Mrs. Grant so she could read the contents for herself. I'd promised Nathaniel's mother I'd do what I could to keep her informed, and for the first time I could truly fulfill the office. "I'm going to need leave and a travel pass, if it can be managed at all. I'll have to go into the office first thing tomorrow and beg."

I couldn't stop the trembling in my fingers. To think of Nathaniel cold and alone in some remote army hospital ripped at my gut. I could only imagine the worry gnawing at his mother, not knowing the condition of her only child. Calling the hospital might let me know if he was still alive, but I seriously doubted they'd be able to give me information beyond that.

"I'm sure they'll manage it for you in the morning, dear. Things may be chaotic right now, but your girls can cover for you. And be proud to do it, I expect."

"Thank you," I said, struggling to take air in my lungs. "I-I need to get to bed."

"Of course, my dear. Try to get some rest. We'll see to it in the morning."

I patted her shoulder in thanks and climbed the stairs to my room, clinging to the banister to keep from shaking.

"You're back late," Margot said from her bed, where she read by a dim light. "I expected you hours ago."

"Late pass, and I decided to take advantage of it for once," I said, rummaging around for a small satchel I could use for a few days' leave in Boulogne-sur-Mer. It seemed prudent to be packed for an immediate departure. Leave was often given at a moment's notice and was usually of short duration.

"Good for you. Though I don't know how smart it was for you to wander the streets of Paris alone."

"I was with Andrew," I said, not bothering to hide the truth from her. I began taking my unmentionables from their dresser drawer and placing them onto the bed.

She sat up and swung her feet down to the floor. "You were out until the small hours with a boy who isn't your intended?" She gasped with mock horror. "My dear, there may be hope for you yet."

"Ha-ha," I replied wryly, adding stockings to the satchel.

"Dinner and dancing?" she asked as I began folding two of my clean union suits.

"Yes," I replied. "And a late breakfast and a stroll about Paris, a museum . . . It was a lovely day."

"It's usually lovelier when the late breakfast comes after the dinner and dancing, but it does sound like a fun day."

"Don't be crass," I said, throwing a boot in my case with a satisfying thunk.

"*Bon dieu*, you spent the night with him," she said. "It's about time. Brava. You two are meant for each other."

"It isn't like that," I said. "He knows we can't have a future together. It would never work."

"For a smart girl, you can be an *idiote*. Why are you packing, then, if you aren't running off to elope with your beloved?"

"Nathaniel has been injured." I tossed the telegram at her so she could read for herself and continued packing clothes, glad my hands had an occupation.

"You're running off to him hours after you . . . give yourself . . . to another man?"

"It's daft, I know. But I'm engaged to Nathaniel. What's to be done about it? Lord, I am an *idiote*, as you say. I've made a horrid mistake."

"Yes, you are. Andrew is a good man. If this is the way you treat him, you don't deserve him."

"So, I'm supposed to leave poor Nathaniel all alone in the hospital? Ignore his mother's wishes despite her never being anything less than kind to me?"

"No, by all means, go to this Nathaniel. And tell him goodbye. You know I have never once heard you tell a fond story about him? Or speak of him with affection—or even fondness. Why are you throwing away Andrew for a man you seem perfectly indifferent to?"

"Because it would kill my parents," I said. "They dreamed of a man like Nathaniel for me, and I don't want to let them down."

She crossed her arms over her chest. "That is the silliest thing I've heard in my life."

"It may be, but my parents have already lost one child. I won't break their hearts a second time."

"I hope you know what you're doing, Ruby. They won't be the ones married to him for the next fifty years."

The morning came all too soon, my sleep having been wrought with the worst kind of nightmares. I must have looked a fright, and I nearly sent someone to shoo off Andrew when I saw he was waiting for me on the stoop. I summoned my courage, however, and descended the steps to him, where he offered me an arm to walk me into headquarters. I refused it, not wanting to give him hope that the previous day's exploits were anything other than a one-night folly. I softened the rebuke by taking his hand in mine and squeezing it affectionately before dropping it.

"Are you all right?" he asked. "You look tired. You weren't up all night suffering from regret, I hope?"

"Not at all," I said honestly. "It's nothing to do with you, I promise."

"I'm glad," he said, taking my hand again for just a moment. "I could live with almost anything else."

"I promise you, last night will always be one of my fondest memories. All the rest of my days."

He brushed a tendril of hair from my forehead. "Why do I get the feeling I'm going to hate the next words out of your lips?"

"Because you're apt to. Nathaniel was wounded at the end of the fighting. It's bad enough that he's still stuck in a hospital in Boulogne-sur-Mer. The telegram arrived while we were out last night. His mother begged me to go to him and let her know the real status of things. You know the army. Sparse on details."

"And drowning in injured men. I'm so sorry, Ruby. Is there anything I can do to help?"

"You really mean that, don't you? I'll never be as good a person as you are. I'm trying to get leave to see him. I have no idea how badly he's hurt, but Nettie deserves the truth."

"I assume you're packed in case your leave is granted quickly?"

"I've been in the army for almost a year. Of course I am."

"I'd have been shocked if you weren't. Bring your satchel and leave it with me. I've got one of the medical-corps trucks for the day so I can fetch some supplies this afternoon. I'll drive you to the office today and on to the station if they process your leave in time to make the morning train. They won't mind a little misuse of government property to help one of our own."

"You have more faith in military expediency than I do," I said. "But it's a good idea." I ran upstairs to fetch the bag and stowed it between Andrew and me on the bench seat.

The air in the truck was heavy with unasked questions. I could tell from the way he kneaded the steering wheel that there were a dozen waiting to be spoken. *Are you going to stay with him? Will you request discharge to take him home? Do you love him?* I supposed those were the most burning among them. It was just as well he didn't ask, because the answers were just as much an enigma to me as they were to him.

Andrew entered the telephone office behind me. It seemed as though Mrs. Grant had called ahead to apprise my supervisor of the situation, because he was already in the process of approving my leave when I knocked at his office door. Margot was on her way already to take my shift, and within the half hour I was back with Andrew in the truck with a pass for three days' leave.

"Scoot closer," he asked in a strained voice after about five minutes on the road.

"Andrew, I can't anymore. I'm so tired of hurting you."

"I know, darling girl. I can see it in your eyes. Just let me wrap my arm around you one more time. Nothing more."

I obliged, allowing him to drape his arm around my shoulders as he drove. Despite driving one-handed, he was steady on the road and never let his eyes waver from his course.

"I never said thank you for last night," he said, his thumb caressing my bicep. "For all of yesterday."

"You don't have to thank me," I said, quietly looking out the passenger-side window. "If anything, the whole thing was selfish on my part."

"How do you figure?"

"Because I did exactly what I wanted without regard for your feelings or his."

"I hope you make a habit of doing it more often. There's no point in living a life if you spend the whole of it trying to please other people."

"You sound like Margot."

"I knew I liked that girl," he said. "She's good for you."

"She is. It's hard to think that in a few months, weeks, or even days she'll be going home and I won't see her every day."

"I know she'll miss you too." He held me even closer. "The thought of you in another city . . ."

"I know," I said.

"It's all been worth it. It's going to hurt like hell, but I'd do it all over again."

"Me too," I said without hesitation. "Even if it was reckless and a bit stupid."

"The best memories start out with reckless and stupid decisions."

"This may be my only chance to get to Cambrai," I said. Andrew's arm tightened around me at the mention of the place where Francis had died. "Unless Nathaniel's condition is too dire for me to leave his side, I have to go. I made a promise."

"That seems like a fantastic idea. It'll be good for you to say a proper goodbye." He brushed his lips against the top of my head.

Too soon the Gare du Nord appeared before us, and Andrew parked the ungainly truck in one of the many open spaces. He exited the truck and opened the door for me, unnecessarily offering me his hand to descend.

"Thank you for the ride," I said, not yet releasing his hand. "Not many men would be so gracious under similar circumstances."

He leaned in and whispered in my ear. "One kiss?"

I nodded my consent.

He kissed me slowly. Savoring. Lingering.

"I'll see you in a few days, I expect," I said, stepping back and trying to stave off trembles.

"No," he said. "I have no regrets about us. Not one. But I'm not made of iron, my darling girl. I'm going to ask for a transfer. A discharge if I have to. I have to leave with some shred of my heart still intact."

The air whooshed from my lungs as though I'd been dealt a blow from a skilled prizefighter. "I understand," I replied, taking a step backward. "I'll miss you."

"My dearest Ruby, I'll remember you always with such affection. I hope you can say the same for me."

I swallowed hard, unable to speak, and took my satchel as he fetched it from the truck. I threw my arms around his neck and took one more frantic kiss.

I kept the tears at bay until the train began to lurch northward, and I let the pain flow freely in time with the rattling tracks that took me away from the man I should never have allowed myself to love.

CHAPTER 29

December 15, 1918
Boulogne-sur-Mer, France

The military hospital in Boulogne-sur-Mer had seen the maimed and dying since the earliest days of the war. Its very walls seemed to tremble with the terror it had witnessed over the past four years, even though the war had finally expelled its last rattling breath. Though there was no longer the torrent of freshly injured men flooding in through the doors, there was still more than enough work for the nurses to do. Their faces were gaunt and gray, their eyes weary from having seen more in their young lives than was right. At an age when their mothers had been courting beaux and attending dances, these young women had given up their youth to save men on the verge of death and to usher those too far gone into its embrace.

One of the nurses saw my uniform, averted her gaze, and stuck her nose into the air. It seemed the nurses in Boulogne-sur-Mer were as fond of the signal-corps girls as the ones we'd met in Chaumont. While on some level I understood their feelings, it seemed a shame that they wouldn't be supportive of their fellow servicewomen.

As I passed alongside the interminable row of beds, I fought against the urge to wrinkle my nose against the stench. I would not let the soldiers see my revulsion, but the air was so thick, so putrid, I felt light-headed, and the world wasn't quite in proper focus. I spotted Nathaniel, painfully thin, his face wan, lying on a cot near the far wall. A nurse by his side gathered up her bandages and supplies when she saw me approach and scurried on to the next patient whose wounds needed dressing.

"My God, is it really you?" he said, trying to sit up on the flimsy cot.

"Don't, don't," I chided. "Lie back and rest."

A nurse handed me a low stool, and I took my place by his left side. He took my hand in his, raised it to his lips, then lowered it back to his side. "I never thought to see you in this godforsaken place," he confessed. "I am selfish enough to be glad of it, but no one as innocent and sweet as you should be near such atrocity. How long do I have you?"

"Just today." I kept my tone gentle, trying to keep in mind all he had endured. "I have just three days' leave, and it may be my only chance to go to Cambrai to see . . . where we lost Francis. To say goodbye for all of us."

"I'm glad for that. He deserves a visit from his family. They all do." There was anguish in the depths of his sage-green eyes that even morphine couldn't dull.

"Are you in much pain?"

"I can manage," he said, though his ashy, sunken cheeks betrayed that his injuries pushed the limit of his tolerance.

"They didn't tell me what happened. Your mother told me only you'd been hurt, no more."

"Our entire regiment fell under the direct blast of the German artillery. We lost more men in an afternoon than we had in months. I was lucky. I took a lot of shrapnel, but nothing vital was hit."

I pulled back his tattered wool blanket to see the extent of his injuries. His right side was bandaged from his foot to the crook of his arm. Had it been his left, his heart certainly would have been hit. It was a miracle his lung had been spared. It was clear from what I could see between the bandages that his flesh would never be the same smooth canvas, untouched by the sun or hard labor. Angry red welts would calm into shining white scars that he would bear for the rest of his life.

"I repulse you," he said. It wasn't a question, nor a condemnation. He spoke as matter-of-factly as he would in response to an inquiry of the weather.

"Not at all," I said truthfully. His scars were earned in service to our country. It would be a poor woman who couldn't look beyond something so inconsequential. In truth, I felt as though I bore worse scars than these. I could only think that Andrew's kisses must have been as visible on my lips as cheap rouge. His musky scent must have been steeped into my very flesh from the hours I spent ensconced in his arms. "All that repulses me is your suffering. I'd bear it for you if I could."

"It's mine to endure," Nathaniel said, screwing on a stoic expression. "And I deserve worse. You have no idea what it was like, Ruby. Out of the dozens of men in my regiment, only a handful survived. I've spent the past weeks wondering why I was spared. What made me more deserving to live than the other men?"

"Don't do that to yourself," I said. "We can't pretend there is anything logical or just about war. It feeds on the good and the wicked alike."

"You have seen a thing or two of war from your switchboards, haven't you?" Nathaniel observed. "I know you're right. In my mind, I know that the only thing that spared me was sheer dumb luck and nothing more. But it doesn't mean I shouldn't take something from it. I want to forge a life that will make their sacrifice . . . if not worthwhile, at least not in vain."

"It's a lovely idea, Nathaniel, but it seems an awful lot to bear on your shoulders."

"That's why I have you. What other woman could understand? I want to do something to make sure the men who come home are taken care of when they return. The hospitals may take care of their physical wounds, but there's more to healing than that. These men need a place to go, to learn how to be a part of good society again. I hope you have only the vaguest idea of the barbarism of the trenches."

"I've more of an idea than I ever wanted to have, but your program is a wonderful idea," I said, brushing his cheek with the back of my finger. "It would do a lot of good for our returning heroes."

"That's exactly what Madeleine—Nurse Johnson—said." His eyes wandered for a moment before returning to my face. I noticed the spark in his eye. It was the one I'd caught so many times in Andrew's when he thought I wasn't looking. I felt a tingling of hope in my heart where envy should have been.

"Is she the nurse who's been attending to you?" I asked, taking his hand. "I ought to thank her."

"She's one of them," he replied, looking away. "But there's no need to thank her. She's proud to do her job."

"As we all are. You're fond of her," I pressed, not letting him evade my eyes.

"As any man would be for an angel of mercy. If it weren't for her, I wouldn't have lived."

I was sure that was true, but there was something in his tone that betrayed that the truth was deeper yet.

"Nathaniel, you needn't keep secrets from me," I whispered. "No one expected you to be a saint while you were deployed. I won't be cross. I swear it." I couldn't admit that I hoped he'd faltered. If he'd given himself to this girl in a moment of weakness, I could shoulder my own sins with less guilt. If he truly loved her, and he knew I'd step aside quietly, the engagement could be dissolved without much discomfort.

"I never was much use at keeping secrets from you," he said. "All the better for you when we're married. Madeleine is a lovely girl, and a kind one. I do care for her. It would have taken a far stronger man than I to master his feelings under the circumstances. But it honestly doesn't matter, my dear. Once the dust settles and we all go home, we'll go back to the way things were."

I felt a wave of nausea. The idea of going back home to Mother's ministrations and the inner sanctum of Philadelphia society made me queasy with grief. That all of them could escape the war so little changed, that the war may have been for nothing, was a tragedy that dwarfed all the personal losses we'd endured.

"I'll want to be married as soon as we can manage," Nathaniel continued. "It may mean a simpler celebration than Mother might have hoped for, but I think simplicity is best, given the times, don't you?"

"Of course," I replied absently. He wasn't wrong. I could no more stomach a lavish society wedding than my own execution. The very thought was perverse. A glimpse of all the arguments with Mother that lay in store flashed before my eyes. She'd be devastated at the prospect of scaling back on her dream wedding.

"Are you certain, Nathaniel? Is this what you want? Am *I* what you want?" I prayed for him to reconsider. Prayed that the war had given him an excuse to value his happiness above more practical concerns.

"Of course, my dear. War could never change that."

"It has changed everything, Nathaniel. There's no use in pretending it hasn't."

He met those words with a piercing silence.

"What about Madeleine?" I insisted. "You don't have to say a word. I can see in your eyes that she means a great deal to you. More than I do." I could picture all too clearly how her special attentions to his injuries had led to stolen caresses, stolen kisses when they thought no one could see them under the cover of night. A proper fiancée would have been riddled with jealousy, but I felt only gratitude toward the woman who'd tended him.

"That's rather unfair. You and I have hardly had an unchaperoned moment together. I learned more in the course of one evening about the workings of Madeleine's heart than I have been permitted to learn about you. But it will be different. We'll be married and able to do what we please. We can fall in love later."

"Doesn't that seem backward to you? Shouldn't you marry the one you fall in love with?"

"That may work in some circles, Ruby, but not in ours. I'm only grateful you and I were thrown together so often and the idea of our marriage wormed its way into our mothers' heads. You've got more life and spark about you than the other girls from our set."

And how long before that spark succumbed to the torrents of convention? How long would I be able to withstand the constant deluge of my mother's expectations and his before I withered to become as meek as any of the old matrons who had long since let themselves be consumed by their husbands' identities? I was no reed lilting in the wind, but I wasn't made of steel.

"I won't try to break your spirit," he said, as if reading my thoughts. "I want you to be happy, truly. If you want to keep working at the phone company, I don't see why that would be a problem. At least until the children come. And even then, there's plenty you can still do to stay active. We'll have resources. You won't be chained to a stove."

He spoke the truth. In many ways, a marriage to Nathaniel was as clear a path to happiness as I could devise. He would never be unkind to me. He would dote on the children. There would be a great deal more sweeping, dishwashing, and penny counting as the wife of an aspiring doctor. But still the idea of being Nathaniel's wife, even with all the comforts of a gilded palace, did not fill me with the same glimmer of delight that it ought to have.

"I believe you," I said at length. "I believe you mean every word of that. I also think marrying me would break your heart and hers."

He rubbed his tired eyes with the tips of his fingers. "Hearts mend, Ruby. I won't go back on my word to you and your family. I couldn't live with the shame."

"You don't have any cause for shame," I said, trying to keep the desperation from my voice. "None at all. I can't say I've honored our engagement as much as I ought to have either. We could release each other from our obligation and be free to marry whom we please."

My confession hung heavy on the air. I could see the questions burning in his eyes, but he was too proud to voice them in such a public setting. It was to his credit I saw no flash of anger in them.

"A medic," I said. "He's from Brooklyn. He has plans to become a doctor. I've seen him work, Nathaniel, and I have no doubt he'll be a brilliant one."

"His name?" Nathaniel asked, his voice strained like a tourniquet over a wound.

"Andrew Carrigan," I said, resisting the fleeting temptation to hesitate or evade the question altogether. I knew the name of Nathaniel's darling; it seemed only fair he knew mine.

"And have you . . ."

"Yes," I said. "And me coming here to you has broken his heart."

"I wish I were a man with enough kindness in my heart to say I'm sorry for that, but I'm not," he said, turning his head away from me.

"Don't you think we're being foolish? You could take Madeleine home, marry her. Start up your veterans' center. With her nursing experience, she'd be a better helpmeet for you in that endeavor than I could ever hope to be."

Hope glimmered in his eyes for a split second, but it went out just as soon. "It's a lovely dream, Ruby, but it's just a schoolboy fantasy. Mother and Father would never welcome her as they should. The rest of their set would be even less kind. You know what the gossip is like. It would crush a sweet girl like her."

"She's spent the last year wading through blood, bone, and death to help us win the war, Nathaniel. You're not giving her enough credit." The nurses in Chaumont had shown us no great affection, but they all had my loyalty. They were as vital as Pershing himself.

"Maybe you're right," he said, looking down at his hands.

"I know I am. You could be happy with her, Nathaniel. Don't throw that away."

"Do you really think this world of ours has changed so much?" he asked. "Do you think Mother and Father could come to accept her?"

"Who could refuse a war hero his happiness?" I countered. "I can't imagine anyone would have the gall to be unkind to her."

"And I suppose you'll go back to this medic of yours?"

"I hope so," I said, looking down at my hands and willing the threatening tears to stay at bay. "I've done a fairly thorough job of breaking his heart. But if he hasn't been transferred to the ends of the earth . . ."

"If he doesn't sweep you off your feet, then he's a fool and doesn't deserve you." He patted my hand. "I truly hope you find happiness, my dear girl."

"I hope you're right, Nathaniel. I ought to go. I'm taking up valuable space here. Tell your Madeleine you're taking her home as soon as you're discharged. If your parents don't welcome her with open arms, I'll talk sense into them myself."

"What I wouldn't give to see that," Nathaniel said with a weak grin. "Seeing you has been a breath of summer in an ugly gray winter, my dear. Pay your respects to Francis and get safely home as soon as you can. I hope you beat me there."

I kissed his forehead and swept down the aisle of the hospital, refusing to ignore the pain and suffering on either side. I met the eyes of the men, smiled at them when they smiled. I would not let them see me wince at the blood and gore that even the end of the war hadn't had the time to erase.

As I neared the door, a nurse with kind green eyes and a loose tendril of brown hair peeking out from her cap looked me up and down. Her hand fluttered to her stomach as though she was pained, but she turned away to attend to a patient with a splinted arm. I saw only the briefest glimpse of her delicate features and the figure she cut as she wended her way gracefully about the hospital administering relief to the wounded. She was lovely. Lovelier than I ever aspired to be. The sort of girl who, had she been born to different parents, would have been Nettie Morgan's pride and joy as a daughter-in-law.

Madeleine was stooped over, wiping with a mother's patience the brow of a man shaking with fever. I knew in my bones that she loved Nathaniel, and I hoped they would find happiness. More, I hoped they would find that Philadelphia had become a far more welcoming place in the time since we left.

CHAPTER 30

December 16, 1918

The train hobbled on from Boulogne-sur-Mer to Cambrai through battle-scarred lands that would bear the marks of our conflict long after our grandchildren and their progeny had passed away from this earth. It was just as well I hadn't thought to grab one of the familiar novels that I'd toted along with me or that I'd borrowed from the girls over the past months. No written words could have held my attention. Being alone with my thoughts proved to be a crueler form of torture than even the Central Powers could have devised for me. If only I'd been permitted to bring Margot with me for support, but servicewomen were afforded no such luxuries. God help me, I'd have even accepted Sadie Porter's company if it would have kept my mind from running free.

I'd broken the one promise I'd made to my parents before leaving for New York—that I would come home as soon as I was discharged from service and devote myself to becoming the ideal consort for Nathaniel. I'd cast aside my chance to become the woman Mother had groomed me to become.

In my mind I drafted the letter explaining the broken engagement a dozen times over. I was glad the want of paper and the jostling of the train made the task impossible, because I was no nearer to an acceptable letter after two hours than I'd been when I boarded. Would I tell Mother about Madeleine? Would Nathaniel resent me letting my parents in on the intimate details of his private life before he had the chance to inform his parents? Engagement or no, they weren't a family we could afford to slight.

There wasn't a doubt in my mind that Andrew would welcome me back into his arms at my first indication that I was free of Nathaniel, but would it be presumptuous to let on that we'd come to any sort of understanding?

So, what was left to include in the letter? *Dear Mother and Father, Nathaniel and I decided, while he was lying in agony on a hospital bed, not to be married. Never mind why, but we're very sure. Please let his mother know he'll most likely be well. Of course, it's never certain, but he seemed stalwart as always. All my best.*

Each variation proved more ridiculous than the last. I considered what the letter might look like if I were to tell them everything, only glossing over the private details concerning Nathaniel's indiscretions. I could tell them the man I wanted to marry was the poor eldest son of two working-class immigrants, a man who, despite a wealth of ambition, was years away from being what Mother and Father considered to be "well established" in the world.

I envisioned the poison-pen letter Mother might write. She'd tell me that I'd forgotten my promises to the family and remind me of all they stood to lose in the face of this broken engagement. Father would send a terse note saying I'd broken Mother's heart and ought to be ashamed of myself.

Worse than the thought of these letters was the realization that they might not come. That Mother and Father would cut me out of their lives, dismissing me as an ungrateful, willful child. They might decide to salvage what would be left of their reputation on the Main Line by making large donations to the right charities and creating their legacy through philanthropy instead of through their children.

The money didn't concern me. Every scenario I'd permitted myself to envision with Andrew involved scrimping by to get started. But to think that I'd never again be welcome in my parents' house. To think I'd never again be granted entry into my father's study for a quiet evening of reading. Even the thought of never hearing my mother offer some biting criticism pierced me.

But for all of this, I couldn't bring myself to get off the train, reverse my course, and beg Nathaniel to reconsider. For years duty and obligation had constricted around my chest like one of Mother's damned cinchers. Once Nathaniel released me, my lungs felt truly full for the first time since the carefree days I spent as a girl romping along the river with Francis. I couldn't face life bound to a man I didn't love—even one as admirable as Nathaniel.

⸻

The cemetery for the Americans killed in action near the Somme was still in its infancy. They'd begun interring the bodies the month before, and it wouldn't be long before the rolling hills were a sea of white markers. One of the soldiers charged with overseeing the burial of his brothers-in-arms directed me toward the sector of the graveyard where I might be able to find Francis, if indeed they'd managed to place his stone.

I walked for more than a quarter of an hour in a light, swirling cloud of snow before I reached the first corner of the graveyard, where the earliest American deceased had been laid to rest. I burrowed into my thick woolen coat as I scanned the names. Peters, Johns, Thomases . . . Smiths, Browns, Wilkes . . . Sergeants, lieutenants, corporals. A flurry of dates from earlier in the year and a few dozen from the year prior, when Francis was killed. I half hoped I wouldn't see his name. That his tall, lanky frame would amble over the hillside with his lopsided grin and mop of curls peeking out from his service cap. I pictured him grabbing me in his arms and twirling me about like we did when we were young. I could take his hand in mine and get him on the first ship home to Evangeline and Mother and have no regrets about anything that had happened in the last year.

But tucked in the farthest corner, I found his name. Francis Charles Wagner. His rank and regiment, and the date he was killed: November 30, 1917. Despite the cold and snow, I sat next to the white marble marker and stared at the letters until they no longer made sense. I felt the breath lodged in my throat, and I tucked my knees into my chest until it finally came rattling out with a violent heave. I removed my glove, reached up, and traced the inscription's disjointed lines and curves with the tip of my index finger. The cold, unyielding marble was another reminder that his warmth was gone from this world.

"I've missed you, Francis," I said once I found my voice. "Do you have any idea how many times I've wanted to talk to you over the past year? I can't exactly tell Mother and Father about Andrew. Nathaniel. All of it. They won't understand what the girls and I have done. I'm going to go home and have to pretend that nothing has changed. And it all has, Francis. All of it. And you've left me alone to hobble along on my own. Did you really have to go and be a hero?"

I leaned my forehead against the frigid stone and shut my eyes against the permanence of the words inscribed on it.

"Mother and Father are crushed, you know. And Evangeline . . . Well, she can tell you herself." From my breast pocket I pulled Evangeline's letter, wrinkled from the months of transport across the ocean and from post to post. I laid it against the base of the stone, where it would lie, forever sealed. I hadn't violated their privacy, and now no one would read Evangeline's heartbroken goodbyes to the man she would always love. The snow would turn the ink into black tears that would seep down into the earth. I hoped Francis could somehow read them, but even if he couldn't, I had to think he knew Evangeline was steadfast in her devotion to him.

What a comfort it would have been to him.

Not for the first time since Evangeline's confession, I indulged in the fantasy of what life might have held for Evangeline and Francis. A tasteful wedding with only our most intimate acquaintances. It would be arranged without Mother's help until the very end, at which point she'd swallow her pride and add the layer of style she always brought to such things. Francis would work with Father to shore up the future of the company. He and Evangeline would live a few streets over in one of the smart little houses where couples of not-yet-considerable means started out. Within a few years, they'd welcome a babe or two and move closer into the heart of the Main Line with the rest of us. Mother and Father would be reluctant at first, but they would have grown to love Evangeline as their own. It wouldn't stop Mother from dropping hints that Evangeline came from an old, respectable family of recently reduced circumstances, but that was her way.

Then I thought of Nathaniel's words about his family's reaction to Madeleine and wondered if all of this was just a fairy tale I'd spun for myself. Mother would have railed against Francis's marriage to Evangeline, of that I was certain. Would Father have been able to talk him out of an alliance that would have denied the family—and the business—the advantages of marrying into one of Philadelphia's grand families? I could imagine the row. It would have been heard as clear as a bell, even in the far reaches of my bedroom. It would have been a hard life for Evangeline, but none of it would have mattered to her. She would have done her best to charm my parents into acceptance and let her children do the rest of the work.

I tried to think what Francis would have done, and there was only one outcome. He never would have wavered in his devotion to

Evangeline, no matter what the consequences were to himself or the family.

And once more, even in death, Francis proved to be my superior. I'd shown no such devotion to either Nathaniel or Andrew, and the shame of it tore at me like the vicious December winds.

I pressed my lips to the stone, traced his name with my fingertips one last time, and stole the courage to stand up and face a future I still had to dig out for myself from the battle-torn soil beneath my feet.

CHAPTER 31

Christmas Day, 1918

Christmas in Paris was simultaneously the most subdued and exuberant I'd ever seen in my life. Though I'd just come from several days' leave, there were more than enough operators to tend to the light traffic we had on a holiday in peacetime. Peacetime. How glorious the word sounded. Though I longed to seek out Andrew, after visiting Francis's grave and breaking with Nathaniel, I couldn't bear learning that he'd already been transferred or had come to think of our night together as a mistake. Perhaps after the holidays I'd be able to face those possibilities, but there was something comforting about holing up in the kitchen with Mrs. Grant.

Together we had procured all manner of good things for our Christmas feast, even a fatted goose with a chestnut stuffing. It filled the kitchen with an aroma I wished I could bottle for perfume. I was no great hand in the kitchen, but I'd rectify that when I got home. If Evangeline was still willing, I'd take the opportunity to learn more from her when my schedule at the phone company allowed. For now, I whipped potatoes and chopped vegetables under Mrs. Grant's direction and tried to make myself useful where I could or, at the very least, not botch her efforts with my lack of skill.

"What magic have you done now?" I asked, finding a bag in the pantry that had to hold at least five pounds of precious white flour.

"I've earned the gratitude of the mess hall, plain and simple," Mrs. Grant said with a wink. "I'd thought to make a fruitcake for you all."

"I have another idea. Will you allow me to make the dessert?" I asked, grateful to find a few oranges in her precious stores.

She turned to me with her head cocked to the side. "Are you sure, dearie? You say you aren't much for the kitchen, and I can't abide wasted flour."

"I promise it will be brilliant," I said. "And you can watch over my shoulder the whole time."

In one of my few lessons at Evangeline's side, I'd learned to make goldenrod cake. She had pronounced my efforts respectable, and Mother and Father had never noticed they weren't from Evangeline's more practiced hand. It was a simple cake made with the usual eggs, flour, sugar, and baking power that was flavored with a hint of orange juice. It was baked into little triangles that were as golden and fluffy as the name suggested and were topped with a simple orange icing. The sweet-tart tinge of the orange cake mingling with the savory, spiced aroma of goose and chestnuts transported me home to the hearth. Papa would be sitting with his pipe, overseeing the opening of presents. Mama would fret over our church clothes until she drove the lot of us to distraction.

But not this year. Mother would have busied herself with the church bazaar and making baskets for the needy on top of her duties for the Red Cross. Papa would hole up in his library, working until his body forced him to sleep. I hoped Evangeline would make them a nice meal. I hoped that she'd join them in the family pew at church, that they would find some way to make merry now that the long war had ended.

When I pulled the cakes from the oven, Mrs. Grant covered her astonishment at the success creditably. "It's a sight to behold, if I do say so myself," she pronounced as we set all the fruits of our labor on the dining table in anticipation of the girls' return. We'd rustled up some evergreen boughs for the table and lit low white candles wherever we could find a space for them. The soft glow made the bulbs of the simple wineglasses shimmer like fine crystal. That night, in our home, there was no sign of the war. I clasped Mrs. Grant's hand in mine and blotted away tears with my flour-streaked apron.

Right on time, the girls bounded in, bursting with the energy of children ready to light into their presents.

"My God, you've managed to summon a feast fit for a king," Addie breathed.

"For queens," Mrs. Grant corrected. "And I know of no ladies who deserve a fine meal better than my girls."

"You're a wonder, Mrs. Grant," Margot said, closing the door behind her. "I hope you don't mind, I've brought a guest."

Andrew emerged from behind her at the entryway. I gripped the chair in front of me to steady my hands, but there was nothing I could do for the beating of my heart that I was sure the whole room was able to hear thudding against my breastbone.

"Lieutenant Carrigan is always welcome anywhere I'm keeping house," Mrs. Grant proclaimed. "Ruby dear, why don't you fetch him the spare chair from the kitchen."

I ducked back into the kitchen, Andrew following in my wake. "Let me carry it," he said before the door closed behind him. He gently took my elbow and lowered his tone. "I'm so sorry, Ruby. Margot wasn't taking no for an answer."

"It's perfectly fine," I said. "Christmas dinner without guests doesn't seem like Christmas."

The expression on his face softened. "You have flour on your cheek. It's not your best look, but it suits you." He reached up with his thumb to wipe it away. For a moment it looked as though he was going to lean in, but he took a step back.

"How was your Nathaniel?" he asked.

"Tolerably well, I suppose. Putting on a bit of a brave face, I expect."

"Seems like a typical man. Eager to get home and tie the knot, is he?"

"I wouldn't say 'eager' is the right word," I said. "But it was certainly what he—and everyone else—expects."

"A good, solid lad from a good, solid family. Of course it's what they want."

"I told him about us, you know," I confessed.

"He's not going to come to Paris to defend your honor in a duel, is he?" he asked. "I'm a terrible shot. There's more than one reason I went into the medical corps."

"Unlikely. I got to see the young nurse who'd caught his fancy."

"What are you saying?" Andrew asked, taking a step nearer.

"He's in love with her. He wants to go home and create a center of sorts to help veterans convalesce. I convinced him that she would be a better partner for the venture than I would." I let out a ragged breath. "He thinks that our circle will never accept her. Or you, for that matter. He said it would be cruel to try."

"I don't care about such things, and neither does she if she truly loves him."

"That's what I told him," I said. "I hope he takes her home and makes good on his ideas."

"So it's over between you?" he whispered.

"Yes," I said. "He wanted to go through with the wedding, but I didn't want him to make the same mistake I did. I care enough about him to want him happy."

He closed the gap between us in a single stride and scooped me up in his arms. His lips came down to mine, and I savored his kiss like it was the last sip of water in the Sahara. He held me to his chest, stroking my hair.

"It's not going to be easy," I said, looking up. "I hope I'm mistaken about what my parents will say, but I don't think I am."

He leaned down and kissed me tenderly. "So long as I have you in my life, I couldn't care a whit about what anyone says, except for your sake. I don't want to alienate you from your parents, but I'm no saint, Ruby. If you love me, I'll do what I can to make them want me as a son-in-law."

"I love you, Andrew," I said, burying my face in his chest.

I felt his arms tremble around me and the breath catch in his throat as he stepped back to kneel in front of me.

"Ruby Wagner, will you please do me the honor of becoming my wife?" He pulled a small box from his breast pocket and opened it to reveal a small aquamarine ring. The center stone was round, flanked by two smaller stones set in filigreed silver.

Unable to speak, I nodded enthusiastically, then pulled him back to his feet.

"You'll think I'm a fool, but I saw this in a shopwindow the morning before you left for Boulogne. The shop wasn't open yet, but I knocked on the window until the shopkeeper had no choice but to open the door for me. I told him it matched the eyes of the girl I wanted to marry and that I had to have it. The sentimental old man all but gave the thing to me. I wasn't sure I'd ever have the chance to give it to you, but I hoped."

"You had it with you when you drove me to the station?" I whispered.

"I couldn't give up hope on us. I don't think I have it in me to stop loving you, Ruby." His lips closed over mine once more, and I reveled in his closeness until a loud clearing of a throat brought us back to our senses.

"I thought it was taking you two an awfully long time to fetch a chair," Mrs. Grant said with feigned annoyance. "Don't tell me I'm going to have to chaperone you."

"I don't think you'll need to chaperone me with my fiancé," I said, unable to keep the smile from my face.

A burst of applause sounded from the next room, and the others, who'd obviously been listening to the whole affair, piled into the kitchen. The girls strained for a peek at the ring and shook Andrew's hand in congratulations.

We moved out to the table to celebrate with a proper feast, though I spent most of the meal with Andrew's hand in mine. I sampled every dish but felt too excited to eat my fill. Thankfully the others had brought their appetites.

"When will you have the wedding?" Eleanor asked between bites of goose and sautéed green beans. "After we're sent home?"

"We've been engaged for five minutes," I said with a giggle. "Hardly enough time to plan."

"And we've no idea when we'll be sent back as it is," Andrew supplied. "I hate to think of leaving things up in the air for months."

"You ought to be married in Paris," Margot suggested. "What a story it would be for your grandchildren."

Andrew blinked and made a few suspicious coughing noises at the idea of grandchildren. His eyes looked bright, and he gripped my hand tighter, daring to lean over and kiss my temple at the dinner table.

A quiet ceremony at the local registry office. No fussing by Mother. No endless lines of guests I barely knew.

"That's the best thing I've heard all day, save for Andrew's little question," I said, pointing to my ring. "I could have you all for my bridesmaids."

A general squeal of delight rose above the table, and I looked over to see Andrew's response.

"What do you say?" I asked Andrew. "It saves the headache of waiting for discharge."

"Are you sure you want to forgo the fanfare of a wedding back home?" he asked.

There certainly would be fanfare. Even if Mother despised Andrew, which she probably would on principle, she would still throw a lavish wedding. She'd never give the slightest hint that the family was anything less than unified. But I'd be subjected to her forlorn sighs and backhanded comments at every turn. *If only you were marrying Nathaniel, you'd be moving into a proper house of your own. If only you were marrying Nathaniel, you'd be able to give up your work at the phone company.* That I enjoyed my work, that I would gladly live in a shoebox with Andrew, would make no difference.

"I'm certain," I said. "I'd rather be married with our friends, so long as you don't think *your* parents will mind."

"Not at all," Andrew said. "We'll give Mama the opportunity to throw us a grand party without all the trouble of an actual wedding."

"Then it's settled," I pronounced. "Set the date, my love, and I'll be at the registry office waiting." Despite hours mulling it over on the train, I still hadn't decided what I would put in the telegram to Mother. I would contrive something when the deed was done, and I hoped she'd find a measure of understanding within her.

"Before the New Year," Andrew said. "If we can manage it. Let's end this horrible year on the happiest note we can."

CHAPTER 32

December 30, 1918

The one thing I could tell Mother about the wedding that she wouldn't find fault with was my wedding gown. Andrew had set about obtaining permission for us to marry from his commander and getting the proper license for us from the French authorities, and I was left to plan the humble wedding by myself—though with the help of a half dozen of the most enthusiastic bridesmaids that ever held the office. I had thought to marry in my uniform like any other soldier, but Margot had grander ideas.

"The other girls and I have a little gift for you," Margot announced, entering our bedroom the afternoon before the wedding. "We weren't sure we'd be able to 'pull it off,' as you say, so I kept it as a surprise."

She held out a large flat box and passed it to me with a smile on her face. "We all pitched in for it," she said as I pulled at the ribbon.

Nestled in sheets of peau de soie paper was a creamy satin dress. I held it up to the light to admire the good French stitching and the cunning cut of the silhouette. It would sit a few inches higher than my uniform skirt, but it seemed to be what the girls were wearing these days. I'd spent so long behind a switchboard and in uniform, I'd not had a spare thought for the latest trends in cuts and fabrics, and I couldn't say I'd missed it all that much.

"You like it?" Margot asked. "It was rather a bit forward of us to buy your wedding gown for you, but time was short, and we were worried you wouldn't get to it."

"Oh, Margot, it's a marvel," I said. "I couldn't have picked a more perfect dress if I had a year and a king's ransom. I thought I'd be married in my uniform."

"No. I could not stand for it. It is one thing for a man, but you want to have pretty memories, no? You have been a soldier for many months, but that should not be true on your wedding day."

"You're probably right," I said, though I wasn't sure if I agreed. If we had an emergency at the office, we'd all be called in, wedding or not. If that didn't make a soldier, I wasn't sure what would. I ran my fingers over the thick satin and felt my throat tighten. "You're the most thoughtful girls in the whole world."

"We have more for you," Addie called from the door. Eleanor and Vera followed in. They produced a lace veil, lovely white shoes, and honest-to-goodness white silk stockings.

"Did you rob a dress shop?" I asked, shaking my head. "Never mind, I don't want to know if you did. If you all get arrested, I'll take it back after the wedding."

"Sensible," Eleanor said. "If we're going to rot in a French jail cell, it might as well have been worth it."

The girls set to work, divesting me of my uniform and dressing me like a doll in my new finery "to make sure it fit." I suspected their motives were far less utilitarian than ensuring the dress wouldn't need alterations, but I couldn't deny them the first lapse into feminine frivolity any of us had enjoyed in months.

"You're perfect," Eleanor breathed. "Like a real model in a magazine." Addie fussed with my hair until the curls laid just right. "Not bad at all," she said. "I expect when he sees you coming down the aisle, he'll see reason enough to stay at the altar."

The girls' giggles carried on the air like champagne bubbles. "It only wants two things," Margot said. She produced a pale-blue sash, the same color as my engagement ring, from the dress box and affixed it around my waist. She then produced a delicate embroidered handkerchief that was yellowed with age but clearly well cared for.

"To borrow only," she explained. "It was my *maman*'s. She said it always brought her good luck, which is why she sent it with me. She had a long and happy marriage, and I am sure you will too."

I lost the battle to restrain my tears and enveloped her in a hug.

"*Ma foi*, I didn't mean for you to use it immediately," Margot chided, dabbing at her own eyes.

"You're sure you won't be sad not to have a big church wedding with all your family and friends?" Addie asked, standing beside me, adjusting my veil. She loved hearing my tales of the society weddings in Philadelphia and all the social gatherings Mother lived for.

"More certain than you know," I said, indulging in a moment's vanity and admiring how the cream lace lifted the color in my face. "I'll have all the family I need right with me. I wish Mother, Father, and Evangeline could be here, of course, but it seems greedy to ask for more than what I'm already getting."

"Andrew is a lucky man," Eleanor said. "A smart, capable girl from a good family? He couldn't do better."

"I'm the lucky one, Ellie," I said, adopting the nickname I'd heard Addie use on occasion. "I almost let him go, simply to please my family. Fifty years of discontent would have been a just reward for such shortsightedness, I think."

"Thank goodness you woke up, *ma chère*," said Margot. "I was tired of coming up with excuses to bring him to dinner. It was becoming rather tiresome. Thankfully Mrs. Grant was always happy to indulge my little schemes."

"What on earth do you mean?" I said, turning to her.

"From the afternoon he came to dinner at the house in Chaumont, pretending his only business was collecting that letter for the poor boy's mother, I knew you were taken with each other. I've not had to work this hard at helping a match along in my life."

"If you try to match up engaged women, it does complicate things."

"Well, if love were simple, it wouldn't be nearly this exciting."

~

The wedding party met at the registry the following morning, some of Andrew's chums from the medical corps there to stand as his groomsmen, and my operators standing up with me as my bridesmaids.

Andrew offered me his arm and bent down to brush his lips against my cheek. "If this is all a dream, I beg you, don't wake me."

I pinched his arm playfully. "You're wide awake . . . Are you sure you want to do this? It's a lot easier to back out of a wedding in your dreams."

"You bet your sweet life, my darling girl."

The registry office hummed with life, as the people of Paris began to rebuild. Couples came to be wed, letters to be notarized, deeds to be transferred. We took our place in line until a crisply dressed older man whisked us aside.

"You are the young American couple who wish to be married?" he asked in thickly accented English.

"That's right," Andrew answered, gripping me closer to his side.

"*Très bien*, the mayor of our *arrondissement* is very pleased you have come. He would like to perform the ceremony himself if you have no objection."

"None at all," I said, my eyes widening. "It would be an honor."

"Come this way, please, then," the man said, leading us through two massive oaken doors that led to the mayor's private chambers.

The mayor—a short, stout man with an impressive mustache—spent several minutes thanking Andrew for his service and shaking my hand enthusiastically. He performed the ceremony so quickly, it wasn't until Andrew kissed me that I was truly aware that it had happened at all.

The medics all clapped Andrew on the back, congratulating him with good-natured ribbing. They would have had any passerby believe I was going to keep poor Andrew a miserable captive for the rest of his life, but he smiled.

Mrs. Grant spoiled us all with a luncheon feast that surpassed even our Christmas dinner, and the house was soon packed with well-wishers from every corner of the American forces stationed in Paris.

"I hadn't expected such a turnout," Mrs. Grant said, flitting about as she attempted to make sure there was refreshment in every glass and nourishment on every plate. "I don't think you needed to worry about missing out by having a quick city-hall wedding."

"I never did," I said with a smile. Andrew hadn't left my side since we'd taken our vows, and I delighted in the feel of my hand in the crook of his arm. "But I confess, I hadn't expected such a turnout myself."

"Celebrations have been so few since the war broke out, I think everyone is starved for a good party," Andrew suggested. "And you've cemented yourself as a top hostess in Paris society, Mrs. Grant. Of all your achievements during the war, I suspect that will be the one that gives you most pride."

She leaned up and kissed his cheek. "I always knew I liked you," Mrs. Grant said. "And I couldn't be happier for the two of you."

The party continued on into the afternoon, but as is wont to happen with military personnel, people were called back to their duties one by one, until only Andrew and myself remained along with Vera, Margot, and Mrs. Grant.

"We should have sent you off in a cascade of rice an hour ago," Vera said. "This isn't much of a farewell."

"It's perfect," I said. "It's all been perfect. I'm happy to have a few quiet moments with you. You gave me the wedding I should have been dreaming about my whole life. Thank you so much for all you've done."

"Now enough of this," Margot said. "You'll be back under this roof in a week. Though it's a shame you can't live as a married couple. It seems silly."

"We're soldiers first, spouses second," I replied. "And it's not like we'll be overseas indefinitely. The war is over, after all."

"Hear, hear," Mrs. Grant said. "You two enjoy your leave. Every second, do you hear?"

"Absolutely," I said, beaming. We all exchanged hugs, and Andrew and I piled into the tiny Peugeot graciously lent to us by a neighbor, Monsieur Ferrier, who was sympathetic to the cause of young love.

"A whole week alone with you," Andrew breathed as he shut his door. "I don't know what I've done to deserve it, but I'm all for clean living if you're the reward, Mrs. Carrigan." He paused on the words, letting them roll on his tongue like fine wine.

"You know how to flatter a girl, Mr. Carrigan," I said, placing my hand on his knee. I resisted the urge to pull it back. He was my husband now, and I could be as familiar as I liked.

"I plan to flatter you for the rest of your life," he said. "And particularly for the next twelve hours in our hotel room."

I giggled, the heat rising to my cheeks. We were to spend our wedding night at a little neighborhood hotel a few streets over, and then the rest of the week at a little resort outside Tours, where we could visit the chateaux and dine on rich cheeses and burgundy.

"It doesn't seem possible that we're going on vacation," I said.

"I know. It was just a few months ago we were staring into the jaws of the lion. My head is still catching up with it all, I have to admit."

It was the same for all of us. Still waking up in the middle of the night waiting for the *alertes*. Cringing at every loud noise. I wondered how we would all manage to reenter "normal" life when we were back home. It seemed so far away now, like a world I hadn't visited in a decade.

"You look awfully pensive for your wedding day, Mrs. Carrigan. A penny for your thoughts?"

"If you're willing to pay that much for them, I'll be managing the household accounts, dear husband."

Andrew replied with a laugh and lifted my knuckles to his lips. "I can tell you're thinking about something far too serious for the events of the day, Ruby. Out with it."

I took a long pause. "Do you think we could stop at the telegraph office before we go to the hotel?" I looked at my pocket watch: the telegraph office would likely remain open for another hour or more.

"What do you need there?"

"I want to wire my parents and tell them . . . tell them we've married." I'd nearly said *what I've done*, like I was confessing a misdeed. In truth, it would look that way in their eyes.

"You wouldn't rather wait until after the honeymoon for such a mundane task? There isn't really any rush."

"I know, but I'll enjoy the trip more knowing I don't have the chore waiting for me when we get back." And the sooner I told them, the less it would feel like I was hiding something from them.

"In that case, I insist," Andrew said, turning the car in the opposite direction from the hotel to the little office that sent civilian telegrams. It would cost a small fortune, but I'd saved the lion's share of my wages since I enlisted. I hoped it would be enough to give us a good start back home. We'd yet to discuss the logistics of where we would live and how we would make things work, but those discussions seemed still so very hypothetical.

We waited in line, and once we were presented with the form, the pen shook in my hand. How was I going to break this news to them? Andrew placed his hand on my back, quickly kissing my cheek as I pondered my message. I took a deep breath and began to form letters, slowly and deliberately, hoping the words I chose were the right ones:

> HAPPY TO ANNOUNCE MY WEDDING TO LT. ANDREW CARRIGAN OF BROOKLYN, NY, IN PARIS TODAY. LETTER SOON. RUBY CARRIGAN.

I wondered if Nathaniel had wired home to tell them we'd broken off our engagement. The wedding would come as a shock either way, but Nathaniel's letter might have served as a bit of warning. The letter I sent them after I'd visited Francis's grave was probably still on its way home, and it wasn't as direct on the subject of my ruptured engagement as it might have been. I shook my head at my own cowardice and handed the clerk my form and my money.

"I'll send one of my own," Andrew said, claiming a form. "I'd hate for my half of the family not to have their share of the good news." He scribbled his message far more quickly than I'd managed to do:

> MARRIED TO MISS RUBY WAGNER OF PHILLY, PA, TODAY. SO VERY HAPPY. LOVE TO YOU ALL, ANDREW AND RUBY.

His message was shorter, but he imbued it with far more affection than mine. Either he wasn't worried that they would disapprove of the wedding, or else he didn't care. I wasn't sure whether to envy his supportive family or his nonchalance, but now that the missives were on the way, I felt worlds lighter.

"That was a smart idea," Andrew said as we returned to the car.

"I think so. Now that Mother and Father know, I feel properly married."

"All the better. I want you to enjoy every bit of our trip. Who knows when we'll have another chance to explore castles and roam the French countryside?"

"A fair point, dear husband. But are you really sure it's the castles and countryside you want to explore?" I asked, winking at him as he turned into the parking spaces by the hotel.

"Another fair point, dear wife. Though I'm shocked at you, Mrs. Carrigan. So bold. So forward."

"Really, Mr. Carrigan? I rather thought you'd like it."

He leaned over, kissed down my neck, and reached under my uniform jacket to feel the soft curves it covered. "Oh, I do, my darling bride. I do."

CHAPTER 33

Tours in the spring would have been utterly magnificent, but it was lovely enough in winter that we didn't mind the chill. We brought our good boots for tromping through the snow, though as I predicted, we spent more time snuggled up in our little pension than we did in the great outdoors.

"A glass of wine for my darling bride?" Andrew asked. He reached for the open bottle that he'd perched on the bedside table after our light lunch of local cheese and a kind of pork pâté. Once we'd eaten our fill, I whispered in his ear that I was in need of a nap, and the wine sat forgotten.

He pulled my mouth down to his, and I fully expected him to lose himself in the kisses once more, but he pulled me to my feet. "Have another sip or two of wine if you like, and then get dressed. We should go for a walk before we grow stodgy."

"Blast you for being right so often," I said, wrapping myself around him before he could pull on his trousers.

"It's a blessing and a curse," he said. "Now get dressed so I can watch you."

I made a show of pulling on my union suit and stockings, slowly buttoning my blouse, and pulling up my skirt. It seemed the opposite of alluring, but he watched every move intently.

"I can understand watching me undress, but why this?" I asked.

"Because only I know what's underneath. Because you share it only with me. When you dress, you're saving that delicious secret just for me."

"That sounds a bit like a caveman, don't you think?"

"I can't help it, my darling girl. That you're mine is still the most remarkable fact I've ever had to wrap my head around. You'll have to forgive me."

"As if I could deny you anything," I said low, reaching up to kiss his ear. "Though if you don't hurry and get yourself dressed, I'm going to haul you back to bed."

"Now who's the caveman?" he chortled. He tossed on his own clothes, and we found our way to the car. The cold was bearable, and snow didn't seem likely, so we decided to brave our way as far as Chenonceau. It was a long drive, but the minutes passed by quickly. The frost-capped scenery was as enthralling in its blacks, whites, and grays as it would have been with the vibrant colors of spring. When we finally arrived at the castle, considerable chunks of ice floated along the River Cher. We stood on the gallery bridge that spanned the width of the river and watched them float by.

I felt revivified by the cold air in my lungs and the blood pumping in my veins, though the warmth of the entryway was welcome.

"Should we ask if we can go inside?" Andrew asked. "It would be quite the thing to say we've seen the inside of a real castle, don't you think?"

"I'm not sure they'd allow it," I said. "It's a home, after all. Even if it's an impossibly grand one."

"Where's your sense of adventure?" he said with a wink. He dragged me up to a surly-looking guard, American at that, and opened his mouth to ask about a quick walkabout inside, but we were waved in at once.

"The *grande galerie* was used as a hospital until last week, and they're still in the process of reassigning everyone," Andrew explained when we were out of earshot. "He saw my medic patch and assumed I had business here."

"Well, let's not make ourselves unwelcome," I said. "Let's take a stroll and go back before we get ourselves or the poor guard in trouble."

"Always the rule follower," Andrew chided. "I thought by marrying me, you'd shown your rebellious side, but I see I still have work to do."

"It would be frightfully dull if you didn't," I said, playfully nudging his ribs with my elbow.

We wandered the hallways for a while, Andrew occasionally slipping into medical talk when officers walked by. If they paid much attention to my uniform, they'd see I wasn't a nurse, but thankfully they seemed busy enough not to take notice of us much at all. We descended into the kitchens, which hummed with activity as the staff prepared food for the remaining troops that were awaiting their orders.

"It's like stepping back into history, isn't it?" I asked, pressed against a corridor wall, watching the cooks and maids rushing about, chopping vegetables with precision, and slinging about brimming-full copper pots as though they weighed no more than a dishrag. "If you put them in homespun wool, this could be Catherine de' Medici's kitchen. I swear I wouldn't be surprised to see her coming in to give a commandment about the menu."

"I'm sure old Catherine was good at that," Andrew mused. "You'd have made a great lady yourself, you know. You can command staff and organize a house just as well as any of the ladies who reigned here. You could have done it if you married Nathaniel, at least on a somewhat smaller scale."

I laughed. "No, even the great Morgans of Philadelphia couldn't claim holdings as grand as these. Though I could well imagine Nettie Morgan ruling over a place like this. A gracious woman like her would be right in her element here." I shook my head. "No, the only staff I want to manage is in the Central Office at Bell. Maybe a helping hand around the house when we're well and truly settled, but nothing more than that."

"I hope you always feel that way, my darling. I couldn't bear to see resentment grow to replace the love I see in your eyes."

"Andrew, the world is changing. Soon the lavish world my mother dreams of will be only a memory, and I'll be left with something far better than broken hopes and yearning for bygone days. I'll have you."

We soon retreated to the car and found the warmth of our bed long after dark had fallen on the Loire. I could tell Andrew's sleep was troubled. I hoped that in time I could convince him that the words I spoke were true.

A week ensconced in each other's arms passed by as quickly as a flap of a hummingbird's wings. We filled the back seat of the loaned car at first light on Monday morning to be able to return to Paris for duty that afternoon.

"I don't expect I'll ever get to see these places again," Andrew mused as the snow-blanketed countryside whizzed past. "A year ago I'd have called you crazy if you told me I'd be sorry for it."

"It's easier to see the charm of a place in peacetime," I said. "Patching up bullet holes doesn't leave much time for enjoying the scenery."

"That's the truth. Maybe we'll have the chance to come back before we ship back home."

"Maybe. And the world seems to be growing smaller every day. I don't think a return trip is as far-off a dream as you might think."

"You might be right, Ruby dearest," he said, his eyes looking out over the vista, not focusing on anything in particular.

"Don't spoil the last hours of our honeymoon by moping," I pleaded. "It's been the best week of my life, and I don't want to waste even a moment."

"Same for me, darling girl," he said, motioning for me to slide up next to him on the bench seat. "I suppose I'm just not ready for it to end."

I nuzzled up next to him on the drive, under the guise of needing his warmth, and drank in his musky scent. Though we'd only been married a week, I knew that I'd sleep poorly every night he wasn't at my side. His soft, even breathing was already my lullaby.

We returned Monsieur Ferrier's car to him and presented him with a heady bottle of red wine from the Touraine to add to his cellar. We walked back to the YWCA hotel, arms linked, before Andrew returned to the hospital.

"I should drop my things off and get to the office," I said after the third lingering kiss in plain view.

"And I should let you," Andrew replied after another kiss. "But I don't seem all that willing to cooperate with my well-intentioned half."

"I like your mischievous half better right now anyway," I said. I drew him in for a final kiss. "But that is for both of you."

I smiled at the skip in his step as he walked back to the street and off in the direction of the hospital. The hotel was empty, save for Mrs. Grant, who whisked me in and offered to prepare me lunch in exchange for a vivid description of the castle country.

"Over dinner, on my honor, Mrs. Grant," I told her. I knew she'd go to the ends of the earth to prepare a sumptuous luncheon, but I couldn't stand the idea of postponing my return to work. I'd do better to grab a sandwich and find my way to the switchboards before the urge to abscond with Andrew and begin our married life in earnest took over my more rational self. "I need to see how badly things have fallen apart in my absence." I winked, knowing that the girls were more than capable of running the place flawlessly without me by now.

"Only if you promise to bring your dashing husband around at every chance," Mrs. Grant said. "I may not be able to offer him houseroom, but I can at least allow you to dine together."

"If he can be spared," I promised, kissing her cheek. I stowed my valise in my room and trekked into the office, keeping up a quick pace against the biting cold.

The switchboards hummed with their usual activity, though all the girls managed to look up to give me welcoming smiles and waves when they saw me enter. I was just about to relieve Eleanor when Addie's hand clasped my shoulder.

"Major Jamison wants to see you," she said, referring to the commanding officer who oversaw the telephone group in Paris. She gave me a quick hug. "We're glad you're back."

The major had been called out on some urgent matter, but an officious-looking sergeant stationed at a desk in the corridor outside his office intercepted me.

"The major was expecting you back yesterday," he said, his tone clipped.

"My leave was through midday today," I said, supplying my papers, though the sergeant had no right to ask for them. "I'm back almost two hours early."

The sergeant looked peevish as he examined my paperwork. "He asked me to pass along these orders, if in fact you were good enough to grace us with your presence."

"Watch your tone, young man," I said. I would have been forced to accept cheek from the major, but not his staff. I took the orders from his hands and opened the sealed envelope.

CHIEF OPERATOR RUBY CARRIGAN (WAGNER) IS TO REPORT FOR DUTY IN COBLENZ, GERMANY, ON 12 JANUARY, 1919.

I scanned over the information about transportation and expenses en route to Germany and could not keep my hands from shaking. "This can't be right," I said. "I've only been in Paris for a few weeks. They can't be reassigning me so soon."

"You're not meant to question orders, Chief Operator Carrigan, merely to follow them."

"We'll see about that, you little maggot." I turned on the ball of my foot and marched down the corridor to where Major Jamison's supervisor, Colonel Davidson, kept his offices.

I didn't wait for the underling outside to give me permission. I rapped smartly on the glass-paneled door.

"Come in," his baffled voice called.

"I'm not going to Germany, Colonel," I announced without preamble. "There is plenty for me to do here in Paris, and I won't be transferred so far from my husband." Given the nature of Andrew's work, I couldn't imagine he'd been given a similar transfer. There were few injured Allied troops still in Germany, and the Germans were tending to their own.

"The United States Army cannot make allowances for married couples. There is no provision for it. We must operate by sending personnel where they are needed. That's how wars are won, Mrs. Carrigan." He folded his weathered hands over the thick piles of manila folders that lined his desk. "We need to maintain communications between the administration here in Paris and our people charged with upholding the armistice in Germany. It's vital work, and we expect you to take your assignments without complaint. I'm surprised, given your reputation heretofore, that this fact has escaped you."

"It has not, Colonel. Nor has it escaped me that the war has already been won. The role I played in that victory wasn't a small one, with all due respect. We have a number of skilled operators who have not had the opportunity to serve at the front. They would be thrilled to serve on the other side of enemy lines. I can give you the name of a half dozen girls from my own group, and I'm sure the other chief operators could do the same."

"The orders stand as they are, Mrs. Carrigan," the colonel said, unflinching. "You speak some German, and we have need of your skills."

I scoffed. My schoolroom German was laughable. "Very well, then I resign my post, effective immediately. I'll secure private quarters in Paris until my husband is discharged."

"Your request is denied, Chief Operator Carrigan," he said, reprising the use of my title. "I suggest you return home to pack. Your train departs in the morning."

I stormed from his office, not bothering to take a polite leave. I passed by the phone office, where I whispered the news of my transfer to Addie, whose eyes widened in surprise.

"What a horrible thing to do to you so soon after being married," she hissed.

"I can't disagree. Take care of things here. I don't expect they'll transfer me back anytime soon."

Rather than follow the colonel's orders to go home and prepare for my departure, I ran to the hospital. By the time I reached it, I was drenched with sweat despite the January cold.

"Miss, you're not allowed in here," a nurse told me, looking up and down my uniform and pursing her lips. "The hospital is for *medical* personnel only."

"I need to speak with my husband," I said. "Lieutenant Carrigan."

"He can't be bothered at the moment, miss," she said. "He has duties to attend to."

I rolled my eyes and barged past her. Andrew was indeed bent over a patient and listening to his heartbeat. He stood abruptly when I stormed in. The nurse tailed me in, but she changed her course when she saw the look on Andrew's face.

"What's wrong?" he said, his look assessing.

"I've been transferred to Germany," I said without making any attempt to soften the blow. "I leave in the morning."

He scooped me up in his arms. "Bastards," he muttered so low that none but I could hear him.

"I tried to resign my post, but they wouldn't let me," I said, wiping away tears I hadn't realized had sprung forth.

"I'm not surprised," he said. "They're in no hurry to send any of us home. They don't want to risk the armistice not becoming a proper peace treaty. Dr. McMurray was worried they'd transfer me after we were married. They've no experience dealing with married couples serving together, and separating us makes things less complicated for them. I just assumed it was me they'd be transferring."

"That's why you were so sullen this morning?" I asked.

"Yes. I didn't want to spoil the wedding or the honeymoon, so I kept it to myself."

"I don't know whether to shake you for it or kiss you," I said, burying my head in my hands.

He cradled me close to his chest. "Both if it makes you feel better. But I'm not sorry we married. They could have transferred us apart just for getting engaged. This way, at least the deed is done."

"True, though I wish you'd told me," I said. "If you think I need coddling, you haven't been paying attention."

"I know, sweetest. I kept it to myself just as much for my own sake as yours."

"I understand. But I hate everything about this."

"As do I. But it won't be forever. Just a few months at worst."

"It sounds like an eternity," I said. "But you're right, of course."

Dr. McMurray came over, took one look at us, and knew precisely what had happened. "Carrigan, why on earth did you report back from your leave a day early? Don't be a martyr. I'll see you back in the morning."

Though Mrs. Grant raised an eyebrow, she said nothing when Andrew followed me to my room. I opened my trunk and tossed in my summer uniform, extra blouses, and every knickknack I'd acquired in my months overseas. I made no effort to treat anything with care.

Andrew intercepted most of my wardrobe and folded it with precision. "I won't have you arriving among the Hun looking like a wrinkled heap," he chided as I tossed one of my skirts into the trunk.

"Very funny," I said. "But thank you."

"I hope you enjoy yourself," Andrew said, earnestly. "Look at the assignment as an adventure. And a chance to make sure this peace lasts."

"Stop being so rational," I said, shaking my head. "I want to be angry right now."

Andrew closed the lid of my trunk now that all my belongings were inside it. I'd not even bothered to unpack my valise from the honeymoon—it would go to Germany exactly as it was. I expected the Germans would have laundry much the same as the French.

"Be angry if you wish," he said, taking a seat on my bed and pulling me down to his lap. "I have other feelings I'd rather explore."

"Mrs. Grant—" I began.

"Is a married woman and knows exactly what we're facing. She'll be happy to give us our privacy. And I expect Margot won't mind bunking with one of the others tonight. They can court-martial me if they want—I'm sleeping in the same bed as my wife tonight."

I curled my head against the nape of his neck, nuzzling softly.

"I'm going to miss you so much," I whispered into the soft curve of his skin.

"Not until tomorrow you won't," he said, covering my mouth with his.

I melted in his arms, and for a few short hours, there was no room left for anger in my heart.

CHAPTER 34

May 21, 1919
Coblenz, Germany

The end of the war meant a slow work schedule for all of us, and though I'd wished for quieter times when we were facing eighteen-hour days at the front, I found it maddening now. I wouldn't mind quiet afternoons, concocting meals and mending uniforms for Andrew in a little pied-à-terre in Paris or back at home, though I'd miss my work. But being trapped in Germany with precious little to do and Andrew so far away gnawed what was left of my patience thin.

I was able to leave work at four in the afternoon that day and was looking forward to a few hours out in the tentative spring sun before dinner. I'd walked every street in Coblenz over the past five months, probably a dozen times over. My wanderings were the thing that gave me peace when I could no longer keep my mind from lingering on how much I missed Andrew, Margot, and the girls I'd worked with for so many months. I longed for home too. Father, Mother, Evangeline . . . even Mother's endless parade of society friends. The one blessing of the war was that we'd been far too busy to pine for home much before now.

I stepped from the office door and nearly square into Margot, who wore a travel-rumpled uniform and a grim expression. I threw my arms around her and kissed both of her cheeks French-style.

"I'm so glad you're here!" I said. "Please tell me you've been transferred here. It's been so dull without you."

"I'm here to stay," Margot said, returning my embrace. "The driver has already taken my things to the YWCA house."

"How wonderful! I'm surprised they sent you, though," I said. "We haven't so much work that it requires another supervisor. But no matter, I'm just glad you're here. Let's get you something to eat, and you can tell me what I've missed. The Germans don't try to welcome us like the French, not that I expected them to. They walk past us like we don't exist."

"Can they make a decent cup of coffee, even for invisible American telephone operators?" Margot asked, her expression wary.

"It's not as good as the French, but a darn sight better than the swill we had at the front."

"*Bon*, I can live with that." She looked as though she were making a noble sacrifice. "Take me to the nearest café if you have any love at all for your old friend."

A couple of weeks before, the girls and I had found, not far from the office, a *Konditorei* that had reopened its doors and was serving respectable coffee and cunning little cakes that would be remarkable once the baker had proper ingredients once more. I ushered Margot there, and she promptly ordered two slices of cake and a coffee for herself. One slice was bright and frothy, made of apricot mousse and cream; the other was dark and rich, a dome of butter cake with cherries bathed in chocolate. She savored her first bite, a look of sheer bliss passing over her face.

"Long trip, I take it?" I asked, taking a bite of my own apple-and-marzipan pie.

"Interminable," she replied. "I haven't had more than one dry sandwich since I left Paris at an ungodly hour this morning."

"I'm so glad you're here. It's been awful without you. It's not that the girls aren't lovely, but it's not the same. Did they give you a reason for the transfer?"

"I insisted on it. And as it happens, I'm a difficult woman to refuse."

"Don't I know that. But it's good of you. I'm sure you were having a much happier time in Paris than you'll have here."

"My reason for coming wasn't merely to keep you company." She set down her cup of coffee and looked at her hands. "I'm afraid I have bad news for you."

"A-Andrew?" I managed to stammer. I could feel the blood drain from my face.

"No, your beloved is well. He sent me this for you." She reached into her handbag and pulled out a small parcel. Inside was a simple silver locket in the shape of a heart with finely etched filigree, not unlike the one in my jewel box back at home that Nettie Morgan had given me before I left. I opened it to find a picture of Andrew and me on our wedding day. The accompanying note said, *A belated wedding gift for my darling bride. Love, Your Andrew.*

"He shouldn't spend his money on such things," I said with a sigh. "Though it's lovely."

"One should not begrudge a man the pleasure of spoiling his wife."

"So, what is this bad news?" I said, affixing the locket around my neck, ignoring regulations. The chance of anyone inspecting us out here was remote, and rules had been relaxed since the treaties had been signed.

"It's your father," Margot said. "The telegram was misdirected to the YWCA house in Paris. We decided it was best to open it." She pulled the yellowed envelope from her handbag and handed it to me. "I hope you don't mind."

"Not at all," I said. I scanned the words several times, trying to absorb meaning from them.

MAY 12, 1919

YOUR FATHER DIED OF A HEART ATTACK LAST NIGHT.
FUNERAL PLANS UNDER WAY FOR NEXT WEDNESDAY.
YOU ARE NEEDED HERE. MOTHER.

The message was terse, but I could not fault my mother for it. There was no graceful way to give such news in a telegram. It was botched often enough in person. I placed the shaking missive into my own handbag and reached for my coffee but thought better of it and placed the cup back on the saucer before I could scald myself.

"I'm so sorry, Ruby," Margot said. "Andrew wanted to come, but they wouldn't spare him. There's no work for him here. And we hoped that if I came, they might let me replace you. To his credit, Jamison agreed to transfer me on the spot, though he couldn't guarantee your discharge."

"My father's funeral is today," I said, calculating the date from the telegram. "I won't be able to be at my own father's funeral."

Margot took my hand. "I know how special he was to you. I wish I could do something to make this better."

"You've done so much already," I said. "You crossed an entire country."

"Not a huge one," she said with a wink. "France is what, maybe twice the size of Colorado? That doesn't sound quite so impressive, does it?"

I smiled despite myself, wiping my damp cheeks. "Can we please go home?"

"Of course," she said. Unwilling to waste food in troubled times, she boxed up the uneaten cake in a small carton procured from the girl who ran the counter, and led me out into the street.

As soon as I entered my little room at the YWCA, I collapsed onto the bed, my knees having used up the last of their strength. Margot curled up behind me and held me and brushed the hair from my face. I waited for the tears to come but found myself hollow.

"What can I do?" Margot asked. "Anything at all."

"You're doing it," I said slowly, deliberately. My tongue felt as though it had been replaced by a stone brick, and the effort to even form words was Herculean.

"I lost my papa too, you know," Margot said. "Just two years ago. I remember the night after he died, my *tante* Isabelle came from Trois Rivières to be with us. She asked me what would ease my sadness. The only thing I could think of was for her to read to me from his little book of La Fontaine's fables that had been in the family for generations. No matter how tired Papa was from cutting lumber, he always had the patience for one more story when he put us to bed. Hearing the words he recited so many times was the greatest comfort I could have asked for."

"That's sweet," I managed to utter, weaving my fingers in hers. "You're kind like your *tante*."

"I never forgot her kindness that night," Margot agreed. "So when you realize what may give you comfort, you tell me."

I nodded in response but said nothing. There was something wholly unnatural about living in a world where my father was gone. I'd received a short note from him in response to my telegram before the honeymoon. It was the sort of formal congratulations one might send a colleague:

> *Congratulations on the occasion of your marriage.*
> *Regards,*
> *Paul Wagner*

Knowing Father the way I did, this was his way of acknowledging my choice, even if he didn't approve. He might have preferred

Nathaniel, but I couldn't think my change of heart would have caused undue strain on him. I clung to this.

I'd heard nothing from Mother, Nathaniel, or Nettie Morgan, not that I'd expected to. I'd written to Nathaniel and his mother to spare them the shock of me arriving home a married woman, and I'd hoped it was a kindness.

"Margot, you d—" I stammered. I buried my face in my hands for a moment to calm my breath. "You don't think my marriage could have caused my father to—"

"Non," Margot interrupted, gripping my hand in hers. "Absolutely no. He didn't keel over in January when he got your telegram. I should think he had plenty of time to get over the shock. He knew you were happy, and at the end of it all, I can't imagine what more a father could hope for his daughter."

"I need to get home to my mother," I said at length. "She'll be glad for my company, I'm sure of it."

"We'll set to work on that tomorrow," she said. "I promised Andrew I'd do what I could to get you home."

"It's so strange. I spent weeks and weeks doing everything in my power to get over here, and now I'd do the same to go home."

"Our job is done," she said simply. "And none of this was worth it if going home wasn't the objective all along."

Margot spent every spare minute advocating for my discharge to anyone who would listen. She brought me all the official forms and sent a telegram to my mother to let her know my whereabouts and my efforts to return, but she insisted that I keep up my duties at the switchboard for at least half a shift every day. At first, I resented her tactics, but I came to recognize it was the only thing keeping me from losing more hours in the confines of my bed than was healthy.

Three weeks later, the discharge papers came. I would be back in Philadelphia in three weeks.

Home.

Three days after my discharge papers arrived, Margot and I waited for the train at the Coblenz *Hauptbahnhof* in the early hours of the morning. I saw the train growing larger on the horizon, and I pulled Margot into a monstrous hug. "I owe you everything."

"Bah, I only did what was right," she said. "Though it would have been smarter of me to be selfish and keep you here."

"There is nothing selfish about you. Do you promise that you'll write? And come see Andrew and me when you're discharged?"

"You have my word, *ma chérie*. And don't forget the post works both ways, *non*?"

I kissed both her cheeks and boarded the train as the whistle sounded. I watched her figure grow small until Coblenz faded into the distance and I set my eyes toward Paris.

Hours later, Andrew was waiting on the platform, his eyes wildly scanning the crowd until they locked with mine.

"My darling girl," he said, sweeping me into his arms and lowering his lips to mine despite the onlooking crowd.

"I'm here," I said, gathering breath. My hands followed the contour of his rough uniform jacket, his arms solid, real beneath my touch.

Andrew pulled me close and cupped my head with his hand. "I'm so very sorry about your father."

The realization that Andrew would never get to meet him, nor would our children, gripped me afresh, but I refused to entertain the thoughts during our short time together. I had to be at the Gare Montparnasse on the other side of Paris in three hours to catch the train to Brest that would take me to the ship.

"I should be taking you with me," I muttered against his chest.

"I'll follow as soon as I can. It won't be long now, I have to think. We've got fewer and fewer men to treat, thank God. Consider it a chance to catch up with your mother before I get in the way." His optimism was enough to make me smile, but getting all our men back home was a tremendous undertaking. Even the biggest ships carried only several thousand men. It would be months before we were all home, and it didn't seem the government was eager to leave the Central Powers unsupervised.

"You could hardly be in the way," I said, taking his arm so he could lead me to the car.

"I'm glad you think so, my love."

The sights of Paris whizzed by as Andrew navigated the winding streets, but my eyes were fixed only on his face. It wasn't Paris's graceful architecture, the imposing churches, the tree-lined streets, or the spires of the Iron Lady I wanted to embed in my memory, but rather the curve of Andrew's jaw, the angle of his nose, and the precise shade of his velvet-brown eyes that I wished I could embroider into my heart.

Andrew took me to a little brasserie outside the train station for a lunch of grilled trout I could hardly eat. He, too, ate without much enthusiasm, preferring to wrap his arm around me and brush kisses against my forehead and cheeks.

"Where do you want to live?" I asked, playing with some of the flaky fish with the tines of my fork. "We haven't got anything like a plan."

"I know," he said. "And it feels unsettling, irresponsible even, but I'm not sure how we can do much until we know when I'll be home."

"I want an idea at least. Do you want to be near your family or mine? Somewhere else entirely?"

"I'll go where it makes you happy. The moon if you insist."

"I don't think there are many medical schools on the moon," I said with a sidelong glance. "And if there were, I don't think the anatomy lessons there would transfer all that well to your human patients."

"Fair point," he said. "But it doesn't matter. Medical school can wait until we're established and have a home."

"No. It will never happen if you don't do it as soon as you get back. You'll get busy in your father's shop, or whatever job you take on, and before you know it we'll be tied down with houses and babies and there's no way we'll be able to send you."

"You make a good case, but I don't see another plan."

"I'll work; you study. We'll be careful about babies until you have your MD and a practice up and running."

"I can't allow you to put me through school," Andrew said, playing with the frayed edge of his napkin. "How could I hold my head up?"

"Proudly," I said, cupping his face in my hands so he couldn't avoid my eyes. "Because you're a big enough man to sacrifice pride for what matters."

Andrew responded with silence.

"Now that we've decided that, where?" I continued.

"University of Philadelphia has as good a medical school as a body can find," he said. "It would mean less of an uprooting for you."

"I'm as uprooted as a person can get," I said. "I don't need to be replanted in the same garden. Aim high. What's your dream?"

"Johns Hopkins," he said. "The things they're doing there are revolutionary."

"Baltimore it is. Not far from either family. An easy train ride."

"This is all big dreaming," he said. "Chances are, I'll end up applying to a dozen schools and be lucky to get accepted into one. But what about you? What is it you want?"

"I've spent so much of my life with my future mapped out for me, I never bothered with dreams of my own. My only hope has been to feel useful and needed, and I've never felt more useful than I have over here. I'm sure that close to the capital I'll find some mischief to keep me busy. For once I like not knowing."

"What did I do to deserve a girl like you?" he asked.

"Incredible luck," I said. "I know Philadelphia Bell will put in a good word for me at the Maryland and DC branches. I'm a veteran now, after all. They'll be happy to take me on. I'll start looking for apartments and everything."

"I'm sure you'll find the perfect spot, my sweetest."

Andrew waited with me until the very last whistle, when I could no longer ignore the pointed stares of the porter, who waited with a martyred expression to take my trunk aboard.

By nightfall I was ensconced on the USS *Von Steuben*, the ship that would carry me home directly to Philadelphia Harbor.

CHAPTER 35

July 2, 1919
Philadelphia, PA

For two weeks I sailed with men eagerly returning from their duties. Some bodies were hale and hearty, others were still nursing severe injuries, but every spirit had been ravaged by the atrocities they lived through.

The pier in Philadelphia was teeming with mothers, fathers, sweethearts, wives, and children all anxious to see their heroes safely home. Toward the back of the crowd a thin figure with ruddy flyaway hair was waving emphatically.

"Evangeline!" I called. I wove through the crowd and crushed her in a bear hug. "I've never been happier to see a face in all my life."

"I'm glad you're home, Ruby," she said, kissing me on the cheek. "Mrs. Carrigan, I understand?"

I tucked her arm in mine. "Yes, and I can't wait for you to meet him."

"Let's get you to the taxi, and you can tell me all about him. You look a treat in your uniform, Ruby. Your mother will burst her buttons."

"Do you really think so?" I asked, cocking my head to the side.

"Well, she should, at any rate."

The early-summer sun bathed us as we walked down the pier to the street beyond, where cars jostled in the never-ending stream of traffic.

"Not a horse in sight," I said.

"Fewer and fewer every day," Evangeline commented. "Sad, but it does make for less of a mess in the street."

"I can't argue with that," I replied, sliding into the taxi. "How is Mother?"

"I've never seen her quieter. When Francis was killed, it wounded her, but I worry her heart is well and truly broken now. But when she heard you were coming home, something of a spark returned in her."

"Well, that's something," I said, my eyes focused on the road ahead. "Did—did Father suffer?"

"I don't think so, Ruby. I found him in his bed in the morning when he didn't come down to breakfast and your mother asked me to go after him. It looks as though he died in his sleep."

"I suppose that's a blessing." I chewed at my bottom lip. "Had he been ill?"

"Not that you'd notice," she said. "Sleeping a little longer than usual, but nothing truly out of the ordinary."

"Do you have any idea if business had been going poorly or anything like that?"

"I wouldn't know for sure, but I could always get a sense of it from his manner if things were bad, and I didn't see any of that in the past few months at all."

I knitted my brow, mentally urging the car forward.

"You don't think my wedding . . ." I wove my fingers together, not able to voice the nagging fear.

"No, Ruby. Your mother got into high dudgeon, but your father didn't seem too surprised by the news. There was no great row on the matter, and they'd not discussed it for some time. At least not in front of me."

"I'm glad for that," I managed to say, feeling my shoulders drop to their natural level. "I couldn't bear to think that I'd caused him that much grief. I knew he wouldn't approve of Andrew on principle, but once they got to know each other . . . I'm simply heartbroken they never had the chance to meet."

I thought of the two of them playing at Father's chess set by the fire in his study, bantering about politics while I curled up on the settee with a book. Andrew would never have the chance to present him with his firstborn grandchild. I ached for all the memories that would never be made.

"What was it like over there?" Evangeline asked after a pause.

"Behind the lines it was stretches of calm between flurries of manic activity. Battles followed by the dread of the next battle. The trenches were as bad as the worst reports you've read in the papers. I won't insult you or our boys by saying it was anything better than the depths of hell."

"Did you ever . . ." Evangeline's eyes shone bright, and she stared, blinking out the window on her side of the car.

"I left your letter with Francis," I said. "He's buried in Cambrai in a proper cemetery."

She took a handkerchief out from her handbag and dabbed at her eyes. "Thank you. I know it was impertinent for me to even ask. I hope it wasn't too much of a hardship to get there."

"Please don't think that way, Evangeline. He was my brother. You were his sweetheart. It was my privilege to deliver your love to him."

"Thank you, Ruby. I just wish they could have brought him home."

"I know, but the task of bringing all our boys home would have been enormous. And this way they can stay in France as a reminder of what we sacrificed for our friends. Let us hope his presence there will help stave off another such disaster."

She took my hand in hers until the car pulled up in front of Mother's house.

The clacking of my heels on the marble-tile entry echoed through the house. The door to Father's study was slightly ajar, and I had to remind myself that his jovial greeting wouldn't come booming from behind his desk. Never again.

I heard the fluttering of pages, so I opened the door the rest of the way. Mother sat behind the desk, her head bent over Father's ledgers. Already the masculine reds and golds of Father's upholstery had been replaced by Mother's ice blues and cool lavenders. The cheerful clutter of the desk was now orderly, no papers askew. Her pen was in a perfect parallel with the edge of the desk.

"Welcome home, Ruby dear," Mother said, looking up from her book. She shut it and came around to the front of the desk, where she kissed each of my cheeks. The low light accentuated the dark circles that ran deep under her eyes. Her hands shook slightly as she held me at arm's length to look me up and down. "You're looking fit, despite the strain of travel. Though we really ought to get you back into some regular clothes, hadn't we? The war is over, after all. We needn't wear such plain things anymore."

"I suppose not," I said. Trading in rough wool for satin, muslin, and lace wouldn't be such a horrible feeling.

"Wonderful, why don't you have Evangeline make you some tea, then lie down for a while before slipping into something more appropriate? The Morgans are finally throwing Nathaniel's welcome-home party this evening, and they want us there."

"Mother, I'm not exactly feeling up to going out this evening. Couldn't we make a private visit in a day or two? I'm sure Nathaniel will understand. He knows what the crossing is like."

"You'll manage well enough for one evening," Mother said. "Nettie said they specifically postponed the party on your account. The poor man has been home for three months, and the celebration is long overdue."

"Why on earth would they host a party on my account, considering everything?"

"He wasn't well enough for visitors when he first came home. And Nettie said he insisted on waiting for you. He is still fond of you, despite the unfortunate turn of events. Everyone will be so disappointed if you don't go." Her pointed expression let me know that she would be among that number.

I wondered if his comely young nurse would be in attendance. If this was to be an engagement party in addition to his belated welcome home, I hoped extending me an invitation was to show there were no hard feelings, and not to make a spectacle of me. It was the last thing Mother could bear.

Evangeline came in, carrying a tray with a single cup of tea and a few little sandwiches. Mother would be taking her refreshment alone.

"Very well." I noticed Mother's dress was a deep claret color, not the widow's black I had expected. "Is it seemly for *you* to attend so soon after we lost Father?"

"No one observes the old rules anymore," she said. "We'd all be locked up for the next year if we didn't press on after the war. It's our patriotic duty to carry on." Mother was such an ardent follower of tradition, I was amazed to hear her speak so flippantly of the shift in customs. Less than two years ago, she'd have been one of the first to cluck her tongue at a family going out of mourning too soon.

"It is," Evangeline said. "And we ought to have a little get-together for Ruby too, seeing as she's returned from service. Something modest, given the circumstances, of course, but it's only fitting."

"Oh, I don't want to take away from the parties for the men coming home," Mother said. "We must have a dozen invitations already. I don't think we could possibly find an open date before the news of your return is old hat."

"No matter," I said, biting back a rebuke. "I expect you'd rather save your efforts for welcoming Andrew home and throwing us a little wedding reception when he joins us."

"Yes, well. That may be quite some time," Mother said. "No sense in fretting about it just yet. Go rest and freshen up, dear, before you run out of time."

My room looked precisely as it had when I left, and it appeared as if it had been disturbed only for Evangeline's weekly dustings. The impractical dresses Mother purchased before my departure still hung expectantly in the wardrobe. I changed from my uniform and into a thin muslin nightgown. I pulled the covers up to my chin, wanting to relax into at least a shallow slumber, but felt too uneasy for rest. The sameness enveloped me. My same clothes. My same furniture. My same knickknacks on the dresser. Nothing had changed, except for me. So much so that the place felt foreign precisely because it had been untouched by the passing of time.

I sank into the soft mattress for all of five minutes before the inactivity became maddening. I took hangers in hand and began making sense of the contents of my trunk. My solemn navy-blue uniforms looked unwelcome amid the gay lavenders and periwinkles in my wardrobe. The blouses could be paired with plain skirts in the future, perfect for a shift at Bell. The woolen Norfolk jackets and uniform skirts from the signal corps would be moth fodder before long, though. We were told it was acceptable to wear our uniforms for "a reasonable period" following discharge, but no one knew what that meant. How long would I keep it in the corner of my closet? When would the memories fade enough that I could bring myself to put it in a collection barrel? Would it feel like I was discarding those months of my life when I finally did? I clutched the sleeve, now adorned with my stripes for service, and squeezed it like the hand of a dear old friend.

Evangeline heard me moving about and knocked softly before entering. She dove into the trunk, separating out the supplies like soap and baking powder that belonged in the washroom or the kitchen.

"I can't imagine Nathaniel really wants me there," I said, hanging the last of my blouses. "It will be awkward for us both. I had intended to invite him for tea in a few days so we could discuss how to smooth things over with our friends. He'll hate pretending things are normal between us."

"He's a refined gentleman," Evangeline said. "Even if he hates you, he knows how to hide his contempt as well as any actor on the stage. It's why I have no use for them."

"Gentlemen or actors?" I asked with a snicker.

"Both," she replied, nudging me with her elbow. "I couldn't have said this before you left, but I think you're well shut of him. He was always too unruffled for my liking. I could never trust a man who couldn't show his temper when it was called for. Your brother was the only one of these Main Line boys worth a second look."

"He was. And I know what you mean. Nathaniel is always even-keeled. A person doesn't want to be made to feel ridiculous for having feelings about things."

"And this Andrew of yours, he doesn't make you feel ridiculous?"

"In a million different ways, he absolutely does," I said. "But it's all the right ways."

"It sounds like you found your match," Evangeline said, smiling as she placed my nightgowns in a drawer.

"I have. I can't wait for you to meet him. We'll send you a train ticket so you can come visit us in Baltimore once we're settled. Maybe he'll have a chum for you back in Brooklyn we can invite out as well who can sweep you off your feet."

"I've been swept off them once, Ruby. I'm not sure I could let anyone follow in your brother's footsteps."

"He'd be heartbroken to hear it." I crossed the room and placed a hand above each of her elbows. "You're a young woman, Evangeline.

If he thought he'd left you to live alone for another seventy years after he passed, he'd turn in his grave. He'd want you to be happy. I promise you."

Evangeline dropped her head. "I know. It just feels wrong."

"And someday it won't. When that day comes, seize whatever happiness you can find. It's what Francis and all the others fought for."

~

A few hours later, Evangeline helped me into the light confection of lavender silk and ecru lace mother had presented to me before I left for Manhattan. It was as feminine and light as Chantilly cream, and I felt so different from the person who had worn rough wool and slept in drafty barracks for over a year. The woman in the mirror looked like a stranger, both to the Ruby who had fought in the war and to the one who came before. But she looked presentable, so there was no avoiding the descent into the parlor to join Mother.

"Lovely," she pronounced, twirling her finger.

I obliged her with a spin.

"I have my beautiful daughter returned to me, and all is right with the world."

"I ought to be in black on Father's account, but Evangeline wouldn't hear of it," I said, shooting her a sideways glance.

"She's quite right. It wouldn't do to show up to a party looking so solemn. You don't want to put a damper on things for him, do you?"

"Of course not, Mother." I was barely able to contain the sigh I so wanted to release. "I'm dead on my feet, though. I hope you don't mind if we make this visit a short one."

"Evangeline will make you coffee before we go," Mother said, which sent Evangeline scurrying to the kitchen. "We mustn't slight Nathaniel. He's a soldier home from war, after all."

I refrained from mentioning that I was no different, but I saved myself the futile effort of trying to reason with her.

Evangeline emerged just a few moments later with the steaming cup of honest-to-goodness American-brewed coffee with a splash of fresh cream. I lingered on the first sip like a lost lover's kiss.

"The taxi will be here in ten minutes, so drink quickly," Mother warned.

Mother had always sniffed at Father's refusal to hire a chauffeur. He preferred to drive himself to the office and the family to social affairs such as these, while I relied on the streetcars for my needs. Mother had always wanted the luxury of being driven where she wanted to go, though it seemed that chauffeurs were going the way of the horse and carriage.

"I ought to get my license," I said, taking another sip of the coffee. "Father's car does no one any good rusting in the garage."

"I've been thinking the same thing," Evangeline chimed in. "More and more girls are doing it, and it seems dead useful. I could do the marketing in half the time."

"If you both want to get yourselves killed trying to drive one of those contraptions, I suppose I can't stop you." Mother fiddled with the contents of her beaded handbag, shaking her head at the notion.

"You ought to join us, Mother," I said. "You might surprise yourself and enjoy it."

"Perish the thought," she replied. "I see the taxi now. Let's not keep him waiting. And Evangeline, I'll want tea before bed."

I followed Mother out into the balmy summer evening with a wave back to Evangeline, who had not been invited. Something else the war hadn't changed.

As expected, the Morgans had gone to every trouble imaginable to make a spectacle for Nathaniel's homecoming. A skilled string quintet played lively tunes that wafted through the hall on the perfume of the arranged flowers that adorned every surface of the stately home. I fiddled with my wedding band nervously as Nathaniel and his parents greeted the horde of guests eager to thank their hosts and greet the returned hero. When his eyes met mine, he pressed through the crowd to our sides.

"So wonderful to see you both," Nathaniel said, kissing Mother's cheeks, then my own. "You're lovelier than ever, Ruby."

"That's kind of you to say," I replied. He still moved stiffly and with the help of a cane. It was plain his injuries would bother him for the rest of his days.

"It's only the truth," he said. "I'm afraid I'm not much for dancing these days, but I'd be grateful if you joined me on the veranda for some refreshment."

I nodded in reply, unable to think of a valid reason for refusing him. Despite the burden of his cane, he insisted on handing me my cup of punch from the table and refused to let me carry his. There were a few people nestled on the thick cushions of cavernous wicker chairs, but they all seemed to find reason to make their way back indoors when they saw us appear. I sat at the large, circular glass table, which had been scrubbed so recently I could still smell the soap. Though I wasn't fond of punch as a rule, I took a sip to give my mouth an occupation.

"Rather sweet," I said, placing the cup of vibrant-red liquid on the table.

"There aren't any spirits in it," he explained. "They've gone quite out of fashion, I'm afraid. Mother has joined the Church Temperance Society and won't keep them in the house. Father is less enamored with the movement, but he tries to humor her. Even my party wasn't enough to persuade her to serve champagne."

"It seems extreme, but I suppose that it could be of some benefit to society."

"Indeed," he said. "Though I'd hoped to steer this conversation away from the blight of drink on the working classes and the like."

I sat up straighter in my chair. "I'd have preferred to have this conversation in a more private fashion. How upset were your parents by the news?"

"More than you can imagine. Mother especially was devastated. She always liked you, you know. Thought you had more gumption than most girls on the Main Line."

"Because I wasn't born to your circle, Nathaniel. And I'm afraid I'm not meant to be a part of it."

He placed his hand on mine. "That simply isn't true. You are a lady and deserve to live as one."

"Is your Madeleine here?" I asked, pulling my hand away. "I don't think she'd appreciate us having such a private conversation." I fiddled with the handle of my cup with my little finger and didn't meet his eyes.

"I broke things off with her before I was discharged home. Came to my senses, you might say."

"Why would you do such a thing? She seemed lovely. It's plain you two were smitten with each other."

"It never would have worked, Ruby. She's a wonderful girl, but she doesn't belong here any more than a blacksmith belongs on the throne in Buckingham Palace." He leaned back in his chair and massaged his injured leg.

"That's an awfully cold thing to say," I retorted.

"It's the truth, and you know it. Mother and the others would have been kind to her face, but you know what sort of gossip happens among this set. Breaking things off with her was a kindness. She will be happier with her own sort of people. You should have been as kind to your mechanic as I was to Madeleine."

"He's a medic," I said through clenched teeth. "The war hasn't changed you one bit, has it? Things aren't what they once were. People don't care about social standing and pedigree like they once did. What matters is what a person does. What a person is capable of doing."

"I wish that were true, Ruby. You always were an idealist, but nothing has changed as much as you think it has. It's time to return to the normal order of things." He reached over and placed his hands on mine once more. "I never thought you'd marry the boy. Certainly not before you came home. I thought you'd have time to realize what a mistake you were making."

"You and I broke things off, Nathaniel. What did you think was going to happen?" I struggled to keep my voice low enough to avoid attracting more attention than we had.

"I hoped that you were smart enough to see that I was in pain and not speaking sense. My . . . dealings with Madeleine hurt you deeply, I'm sure, but I didn't think you'd be so rash."

"Well, there is no returning to things as they might once have been. Not for me. I'm a married woman now, and very happily so." I pulled my hands away from his and knitted my fingers together in my lap.

"Even the most grievous of mistakes can be undone under the right circumstances. There are more than a few imprudent marriages that have sprung up since the war broke out and judges who are sympathetic to those seeking a quiet dissolution. No one here really knows of your marriage to the medic. It can all be done very discreetly, you know."

"But I love my husband," I said. "And I have no intention of divorcing him."

"An annulment," he corrected. "'Divorce' is such an ugly word. Love is admirable, my dear, but do you honestly think it can last with such a man? You've been raised to be a pillar of society. To make a real difference in the world through good works and service. Don't throw that away for the chance to live in a New York hovel, doing the wash for six underfed children."

"You paint a vivid picture," I said. "But I won't cast Andrew aside as carelessly as you cast aside poor Madeleine. He deserves better from his wife. Just as Madeleine deserved more from you."

"You're breaking your mother's heart, you know. She was here the night I came home off the ship, and she begged me to find a way to make things right. She's lost her husband and her son. For you to act so selfishly is more cruel than any pain I might have inflicted on that poor nurse."

"That's a nasty trick to play, Nathaniel. Mother can take care of herself, probably better than you or I can." I shifted in my seat. "You loved Madeleine, didn't you?"

"I was foolish and in pain. She eased my suffering and kept me from being lonely. It's hard not to let yourself believe you're in love in situations like that." He removed a silver case from his pocket and took out a cigarette, which he lit deftly before offering me one. I waved it away. He'd never smoked before the war, but he wasn't the only doughboy to pick up the habit overseas.

"You've persuaded yourself that you don't care for her, but I don't think it's true."

"What does it matter, Ruby?" He took a long drag on his cigarette, his sage-green eyes never meeting mine. "It's done. She's back in Milwaukee with her family, and better off for it."

"What about your plans to help the veterans when they return? That was a marvelous idea. I've heard the hospitals can't serve a fraction of the men that need help. You could do so much good."

"I'm sure the government will do what they can for them. But it's become clear I'm needed here. I'll be seeing to Father's affairs now, almost entirely. The stress of the war aged him greatly, and he needs a steady hand to take over the helm, so to speak."

"You've been groomed for it your whole life," I said. "But will it make you happy?"

"A more irrelevant question I can't imagine," Nathaniel said, swallowing a titter and shaking his head as smoke coiled from his nostrils.

"It's the *only* relevant question," I said. "This isn't about sitting next to someone you find tedious just to please your mother. This is your life's work. Can you honestly say that, on your deathbed, you'll look back on taking over your father's business with the same amount of pride and satisfaction as doing something for your fellow soldiers?"

"Perhaps not, but you speak as though I have a choice. I don't. But you could help. Stay with me, and be the bright ray of sunshine in my dull life."

"No, Nathaniel," I said, pushing back my chair and standing. "I refuse to marry a man who spends his life in a dark room, longing for the sun but lacking the backbone to stand and open a window."

CHAPTER 36

I kept my eyes on the road with as much attention as the driver until we were in the privacy of home. Mother's home. She indicated I should follow her into Father's study, and I took my seat in one of the plush chairs across from his seat at the desk.

"Nathaniel spoke to you, I take it?" she said, pouring a generous measure of brandy from one of Father's decanters into two crystal glasses. Temperance hadn't yet become the fashion with her, apparently. She placed one in front of me and reclined in Father's seat with hers.

"He did," I admitted. "Was the annulment your idea or his?"

"His," she said. "I figured the marriage was a fait accompli, but he held out hope."

"Did you honestly think I'd toss out my marriage like that? That I could possibly be so fickle?"

"No," she said, taking a healthy swig from the glass. "But he was determined to ask, and I figured letting him wouldn't hurt anything at this point. I knew it was doomed to failure. You're the steadfast sort, like your father. Honorable. But at least this way he can move on knowing he tried. I thought we owed him that much."

What we owed him for I couldn't begin to guess. I drained the contents of the etched tumbler and set it hard on the mahogany finish of the desk. "So let's have it, then. Bring out your best hellfire-and-brimstone lecture. I faced the Hun for year and a half—I think I can handle you in high dudgeon."

"No, Ruby. I'm done with all that. You're a woman grown. And frankly, I'm tired of it." The dark circles under her eyes gave credence to her claim.

"Who are you, and what have you done with my mother? If it's ransom money you're after, you're going to be sorely disappointed."

"Very funny, dear. I'm not an impostor; I'm simply done trying to make you into someone you're clearly not interested in becoming. You're free to make your own decisions. And, make no mistake, free to suffer the consequences of them too if they end up biting you in the rear."

"How very logical of you, Mother," I said. "I'm glad you finally noticed I grew up."

"You think this medic of yours can take care of you?" she asked, swirling the cut-crystal tumbler in her hand against the glow of firelight.

"Yes," I said. "Though I don't need it. And I can take care of him. He wants to go to medical school, and I'm going to see to it that he does. If I have to work double shifts for the next four years to pay for it, I will."

"You think a working-class boy from immigrant parents really has it in him to finish a four-year medical course?"

I could have taken the bait. Yelled. Thrown one of the tumblers against the wall and let the crystal shards rain down on Father's plush rug. Instead, I leaned back, laced my fingers behind my head, looked up at the intricate wood-paneled ceiling, and exhaled all the social venom the evening had set coursing in my veins. "You should have seen him in the hospital, Mother. Hands as steady as a mountain goat's hooves and determination to match your own. He was born to be a doctor. He'll be a damn fine one too."

"I hope you're right," Mother said. "But I can say without boasting, I didn't raise a fool. If you think he's the decent sort, I'm sure he is."

"Why the change of heart?" I asked, craning my neck to look at her.

"I lost my son. I lost my husband. If I let us become estranged, what's left?" She took one of the pens from its place in the lineup and twirled it between her fingers. "There is nothing more pathetic than a childless widow trying to cling to the glory of her past. I can stand to be many things, Ruby, but pathetic isn't one of them."

"No one would dare call you pathetic. They know they wouldn't survive to utter the third syllable."

"It's nice to know someone still thinks I instill fear into the hearts of man." She leaned back her head and let out an unreserved, full-throated laugh. I hadn't heard her do that in years. "You know your father used to say that if I'd been of age fifty-odd years ago, Lee wouldn't have surrendered. He would never have dared set foot on Union soil in the first place."

"That sounds like him," I said, remembering our plot to send her over as General Pershing's secret weapon. My shoulders began to shake with giggles. "He knew you were as stubborn as a worn-out donkey, and he loved you for it."

"God, I miss him," she whispered. "Whatever you might have thought about us, I always loved that fool man."

"You made him a better man," I said, sitting up in my chair. "He'd never have accomplished what he had if it wasn't for you. He knew you were the making of him. He'd never have denied it."

"I'm glad you think so, Ruby. I only wonder if I shouldn't have taken a few lessons from him as well. He was a far kinder person than I am. I hope you know I only ever wanted what was best for you. Even though I misjudged what that was."

"I know, Mother. Even when you drove me mad, I knew that every single thing you did was to give me the advantages you didn't have as a girl. I'm sorry I seemed ungrateful at times, but deep down I always knew."

"I'm happy to hear it," she said, wiping a tear from the corner of her eye with her crimson sleeve. She pulled a bank ledger from the top-right drawer. She sat pensive for a few moments, then uncapped her pen and wrote something in her practiced, loopy script. She folded the top third of the page along the perforated lines, tore it off, and passed it across the desk.

"I won't make such a gift a second time, so I expect you to use this wisely. That's the sum your father and I set aside for your wedding and to help you get settled. Since there wasn't a wedding, I suppose you can use it to help this Andrew of yours get started in medical school, if that's what you want. I don't want you to ruin your health working double shifts for any man, worthy or not."

I looked down at the check and wiped my tears before they could blotch the ink. "Mother, you don't have to do this. You should save the money to take care of yourself." I didn't know what provisions Father had left for her, but even a generous estate could be depleted by a long-lived widow.

"Your father would have wanted this," she said. "And this way I can guilt you into taking me in when I finally slip into dotage, can't I?"

"This check comes with substantial strings, in other words," I said, snorting as I dried my tears. She'd made the check out to Ruby Carrigan. It still looked foreign to me after six months, and I still occasionally formed part of the "W" in Wagner before I caught myself.

"More like iron cables and dipped in steel," Mother said with a snicker. "But I won't be a nuisance. The tiresome mother-in-law is such a boring cliché. Just promise that the pair of you will come see me sometimes?"

"As often as we can, Mother," I promised, reaching across the massive desk and taking her hand in mine. "I know you'll love Andrew. He's really a wonderful man."

"He'd better be," she said. "I'd be heartbroken to part with you for less."

CHAPTER 37

August 15, 1919
Washington, DC

"It is a good thing for my prison record I didn't have your little *pistolet* with me today at the War Department," said Margot. "I went to ask about the bonus certificates, since my letters went unanswered. After an hour they finally sent one of their lowliest clerks out to speak with me in the lobby. He informed me that we were 'not properly in the army.' Can you believe this?" Margot had stormed into the apartment she shared with Evangeline—and where I spent most of my free time. She had launched into her grievances the second she saw me.

"What on earth do they mean 'not properly in the army'? It's not like we stowed away on the boat and played soldier for the better part of a year and a half." I sat up straighter on the sofa where Evangeline and I lounged after our long shift at the DC branch of Bell's Chesapeake and Potomac Telephone Company.

"They said we were not *really* under oath." Margot pulled off her gloves with such vigor I was surprised she didn't tear the fingers from the palms. "That we could not legally be in the army because the army's requirements specifically use the word 'man' in them. Not 'person' like the navy and the marines. All that hand-on-the-Bible nonsense was just for show, apparently."

"What poppycock," Evangeline said, now clutching a throw pillow to her chest. "How can they do such a thing? They plan to pay healthy bonuses to men who served. They can't find a bit more for a couple hundred operators?"

"It seems easy for them to ignore us. I heard that Addie McMillan wasn't allowed treatment at the veterans' hospital either. She hasn't truly been well since she got the flu." Margot poured herself an iced tea and flung herself in the secondhand armchair she'd bought for a song when they began furnishing the place.

"It isn't right," Evangeline said. "She fell ill while in service. The lowest private who wandered into France on the day before the armistice would have been treated if he'd contracted the sniffles on the boat over. But Addie's on her own?"

"The hospitals are overrun with soldiers still in need of medical care and rehabilitation," I pointed out. "But that doesn't make it right. Something needs to be done. They can't just discard us like this."

"You're right about the hospitals," Evangeline said. "Andrew is going to be a busy man when he gets home. Even with taking the time to finish medical school."

"True enough," I said. "I'm just glad he'll have something to do." So many of the returning soldiers didn't find solace in the quiet of peacetime. They only found the time and the opportunity to become better acquainted with the demons that accompanied them back from Europe. I wished Nathaniel hadn't abandoned his notion of an organization to help restore the returning combatants to a normal life. His wealth, his influence, could have done so much good, but I'd yet to hear anything from home to indicate that he'd reconsidered. "First the victory medals, now this. I'm not going to let them get away with such treatment. We worked too hard to be dismissed like dogs at the dinner table."

I looked out the small window. The Potomac was visible if you craned your neck the right way. The girls liked to boast of their "river view" apartment. The apartment I'd rented for Andrew and me next door was a bit larger, but we couldn't claim the view unless we climbed out onto the fire escape with binoculars.

"How in creation would we even begin to take on the US Army?" Margot asked. "I wouldn't know how to take the first step, let alone see the thing through."

"There has to be a way," Evangeline said. "They aren't above the law. They have to be made to do the right thing."

"I'm not sure, but I'll pester every lawyer in this city until one of them helps us with the case," I said. "It's not a fantastic sum of money, but by the time they pay out the certificates in 1945, we might be grateful to have it. We won't be young women then."

"I expect the same is true for most of us," Margot said. "We'll need all the girls' support to make this work. I'll start writing letters. It won't be too much trouble to trace down Gloria and all the other girls who went over in our group, and we can start finding the operators from the other six groups once we've managed that."

"Very good," I said. "It's a start, anyway."

The light in Margot's eyes was once again bright, just as it had been back in Manhattan when the thrill of our deployment was still ahead of us. I wondered if the others would be as eager to help, or if they would be happy to forsake a few hundred dollars to leave the war behind them. There were lives to return to, families to start. Some might be angry now, but it would be easy to move past the army's slights once there were babies in arms and toddlers crawling on the floor.

A knock sounded at the door, and Evangeline stood to answer it.

"May I help you?" she asked a moment later.

A familiar tenor voice wafted from the door. "I believe you have my wife."

It was a mercy I didn't knock over the sofa in my flight over to Andrew's arms. He spun me around like a child as I pelted his face with kisses.

"You're home safe," I breathed, burying my face in his chest. "You're finally here."

"The USS *Eddelyn* made berth in New York this morning, and I got on the first train to Washington that had an open seat." He wrapped his arms tighter around me. "God, it's good to be home."

Still tucked in his arms, I introduced Evangeline, once I had stemmed my tears enough to speak.

Margot produced a bottle of champagne that she'd brought home from France, the last of her small stash. Likely the last we'd have, as Washington was the model of prohibition for the rest of the country.

"To our returned soldier, and the happy couple," Margot said, raising her glass.

"And to Johns Hopkins's newest student," I chimed in.

"Don't count your chickens, dearest wife," Andrew said, clinking his glass to mine and kissing my temple.

"I'm doing no such thing. Your acceptance letter is on the kitchen table next door." I reached up to return the kiss. "I sent in your application the very week I got home. I wasn't going to let the temptation of regular work keep you from going back to school." I didn't add that I'd sent in his deposit money from the proceeds of Mother's gift. Such an admission might be too much for his pride to tolerate, but I'd have to convince him it was no different from accepting scholarship funds.

"I got accepted?" he asked, blinking as he pulled me closer.

"With your service record, they're happy to have you. Classes start in September." I laced my fingers with his. "You can spend all of August learning your way around the city and putting on a few pounds. I won't have your professors mistaking you for a patient on your first day. And if we don't visit your parents within the week, I'll never be forgiven. My mother too."

His arm still around me, Andrew looked pensively at the bubbles floating gracefully to the surface of the pale honey-hued liquid. "I wish I could think of something to say."

"In my experience, the correct answer to such things is 'thank you' when a Wagner woman is involved," Evangeline suggested sagely. "And if you'd been wise enough to let me know of your wedding, I could have warned you in time: it's best to let the women in this family lead when they want to. They know where they're going."

"In that case, I'd be happy to follow my wife home. Care to show me the way, Mrs. Carrigan?"

"All too happy, my love."

Over the next days, we settled in to the apartment next door. There was no gilded staircase leading to palatial bedroom suites or priceless works of art on the walls. There was a roof that leaked in bad weather and a floor that squeaked. We comforted each other when the specter of war haunted our sleep, and when the idleness of peacetime grew fatiguing. We made a point of celebrating the small triumphs and joys like they were monumental. The war had changed us, changed the world, but together we would find ourselves and the place we were meant to take in it.

EPILOGUE

August 18, 1920
Washington, DC

I wove my way through the crowds that lined the streets near the Capitol, hand in hand with Andrew. Though it was the middle of the week, he'd managed to secure a day off from his classes, and I from the switchboards. Thanks to his experience as a medic, he was able to earn some income assisting the professors as they treated their patients, and he'd wowed them with his bedside manner and stamina. The war had taken much, but at least it had given Andrew these gifts. His hours were long, but so were mine as supervisor at the Central Office. Sunday was our only real day of respite, but we found that any more than that was much too quiet to bear. In those times, Andrew found his voice again, and it gave us both solace.

Still, to the army, I was no soldier.

"Ruby!" a clear voice rang out over the crowd assembled at the Capitol steps. I looked up to see Evangeline's vibrant red hair above the crowd.

"Here!" I shouted, though Andrew, with the advantage of his six feet in height, had more luck catching her eye.

She and Margot jostled their way through the throng and took their places by our side, with Andrew, Margot, and me holding our ground amid the bustling crowd. The cheers were jubilant as garland and bunting unfurled from balconies. Andrew stood behind me, his hands on my waist, as we watched the women marching with American flags in tow, carrying banners proclaiming our hard-won victory. I took Margot's hand in my left and Evangeline's in my right as we watched the parade.

"It's finally happened," Evangeline said, wiping a tear with her free hand. "My mother had always told me this day would never come, and here we are."

"Far too long in coming," Andrew said, placing a kiss atop my head. "Now that you ladies have the vote, perhaps you can turn this country around for us."

"It's time we had the chance to try," I said. "And there's a lot to be done."

"Hear, hear," Margot chimed in, her lips drawn in a line.

Margot and I had written hundreds of letters if we'd written a single word, yet so far little had been achieved in our quest to have our veterans' benefits reinstated. No pensions, no victory medals, no promised bonus pay. The army was still adamant that we had not served as soldiers. I certainly had felt like a soldier when I took my oath of service. I certainly had felt like a soldier when bombs crashed and bullets flew overhead. I certainly felt like a soldier when I was denied my request to resign my post.

I stood in solidarity with the suffragettes, but I did not join the hundreds of women in wearing a flowing white dress. Though my experience with the suffrage movement was limited to my brief, disastrous involvement at Bryn Mawr, I always had admired their careful, feminine dress. They eschewed the idea that only heartless, man-hating shrews coveted the male voice in government. The suffragettes had hoped to ensure the support of men by showing them that the vote wouldn't make them any less feminine. They wanted to make their movement fashionable to attract more women to their ranks. Evangeline wore her best white dress, but Margot and I had decided to make another statement. Hand in hand, we wore our uniforms for the last time.

We would show the world we were soldiers.

AFTERWORD

It would not be until 1979—when a stalwart young lawyer by the name of Mark Hough took on the case of the "Hello Girls"—that the women switchboard operators of World War I would be given the benefits and honors they had earned for their service.

Of the 228 women who served as operators in the US Army Signal Corps, only 28 of them lived long enough to hear the verdict on their case.

AUTHOR'S NOTE

In American history books, the First World War—the Great War—is rarely depicted as "great." It often reads like a filler chapter to maintain the timeline between the landscape-changing events of the American Civil War and the drama and romance of the Second World War, which cemented America's place as a world power. That the First World War does not hold the same place in the American psyche as it does in other countries' stands to reason. As I'm apt to say, "The US Army didn't go to fight in World War I; they went to end it." While we entered the war in April 1917, it wasn't until the following year that we truly joined the battle on a grand scale. The losses suffered by France, Canada, and England over the four years of conflict left an indelible mark on the faces of those countries, something the US simply couldn't claim.

Despite the lack of airtime given to it in many American history classes, the Great War *was* immensely important to the future of the Unites States. Originally, Britain and France had thought to add the AEF troops to their own armies, to be led by French and British generals. General John J. Pershing was having none of that. He wanted to lead his own men into battle and to prove our mettle as an independent fighting force. In so doing, he established that we were a dominant military power, more than capable of managing our own affairs.

We see the posters of Rosie the Riveter and hear about the women taking over jobs in factories to help free up men for the war effort in World War II, and it would be easy to believe that this was the conflict that saw the rise of the women's rights movement. These events were a huge step forward in the movement, to be sure, but the involvement of women in the Great War is perhaps of even greater significance. Prior to our entry in the war, the women's suffrage movement was growing, but little change had been effected. The one argument the antisuffragist groups clung to, which continued to resonate with many people, was that women were not able to fight in wars to defend their country and, as such, should not have the right to vote directly in its governance. This was the war that changed all that. The army's regulations at the time specifically mentioned that service members had to be men, but the same was not true for the other branches of service. Women went over to Europe not only as nurses, operators, and clerical staff to support the combatants, but also as "marinettes" and "yeomanettes" in the marines and navy. They fought and died for their country. The last real argument against women's suffrage died along with them.

I began working on this book at the insistence of a friend who is a former member of the US Army Signal Corps. He was one of the earliest champions of my first novel and sent me an article on the "Hello Girls" through Facebook, saying, "This is fodder for your next book. Celebrating unknown women heroes—this is what you do." I started reading further, and he was right. Not only were these women groundbreaking in what they accomplished; they really were the catalyst for major changes in women's rights for the next century. Once I grabbed hold of the idea for this book, there was no letting go.

I joke that I'm the woman who always shows up a day late when it comes to research. I'm skilled at finding wonderful symposiums or museum exhibits on my topics of interest just after they've passed through town. For *Girls on the Line,* I may have used up all my research luck in one single trip. Once I had a solid outline and characters in hand, I hopped on a plane to the National World War I Museum to pore over the contents of the archives. The amazing archivists Jonathan Casey and Alex Bergman briefed me on what they had on hand . . . oh yes, and mentioned that Mark Hough, the lawyer who won the case to reinstate the Hello Girls' veterans' rights in 1979, would be there for an interview in the next fifteen minutes. I had the privilege of listening to filmmaker Jim Theres interview Mr. Hough for several hours for his documentary on the Hello Girls that debuted in March 2018. Mr. Hough's anecdotes about these courageous women and their legal struggles to be recognized as soldiers brought more than a few tears to my eyes. It was certainly one of the top ten days of my professional life.

Mr. Theres was also kind enough to put me in contact with several of the surviving family members of the Hello Girls who contributed to his documentary. Carolyn Timbie, granddaughter of the inimitable Grace Banker, the chief operator of the First Telephone Group, entrusted me with a copy of her grandmother's journal. This priceless document served as the timeline for much of Ruby's war experience from her days training in New York through the armistice. Candace McCorkell, granddaughter of operator Melina Adam, shared with me scads of her grandmother's letters and photos from the war. What was remarkable about Melina (better known as Addie) was that she managed to find the love of her life in the midst of this horrific conflict. Like Ruby, she was married in Paris before returning home and found a very disappointed former suitor waiting for her at home. Some research threads are simply too good to leave out of the book.

In addition to these research treasures (and I don't use that term lightly), I had access to Supervisor Berthe Hunt's journal as well as hundreds of legal and military documents, private letters, and photographs. From these, it was possible to piece together an idea of what daily life was like for these women and what the conditions in which they lived were. They worked strenuous hours and were often housed in less-than-optimal conditions, especially toward the end of the war, but they never shirked their duties. Though the war was a strain on them all, their experience overseas wasn't always grim. The presence of these women provided much-needed social opportunities for the exhausted soldiers. The women saw boosting morale as an important duty and hosted dances and dinners as often as they could. They were certainly hardworking and serious, but still as fun loving and vivacious as young women their age ought to be. Many of the anecdotes you read in this book—including the faux court-martial, the visit to the fields to see the practice gas attacks, and the incident with the bedbugs—were my fictionalized recounting of actual events found in the source material from various operators. Unfortunately, the Spanish flu, the oppressive mud, and the fire in their bone-dry barracks were parts of their experience as well.

Ruby was a character who came to me clearly and with a lot of ideas in her head. She is a woman with her feet in two eras—that of her mother and her Victorian ideals, and that of a postwar world full of the modern views she adopts overseas. She wanted her story told, and I was grateful she chose me to tell it. Her love interests, Andrew and Nathaniel, also represent the values of the new world and the old. They struggle to find their places in an age that scarcely resembles the one in which they were born. While the story between Ruby, Andrew, and Nathaniel may seem merely an ordinary romance set in extraordinary times, my hope is to convey the seismic-level shifts in the social construct through these relationships. It isn't hyperbole to say that the First World War sounded the death knell for the class system. While the effect was certainly more apparent in countries like England, which have an established aristocracy, the Main Line set would have felt the effects of the changing world very keenly. Ambitious, intelligent men like Andrew had more opportunities than ever, while the privileged Morgan family would have found that their family legacy counted for less and less in the postwar world.

Even in 2018, women's rights are still far from finished business. Compared to other countries in the Western world, the United States is behind the times in understanding that women's rights truly are *human* rights. Though we have much work to do, the Hello Girls ushered in a monumental leap forward for all womankind in the pursuit of equality. It is my fervent hope this book does justice to what all the women of the US Army Signal Corps did to give the daughters of this country the precious gift of suffrage and that we honor their legacy by using that gift at every opportunity.

Thank you so much for reading,
—Aimie K. Runyan

ACKNOWLEDGMENTS

A book starts as a solitary endeavor and becomes the work of many. I humbly wish to thank:

As always, my incredible agent, Melissa Jeglinski, for her constant support. Your enthusiasm for this project means so much!

The wonderful Chris Werner and Jenna Free for their scrupulous edits. You really helped make this book shine much brighter.

Danielle Marshall, Gabe Dumpit, and the whole Lake Union team for making my publishing experience an exemplary one.

Sean Vogel, former US Army Signal Corps captain, whose support of my first novel gave me the courage to pursue my dream of becoming a published author, and who passed along the article that inspired this very book.

Alex Bergman, Jonathan Casey, and the entire staff of the National World War I Museum in Kansas City, Missouri, for their guidance and gracious welcome.

The Timbie and McCorkell families for being so incredibly generous with your grandmothers' stories. Their diaries and letters helped bring Ruby to life. I am forever grateful.

Jim Theres for putting me in contact with the surviving family members of these remarkable women and for being so active in making their story known.

Elizabeth Cobbs for being so generous with her expertise.

Mark Hough, for letting me listen in on his firsthand accounts of working with the "Hello Girls," for giving them a voice, and for helping them win their final battle. Meeting you was an honor and a highlight of my career.

The Tall Poppy Writers, Ladies of the Lake, and the BWW for being my lifeline in a hectic business.

The founders, organizers, and members of amazing reading communities such as Bloom, Great Thoughts Great Readers, Bookworms Anonymous, A Novel Bee, Women Writers Women's Books, and Reader's Coffeehouse. You bring joy and validation to the writer's heart.

Stephanie, Todd, Carol, Melony, and Jamie for your support and friendship.

My parents, Kathy and Wayne Trumbly and Bob and Donna Runyan, and my sisters, Katie, Maggie, Denise, and Tammy, for being the world's greatest cheerleaders.

Ciarán and Aria for making me laugh. (A special thanks to my Aria for sharing her big day with Ruby this year. You two would get along famously.)

And my Allan—always.

BOOK CLUB QUESTIONS

1. How does Ruby's demeanor change between home and the workplace? Why do you think this is, and how does it show?
2. What do you feel are the catalysts for Ruby's decision to serve overseas?
3. What does it seem were the reasons behind General Pershing's decision to send women over as operators?
4. Ruby is thrust into a leadership role early on in her deployment. Does she seem confident in her abilities? What do you think influences her perception of herself as a leader? Discuss times Ruby demonstrates her strengths and weaknesses as the head of her telephone group.
5. How do Ruby's memories of her brother, Francis, drive her throughout her time overseas?
6. What do the two leading men, Nathaniel and Andrew, represent? How is this apparent?
7. There is constantly tension between the women of the signal corps and the nurses they encounter. Why do you think this might be?

8. What do you feel are the reasons Ruby seems so bound to her promise to her parents to marry Nathaniel after the war? Do you feel she was ultimately justified in her decision?
9. Why do you think the army reacted so strongly in the face of Ruby's wartime marriage? Do you think their decision to transfer her was justified?
10. Ruby's mother eventually comes to peace with her daughter's decisions. Why do you think that, despite all her misgivings, she makes the financial gesture toward Andrew and his education?
11. Why do you feel the army was so reticent to recognize the (relatively small) number of female telephone operators as veterans?

ABOUT THE AUTHOR

Photo © 2017 Melony Nottingham Black

Aimie K. Runyan writes to celebrate history's unsung heroines. She is the author of three previous historical novels, including the internationally bestselling *Daughters of the Night Sky* and *Promised to the Crown*. She is active as an educator and speaker in the writing community and beyond. She lives in Colorado with her wonderful husband and two (usually) adorable children. Visit her at www.aimiekrunyan.com.